ROCK HARD

NALINI SINGH

NEW YORK TIMES BESTSELLING AUTHOR

eISBN: 978-1-942356-05-9
ISBN: 978-1-942356-16-5

Cover image by: Jenn LeBlanc/Illustrated Romance
Cover design by: Croco Designs
Book design by: Maureen Cutajar/www.gopublished.com

Other Books by Nalini Singh

Rock Addiction
Rock Courtship: A Novella

The Psy/Changeling Series
Slave to Sensation
Visions of Heat
Caressed by Ice
Mine to Possess
Hostage to Pleasure
Branded by Fire
Blaze of Memory
Bonds of Justice
Play of Passion
Kiss of Snow
Tangle of Need
Heart of Obsidian
Shield of Winter

The Guild Hunter Series
Angels' Blood
Archangel's Kiss
Archangel's Consort
Archangel's Blade
Archangel's Storm
Archangel's Legion
Archangel's Shadows

For detailed descriptions of these books, as well as additional
titles, visit Nalini's website: www.nalinisingh.com.

ROCK HARD

Part One

1

CHARLIE-MOUSE MEETS T-REX...
AND THINGS HAPPEN

CHARLOTTE CLOSED THE FINAL updated folder with a smile.

Pushing back from her desk after shutting down her computer, she stretched to loosen up the kinks, then decided to visit the restroom before heading out to catch the 6:15 bus home. It was a good bet it'd be blissfully empty this late on a Saturday since most people were coming into the city while she was heading in the opposite direction.

She could sit against the window and people-watch as the bus snaked up and out of the city's central business and entertainment district. Maybe she'd read the little booklet that described the spa treatments she planned to indulge in tomorrow. Her best friend had given her a gift card months ago, back on her birthday, but with work being so frantic as the interim management team tried to hold things together, followed by all the prep for the arrival of the new boss on Monday, she'd had no chance to use it.

Nudging her wire-framed glasses farther up her nose as she exited the restroom, she let herself back onto the floor, her

3

mind already on the spa treatments she'd booked. The idea of a therapeutic mud bath had her close to a giggle—she'd chosen that one just so she could tell Molly she'd blown the gift card on fancy mud. Her friend would get a kick out of it.

Tonight, however, she had a date with the oven; she was itching to try out her new recipe for banana-nut cupcakes with buttercream frosting. All she had to do was grab her purse and coat and catch the elevator down. An easy five-minute walk to the bus stop, and if the service was running on time, she'd be on her way home soon afterward.

It was as she passed the fourth cubicle down that she heard it. A door slamming lightly against a wall, as if someone had pushed it a little too hard... or bumped it while trying to move with stealth.

Impossible.

There was no one else here. And no one was likely to have come in during the few minutes she'd been away from the floor. The others who'd been in today were long gone, their workstations silent. She had to have imagined it.

Another noise, this one duller. The kind an overstuffed manila folder might make as it fell to the carpet.

An invisible hand choked her throat.

Her body shook.

And her mind threatened to blank.

No. She straightened her shoulders. *I am not a victim. Not anymore. Not ever again.*

Repeating the mantra that had kept her sane for the past five years, she reached into a pants pocket to retrieve her phone. She never went anywhere without it, not even into the shower at home, having bought a waterproof case the same day she'd bought the phone. It was a crutch, but as Molly had said, so what?

If having the phone within reach allowed her to function, to step outside into the world, to not live in a cage, then no one had any right to judge her. It had taken Charlotte time, but she'd stopped judging herself for the need, too. In the grand scheme of her screwed-up psyche, her reliance on the safety net of a phone was a blip on the radar.

Unlocking the screen with icy fingers, she crouched behind the dark blue wall of a cubicle that belonged to a temp in Accounts and speed-dialed her best friend. "Pick up, pick up," she muttered near-silently as she chanced a peek around the corner.

When she concentrated, she was able to track the sounds of ongoing movement to the records room. As the records clerk, Charlotte had intimate knowledge of what was inside that room: computers full of sensitive commercial information as well as rows and rows of legal documentation including contracts and draft tenders, not to mention the personnel files for every employee who worked for Saxon & Archer Corp.

When Molly's answering machine came on, Charlotte realized she'd accidentally called Molly's home line rather than her friend's cell phone. She glanced at her watch. Molly was a librarian who worked Saturdays, but she should've been home by now, might just be in another room. "Molly," she said when the beep sounded, her voice trembling despite herself. "Please pick up."

Nothing. No response.

About to hang up and try Molly's cell phone, she heard the sound of the receiver being handled. Molly came on the line a second later, her tone sharp with concern. "Charlie, what's wrong?"

"Oh, you're home." Charlotte swallowed in a vain effort to wet a throat so dry it felt as if it were lined with broken gravel. "I just…" Taking a deep breath when her pounding heart threatened to drown out everything else, she said, "There's someone else in the office, and there shouldn't be. I came back from the bathroom and heard them moving around."

"Leave." Molly's voice was urgent.

It was good advice, but Charlotte didn't want to run, to hide. Didn't want to be a coward as she so often was.

Finding courage from the intense, painful frustration inside her, she said, "No." And though her skin was hot and her breath shallow, her pulse in her mouth, she rose from her crouch. "It's probably only the building security guard doing an unscheduled round," she added in an attempt to convince herself there was no reason to fear, "but could you stay on the phone with me while I go check it out?"

"I'm right here."

Grabbing a large stapler from the cubicle opposite where she'd been hiding, Charlotte slipped out of her low-heeled slides and padded down the beige of the carpet, trying to calm herself with rational thoughts. There was *no reason* for an intruder to break in to commit industrial espionage—everyone knew Saxon & Archer was in trouble; trouble so bad that even the sharks who usually circled dying companies had declared them of no interest.

That dire state of affairs was why the new CEO with his reputation as a ruthless negotiator with a razor-sharp mind had been brought on board. Rumor was the powers that be had been so desperate to secure his services they'd given him a chunk of the tightly held company as part of his pay package.

Of course, those shares would be worthless if he didn't manage the herculean task of hauling Saxon & Archer out of its death spiral—and Charlotte couldn't think about that, about the possibility of losing her job, without breaking into a cold sweat, so she shoved that line of thinking aside to focus on the here and now.

Right now it made no sense that someone would want to steal data on a floundering company. And there was nothing else here to steal. Unless this was one very aggressive recruiter who planned to poach Saxon & Archer personnel and was laying the groundwork. Yes, that was going to happen. *Not.*

It had likely just been files falling to the floor, or a door moving because of a draft generated by an air-conditioning vent, or—

Screaming as she saw the shape of a very big, very muscular man move out from inside the records room, she threw the stapler.

He caught it in one big hand, stared at it with steel-gray eyes, then at her. A single raised eyebrow. "Perhaps you'd better answer that."

Charlotte realized he was talking about her phone. Her fingers had a death grip on it, and she could hear Molly yelling her name even from this distance. Bringing it to her ear as her face flushed to a no doubt horrific shade of red, she said, "I'm fine" to her best friend.

"I'm glad to hear that." With those words, the dark-haired and very familiar man across from Charlotte held out the stapler. "You might be needing this... Ms.?"

"Baird," she said in a croak of a tone. Coughing, she managed to clear it to a rasp. "Charlotte Baird." She held the phone against her chest and forced herself to meet the penetrating gaze of the six-feet-five, broad-shouldered, and dangerously gorgeous man she'd recognized a split second *after* she threw the stapler.

There were few people in the country who wouldn't recognize Gabriel Bishop, former pro rugby player, decorated captain of the national team, and holder of on-field records unbroken in the seven years since he'd been forced to retire because of a severe Achilles tendon injury. "Thank you... sir."

A nod, his hair glinting blue-black in the overhead light. He was gone a second later, a legal file held in his hand.

Walking back to her cubicle on shaky legs, Charlotte collapsed in her chair and buried her face in one hand, elbow braced on her desk. "I just met my new boss," she groaned into the phone. "Or more specifically, I threw an industrial-strength stapler at his head."

Molly laughed in open relief.

"Oh God, Molly, what if he *fires* me?" Charlotte didn't know how she'd find a new job. Interviewing for this one would've left her a nervous wreck if the human resources manager at the time hadn't been an older man on the verge of retirement who'd reminded her of her father.

"He's not going to fire you," Molly said. "You were in the office being a diligent employee, remember?"

"Right, that's right. I—"

"Ms. Baird."

Jerking around at the sound of that deep male voice, Charlotte said, "Yes." It came out a squeak.

"Have you been here all day?" Gabriel Bishop's eyes—cold, hard, incisive—pinned her to the spot, his big body blocking out the light.

She nodded, her voice having deserted her totally by this point. The man was a wall of pure muscle, like some Greek god carved by an adoring artist.

"In that case," he said, "I'm sure you're hungry. We'll go to a bistro I know nearby for dinner." It wasn't an invitation but an order. "You can bring me up to speed on certain issues." His eyes went to the phone in her hand. "Five minutes."

Waiting until his footsteps disappeared, Charlotte repeated his order into the phone, her stomach in knots. Even condemned prisoners got a last meal. Maybe Gabriel Bishop did the same for employees he was about to fire?

"Go," Molly said. "And order the most expensive thing on the menu."

"I'll probably throw it up." Her nerves twisted, then twisted again and decided to tie themselves into knots for good measure. "I better go—he said five minutes."

Molly wished her good luck and they hung up. Tidying herself up by redoing the ponytail in which she wore her barely shoulder-length blond hair, the strands so fine they tended to escape and curl around her face, she got up and slung the strap of her purse over her shoulder. Picking up her warm but shapelessly blocky brown coat afterward, she slid her feet into her abandoned shoes, then walked to the elevator.

She had a feeling her new boss intended for them to go to a particular upmarket bistro—the gossip pages liked to spy on him, though he didn't court the attention, and he'd been photographed there a number of times. Mostly with business associates.

Every so often with a stunning model or pro sportswoman or heart surgeon. Once, he'd been seen with an up-and-coming member of Parliament. *That* had sent the gossip into the stratosphere.

His only "type" appeared to be tall and beautiful.

This would be the first time with a short, glasses-wearing blonde dressed in a badly fitting sweater.

At least she didn't have to worry a journalist looking for a scoop would snap a picture, Charlotte consoled herself. The fact she wasn't a date couldn't be clearer if she'd painted it on her forehead. Another piece of good news was that the bistro was only a two-minute walk away, so she didn't have to put on her coat; carrying the heavy brown mass gave her a way to hide her hands, which kept fisting and locking together when they weren't trembling.

"Ms. Baird."

Startled for the third time in seven minutes, she looked up to find her new boss—whom she'd *attacked with a stapler*—had taken the stairs to this level, when she'd expected to meet him in the lobby downstairs. "H-hi." Not so much a squeak this time as a croak.

Charlotte didn't think that was an improvement.

Pressing the elevator button, Gabriel Bishop nodded at her coat, his chiseled jaw bearing a hint of dark stubble. "It's windy out."

Hands feeling white-knuckled, she managed to say, "I'll be okay." It wasn't a total lie. Instead of her usual work outfit of a loose skirt-suit, she'd worn jeans and a round-necked navy sweater. Saxon & Archer had always been a little old-fashioned about appropriate office clothing, but everyone was more casual on weekends.

Even the boss wasn't wearing a suit, but well-loved jeans that had a rip at the knee and a stone-gray shirt with the sleeves rolled up to the elbows, his tanned forearms dusted with fine black hairs. What wasn't on display was the tattoo she knew covered his left pectoral muscle and his shoulder before flowing partway down his arm. Thick veins ran below the skin of his forearm, his strength apparent even at rest.

Gabriel Bishop was definitely not a "normal" CEO in any sense of the word.

The elevator arrived then, and he waved her in before stepping in himself. The cage had never before struck her as tiny, but then she'd never before been in it with a man whose shoulders were twice the width of hers; it was obvious he stayed in shape despite not playing professional rugby anymore. Not that she hadn't already known that from the photos she'd chosen for the new company brochure.

Anya was supposed to have organized that, but going through photos of the new boss was one task Charlotte hadn't minded handling for the other woman, even if she had allowed herself to get sidetracked by searching out images from his playing days. She'd thought she'd appreciated the impact of him, but it was different seeing him in person.

The photos didn't do him justice.

Gabriel Bishop wasn't simply strong and tautly muscled—he was a force of nature.

The photos of him on the rugby field were unbelievably hot, but the seven years since then had honed him, made him impossibly more gorgeous. No wonder women across the spectrum fell at his feet. Only last week, Charlotte had seen a report of a flirtatious blog post where a singer with a recent platinum album had named Gabriel Bishop as the one man she wouldn't kick out of bed for eating crackers.

Stepping out when the elevator doors opened on the ground floor, she gulped in a cool draft of air and managed a shaky smile at the security guard when Steven rose from his post behind what was the main reception desk during weekdays.

"Mr. Bishop, Charlotte, have a nice night."

"Thank you, Steven," Gabriel Bishop responded. "I'll see you tomorrow."

Then the two of them were walking to the sliding doors that led out onto the city's main street. It was relatively quiet outside, the tourists and shoppers having gone home and the retail stores closed or closing up, while the clubbers and partiers hadn't yet hit the streets. Before them would come the wave of people heading out to dinner at the restaurants in and around this area, as well as down on the waterfront.

Across the road, she glimpsed a group of men and women dressed in striped rugby jerseys, team scarves around their necks. It reminded her there'd been a special doubleheader at Eden Park today—it looked like fans who'd attended the first match had already started to trickle into the city for a post-match drink.

And all this mental procrastination wasn't doing anything to lessen her awareness of the large, powerful man at her side. Twisting her hands under her coat, she told herself to make small talk, lessen the chance of being fired, but every time she went to open her mouth, nothing came out.

Finally, frustrated with herself to the point that she could feel tears building behind her eyes, she blurted out, "I'm sorry. I thought you were an intruder."

"I survived." No anger in his voice, though the eyes he turned on her were assessing. "The stapler was too heavy for you to throw with any accuracy. Next time, try a hole punch."

Was that a *joke?*

Since she had no desire to rock the boat if he truly wasn't furious, she didn't say anything else and they were soon at the bistro where he was greeted by name and shown to a plum table by the window, though he couldn't have made the reservation any more than a few minutes earlier.

"Your coat?"

Coloring at being caught holding on to it like a security blanket, she handed the coat over to the male server who had the training not to turn up his nose at the distinctly non-designer cut. "Thank you," she said and pulled out her own chair before Gabriel Bishop could do it, not sure she could handle him at her back. He was too big, too overwhelming— and she hated strangers at her back regardless.

He watched her fight to pull the heavy chair back in under her but didn't comment.

Face hot, she tried to focus on the words handwritten on the thick, textured paper of the menu, but it might as well have been in Swahili.

"Have you made your choice?"

Because he was looking at her as if waiting for a decision, she pointed randomly at a line on the menu and hoped she wasn't ordering brains in a lovely mint sauce or something else equally unappetizing. The menu was whisked away a second later, water brought to the table.

"Now, Ms. Baird."

She looked up, hearing something in his voice that told

her he expected attention. Those steely eyes were focused on her to the exclusion of all else. "Y...yes," she said, the word barely audible.

"Tell me about the current situation with the Hamilton land negotiation. It's obvious the potential buyers want the site of the old factory. It's equally obvious Saxon & Archer needs the capital. What's the holdup?"

The file opened in Charlotte's mind, her visual memory acute. She could hear her mental voice laying out the facts in a clean, crisp manner, but nothing came through her vocal chords; instead, her fingernails dug into her palms. Panic fluttered in her chest, a trapped bird with a sharp beak that pecked and pecked at her.

2

THERE IS GROWLING

"LET'S TABLE THAT QUESTION for now," Gabriel said when it appeared Ms. Baird was about to hyperventilate. "It's Saturday night, and you've already pulled a full day."

She gave a jerky nod and gulped down some water, her eyes anywhere but on him.

Gabriel was used to inciting a reaction in women. The tall, confident, sexy ones flirted with him. The not-so-confident ones smiled shyly at him, and even women put off by his physique generally changed their minds after speaking to him for a few minutes and realizing he wasn't all brawn and no brain.

He knew many of the women who hit on him weren't actually interested in him as a person. A few just wanted "a bit of rough" in bed, while others were after a trophy sports-star husband—enough to overlook the fact he was no longer on the playing field. Then there were the ones looking for a wealthy CEO who could keep them in diamonds.

The fact he was young and in good shape was a bonus to the fortune hunters; it was his money that was the draw. As long as they had access to a healthy bank account, those women would coo sweet nothings into the ear of a toothless old man of ninety-eight. So while Gabriel knew he was attractive enough and had never had trouble finding a woman with whom to heat up the sheets, it wasn't as if he thought of himself as God's gift to women. However, neither was he an ogre.

Except Charlotte Baird, whose personnel file he'd looked up after meeting her, seemed to strongly disagree with the latter. Petite and pretty, she'd been sitting so petrified through dinner that anyone would think he'd attacked her rather than the other way around. Her fear roused his temper, which only made her fingers clench tighter on her cutlery, until the fine lines of her bones were outlined against creamy skin dusted with gold—which further exacerbated his temper.

Realizing she'd starve if he didn't allow her to leave, he motioned the waiter to their table. "Box Ms. Baird's meal to go. Add the blackberry cheesecake."

Her eyes flicked up, hazel and clear behind her glasses, her lips parting. "No, it's okay," she said in a rasp of a voice even as the waiter cleared away her meal.

"I'm paying for the damn meal, Ms. Baird. You might as well enjoy it." He didn't care about the cost; what he cared about was that the woman across from him had eaten exactly two tiny bites in fifteen minutes. It wasn't as if she had flesh to spare—though she wasn't skin and bones. No, she was just small, her weight in perfect proportion to her bone structure. So she ate. Just not with him.

Having shut up at his snarl, skin paling, she didn't say another word until they'd left the restaurant.

"Where's your car parked?" he asked, not wanting her on the streets alone given the high number of sports fans who'd

16

poured into the city while they were in the restaurant. Most were fine, in a cheerful mood, but it was obvious a few had started drinking early.

"I catch the bus," she said, shoulders hunched under that hideous brown coat that swallowed her up. "I only live just past St. Lukes."

Gabriel's first instinct was to offer to drive her to the suburb. It was what he'd have done with any other woman in this situation. However Ms. Baird's bones might well chatter themselves out of her skin if he suggested she get into a confined space with him for longer than a few seconds.

Leading her to a taxi stand instead, he said, "Take a cab and file an expense report on Monday."

"I didn't—"

"*Take* the damn cab." It came out through gritted teeth. The idea of any man hurting a woman made Gabriel see red. The fact Charlotte seemed to think *he'd* hurt her scraped against his every nerve.

Flinching, she didn't argue again when he pulled open the back door of the cab and told the driver she needed to go toward St. Lukes.

"Ms. Baird," he said once she was seated, "don't forget that expense claim. I'll be checking on it personally."

Huge hazel eyes locked with his for a second. Beautiful eyes, he thought, clear and striated with gold and green behind the transparent lenses of her spectacles. Her eyes went with the soft blond curls she'd tied into a ponytail, a few wisps having escaped to kiss her flawlessly clear skin.

A petite but tempting morsel. Too bad she was terrified at the sight of him.

CHARLOTTE DIDN'T SAY THANK you to Gabriel Bishop for the cab, instead sitting frozen in her seat until he shut the door and the driver pulled out. Probably not the best thing to do if one was trying not to get fired, but her nerves were shot. One more minute in his company and she might just have burst into tears.

Pathetic, Charlotte. You are a pathetic excuse for a woman.

Her teeth clenched at the ugly echo of Richard's voice; her hands fisted so tight her bones hurt. She hated that despite all the work she'd done, all the success she'd achieved in overcoming that horrible year of her life, fear could still creep into her heart like this, incapacitate without warning. Hated even more that Richard's voice could infiltrate her thoughts even now, the ugly things he'd said dripping venom into her veins.

Monday would be a nightmare. All she could hope was that Gabriel Bishop would forget about the inconsequential mouse he'd taken to dinner and stay focused only on the higher-ups.

3

T-Rex Goes on a Rampage

SHE'D FILED THE EXPENSE claim. Putting down the phone after checking with the accounts department, Gabriel wondered what Ms. Baird would do if he decided to pay her a visit and ask her how her Sunday had gone. Probably jump out of her skin, her bones clattering against one another.

Scowling, he continued to go over the documents in front of him. Saxon & Archer was an old company with a good, strong core. Unfortunately, that core was buried under multiple layers of mold, courtesy of serious mishandling by the past CEO—a man who'd given the *appearance* of competence, but who, from what Gabriel could tell, had spent the majority of his time playing golf with his cronies. He'd all but driven the company straight into bankruptcy.

As a result, the luxury department stores that had long been the jewel in Saxon & Archer's crown were faltering; retail and corporate employee morale was so low that attrition was at an all-time high. As for the supply centers that created branded Saxon & Archer goods—once considered a premier brand—they'd been badly managed to the point that online review sites had begun to joke about knockoff Saxon & Archer goods being better than the originals.

When the board had woken up at last and terminated the idiot CEO's contract, they'd also voted unanimously to offer the position to Gabriel. Two major reasons underlay their decision. The first was his consistent track record in hauling ailing businesses out of financial hot water and putting them on the path to stellar success. The second was his ability to fire people who needed firing.

After spending the past week going over the personnel and financial files at his home office, then rechecking details this weekend, Gabriel had a long list. "Anya," he said into the intercom, "get Legal up here."

The portly and bald sixty-year-old in-house lawyer was in Gabriel's office five minutes later, his shoulders stiff and his lips pressed into a thin white line against the deep brown of his skin.

"I'm not firing you," Gabriel said, waving the older man into a seat. "You're actually one of the few competent people on the senior staff." Age didn't matter to Gabriel; it was what the individual brought to the table that counted.

Blinking quickly, the lawyer took a seat and pulled out a sheaf of documents from the briefcase he'd brought with him. "I'm assuming you want to know if there are any legal or contractual issues you need to be aware of before you begin to terminate contracts?"

Gabriel smiled what one business opponent had called his "shark" smile. "Like I said, you're competent."

CHARLOTTE HID OUT IN her cubicle after reaching it without running into Gabriel Bishop. Word filtered down by midmorning that he was causing carnage in upper management. More offices had been cleared out in the past two hours than in all the time Charlotte had been working at Saxon & Archer.

"Psst."

She looked up at the furtive sound to find Tuck leaning with his arms on top of her cubicle wall.

Smiling at him, the lanky nineteen-year-old mail clerk one of the few men with whom she was totally comfortable, she said, "Careful you don't get caught 'lazing about' or Mr. Varma might decide he doesn't really need a clerk." Charlotte herself had been working nonstop since arriving at her desk; Anya had been driving her hard as Gabriel Bishop made demand after demand.

"Nah." Tuck looked left, then right, before leaning even farther over the wall to whisper, "Mr. Varma's too worried about his own job. Did you hear the new boss just fired Mrs. Chang?"

Charlotte's eyes widened. "Wow." Dolly Chang had been running the PR department for over ten years… though she did have a tendency to take long lunches with her friends and bill it to the company. Not to mention she constantly copied the old campaigns of offshore companies, making just enough minor adjustments to get away with it. The fact most of those campaigns had no relevance in the New Zealand market seemed to either escape her or cause her no concern.

"I guess I'm not too surprised," Charlotte said slowly. "Mr. Bishop does have a reputation for coming in and cleaning house."

He cemented that reputation over the next eight hours. Two-thirds of senior management was gone by the end of the day, the remaining third too busy to worry about anything but work. Five members of the junior staff received unexpected promotions, while others were demoted or warned to improve their performance if they wanted a job at the end of the month.

Once again, Tuck had the gossip. "I heard one of Dolly's juniors say the boss said he wouldn't blame her for her shoddy work to date since she'd had a bad supervisor," the teenager told her as they left the office together.

"That's kind." Not a word she would've associated with the man who'd snarled at her to take the damn cab. Like a bad-tempered T-Rex, she thought.

Tuck zipped up his multicolored jacket with its dozens of pockets. "Yeah, but then he said if she didn't improve over the next three months, she'd be out." He drew a line across his throat. "I figure that's fair, right? Especially now that she has a chance to get a promotion since Dolly isn't around to push her favorites into the best spots."

"Yes," Charlotte said. "It's very fair." Harsh, but reasonable.

However, if she'd thought that first day was the end of it, she was wrong. She came into work the next day and quickly learned that T-Rex wasn't finished. The atmosphere on her floor was muted and tense and hyperactive all at the same time as people tried to show they could do their jobs.

Anya kept Charlotte busy until Charlotte barely had five spare minutes to gulp down lunch at her desk. Charlotte wasn't naïve or stupid; she knew full well the other woman was taking advantage of her. Charlotte's job was in Records, not as Anya's assistant—but as long as Anya was too lazy to do her job, Charlotte's would be secure. The fact was, with Records now so well computerized thanks to Charlotte's own work, she'd worried she'd be seen as redundant, her head on the chopping block.

Especially with Gabriel Bishop on a mission to clean house.

He really was a T-Rex, stomping through the company, chewing up people and spitting them out left, right, and center. But the T-Rex wasn't looking Charlotte's way, and that was fine with her. She'd just be a quiet, industrious little mouse in the corner, not worth bothering with but too useful to fire.

Then the carnivorous creature decided to notice her.

Tuck was handing her a stack of mail that afternoon when the dreaded call came. "Boss wants to see you," Anya said, a smirk in her tone. "Now. And bring your laptop."

Her pulse in her mouth and her cheeks hot, Charlotte smoothed her hands down the dark brown linen of her calf-length skirt before pulling on the matching jacket over her white shirt. "Off I go to get eaten alive," she said to Tuck, trying to make a joke out of what was no doubt her execution and failing abysmally.

The idea of those hard gray eyes on her, that icy focus... Goose bumps broke out over her skin as she picked up her laptop and slid it into a bag. She wasn't sure she could carry it in her hands without it slipping out of her grasp; the fine tremor in her bones had her barely able to sling the strap of the bag over her shoulder.

"If he fires you," Tuck said, his brown eyes stark with distress, "he's an idiot."

Charlotte wondered if Tuck would still say that if he knew she'd thrown a stapler at the boss's head. As far as first impressions went, it couldn't get much worse. Unless, of course, said stapler-throwing employee then lost the ability to speak while out at dinner with the same boss, instead doing an excellent impression of a statue.

Stomach knotting at the reminder of how badly she'd screwed up, she stepped out of her cubicle. Her skin prickled. It was obvious from the number of sympathetic eyes on her that people had guessed where she was headed and why. Not surprising. Three others from this floor had made the trek. None had returned, their belongings packed up by assistants assigned the task.

Some of her colleagues called out soft words of encouragement, but she could tell that despite their sympathy, they all thought she was a goner.

One of the senior people in Legal was more blunt when Charlotte passed her office. "I told you to apply for Anya's position when it first opened up."

Yes, she had, not seeming to realize the extent of Charlotte's shyness. Charlotte's inability to sell herself as an employee was pathetic. After being fired, she'd probably end up working for a mail-order business out of her home, never speaking to any other human except Molly. Eventually, she'd turn into a crazy woman with bird's-nest hair who frightened small children and random telemarketers.

Shut up, Charlotte. This is not helping.

A second later, she was off her floor and climbing the stairs that led up to the managerial level. Taking several deep, gulping breaths when she reached the landing, she gripped the strap of her laptop bag and entered the floor. Everyone was too busy up here to stare at her—and quite a few offices were empty, the occupants booted out.

All too soon, she was in front of the automatic glass doors that guarded the CEO's domain, the walls on either side of the doors also clear glass. The expensive renovation had been done by order of Bernard Hill, the previous CEO. Anya's office lay in the section immediately beyond the glass, and it had a glorious view on the right as you walked in, courtesy of a floor-to-ceiling window that drenched the area in natural light.

The CEO's office with its rumored even more spectacular view of the city lay behind the PA's office and attached waiting area. It had its own door, no glass anywhere in sight. Likely so Bernard could nap in quiet privacy while Saxon & Archer fell into ruin.

Anya noted her entrance and waved her into the den of the T-Rex without bothering to rise from the clear glass—of course—sprawl of her desk. The other woman was all perfect makeup and poise, her glossy brown hair expertly blow-dried and her grape-colored dress hugging her svelte form while appearing businesslike.

According to the rumor mill, the other woman had set her cap for Gabriel Bishop. One of the general admin staff had heard Anya talking to the CFO's personal assistant about her ambition to be Mrs. Bishop. She'd said something along the lines of having him eating out of her hand inside a week.

Charlotte didn't think anyone could manage Gabriel Bishop if he didn't want to be managed, but physically at least, Anya fit his type: tall, beautiful, together.

"Go in," Anya said with a roll of her eyes when Charlotte hesitated in front of the closed door to the CEO's office. "It'll only take him a minute to give you your marching orders."

Then who'll do your work?

Throat dry, Charlotte didn't utter the snarky thought. Instead, determined not to let Anya see her flinch, she swallowed and, opening the door after a quick knock, went in. She made sure to close the door behind herself. If she was about to be fired, she could at least save herself the humiliation of having Anya listen in.

The view *was* spectacular, and the previous CEO's pristine glass desk was gone. Charlotte knew about that desk because she'd seen it being brought in by the movers. It had been a stylish designer piece that Tuck had seen in the office itself. Apparently, Bernard had kept it clear of everything but his phone and a single gold-plated pen, the desk's surface shining and clean.

Gabriel Bishop, in contrast, was seated behind a heavy and scarred mahogany desk covered with paper and binders as well as two laptops running different programs. He was currently scowling at what looked like a contract with one of their suppliers. His dark blue tie hung loosely around his neck, as if he'd tugged impatiently at it, and the sleeves of his white shirt were folded up to his elbows to reveal just a hint of the extensive ink on his body.

He seemed unaware of the breathtaking view at his back, the waters of the Hauraki Gulf glittering under the icy-white autumn sunlight.

"Ms. Baird," he said without looking up, "for what earthly reason do we still have a contract with McElvoy Shoes when the stores have had to send back multiple shipments for shoddy workmanship?"

Palms sweaty, Charlotte gripped the strap of her laptop case even tighter.

T-Rex raised his head, those steely gray eyes laserlike in their intensity. "Sit down before you shake apart." A snarl.

Charlotte sat.

And he went back to flipping through the contract. "Ms. Baird, an answer before I'm eighty-five would be nice."

Realizing his question hadn't been a rhetorical one, she closed her eyes so she couldn't see him and blurted out, "Mr. Hill was friends with old Mr. McElvoy, and when McElvoy Senior was in charge, the workmanship was exemplary, the delivery dates never missed. But now he's handed the reins to his son and things are slipping."

"The many and various people in management who had to be aware of this didn't bring it to my inept predecessor's attention?"

Peeking out and seeing he was still looking through the contract, his scowl even heavier, Charlotte said, "I think they tried, but Mr. Hill was very loyal to his friend." Or too lazy to handle the matter when it was so much less stressful to let it slide and go play golf instead.

Given his work habits—or lack of work habits—Charlotte had no idea how Bernard Hill had managed to rise to the position of CEO of Saxon & Archer, but then, as shown by Anya, the world didn't always reward those it should.

Her skin grew cold at the reminder that she was about to end up just as unemployed as Mr. Hill.

"One thing's clear," Gabriel Bishop said now, his jaw set in a brutal line. "McElvoy Junior has been hosing us with these charges." Grabbing the phone, he made a call to Legal. "Terminate the McElvoy contract. They're in breach for the tenth time—and get the damn penalty payments."

Having utilized the momentary break to retrieve her laptop from the bag, Charlotte waited to be asked to hand it in since it was company property. Why he'd made her carry it up herself, she didn't know. Everyone else had been called up as they were. Maybe he wanted to punish her in some extra way because she'd thrown a stapler at his head.

"Tell me about the Khan negotiation," he said, setting the McElvoy contract aside to pick up a different one on which it looked like he'd already scrawled notes in deep blue ink. "Hill's personal file on the situation is fragmented at best. Far as I can figure, Khan is happy to sell us the land for a parking lot but has a sentimental attachment to the building currently on-site. I'm assuming you kept better records as part of your job?"

Charlotte stared.

Gabriel Bishop shoved a hand through his hair, then leaned forward, forearms braced on a desk that had so many nicks and dents that she knew instinctively it had followed him from company to company as he did what he did best. "Ms. Baird," he said, those cold eyes watching her with a relentless focus that made her every muscle tense to breaking point, "from the memos I see on these files, all of which were apparently created at your workstation, you're highly intelligent. I don't want to fire you, but I will if you can't give me the information I need."

4

In News That Surprises No One, Anya Is a Bitch

CHARLOTTE WAS FLABBERGASTED THAT he'd made a point of checking the origin of the memos for which Anya always took credit. She was so shocked that she might have frozen into silence again; it was the critical sentence "I don't want to fire you" that gave her the courage to speak.

"Mr. Khan," she said, coughing to clear her throat and pinning her eyes on the knot of his tie so she wouldn't have to hold his gaze, "is playing hardball because he knows Saxon & Archer needs that land. There's nothing else available."

"Reasons for your conclusion?" Gabriel Bishop asked, making edits to another document as he spoke, his strokes sure, the red ink like blood on the page.

It was easier to speak when he wasn't looking at her. "I've seen three or four of the e-mails he exchanged with Mr. Hill." Bernard Hill had been terrible about saving crucial e-mails, but Anya had forwarded Charlotte the odd one to add to the file. "It's obvious if you read between the lines. He says things like 'I'm sure we can come to a compromise. I know how useful the land would be to Saxon & Archer, and I'm a reasonable man.'"

Her new boss put down his pen and leaned back in his chair, his attention now fully on her. "I see. Did Hill explore any other options on the parking situation?"

God, it was hard to think when the force of his personality was smashing against her senses. Lowering her gaze to the knot of his tie again, she said, "No," then bit her lip and went with her gut. It might be twisted into a pretzel by now, but since he hadn't fired her yet... "I did once see a memo from Brent Sinclair"—a very junior member of staff—"that suggested we implement a complimentary shuttle system from a major commercial parking lot about fifteen minutes away."

A frown from the man on the other side of the desk. "I haven't seen that memo. Forward it to me."

Having already popped open her laptop, Charlotte was able to quickly locate and forward the memo, and after Gabriel scanned it, he asked her countless more questions about other ongoing situations. She barely had time to breathe for the next two hours. She certainly didn't have time for nerves. The man's mind was a steel trap, and he expected the same from her. How he even *knew* to ask the questions, some of them incredibly detailed and obscure, she didn't know.

She answered everything as best she could, having to access the electronic records system for the more intricate details. Just when she thought they were done, he asked her how she'd book a last-minute Friday business trip to Saxon & Archer's Sydney offices for him, with a dinner party thrown for corporate partners upon arrival.

Charlotte blinked but managed an answer; she'd handled such details multiple times. Anya usually drafted up what she needed, and Charlotte made it happen. Maybe, she thought suddenly, T-Rex intended to make her Anya's official assistant. Not her dream job, since she'd be stuck in an office near the condescending Anya all day, but better than being unemployed.

"Enough." Gabriel Bishop glanced at his watch. "Tell Anya to get Sinclair up here."

Charlotte escaped as quickly as possible, sneaking away for fifteen minutes to go grab a stabilizing coffee from her favorite café half a block over. Walking around the entire block to calm herself, she returned to her desk to find an e-mail from Anya requesting a concise summary of a labor dispute the previous CEO had ignored for well over half a year.

The other woman had added: *p.s. Guess you haven't been demoted to being the tea lady just yet.*

Relieved at the normality of the request and of Anya's bitchiness, Charlotte knuckled down to work.

HAVING SENT SINCLAIR OFF to draft a more detailed breakdown of his plan after grilling the younger man and confirming the strength of his idea, Gabriel considered the mouse who'd been in his office not long ago. Ugly brown suit, soft blond hair that was in a bun today, and clear hazel eyes shielded behind the lenses of her wire-rimmed spectacles, Charlotte Baird did her best to disappear into the woodwork.

What Gabriel had discovered today was that the mouse wasn't only hardworking but was also highly perceptive and had a keen intelligence. In the miniscule fractions of time in which she forgot to be terrified of him, she'd… sparkled. Like there was a brilliant light deep inside her, stifled by a crippling lack of confidence.

An intriguing mouse was Ms. Baird.

Gabriel found himself interested, and he'd never before found a mouse interesting.

Setting aside the problem posed by having an employee who was clearly in the wrong position for her skill set, he turned his attention from the mouse to the flashy bird of paradise.

"Anya," he said into the intercom. "Come into the office. And bring your laptop."

FEELING AS IF SHE'D been through the wars, Charlotte ate a whole bag of chocolate raisins at her desk that evening while finishing up some work for Anya. Her brain felt like it had the consistency of noodle soup.

It wasn't the work that had exhausted her. No, that had been hectic but interesting. It was the stress of not knowing whether she'd still have a job at the end of the week. Anya's "tea lady" comment had been pure spite, but given Charlotte's abysmal interviewing skills, she'd be lucky if future employers even trusted her to make tea.

That morose thought was still uppermost in her mind when Molly called at seven to ask if she'd like to grab dinner down at the Viaduct. "Yes!" she said to her friend, and decided then and there that she'd put the whole employment situation out of her head for the next few hours.

She did slip up and mention the fact she thought Gabriel was a T-Rex, which Molly found hysterical, but her news about work drama paled in comparison to Molly's bombshell. After deciding on dessert before dinner, the two of them walked down to sit by the water, ice creams in hand as they waited for a super yacht to come in. That was when Molly confessed the aftermath of a cocktail party they'd attended the previous Friday night.

In short, her best friend had taken Zachary Fox, rock star and man voted "Reigning Sex God" by a men's magazine three years running, up on his offer of a one-night stand.

Charlotte's mouth fell open. "You—with Zachary Fox—" Throwing one arm around Molly, Charlotte smacked a big kiss on her best friend's cheek, Molly's skin a pure cream now touched with color. "My hero!" She pulled back her arm a second before her ice cream would've toppled over. "At least one of us will have outrageous stories with which to shock any grandchildren we might or might not have."

Molly giggled and leaned into Charlotte, her wild tumble of black hair pulled back into a tight braid. Then, eyes on the water rippling with color from the lights of nearby businesses, Molly told her how the one-night stand had turned into a much more complicated arrangement that held the potential to tear open old scars so jagged and raw that Charlotte wasn't sure the wounds had ever truly healed.

"Do you think I'm being ridiculous?" her best friend whispered. "About not being caught by the media with Fox?"

"Of course not." Charlotte finished off her cone, balled up the napkin it had been wrapped in, and took Molly's to the trash as well before coming back. "I was there, remember?" She closed her hand over Molly's, heart hurting for her friend. "Did you tell Fox about what happened? So he knows it has nothing to do with him?"

Shaking her head, Molly pointed out the gleaming super yacht that had appeared in the distance. They watched the sleek craft glide in, the words they exchanged in the ensuing minutes layered with old pain.

Driven by her love for the woman who'd been her best friend since they first met in nursery school over two decades ago, Charlotte said, "I'm scared, Molly. All the time." Until she couldn't breathe sometimes. "You know why."

Molly hugged her close, her voice fierce as she said, "We don't have to talk about it."

"No, it's okay." She turned to face Molly, looking into the warm brown eyes that had been the first thing she'd seen after she woke in the hospital bed just over five years ago. Molly hadn't left her bedside for a single minute. "I miss out on so much because I'm scared—and the thing is, I'm intelligent enough to know it." To be painfully aware she was living in a cage of her own construction. "That just makes it worse."

"You're selling yourself short." Molly scowled. "You said I was brave, but I wouldn't have made it through high school and foster care without you. You were my rock."

"You were mine, too." Charlotte shook her head, refusing to allow her friend to be sucked under by the trauma and anguish that had blighted her teenage years. "Don't let that tough, strong, fifteen-year-old girl down, Molly. Don't shortchange yourself like I do." Charlotte knew it was too late for her to break the bars of her own cage, but Molly had a shot and Charlotte would do everything in her power to make sure her friend took it.

"Is it worth it," Molly said at last, the agony of memory in every word, "for a single month?"

"That's for you to decide," Charlotte said, then fanned her face. "But I vote for breaking the bed with Mr. Kissable."

Molly burst out laughing, the sound a little wet. "Maybe you need a rock star of your own."

"No way. I'd rather go to bed with T-Rex." It was a flip comment that hid countless fantasies. And fantasies they would remain, she thought, as she and Molly found a place to eat after her best friend finished grilling her about her new boss. Because the fear inside her, it would permit nothing else, permit no extraordinary life where she caught and held the attention of a man like Gabriel Bishop.

THE NEXT MORNING, CHARLOTTE was still thinking about Molly and hoping her friend would find a way to talk to her rock star about the past, when geeky, sweet Tuck poked his head around her cubicle wall. "Charlie, did you hear?"

Put on guard by the awed shock in his tone, she said, "What?"

"Anya," he whispered, eyes all but popping out of his head and dark blond hair disheveled. "*He* fired *Anya.*"

Charlotte collapsed into her chair, her knees like jelly. "Oh, no." If Anya was gone, she had to be next. She jumped a foot when her phone rang even as the thought passed through her head.

"Ms. Baird. In my office."

Hanging up with trembling hands, she pushed up her glasses and told herself she could deal with T-Rex and the chopping block. After all, she'd survived far worse. That's what she had to remember. She'd *survived.* "I have to go upstairs," she said to Tuck.

The nineteen-year-old's face telegraphed his distress. "God, Charlie."

"It's okay. I'll come see you afterward." If she was even allowed back on the floor and not just shown the door.

People didn't stare at her this time. She might've taken that for a vote of confidence if not for the funereal gloom on their faces when they glanced at her out of the corners of their eyes. Most of them had already been through the gauntlet, come out safe on the other side.

Most of them weren't in a redundant position.

The walk upstairs and down the corridor felt like it took an eon, and then she was entering the T-Rex's den, his door having been open. He was standing with his back to the glass wall with its incredible view, his cell phone to his ear. Today's suit was a deep charcoal gray paired with a steel-gray shirt and a charcoal tie. Austere and dark, it threw his features into stark relief.

Gabriel Bishop was a gorgeous man.

Charlotte could admit that in the privacy of her own mind. Too big and muscled and dangerous, but gorgeous. Like a tiger was gorgeous. Right before it ate you.

Walking over to his desk, still involved in a discussion that—from the context—she guessed was with one of their South Island store managers, he picked up a cup of takeout coffee and held it out to her. She took it on a surge of hope. Despite her thoughts when they'd first met, T-Rex *didn't* have a policy of offering his victims a last meal—or last drink. Since she wasn't sure her jelly knees would continue to support her, she took a seat while he paced and talked.

After she girded herself to sip at his version of coffee, having glimpsed the tar-black stuff in the open takeout cup on his side of the desk, she found her taste buds blooming. He'd handed her a frothy, creamy latte—one of her favorites.

At this point, Charlotte had given up guessing how he knew things. But *surely* he wasn't planning to fire her... unless he got off on being cruel. On raising hopes only to dash them. There were men like that. She knew. God, she knew.

Stomach a ball of ice between one thought and the next, she held on desperately to the cup as he ended the call and pinned her with his gaze.

"Ms. Baird, we need to have a serious discussion about your future."

5

CHARLIE-MOUSE VS T-REX:
ROUND 1

GABRIEL WATCHED CHARLOTTE'S SLENDER fingers tighten around the takeout cup so hard that she dented it.

Her cheeks had gone pale, but she kept her shoulders up and she found her voice. "Yes, sir?"

Good, he thought. The fact she was shy and uncomfortable around him was a distinct negative when it came to the position he was about to offer her, but she had guts and she had brains. He could work with that. "I need a new PA."

She blinked, her fingers easing their death grip on the takeout cup. "Do you want me to help HR screen applicants?" The faintest hint of a relieved smile. "I have a good idea of what Anya's job entailed."

"No," he said, taking a seat since he could tell his size intimidated her. Not that he was much smaller sitting down. "There won't be any applicants. You are going to be my new PA."

She just stared at him, her soft pink lips parted in a silent gasp. Bitable lips. That, he told himself, was a highly inappropriate thought, but for some reason, he couldn't wipe it from his brain. When she wasn't quivering in terror, Ms. Baird with her agile mind and her sparkling eyes was very, very intriguing. As for the rest of her—her shapeless clothes couldn't hide the fact she was built like a pocket Venus. Undo her ponytail, take off the glasses—or maybe he'd leave them on—and she'd be a petite, curvy, *bitable* package.

Of course, his attraction to this pretty mouse wouldn't have saved her position if she'd been incompetent. Though had the latter been true, he wouldn't have found her anywhere near as intriguing. Smart women were his catnip.

Too bad he was her boss. "You'll take over Anya's role, effective immediately."

Eyes going wide, she squeaked out a protest. "I can't do Anya's job!"

Gabriel raised an eyebrow. "Really? Strange, since it appears you *have* been doing it for the past three years." There was nothing he hated more in the business world than people who took credit for the hard work of others. "Anya couldn't answer the majority of the questions I posed to you yesterday."

Worse, unlike Charlotte, the other woman hadn't known where to go or which files to access to get the information. She'd just smiled serenely and said she'd have the research on his desk first thing in the morning, then had no doubt gone out and e-mailed Charlotte the work requests.

Gabriel's suspicions had been roused Monday—by the fact his PA was always available and smiling and put together in spite of the fact he'd thrown an avalanche of work at her. Any other man or woman in her position would've snapped at him at least once, and never, *never* would she have been able to leave the office at a reasonable hour. It had taken him less than five minutes to access the file records of the memos hitting his desk.

The last access code was always Anya's—when she'd printed out the document. Everything below that linked back to Charlotte's workstation. It was to make dead certain of his suspicions that he'd put both women through the same interview yesterday. He didn't need a polished liar by his side; he needed Charlotte with her intelligence and her deep knowledge of the staff and their skills. Without her, it might've taken him weeks to discover Sinclair.

Anya hadn't known the Sinclair proposal even existed.

"But," Charlotte began on a rush of breath, as if she'd built herself up to get it all out, "I don't know how to deal with suppliers and management and—"

"You'll learn." Gabriel couldn't figure out why a woman so damn good at her job was so diffident about her abilities. "There's really no choice. You accept this position or you pack up and go," he said, testing how far he could push her. "You've done too good a job in your current role—there's no longer any need for a full-time employee there." An absolute truth. "It's be my PA or hand in your access card to the building."

She put her coffee on the desk he'd moved in on Sunday, her fingers curling into fists and hot spots of color on her cheeks. So, there was a temper there. Good. She'd need it to deal with him—Gabriel knew full well that he wasn't the easiest of bosses. When she swallowed without unleashing the temper however, he wanted to growl at her.

Throttling back an impulse that would only terrify her, he said, "Yes or no?"

A long, indrawn breath. "Yes," she said on the exhale.

CHARLOTTE DECIDED SHE MUST'VE lost her mind as she set herself up at Anya's former desk, T-Rex having given her fifteen minutes to get herself sorted. A gleeful Tuck helped her move her things.

"I knew the Bishop was *the man*," he said, unadulterated hero worship in his tone as he used T-Rex's famous on-field moniker.

The Bishop, Charlotte thought mutinously, was a bully. One who kept her on her toes the entire day. Five o'clock came and went with no sign of stopping. At six, unsure of the protocol of being a PA, she looked through his door—which he tended to keep open except when in private meetings—and saw him scowling at the screen of the sleek laptop he preferred over a desktop.

His tie was gone, the top two buttons of his shirt undone to offer a glimpse of the tanned skin at the vee of his throat. Fine as the fabric of the shirt was, she could make out a hint of his tattoos under the surface, see the flex of muscle as he worked.

Why did T-Rex have to be so big and gorgeous?

Throat dry, she nonetheless made herself knock. "Sir."

"Do you know how to fix this?"

Walking over, she realized the problem straightaway. It was something that had happened to her a couple of times and she'd learned the trick of fixing it from their tech support team.

"I can…" She made to go around his desk.

He pushed away, thrusting both hands through his hair before he picked up a pen to sign a contract she'd handed him earlier. Relieved at not having to deal with his large,

41

powerful body close to her, she quickly fixed the computer glitch and went back around to the other side of the desk.

He handed her the contracts. "Get that to the courier for morning delivery. And where's Merrill? I need to see her."

"She headed home a few minutes ago to have dinner with her family." The CFO had stuck her head in to say good night. "She said she'd finish off the financial report once her kids are in bed, e-mail it through. Do you want me to ask her to return to the office instead?"

"No." Scowling, he glanced at his watch, as if he'd completely missed the fact it was getting dark outside, the sweeping view of the harbor lost on a man who barely seemed to notice it. "Do you have to be anywhere?"

Charlotte had intended to meet Ernest for dinner, but that didn't seem like something she should say to her boss right after a promotion. "No," she said, consoling herself with the reminder of the considerable pay hike she'd received today.

"In that case, can you find me these contracts?" He rattled off a list.

Heading out to Records, she located the originals and gave them to him, then returned to her desk to make a call to Ernest. "We'll have to reschedule," she told the kind, gentle man with whom she had no trouble speaking or interacting. They'd been dating for a year, and never had he made her feel in any way threatened or overwhelmed.

"I'll miss talking to you," he said. "But congratulations on the promotion."

"Thanks, Ernest." Hanging up soon afterward, she felt the hairs rise on the back of her neck and glanced back to realize

Gabriel had come to his office doorway. "Did you need anything further?"

Instead of answering, he raised an eyebrow. "Boyfriend?"

Her cheeks heated. "Yes."

"Funny name."

"What?" She frowned. "Ernest is a perfectly nice name."

"Oh, I thought I heard you call him Ermine." Passing her a sheaf of paper with that oh-so-offhand comment that had her eyes narrowing, he asked her to input the changes and flick the file back to him so he could finalize a contract with a London-based supplier.

After that came another task, then another. It was ten by the time she could leave. T-Rex was still in his office and showing no signs that he'd be heading out anytime soon. They'd eaten earlier, after he'd had her order in meals from a top local restaurant. Now, though, she worried he'd get hungry later. It wasn't as if he was a small man, and his brain probably burned as much fuel per hour as most men did pumping iron.

Putting down her handbag, she went to the staff break room and hit the vending machine before returning to his office. He was standing in front of an easel on which an architect had earlier that day placed a number of design specs for the renovations of their flagship Auckland, Queenstown, and Sydney locations.

"Good night, Mr. Bishop." She drew in a quick breath. "I got you some granola bars." It had been the healthiest snack she could find in the machine—she'd have to speak to the stockers about filling it with more nutritional items.

"Thanks." A frown in her direction. "A cab, Ms. Baird."

"I called one." That was the one company perk she'd never felt bad about using, not when she worked late. It was a matter of safety.

"I'll walk you down." Stretching his shoulders, he came over.

Charlotte wanted to say there was no need but decided it wasn't worth using up her small store of courage. She kept herself from hyperventilating during the elevator ride down by silently doing the exercise her therapist had taught her. That was the *only* useful thing she'd gotten out of therapy.

Almost tumbling out on the ground floor, the warm, intrinsically male scent of Gabriel Bishop in her every inhalation, she released a relieved breath when she spotted the cab through the glass of the main doors, the bearded and grandfatherly Indian cab driver familiar. Gabriel Bishop walked her down the steps and opened the back door to the sedan.

"I'll see you tomorrow," her boss said and shut the door.

As the cab pulled away, she saw him stride down toward the waterfront, hands in his pockets, tall and strong and a relentless force.

GABRIEL RARELY SECOND-GUESSED himself, but he was doing so tonight. Charlotte Baird was highly competent, to the point that he'd blasted through far more work than he'd expected to complete today, so he'd made no mistake there. She was also petrified of him, had once again almost hyperventilated herself into a faint in the elevator. Logically, he should transfer her to a less frontline position within the company, but he hated the idea of all that talent being buried away or taken advantage of by another Anya.

Striding across the flat paving stones of Auckland's central public-transport hub, he crossed the street to the ferry terminal and stood watching the evening water traffic as he considered the problem. Not only was Charlotte spectacularly easy to work with, anticipating his requests even after only a single day working together, she had an excellent sense of what was important and what wasn't. He'd had far fewer interruptions from other staff today as a result.

Quite aside from that, and even disregarding his physical attraction to her when she wasn't being a mouse, he liked Ms. Baird. He'd heard her talking on the phone with a woman called Molly for a few minutes late this afternoon, caught a glimpse of a dry wit that had made him grin. Yeah, he liked the woman behind the mouse.

However, that woman tended to go into hiding around him.

Tapping his fingers on the metal railing, he turned and almost ran into a statuesque blonde in a sparkly dress. "Hi," she said, the look in her eyes making it clear she'd recognized him, two women who were clearly her friends standing a short distance away. "My friends dared me to ask you out, but I was planning to do it anyway." Her smile deepened. "Join us for a drink."

"Appreciate the offer," Gabriel said, "but I've got to return to the office."

"If you change your mind, we'll be in there." She pointed out a waterfront bar. "We're all huge rugby fans, would love to watch tonight's Argentina-England game with you." Biting down on her lower lip, she leaned in a little closer. "If you'd rather watch in private, my apartment's not far."

Gabriel could tell from her tone and smile that watching sports wasn't the only thing on the menu. "Thanks."

It wasn't until he was back in the office that he realized he hadn't even been tempted by the stranger's offer... because he had another blonde on his mind. *That* could prove problematic, but it had nothing to do with Charlotte's suitability for her position. He'd give her a week, see if she stopped quivering in terror. Any longer and he'd probably give in to the urge to snarl.

That thought in mind, he went over to the design specs again, was trying to figure out why the second-floor design wasn't working for him, when Charlotte's office phone rang. Guessing that an international contact who'd e-mailed him earlier to ask if he'd be in had called the wrong line, he walked out to his PA's desk and picked it up. "Bishop."

"Son?"

His entire body went rigid at that single word, the gravelly voice one he hadn't heard in over a year, since the last time Gabriel had told him to get lost. "I have a father," he said, "and it's not you."

Hanging up, he returned to work, shoving aside unwanted reminders of his origins with the habit of long practice. The boy he'd been was long gone. In his place stood a man who knew who he was—and what he wanted. Hauling a certain mouse out of her burrow was high on that list.

6

LACE PANTIES AND POOR ERNEST

CHARLOTTE ARRIVED AT WORK at seven thirty the next morning to find Gabriel Bishop's office door open, but no carnivorous predator inside. A fresh suit was hanging on the back of his door, however, which meant he'd been in already.

Deciding to catch up on e-mails that had come in overnight from international suppliers as well as stores involved in a stock take, she was typing a reply when a sweaty Gabriel arrived fifteen minutes later. He was dressed in black running shorts and a faded University of Auckland T-shirt that was currently sticking to his body.

She'd known he was in shape, but now she realized none of it was an illusion created by his well-cut suits. Okay, she'd already known that, but seeing his muscled body in the flesh was a whole different ball game. He was built like a tank, hard and powerful.

Each of his thighs was thicker than both of hers put together, his biceps toned, his shoulders appearing even wider than usual. Everything about him was *big*. Civilized clothing didn't make him look better, she realized—it toned down his intense masculinity. Out of his suits, with the ink on the upper part of his left arm exposed, as well as that on his opposing thigh and…

Her skin hot and lower body clenching, she just nodded in response to his "Good morning."

Disappearing into his office, he returned with his suit pants and a fresh shirt slung over his arm, along with a sports bag. "Push the meeting with Sales to nine, will you, Ms. Baird? I need to talk to HR about something before then."

"Yes, sir," Charlotte said almost soundlessly, but he was already gone, heading toward the employee shower one floor down.

The thigh tattoo went all the way around, the design intricate.

Heart rate a rapid stutter, Charlotte got up after he disappeared and decided to go grab him a coffee. He'd bought her one yesterday after all. She was just being nice. "Oh, shut up, Charlotte," she muttered once she was in the elevator, and slumped her face into an upraised hand.

The truth was she was running away. Only for a few minutes, but that's what this was: strategic retreat. Gabriel Bishop was overwhelming. Once, before she'd ever met him and under the influence of cocktails, she'd told Molly she wanted to rip off his shirt and sink her teeth into his pecs.

That desire hadn't waned even now that she knew he was a T-Rex. Of course, the desire was all strictly in her imagination. The idea of actually handling him in real life? So impossible as to be laughable. Charlie-mouse was not about to play with a predator who could eat her alive and not even notice the bones. The good news was that she could admire him in relative safety—there was no chance in hell he'd ever notice her as a woman.

Getting the coffee from a nearby café, she took it back upstairs. He was in his office when she entered, the striped dark gray of his tie hanging around his neck and his damp hair roughly combed. The scent of clean, fresh soap over warm skin permeated the office. Shooting her a smile that turned him from gorgeous to flat-out devastating, he flipped up the collar of his white shirt to get the tie in place. "Thank you, Ms. Baird."

Nodding, Charlotte escaped, though she *really* wanted to stay. She'd never realized how erotic it was to watch a man dress until this precise moment. And she shouldn't be having these thoughts about her boss—especially since she couldn't keep from quivering like a rabbit in his presence. Sometimes she just *annoyed* herself.

"Get to work," she muttered and knuckled down.

Gabriel was fine for the first hour, but then he began barking orders even a six-armed woman with a split personality would have had trouble handling.

Finally, pushed to the edge, Charlotte snapped. "I'm going as fast as I can!" she yelled when he asked her for something a minute after he'd asked her to complete another task.

He scowled and held out a file. "This is a priority."

Grabbing it from his hand, she said, "Fine," and slapped it down on her desk.

It was over an hour later that he disappeared for ten minutes. When he returned, it was to put a small bakery box on her desk. "I think you need something to sweeten your mood today, Ms. Baird."

What she *needed* was for the T-Rex who was her boss to stop snarling and growling, she thought as he returned to his office.

Not opening the box until her curiosity had almost killed her, she found it held a slice of decadent chocolate cake with a white-chocolate ganache topped with curls of both white and milk chocolate. "I cannot be bribed with cake," she muttered, eating a bite nonetheless.

Cake aside, he didn't let up. Needing a break lest she give in to her new fantasy—that of dumping a jug of ice-cold water on his aggravating head, she didn't cancel her lunch date with Molly, the library where her best friend worked only a five-minute walk away. First, she wanted to catch up on what was happening with Molly and Fox. Second, T-Rex needed to know he couldn't stomp all over her.

Her conversation with Molly had her smiling in no time. Sandwiches eaten, she dragged her best friend into a fancy lingerie shop where she'd window-shopped more than once. Fine, she might have given in to temptation a couple of times, but no one had to know about her small addiction to pretty lace panties and bras.

In fact, she thought gloomily, at the rate she was going, no one ever *would* know.

"What's the point of buying lingerie that'll stay on for five seconds at most?" Molly muttered at one point.

"Five *seconds?*" Charlotte put a hand over her heart, her mind suddenly supplying her with images of Gabriel's big hands tearing off the lace that cupped her breasts. "Wait while I have an orgasm." It came out a little higher than she'd intended, her face flushed.

"What, you still haven't jumped T-Rex? Even now that you two are attached at the hip?"

Charlotte pursed her lips while inside her head, fantasy

Charlotte punished the boss for his bad behavior by tying him up naked. "Why would I want to jump a man who yells at me one minute," she said, deciding she was losing her mind, "and leaves chocolate cake on my desk the next?"

"What?" Paying for a bra and panty set that would look phenomenal on her knockout curves, Molly pointed a finger at her. "You've been holding out on me."

"Hah! More like I've been protecting you from the madness," Charlotte said as they walked out into the sunshine. "This is only my second day in the position, but he's already driving me insane. Yesterday he made me work till ten at night, caused me to miss a date with Ernest—"

"What you and Ernest are doing isn't called dating, Charlie."

Charlotte folded her arms, trying not to think about the fact she'd been fantasizing about the wrong man ever since Gabriel Bishop walked into her life. "So maybe he hasn't made a move—"

"After a *year*." Molly's voice was gentle but firm. "Doesn't Ernest spend the whole time telling you about his model-airplane collection?"

Glaring at Molly, Charlotte said, "I admit he's a bit obsessed with his models, but he's small like me, kind, and he doesn't raise his voice at me."

"You know I like Ernest; he's a lovely, sweet man." Molly shoulder-bumped her. "I understand why you *want* to be attracted to him, but the truth is you aren't."

Charlotte ducked her head, not wanting to face a fact she'd been happily avoiding for a year. As long as she was "dating" Ernest, she had a safety net, a way to pretend she was normal for at least a fraction of time.

"You convinced me to be brave," Molly whispered. "I think you can be too."

"I'm not like you, you know that."

"Do I?" Her best friend shook her head. "You said you were in awe of me for standing up to Queen Bitchface, but I remember you telling off the worst clique in the school until they crawled off with their tails between their legs."

"It's different when it's someone I love." She'd take on anyone who hurt someone who belonged to her. "When it's me..." Charlotte swallowed, her next words a rasp. "He scares me." It was a confession torn out of her soul.

Molly's expression suddenly somber, she drew Charlotte to a bench in the nearby square, the water fountain to the side creating a gentle background melody. "T-Rex?"

At Charlotte's nod, Molly put her hand over Charlotte's. "Are you afraid to be around him?"

"No," Charlotte said, realizing her best friend had taken the wrong meaning from her words. "No, not like that." Stomach tense and chest tight with the weight of what she was admitting, she glanced at her watch. "We better go—we'll be late getting back to work."

"I'll make up the time." Molly squeezed her hand. "And since T-Rex didn't let you leave till ten last night, I'm sure he can't argue against a long lunch today."

"Yes, he can." The man was totally unreasonable.

"Do I need to storm the battlements and steal you away from his clutches?"

"Ha-ha." Teeth sinking into her lower lip, Charlotte just blurted out the truth. "He scares me because of the way he makes me react. Sometimes I want to grab that tie of his and—"

"Do the kind of things I've been doing with my rock star?"

Charlotte blushed. "Only in my more insane moments." She pushed up her glasses. "Have you *seen* how big he is?" Even thinking about his body made her breath catch, and it wasn't in fear.

"Sexy big." Molly waggled her eyebrows. "Also, you shouldn't expect rational advice from me—I brought a man home after meeting him in an elevator."

Charlotte laughed, gleeful. "Now you're about to head off with him for a dirty, dirty weekend." She was so happy for her friend.

Dropping her head in her hands, Molly moaned. "What am I doing, Charlie?"

"I told you, being the brave one." She jumped as her cell phone rang. "It's His Carnivorousness," she muttered after reading the caller display. "Hello," she said in a far more professional tone. "Charlotte speaking."

"Ms. Baird, where the hell are you?" came the growl down the line. "Do you not realize I pay you to be available when I need you?"

Charlotte's hands itched for that jug of ice water. "Yes, I realize that," she said, managing to keep her tone polite. "However, I did work well beyond my contracted hours yesterday."

"What? Ermine complaining already?" A snort. "Don't tell me you're pacifying your boyfriend when you should be at your desk."

Charlotte saw red. "Yes, I am," she said, her mouth moving ahead of her brain. "In fact, we're about to check into a hotel." Stabbing the End key, she turned to find Molly staring at her.

"Did you just tell your boss you were about to check into a hotel with Ernest?" her best friend asked in an awed whisper.

Charlotte froze, suddenly realizing what she'd said. "Oh *God!*" It was a mortified wail, her breath stuck in her lungs. "I told you he was driving me insane."

Molly nudged Charlotte's head between her knees. "Breathe, Charlie."

Charlotte tried, but she could tell her face was still bright red when she sat up. "I can't go back to the office now." How would she even face Gabriel Bishop? "I'll have to quit." Interviewing for a new position couldn't be any harder than trying to explain to the boss that she hadn't in fact been about to check into a hotel with her boyfriend who wasn't really her boyfriend.

"No, you don't." Hooking her arm through Charlotte's, Molly dragged her to her feet and escorted her to the Saxon & Archer offices.

"Be brave," Molly mouthed when Charlotte paused in the doorway, breathing choppy again and her heart thumping.

Charlotte had never been brave, but she couldn't let Molly down, especially when her best friend was trying to aim for her own dreams. *Be brave*, she mouthed back, and forced herself to the elevator.

The walk down the corridor to her office was as bad as the day she'd thought she was about to be fired. Even when Brent Sinclair caught her in passing to say a heartfelt thank-you for her part in getting his idea in front of the boss, it didn't stop the sick feeling in her gut.

Not only had she thrown a stapler at the boss's head, she'd hung up on him after saying she was heading out for some afternoon delight.

Wanting to whimper, she walked through the doors to her office and took off her coat while placing her handbag aside. Then she cleared the messages on her phone and sat down to finish up work she'd left half-complete when she'd gone out for lunch. Taking it into T-Rex's office, she placed it on his desk.

He looked up, a gleam in his eye. "Nice lunch?"

Feeling her cheeks turn tomato red, she managed to say, "Yes."

The T-Rex didn't bite, his attention back on his work. "I need you to set up a conference call at four with Sydney and Queenstown. Make sure it's attended by the entire management team at both locations."

Stunned at having been let off so easily, she said, "I'll get started now."

She'd almost made it to the door when Gabriel Bishop said, "Looks like Egor is a quick draw, Ms. Baird. There are pills for that, you know."

Goddamn it, where was that jug of ice water?

7

THE INFAMOUS SLAVE CLAUSE

CHARLOTTE WAS SURPRISED TO find on Friday afternoon that she'd survived almost an entire week working for T-Rex. Earlier that day, he'd fired her, then in the next breath asked her to track down someone at a regional branch office. When that happened a second time, she ignored being fired and kept on with her job—though she might have glared daggers at his back a time or two.

As for the gourmet passion fruit and dark-chocolate French macarons that appeared on her desk after she'd worked through lunch, she bit into one with relish, imagining it was a particular carnivore's head.

"Hey, Charlie." Tuck came in right then. "Got the mail for you."

Seeing him eye the macarons, she held out the box. He grinned and took a couple, bit into one. "Wow, these fancy cookies are pretty great." A gulp and the sweet confection was gone. "Want to go on coffee break together?"

"Sorry, Tuck. Have to work."

"It is so *awesome* that you got this job." He beamed at her.

"You're like my favorite person in the entire building."

Charlotte smiled at him as he headed out with the mail cart. "We'll do lunch together next week, okay?"

Tuck gave her a thumbs-up, the doors closing behind him.

"Cheating on poor Ebenezer, Ms. Baird?"

Charlotte didn't jump at the deep voice from the open office doorway—the tiny hairs on her arms had risen a second before he spoke. As an early warning system, it was infallible.

"*Ernest*," she gritted out, pushing back in pure self-defense. "His name is Ernest." As long as she didn't look at the man who was driving her insane, she'd be fine. But as she couldn't totally ignore her boss, she did finally angle her chair toward him.

"I'll be sure to remember that," he said, that dangerous gleam back in his eye.

"Did you need me to do something?" she asked, busying herself at her desk once more because staring at Gabriel Bishop for too long had a way of adversely affecting her nervous system.

"I need you to come in to work tomorrow." A faint scrape of sound that told her he was rubbing his jaw. He always ended up with a five-o'clock shadow around four and kept an electric shaver in his desk drawer in case he needed to attend a late meeting or business dinner.

He hadn't shaved last night when he'd actually left at a reasonable hour in order to make a personal dinner. His dates probably didn't mind the stubble. Charlotte didn't— and God, that was a singularly improper thought. Not just because he was her boss, but because he'd spent the day infuriating her in myriad ways.

"You also need to book us return tickets to Queenstown on Sunday," he told her before she could respond to his first request. "I want you with me for the lunch meeting I'm having with a number of hotel managers there."

"On Sunday?"

Another rub of his jaw, his voice grim as he said, "Saxon & Archer boutique contracts are coming up for renewal, and it's going to be a hard sell to get them to give the company another shot after Hill's idiocy." That shark smile again. "Might as well ply them with champagne before I get them to sign on the dotted line."

"I'll organize it now. Is it overnight?"

"No. Back on Sunday night—latest flight you can get."

"Okay." Having somehow reined in her rioting thoughts, she got up and handed him a piece of mail she'd seen at the top of the pile Tuck had dropped off. "It's marked personal."

His expression darkened as he took in the plain white envelope, the writing in front elegant and full of flourishes. "Thank you."

Charlotte almost asked if something was wrong, if the letter was connected to the phone calls he'd received over the past two days from an older-sounding man. However, he'd turned to head back to his desk by the time she parted her lips to speak. Closing her mouth on the words, she'd begun to book the tickets when it hit her.

He wanted her with him in Queenstown.

The city was famous for its skiing, water adventures, and breathtaking alpine scenery, the Saxon & Archer boutiques there as important to the company's bottom line as the flagship stores. Each was located in the heart of a five-star hotel and was meant to function as a designer haven for well-heeled travelers.

As a representative of Saxon & Archer, she'd be expected to look the part.

Spots appeared in front of her eyes, her heart pumping hard and fast. She'd known she'd be expected to accompany him to meetings, but the reality of it was nerve-racking enough that she took off for a walk the instant she'd finished booking the tickets. Once out on the street, she called Molly.

Her best friend was out of the country but picked up quickly. "Charlie? What's up?"

Charlotte wanted to ask Molly how everything was going with Fox and the concert setup, but in full panic mode now, she said, "I need help!"

"To seduce the Bishop?"

"*Molly.*" Her stomach twisted at the thought of being so close to all that raw male heat, desire entangled with a fear that seemed woven into her bones. "No," she said to her best friend. "Clothes, I need help with clothes."

"You're changing your wardrobe?" This time the question was gentle, hopeful.

Biting down on her lower lip, Charlotte fisted her hands. "I can't go to a major meeting like this." She waved a hand over the baggy black dress she had on, forgetting Molly couldn't see her. "Mr. Bishop—"

"*Mr.* Bishop?" Molly repeated. "I'm your best friend. I know you don't think of him as *Mr.* Bishop."

The teasing was just what she needed to get back on an even keel. Making a face over the phone line, she said, "I was going to say T-Rex has been very patient." Unexpectedly so. "He could've ordered me to get a better wardrobe the day he gave me the promotion." She scowled. "The day he *forced* a promotion on me."

"That job was always yours. He just made sure you're getting paid for it now."

Charlotte rubbed her hand free hand over her face. "I just don't know if I can do it." Her messed-up psychology wasn't that complicated; she knew exactly why she wore what she did. Knowing that clothes made no difference, wouldn't have changed what had happened to her, didn't alter anything. The clothes she chose made her feel invisible, and even if that was a lie, it was a lie she needed to function.

"You know it wasn't your clothes that made Dick do what he did." Anger thrummed through her friend's voice. "You could've worn a potato sack every day or a high-powered suit or a miniskirt, and it wouldn't have changed the fact that he's a vicious asshole."

Charlotte knew that if Molly'd had her way, she'd have found and kicked the living shit out of Richard. "It's not logical," she admitted to the best friend who had always, *always* been there for her, "it's about control. I just feel like I'm doing something to protect myself when I dress this way, even when I know what I'm actually doing is hiding."

"Hey, you know my rule—no putting yourself down."

"I wasn't. I was being brutally honest." She blew out a breath. "It's time I faced my neuroses head-on."

"A little neurotic behavior makes us interesting."

"Who said anything about a little?" Glancing at her watch, Charlotte walked quickly toward a small store that usually had a good petite selection; she wasn't sure she'd get a chance tomorrow and they had an early flight to Queenstown on Sunday. "I'll send you photos from the changing room." She could do this, could lose her cloak of invisibility and survive.

Going backward was no longer an option.

Not when she'd fenced with a T-Rex and come out alive on the other side.

HAVING SHREDDED—UNREAD—THE letter from the man who thought he should have the right to call himself Gabriel's father when he'd done fuck all to earn that right, Gabriel called the man who *was* his father, though they shared no DNA. It was Joseph Esera's heritage that Gabriel wore on his body, the design drawn by his stepfather and inked by a stepuncle who was an artist specializing in Samoan tattoos.

Every line had a meaning, a history.

Each part of the overall design had been given to him as a gift on a momentous occasion in his life, starting from his rugby selection at eighteen. Some of the tats had hurt like a bitch, but Gabriel's pride in honoring his stepfather—in being embraced so absolutely as Joseph's son—was deeper than any fleeting pain.

"Hey, Dad. What did the doc say about Danny?" His youngest brother had been benched to make sure he healed properly from a hamstring injury that had occurred in an earlier game. Though only twenty-one, Daniel Esera was already making a name for himself as a halfback to watch, and his coach had taken the "better to be safe than sorry" approach. It was the right decision, but Danny had been itching at the bit for the past two weeks.

"Cleared him." Joseph's response was jubilant. "He'll be on the pitch tomorrow."

Gabriel grinned, making a mental note to message his baby

brother in congratulations. "Are you and Mom still doing that movie thing?"

Joseph and Alison had found one another when Gabriel was eight and his brother, Sailor, six. A marriage as soon as his mom's divorce was final, two more kids, and more than two decades later, they were still nuts for one another. Enough that Joseph, a big man's man who'd earned a name as an enforcer on the rugby field, had agreed to "romcom date nights" with Alison, regardless of the fact he'd rather have rusty metal spikes driven into his eyeballs.

"Of course we're doing the movie thing," Joseph said now. "You think we're about to celebrate our twenty-fifth wedding anniversary because I'm an idiot?"

Laughing, Gabriel talked with his stepfather for a few more minutes before ending the call and messaging his brother. The twin interactions wiped away the anger he'd felt at seeing that letter, that ridiculous handwriting that was all flourish and no substance, just like the man who'd formed the words.

"Ms. Baird," he said, going to the doorway so he could playfully needle his PA—who was starting to no longer quiver in his presence… and who was getting more and more attractive every day.

Her desk, however, was empty.

CHARLOTTE WAS ZIPPING UP a dress in deep magenta when her cell phone rang, a familiar name flashing on the screen. "Mr. Bishop?"

"I can't find the damn Baxter file." It was a snarl.

"I put it on the left corner of your desk."

A pause.

She took the chance to check out the dress in the mirror, was shocked to realize the vibrant color looked good on her. Not that she could wear it yet. It was one thing to remove the cloak of invisibility, another to shout her presence.

"Got it." Gabriel's voice back in her ear. "I need you back here ASAP."

"Why?" It was much easier to dig in her heels when she wasn't face-to-face with him.

He growled—actually *growled* down the line. "Because you're my damn PA."

"I didn't see a slave clause in my contract." Charlotte had no idea where this was coming from. "I didn't take a lunch break, so I'm having a short break now." She went to unzip the dress, stopped when she realized he might hear her.

"Eat fast."

She dressed and undressed fast instead, sending Molly photo after photo. Fifteen minutes later and she had a couple of new outfits. Making plans with her best friend to do some further shopping once Molly returned to the country, she girded her loins and returned to work. To find T-Rex's door shut.

Wondering what was up since he didn't have anything scheduled, she sat down at her desk and decided to take the time before the inevitable confrontation to check her e-mails. The routine task would calm her the same way the other routines did in her life.

Except the e-mail at the top was from Gabriel Bishop, complete with an ominous subject line: *Changes to the terms of your employment.*

Clicking it with her heart in her throat, she got ready to be penalized for snapping at the boss... and burst out laughing. A hand over her mouth to muffle the sound, she glanced at Gabriel's closed door. The man was lethal.

Turning back to the screen, she read the e-mail again.

Dear Ms. Baird,

As of today, you do have a slave clause in your contract. It means you do everything I say. Under no circumstances are you to eat, sleep, take breaks, or check in to hotel rooms with men named Eggplant.

Sincerely,
Gabriel Bishop

Hitting the Reply key, Charlotte typed a message and sent it before she could second-guess herself. Afterward, she printed out both his e-mail and her own and put them in her handbag.

8

OH, THOSE RED, RED ROSES...

G ABRIEL WALKED VIV GRIMES to the door, having just spent an hour discussing her options with Saxon & Archer. The previous CEO had misused the intelligent supply manager to the point that she'd been about to resign when Gabriel came on board. He'd just convinced her that she could trust him to watch her back. Which he would.

Unlike his predecessor, Gabriel understood the value of good people.

He glanced toward Charlotte's desk as Viv left. Seeing her chair pushed back and an open file beside her computer, as if she'd stepped out for a quick minute, he wondered if his suddenly mouthy assistant—he grinned at the memory of that phone call—had seen his message.

Before he could check his e-mail for a reply, she walked into his office with a bottle of water, a foot-long sub, and a scowl on her face. "Since I know you didn't stop for lunch." She put both on his desk.

"Where's my coffee?" he said, needing the hit.

"You mainline it," she muttered. "Drink some water for a

change." With that, she turned and left.

He decided he liked her back view as much as the front.

Except for the fact her ugly sack of a dress hid every feminine curve he wanted to see. Whoever Ernest was, he was a damn idiot if he hadn't taught Charlotte that she was sexy as hell.

Gabriel wasn't going to hit on a vulnerable employee, even when he wanted to more every damn day, but he was allowed to admire her when she couldn't see him. It probably wasn't behavior HR would agree with, but Gabriel wasn't exactly planning on telling them.

Since he was starving, he ate the sub and drank the water in the five minutes he had before leaving for a meeting with the board. It was a waste of time as far as he was concerned, and he was annoyed enough today to tell them.

"No more fucking meetings," he said, bracing his palms flat on the table.

The men and women around the table flinched. "Mr. Bishop, we hired you and—"

"And you need to let me do my job," he said, well aware his percentage of the company wasn't the majority—and also aware they needed him more than he needed them. He had shares in multiple national and international companies, a property portfolio that would make their eyes bulge, as well as a number of other highly profitable investments.

The only reason he worked with failing companies like Saxon & Archer was for the challenge of rescuing them from the scrap pile. His patience with idiots who kept him from doing that only went so far. "I am not a trained poodle who'll perform for you," he told them. "If you can't handle that, then fire me, otherwise this discussion is over." He paused—to shocked silence. "I'll give you a monthly report as agreed in our initial discussions. Any questions?"

There were none.

He left with a cordial "Good afternoon." Yeah, they *could* fire him, but they wouldn't. He was very, very good at saving sinking companies, and Saxon & Archer was definitely sinking, or had been until he came on board.

He checked in with Charlotte as he walked to his vehicle, the meeting having taken place away from headquarters so as not to spook the market. "Anything I need to handle?"

"Katherine Newton from Accounts called up to say she needed to check some expense reports with you—"

Gabriel groaned. "Did that idiot Hill micromanage all the stuff he shouldn't and ignore everything he should've handled?"

"—which is why I told Katherine to send the reports to me. I've authorized them on your behalf."

"As long as no one's charging strippers or Tom Jones CDs, that's fine," he said and thought he heard a quickly muffled laugh. Cheeks creasing, he said, "I'm on my way to the Queen Street branch." The company's oldest store was now smaller than the Sydney branch, but it had a sense of history about it that nothing could alter. "Don't interrupt me unless absolutely necessary."

"I'll make sure your calls are diverted for the interim."

"Thank you, Ms. Baird." God, he loved her voice.

Why the hell had he promoted her instead of firing her? If he'd done the latter, he could've pursued her straight into his bed, naked and sweetly curved and with that soft skin he wanted to mark all over with his kisses and his touch.

67

Scowling because ethics made for a damn cold bed, he headed to the store.

It wasn't until seven at night that he finally had a chance to check his e-mails. He'd texted Charlotte at five to tell her to take off, so he was alone in the office when he read what she'd written.

Dear Mr. Bishop,

Thank you, but I must decline your new contract terms. I believe the following to be a much more equitable alteration to the terms of my contract:

Charlotte Baird is to get a twenty percent pay raise effective immediately, in consideration of the fact her boss does not sleep and therefore expects her not to need sleep either.

Yours sincerely,
C. Baird

Leaning back in his chair, arms folded behind his head, he grinned. Oh yeah, he liked the woman beneath the shapeless suits and the prim metal-framed glasses. Actually, he liked those cute glasses too. The idea of seeing her with her soft blond curls loose around that face with its pointed chin and golden skin, her glasses on her nose and the rest of her bare...

"Inappropriate, Gabriel," he groaned, his cock shoving against the zipper of his pants.

He seriously needed to get laid.

Unfortunately, his body was showing a decided preference for the one woman he couldn't have.

SUNDAY MORNING, CHARLOTTE SMOOTHED her hands over the gray wool shift that was one of her new purchases; she'd jazzed it up with a double string of turquoise beads recommended by the shop assistant.

Her hair was up in a plain bun, but she'd spent last night practicing with bobby pins so her curls didn't escape. Makeup remained beyond her after so many years of not wearing it—not that she'd ever been anything but an amateur—but according to Molly, her skin didn't need it.

Carefully putting on the pale pink lip gloss she'd decided to chance, she took a deep breath and looked in the mirror. Okay, she wouldn't win any fashion prizes, but she looked professional, wouldn't embarrass Gabriel at the meeting.

Grabbing her purse, she set the alarm and locked up. The cab she was catching directly to the airport arrived seconds later. With it being so early on a Sunday, the drive was a breeze, and she was soon through security and waiting for Gabriel at the gate. He arrived close to takeoff, and from then on, it was all go.

They worked throughout the just under two-hour-long flight, landed, and went straight into unannounced site visits to a number of the boutiques before making their way to the restaurant she'd booked for the lunch meeting. The hotel managers, when they arrived, proved uniformly intelligent and financially savvy, but in the end, Gabriel got exactly what he wanted, his charisma potent.

"Looks like we have two hours to spare," he said afterward. "Come along, Ms. Baird, you can help me choose a gift for a beautiful woman I know."

Charlotte couldn't think of anything worse. "I'm sure you have excellent taste, Mr. Bishop."

"I insist."

That was how she found herself traipsing from one high-end jewelry boutique to another. She pointed out items just to end the whole excruciating exercise, but he wasn't satisfied. In the end, he bought the only piece she'd truly loved. It was her own fault: she'd been sneaking a photo of the delicate, one-of-a-kind bracelet when he'd caught her.

And now, she thought as she collapsed into her bed that night, he'd give the exquisite piece to some woman who probably wouldn't appreciate the delicate artistry of it. Punching her pillow into shape, she glared her way into sleep. Her mood wasn't much better the next morning.

Having arrived at the office before Gabriel returned from his run, she'd just made herself a cup of coffee and taken a seat when he came in. He looked as rawly sexy as he always did. He even smelled good, and that should've been impossible. The scent of clean sweat over warm skin worked where Gabriel Bishop was concerned. Charlotte didn't think any woman would push him away if he hauled her close for a kiss right now.

"Morning, Ms. Baird."

"Morning, Mr. Bishop." At least she could speak now in his near-naked presence.

Grabbing what he needed for the shower, he pushed a hand through his sweat-damp hair and turned at the glass doors. "Ms. Baird."

Charlotte jerked her eyes guiltily up from his thighs, face red. Thankfully, he was scowling at something on his phone, which he must've picked up from the office since she knew his run was the one time of day when he made himself unreachable. As a stress-relief measure, she approved. The fact she got to start her day by seeing him sweaty and hot and in running shorts? A bonus.

"I'm sending you an address," he said now. "Have a dozen roses delivered."

Her happy mood dived. "What color?"

"Red, of course."

For once, she didn't watch him leave, didn't give in to the temptation to sneak a glimpse of the seriously built male who was her boss. Instead, she checked her e-mail to see who was about to receive a dozen red roses from Gabriel Bishop—likely the same woman to whom he'd given the bracelet.

Fabiana Flores.

Charlotte would've had to have lived under a rock for the past week not to recognize the name of the glamorous model with the bee-stung lips who was in the country for a perfume launch. As she contacted a florist to place the order, she told herself not to be surprised. Athletes and models—it was a predictable combination. And why not? Both took care of their bodies, were often of heights that complemented one another—

"Stop obsessing, Charlotte." After all, fantasies about him aside, it wasn't as if she'd entertained any serious hopes of Gabriel looking in her direction. In fact, she couldn't think of anything worse: the brutal truth was that she'd most likely panic, fear clutching her throat and stealing the air from her lungs, and it would wreck everything.

It hurt to admit that, admit her deficiencies so bluntly, but Charlotte had stopped lying to herself the day she'd broken things off with Richard. Lies and false hope only ever led to pain and betrayal.

Gabriel Bishop was simply out of her league.

Part Two

9

THE MOUSE GROWLS

TWO AND A HALF MONTHS later, and Charlotte had sent countless bouquets of red roses on Gabriel's behalf, each one to a different woman. Models, actresses, television anchors, two doctors, a long-haul commercial pilot, three fellow CEOs, and a chef. The chef returned the roses with their heads lopped off.

Seeing the beheaded stems when she took the open box into his office, Gabriel winced. "You see why a second date would've been a bad idea, don't you, Ms. Baird?"

Charlotte didn't know why she said what she did when she'd been the *perfect* personal assistant for so many weeks, discreet and efficient and invisible except when he needed her. Well, okay, there had been that incident with the muffin, but he'd driven her to it, so it didn't count.

She couldn't explain today's response as easily. Maybe it was the sad, beheaded roses. She felt an acute sympathy for the angry chef, for all the red-rose women. Or perhaps it was the fact the florist now knew her by name, saying, "The usual?" when Charlotte called.

There was only so much a PA could take.

"It appears, Mr. Bishop," she said from her standing position on the other side of his desk, "that you don't believe in second dates at all." The parade of stunning women in his life was endless—and no face was ever repeated.

One date and they were out.

Leaning back in the black leather of his executive chair, arms folded behind his head and the fine gray cotton of his shirt stretched across the defined ridges and valleys of his chest, Gabriel grinned. It was as devastating as usual, but Charlotte had learned to deal with the dip in her stomach that was her response to her boss's smile. Unfortunately for her, her susceptibility to him had increased rather than decreased in the time they'd worked together.

His physical attractiveness was only a small part of it.

Gabriel might not know the meaning of commitment when it came to women, but you could take his word to the bank in business. His employees—and the entire board for that matter—remained more than a touch intimidated by him, but they respected him and his promises. Not only was he fair, he worked harder than any one of them, and the company was going from strength to strength under his leadership.

Smart, driven, gorgeous, he was more compelling than anyone she'd ever met. He was also the most arrogant.

"I wouldn't want anyone to get ideas," he said, the glint in his eye familiar. "Second date and women start thinking about monogrammed towels and engagement rings."

Charlotte rolled her eyes.

He caught it, of course. "You disagree?"

"I wouldn't presume to comment on your private life." No matter how much she wanted to.

"Come on, Ms. Baird, don't get shy now."

Charlotte didn't trust that tone in his voice—it was a dare. Charlotte didn't take dares. Especially from T-Rexes with very sharp teeth. "Would you like these in water?" she asked, holding up the box of stems.

"You have a mean streak." Lowering his arms with a scowl, he glanced at the face of the heavy metal watch he always wore. On him, it was in perfect proportion, suiting the heaviness of his bones, the taut lines of muscle in his forearms.

"Damn, I have to deal with the mess Clarke's made in his region."

"I'll get the files." She stopped in the doorway, the same strange something that had made her comment on his dating tactics poking at her until she said, "Want me to call up the chef and ask her to send you dinner tonight?"

HE WANTED HER.

Petite, intelligent, with a hidden fire in her eyes when he pushed too hard, and a smart mouth he wanted to taste, Charlotte Baird was Gabriel's version of perfect. "Thank you, but no," he said to her retreating form. "I prefer not to die from food poisoning."

Nearly three frustrating months on from their first meeting, and Charlotte was at last no longer so skittish around him. Her quips today cemented his conclusion that she was ready for the next step in this game they were playing, a game of which she was currently unaware. The fact she remained his subordinate at work meant he'd have to take care when it came to how he went about this, but he was going to have Charlotte Baird.

No one and nothing had ever stood in his way when he set his mind on something, and his mind was set on Charlotte, had been for a long time. The patience he'd displayed these past months... she had *no* idea.

Once he had her, he was going to take her. Over and over and *over*.

"Ms. Baird, I'm growing a beard while waiting for the file," he called out, well aware she was printing the latest dispatches on the situation so he could get a full picture.

She strode inside a minute later and placed the file very carefully on his desk, though he could tell she wanted to slam hard, maybe kick him while she was at it. He wouldn't mind if she tried—he really liked her legs.

Scowling at the professional but bland three-quarter-length black skirt that hid most of the view, he grabbed the file and flipped it open. "This is missing the second half. The entire section to do with the tactless incident that landed his branch on the six-o'clock news." He'd thought he'd weeded the idiots out of Saxon & Archer, but clearly not.

"I didn't print out all the documentation, since it'll be easier for you to click through to related files using the link I've just e-mailed you." She gave him a smile so sweet he was quite certain his PA wanted to strangle him. "I basically set up a private internal wiki for you."

He was impressed, but he was also having fun riling her up. "Fuck that," he said and watched her cheeks go bright red, her eyes fiery. "I want a printout of everything and I want it now. I have to read the entire lot before I go screw his head on straight."

"Here." Striding around his desk as if she'd lost patience with him—and he'd been trying for a hell of a long time to get Charlotte to lose patience—she picked up the tablet computer he used mostly to watch rugby games when he needed to clear the cobwebs, and switched it on.

Tapping on it, she said, "Input your password."

He raised an eyebrow. "I am your boss, Ms. Baird," he said, just to see if she'd give in and kick him at last.

Because that would be first contact, and then he could go after her no holds barred.

Instead, she said, "Please, sir," in such a sincere voice that he narrowed his eyes.

Tapping in the code, he watched her download his e-mail, frown, then lean forward to access his computer. He didn't like anyone in his personal space that he hadn't invited in, but he liked Charlotte there just fine. Leaning back in his chair, he enjoyed the shape of her ass as she worked.

The skirt was tight enough at least to stretch nicely over the curve of her butt.

The urge to stroke his hand over those luscious curves was seriously tempting, but he wasn't stupid. After all these weeks of very careful strategy to get her to stop seeing him as her boss and start seeing him as a man, no way would he give Charlotte any excuse to pull away. Not only did he have no intention of losing the best damn PA he'd ever had, how the hell was he supposed to get her permanently into his bed if he didn't have access to her twenty-four seven?

No, he'd wait. And he'd do his stroking in private, after he had her bent naked in front of him, that pretty butt tilted up for his pleasure and hers. He wanted to hear Charlotte moan his name and then ask him to do dirty things to her, her prim little spectacles fogging up with heat.

"There!" Getting up, that stupid skirt sliding over the heart-shaped beauty of her ass to hover around her calves—what woman-hating designer had created that abomination?—she grabbed his tablet and tap-tapped once more. "All the files at your fingertips."

Gabriel took the tablet, swiped through. "It'll do," he said, though he was seriously impressed at how she'd put everything together in a way that made it effortless for him to access what he needed.

He saw her hands curl into fists, but once again, she restrained her violent impulses. A pity. He'd have liked the excuse to tumble her into his lap when she took a swing at his jaw, that sweet ass coming down over his thighs.

Putting down the tablet on that pleasurable thought, he picked up the digital recorder he'd been using before she came in with the rose stems. "I want you to personally type this up." He didn't trust the pool of typists who handled most of the general data input, not with a document that needed to say exactly what he wanted it to say without him having to go over it ten times to make sure they hadn't misplaced a comma or inserted a word.

"Of course." Her eyes flicked to her watch after she checked the length of the recording. "Did you need it tonight?"

"Why, hot date with Ebenezer?"

Red cheeks again, her chest rising as she took a deep breath. "My personal life," she said after she exhaled, "is none of the company's business."

No, but Gabriel was going to make it *his* damn business. He'd been trying to put the kibosh on her dating thing with Ernest ever since she became his PA—but though he hadn't managed to cut that off, the man clearly wasn't taking care of her. If he had been, she wouldn't feel the need to wear calf-length skirts with white shirts that buttoned up to her neck or shift dresses two sizes too large. The clothes might be professional and absolutely unobjectionable from a business standpoint, but they totally overwhelmed her petite frame.

In point of fact, Gabriel was dead certain Ernest hadn't made any kind of a move. Charlotte just didn't act like a woman who was taken—and every time Gabriel called her late at night to check on something, she was at home. That meant Ernest was a dimwit, because what kind of man *wouldn't* make a move on Charlotte if he had her?

Yeah, well, the dimwit's luck was about to run out.

"Yes," he said aloud, "I need it tonight." It wasn't a lie, not this time. "This agreement could significantly cut our transport costs, but we're on a strict timetable."

A quick nod. "I'll start on it right away."

CHARLOTTE SAT DOWN AT her desk, a desk no one in the company had ever expected her to possess, least of all Charlotte herself.

Just like she'd never have predicted she'd one day just grab her boss's tablet and force him to move into the twenty-first century, but he'd been pushing and pushing and pushing until she couldn't take it anymore. Using the headphones she preferred over earbuds, she connected the sleek black recorder he liked to use, and his deep voice filled her ears.

It still made her stomach flip, even after close to three months in his proximity.

Blowing out a quiet breath, she began to type, focused on getting the details exactly right. It was why she had this office, this position, despite her shortcomings... despite the fear that lived inside her even after all the other strides she'd made, a sinuous, mocking beast that still woke her some nights in a cold sweat.

Last night had been a bad one.

Heart pounding hard enough to make her feel sick, she'd had to get out of bed, check she was alone in the house before she could close her eyes again. But no matter the fear, she was living a good life. Maybe it wasn't exciting, she admitted, and maybe her timidity and continued inability to *not be afraid* was increasingly frustrating... and maybe she'd never have the passionate connection Molly had found with her rock star, but—

"Ms. Baird."

Jerking at the sound of Gabriel's voice mixing with that on the tape, she removed the headphones to see him scowling at her. "I'm almost done."

"Good. Once you finish that, I need you to find Finley and get his ass in here."

Realizing the scowl hadn't been for her, she finished up the document, proofed it, then printed it off and handed it to him. Simon Finley had left the office at five, was having a beer at home when she located him.

"Jesus Christ," he muttered. "That bastard has no life and thinks no one else does either."

Hanging up on the other man after getting a promise he'd be in within a half hour, she knew Finley was wrong. As shown by the parade of red roses, Gabriel did have a life outside work, one filled with long-legged beauties who not only had va-va-voom bodies and faces but brains. Even the models Gabriel dated weren't simple clotheshorses; they all had their own perfume or clothing lines, other business ventures.

Yeah, she was never going to be in that league, she thought, picking up the phone to answer a query from the security guard downstairs. "Charlie, delivery guy just dropped off takeout for the boss. I can't leave my post right now with Steven on break—you okay to come grab it?"

"I'll be right there."

After picking up the food, which she saw was from a top-tier restaurant Gabriel liked, she brought it up and carried it through to his office. It was a routine they went through at least three times a week, Gabriel pulling more hours than anyone else in the company.

As usual, the last container was marked "Charlotte." Normally, she was the one who placed the order, but on the rare occasions he did so himself, he never forgot to order for her, and he never got it wrong. She had no idea how he'd noticed she liked certain things and not others, but he had.

"Finley?" Gabriel asked without looking up from the computer screen.

"On his way back into the city. He's in Albany, so it'll be twenty minutes at least with the current traffic."

No answer, his concentration on work. Taking her dinner back to her desk, she opened it to reveal fragrant jasmine rice with a plastic tub of Thai green curry beside it, a prettily cut cucumber on the rice as a garnish. Mouth watering, she grabbed the included fork and began to eat at her desk.

"Ms. Baird."

She almost dropped the fork at Gabriel's quiet but penetrating call. Damn man. Leaving her food, she went to the doorway of his office. "Is there a problem with the document?"

"No. Bring your dinner in here."

Blinking, she went back to retrieve the container. They never ate together—he was usually working and eating at the same time, and she had to eat quickly in case he wanted her to enter last-minute changes or organize meetings or phone conferences as soon as he was done with whatever he was working on.

Last week, she'd had to call suppliers in London, Namibia, and Finland, all in the space of a single—long—day. Saxon & Archer was once more being lauded as *the* luxury department store in Australasia, and it had a great deal to do with their rejuvenated supply chain as well as the rising staff morale. All driven by the inexorable force known as Gabriel Bishop.

When she returned to his office, it was to find he'd come around to the black leather seating area to one side that he sometimes used for more casual meetings. His tie was off, the top two buttons of his shirt unbuttoned and his sleeves rolled up as was standard by this time of day. Dark stubble shadowed his jaw. The sensual curve of his lower lip was the only point of softness on him.

In her madder moments, Charlotte sometimes wondered if he was rough in bed or if he had tenderness in him.

"You know he's hot, right?"

Molly had said that to her when Charlotte had been complaining about Gabriel back at the start. While Charlotte had denied it at the time, they'd both known she was lying. Now, if she could only forget his attractiveness and focus strictly on the job, she'd be well on her way to a successful long-term career.

Taking a seat on the sofa opposite him on that reminder, she ate in silence as he alternately frowned at the document he was still reading and went through his food quickly and neatly, as if it was simply fuel. It was a tragedy, the meal exquisitely prepared by one of the top chefs in the country.

"Ms. Baird, why are you staring at me as if I'm killing baby kittens?"

10

HALF-NAKED T-REX AND ICE CREAM (SADLY NOT AT THE SAME TIME)

HE REALLY SHOULD STOP doing that to his pretty little admin, Gabriel thought with an inward grin. Every time he caught Charlotte staring at him, she turned bright red and couldn't speak for at least a minute. He didn't mind the red—it made him wonder if she blushed all over her body—but he minded the way she still went mute around him every so often. Usually, it was simply because he'd inadvertently startled her, but sometimes, he scented fear and it pissed him off.

Gabriel didn't hurt women, had never hurt women. Hell, even his piss-poor excuse for a biological father wasn't violent. Brian Bishop might have used his wife like she was an automatic teller machine, but he'd never lifted a hand to any of his family.

That was the only good thing Gabriel could say about the man.

Charlotte hadn't been so lucky. Someone had brutalized her to the point that the scars lingered deep within; he'd like to get his hands around the neck of the fucking bastard, give him a taste of his own medicine. One day, when she trusted him enough, she'd tell him, and he'd make sure she had no reason to fear her abuser again.

"You should appreciate your food. Someone put a lot of time and effort into it."

He was so surprised at the feminine rebuke that he leaned back and looked at her. Breaking the eye contact almost at once, she focused on her own meal. He watched the fork travel through her lips and thought about that pretty, pretty mouth on his cock, her tongue licking along the vein that ran along the bottom.

Christ. Wrenching his mind off that particular trajectory before it became rigidly obvious what he wanted to do to her, no doubt terrifying her into running, he started eating again. "I appreciate food when I have the time," he said, considering once again how to take this to the next level. Charlotte had finally stopped jumping when he was nearby, and today, she'd shown more than a hint of temper. He wasn't about to allow that progress to stall. "We might have time for a proper meal together in Rotorua next week."

Her eyes flicked up at the mention of the city famous for its high geothermal activity, complete with geysers and bubbling mud pools. "Rotorua?"

"Uh-huh." Glancing over her shoulder, he said, "Come in, Finley. Ms. Baird and I were just finishing dinner." He picked up the printout he'd edited earlier, as Charlotte put down her fork and closed the lid on her empty container.

Handing the pages to her, he said, "Can you input these changes tonight?"

"Yes, of course. Would you like me here for the meeting at ten?"

He took a second to run through the details in his head. The call was scheduled so late because of the time difference with London, home of the man with whom Gabriel was doing a deal critical for Saxon & Archer's future growth. "Yes," he said, "I might need you."

Glancing at his watch, he saw it was almost eight. "If you like, you can go home for an hour and a half after you finish the edits, get back here ten minutes before the meeting."

Nodding, she left, closing the door behind her, and Finley took her place. Whereupon Gabriel looked the man in the eye and said, "Would you care to explain to me why there's a hundred thousand dollars missing from the operating budget for your department?"

CHARLOTTE DIDN'T GO HOME as Gabriel had suggested. Instead, putting on her coat, she took a walk down to the waterfront, the city streets vibrant with life despite the winter chill, the sea wind refreshing against her skin. Leaning against the railings by the ferry terminal, she watched the ferries come in and thought about how many ice creams she and Molly had shared on the nearby steps.

She missed her best friend each and every day, but she was fiercely happy that Molly had made the brave decision to fight for her dream and moved to LA. They still spoke or e-mailed every day, and Charlotte had no fear that would ever change. No matter if Molly was now with one of the biggest rock stars on the planet, she was still Molly, still Charlotte's sister of the heart.

One who'd sent her a message two days ago that said:

Fox told me today that the band decided to get their own private jet. Yes, my jaw fell too. But apparently it's a good investment—and the best news is that you can fly in style when you visit. I can't wait until you can take a vacation and come over so I can show you LA!

Has T-Rex fired you this week? Or has he been behaving? Tell me all! I get suspicious when you go quiet on the subject of Mr. Tall, Dark, and Carnivorous. Oh, hope the fancy cake you wanted to make came out okay. I miss your baking, especially those chocolate chip cupcakes with orange cream frosting.

And talking of baking, your new cooking class buddies sound like a hoot! Juliet and Aroha are my kind of women. Hope your next coffee date is just as much fun.

– Love, Molly
p.s. A pressie attached for you. VERY NSFW.

The attachment had been a shot of Gabriel in his rugby playing days, sans his playing jersey. It had *definitely* been very not safe for work. The jersey had ripped during what Charlotte knew had been a particularly brutal tackle—she'd watched that game with her father by her side, both of them wincing at the punishing hit Gabriel had taken.

He hadn't gone down, however. No, he'd made the try. Afterward, the fresh cut on his cheekbone still bleeding, he'd pulled the torn jersey off; the shot Molly had sent was of him pouring water on himself to cool down while a member of the team staff went to grab him a replacement jersey.

Charlotte had turned into a puddle in her bed at home when she'd pulled up the message and downloaded the image. The water dripping over the breadth of his shoulders, over his pecs, along the hard ridges of his abs, into the waistband of his playing shorts…

Charlotte waved a hand in front of her face.

Yes, the man was hot. Seriously, dangerously hot. A week ago, she'd walked in on him while he was changing into a fresh shirt to attend a dinner party he was heading to straight from work.

Her mouth had watered before it dried up, her skin taut over her body. She'd lost the ability to speak, so it was as well that he hadn't been annoyed at the interruption, had simply started giving her instructions about something he needed done. Charlotte had heard none of it, though later she discovered she'd taken notes.

All she'd seen right then were the impossibly beautiful ridges and planes of his body, followed by the efficient movements of his fingers as he did up the buttons. She'd almost whimpered as he slipped each small disk into its hole, the view disappearing before her eyes. His chest was lightly furred with dark hair, just enough that her nipples throbbed at the memory even now, her body happily informing her the rasp of sensation would feel exquisite.

As for his hands, they were big and strong and a little rough from the rugby he still played when he coached a local high school team twice a week. With the season in full swing, she had standing orders to juggle his schedule so he could make all the training sessions; she knew he attended all the team's weekend games as well.

Apart from the parade of one-date women, that appeared to be his only downtime.

If she sometimes imagined what those capable, strong hands would feel like against her skin, that was her secret fantasy. No need for anyone to know. *Especially* not Gabriel.

"You know, Charlotte, there's probably a law against ogling the boss," she muttered to herself, but knew she wasn't going to stop.

A woman had to have some vices, and her ridiculous fantasy crush was Charlotte's. Because that was all it was, she told herself for the hundredth time: a crush on a gorgeous man who scrambled her neurons. She refused to consider how much she liked and respected him, how fascinated she was by his brain. Going down that road would lead only to heartbreak.

No, far better to focus on his thickly muscular thighs, the lickable broadness of his chest, the strength of his forearms. Suiting action to words, she took out her phone and pulled up the image Molly had sent her, sighed. And thought about what it would be like to have him tied to her bed so she could kiss and pet him all over as much as she wanted while he called her "Ms. Baird" and gave her increasingly aroused orders in that deep voice that made her nipples go tight.

Overheated despite the crisp sea air, Charlotte walked back to the office about forty minutes after she'd left. Swinging by a convenience store on the way back, she bought a single-serve tub of chocolate macadamia ice cream for herself, then, for no reason that she could consciously articulate, a tub of boysenberry swirl for Gabriel. He didn't like chocolate, but he always ate the fresh berries she often included as dessert when she ordered him lunch.

His office door was still closed when she arrived. Grabbing her laptop, she headed down the otherwise deserted hallway to the staff break room and put the ice creams in the freezer, then sat down at the table set beside a tall window that overlooked the sparkling cityscape. She had a good idea why Gabriel had pulled Simon Finley in, and she didn't particularly want to be there when the man exited.

She'd just finished booking airline tickets for Gabriel's next trip to Sydney when a shadow fell across her screen.

"You didn't go home," he said, opening the fridge then shutting it without taking anything out.

"I got you boysenberry ice cream."

He opened the freezer compartment. "Shut down the laptop, Ms. Baird. It's time for ice cream."

Obeying, she moved the computer to the side of the table and picked up her ice cream as he grabbed spoons and took a seat across from her. His legs sprawled out on either side of her own, his big body taking over the room, but he didn't push at her as he usually did in subtle but maddening ways.

For the first time since she'd met him, he actually looked tired.

"Finley," she said quietly. "It was about the money, wasn't it?"

A nod. "When did you figure it out?"

"When you asked me to pull his expenditure reports. I didn't understand all of it, but I could tell something was off."

"He'll be paying it all back over the next year or he'll be going to jail." Jaw grim, he said, "I dislike thieves, but it's not worth the bad press for the company if this gets out. Not now, when I've finally got Saxon & Archer in a viable position."

Charlotte nodded, the two of them not speaking for the next couple of minutes. It was odd to be quiet with him when her skin thrummed in shivering awareness of his presence, but funnily enough, it wasn't difficult.

"Here, try this."

Looking up, she saw he was offering her a scoop of his ice cream. "No." She blushed despite herself. "Mine's good."

"Be wild, Ms. Baird." The spoon brushed her lips, and when she parted them to reply, he slipped it in, the sweetly tart flavor bursting on her tongue. "That wasn't so bad, was it?"

Heart in her throat, Charlotte shook her head. It had to be her imagination, but she could almost believe he was flirting with her. Idiot. A man like Gabriel Bishop didn't flirt with mice like her, even if her best friend, Molly, was convinced otherwise. Molly, however, had been sure something was up from the start and nearly three months later, Charlotte was still single and Gabriel Bishop was still spending a fortune on red roses.

No, what he was doing was amusing himself by driving her insane. Every time she tried to see Ernest for dinner, he suddenly needed her to stay late—she swore he had radar when it came to her seeing Ernest. It was as well that Ernest was so sweet about the way she had to keep canceling or postponing their plans.

Too sweet.

Molly had been right all those weeks back when she'd pointed out that while Ernest might be someone Charlotte wanted to see as a man she could be in a relationship with, theirs was more of a friendship, nothing else. And she did occasionally want to see her friend, especially now that Ernest was *actually* dating a woman—and he wanted her advice on how to propose.

Charlotte was the least qualified person on the planet to offer relationship advice, but poor Ernest didn't know any other women except his girlfriend, so Charlotte was it. That in mind, she girded her loins against the battle about to come. "I can't work late on the fourteenth."

Gabriel raised an eyebrow. "Ervin?"

"*Ernest.* And yes." When he snorted, she'd had it. Slamming down her tub of ice cream, she glared at him. "He's a very good friend, and since you know nothing about him, I'd appreciate it if you kept your opinions to yourself!"

Gabriel's eyes—that steely gray that could almost be silver when he laughed—glinted. "You're dating him and you still call him a friend?"

So maybe it was a teensy bit her fault he thought she was still dating Ernest. Blame her pride. Ridiculous as it was, she hadn't been able to bear for him to think no one wanted her, especially when he was out with a different glamorous woman every time she turned around.

It would, however, be a little difficult to explain why she would soon be attending the wedding of the man she was "dating."

"Ernest is my friend," she muttered, stabbing her spoon into her ice cream. "It's his birthday on the fourteenth."

She should've known Gabriel wouldn't let the subject drop.

"So you're not dating?"

He didn't have to rub it in. "No," she admitted, then said something she wouldn't even have thought about saying before a certain T-Rex entered her life. "Unlike you, I don't change partners on a daily basis."

"I don't change partners," Gabriel said, leaning back in his chair and eating a scoop of ice cream. "I've never had one of those."

"Probably because that would require more than an endless series of one-night flings." Charlotte froze as the words left her mouth—that had been a singularly discourteous thing to say to her boss.

"Don't stop now, Ms. Baird," he drawled, scooping up another spoonful of ice cream and holding it out to her lips.

She pursed those lips. He smiled, knowing she'd have to part them to speak. "I—"

He slipped the spoon into her mouth, the creamy dessert cold, the spoon warm from his own lips.

The intimacy of it made her stomach flutter. "That's very improper behavior."

"No argument," he said, eating a spoonful. "Does it make you uncomfortable?" A serious question.

Charlotte wanted to say yes, and back when she'd first begun working for him, it would have unnerved her. But he hadn't talked like this with her then—no, he'd been T-Rex. Now, though she tried to think of him as T-Rex, she saw Gabriel instead. "I can handle it," she murmured, and when he smiled, added, "Don't take that as support for further inappropriateness."

His smile was slow, creasing his cheeks and bringing the silver into his eyes. "I'm afraid it's too late."

Charlotte looked down at her ice cream, her confidence running out all at once, as if a tap had been opened and leached it all out onto the floor. She didn't play games with men, didn't know how to; she wasn't even sure if Gabriel *was* playing with her or if he was just passing the time.

A quiet buzz of sound that had become intimately familiar over the months she'd worked for him.

Pulling out his cell phone, he glanced at the screen and said, "Other side's calling early."

As she listened, he completed a complex international deal over the phone, pulling things from memory she'd have thought would be impossible if she hadn't seen him do the same thing multiple times. The man's mind was a steel trap—and he expected the same from her.

Since her laptop was formed of a large tablet and keyboard clipped together, she'd already removed the tablet section and pulled up the file with the buyout terms he was discussing. He glanced at it when she turned it to him, nodded, and made a finger movement that, from the context of the conversation, she translated to mean he needed to glance at another particular section. She found it, turned the tablet his way again.

He scanned the text, but she could tell he didn't need the confirmation. The deal was done two minutes later, and Gabriel hung up with a smile. "Well, that went better than expected."

Charlotte laughed. "You got everything you wanted."

Eyes lingering on her face, he grinned. "Yes, I wasn't expecting total capitulation." He slid away his phone. "It seems I've kept you late for no reason."

"It's all right. You couldn't have known they'd roll over." Tonight's overtime had been a real request. "I'll call a car."

Gabriel shook his head. "I'll drop you home."

It was the first time he'd made the offer. Every other time, he'd escorted her to the executive cab, then called to make sure she was safely home. Swallowing, she said, "No. You live in the city." Only a few minutes away. "It'll be an extra drive for you."

"I could do with a drive after revving up for a negotiation that turned into a cakewalk." Rising, he took her ice cream container and threw it into the trash along with his. "Come on, Ms. Baird. I promised early on that I wouldn't bite." A slow smile. "Unless you make the request, of course."

11

LIONS, GAZELLES, AND
BESPECTACLED MICE

CHEEKS BURNING, CHARLOTTE GOT up and walked out ahead of Gabriel, able to feel him behind her every inch of the way. It was probably what a gazelle felt like when she had a lion on her tail. A big, good-looking lion who'd almost convinced the gazelle he was harmless... right before the glint in his eye reminded her he had very sharp teeth.

"Your coat in the closet?" the lion asked.

Charlotte nodded, realizing she was mixing far too many metaphors where Gabriel was concerned. Nerves did that to her. Next thing you know, she'd be imagining a bespectacled mouse quivering in mingled terror and anticipation as it sat at a dinner table with a lion who looked ravenous. And suddenly the mouse was a woman who looked an awful lot like her, and the lion was a shirtless man with water running down the chiseled planes of his chest.

Thank God they'd reached the closet.

Built into the wall, it didn't break the clean lines of the outer office, and she made sure not to leave her things lying around. It was something she'd learned from her predecessor.

All her other faults aside, Anya had known how to look like the perfect PA.

Big hands reached past her for her coat, Gabriel's warm, masculine scent seeping into her pores to make her already racing heart stutter, her breath catch, and her thighs clench. Her body didn't seem to have received the memo that she wasn't interested in sex with a T-Rex. Probably because she kept fantasizing about all kinds of things that could lead to nakedness with said T-Rex.

"Here." He shook her coat open and held it out.

No man had ever held out her coat. What was she supposed to do with her arms? Moving slowly, she raised one arm then the other... and he slipped it on as effortlessly as if he did this every day for her, his fingers brushing her shoulders before he reached into the closet for his own coat. She'd hunted it up earlier that day, along with his suit jacket. Whichever suit he wore, the jacket never stayed on during the day, but he needed it unwrinkled for meetings.

Leaving the jacket in there, he shrugged into his coat as she picked up her purse. She wasn't surprised when he walked into his office and returned with a black briefcase—Charlotte wasn't sure the man ever stopped working. Except, of course, when he took home the women who received red roses the next day.

Hand tightening on the strap of her handbag, she nodded when he said, "Ready?"

The elevator felt tiny with him in it, his sheer presence taking it over. She wasn't sure she'd survive the drive to her house—she'd been in the car with him before, but tonight, with the night enclosing them in a dark cocoon, everything felt different, felt strangely intimate.

Red-rose women, she reminded herself before she could get too stupid. *Unless you plan to grow a foot and magically sprout bigger breasts, there's zero risk of him actually having any interest in you.*

The thought made her eyes narrow as they stepped out into the cavernous underground garage and Gabriel led her to the gleaming black all-wheel drive parked in the CEO's spot. A crouching beast of an SUV that meant Charlotte always had to use the step at the side to get into the passenger seat, it wasn't the usual CEO-type car, but he probably wasn't comfortable in a smaller car. This one suited him.

It probably suited his leggy dates as well.

Stop it, Charlotte, she ordered herself.

"Ms. Baird." A penetrating glance as he unlocked the car with a remote and opened the passenger-side door. "What's the matter?"

"Nothing." She gasped as he gripped her by the waist and hitched her into her seat.

"You sure?" he asked, hands still on her and expression incisive.

She nodded, sucking in a rushed breath when he finally released her and shut the door. Then he was in the driver's seat, handling the large vehicle with ease as they left the garage. Using the controls on the steering wheel, he turned on the radio, jazz pouring out of the speakers at a soft volume. "You okay with jazz?"

"I haven't listened to it much," she admitted, "but I like this sound." Smoky and sensual and slightly cynical.

"There's a small club up north that has the occasional jazz musician play a live set," he told her, turning left to go up a hilly street. "I'll take you sometime."

Guessing he was simply making conversation, she said, "I've never really seen live music. Molly says it's amazing."

Gabriel shifted gears, the car smooth as a cloud on the city streets. "Do you plan to visit her?"

"If my boss ever permits me a vacation."

That boss grinned. "I just can't live without you, Ms. Baird."

Not wanting to think too hard about the way her stomach fluttered at those playful words, she said, "How about you? Do you have a best friend?"

"My brothers and I are all close, and I have a few mates who might as well be blood. We met playing rugby in high school."

"Do you miss it?" she asked softly. "Playing professional rugby?" Charlotte would've never brought up the subject if she'd thought it would make him sad, but he still seemed to find pleasure in the game.

Two weeks ago, he'd called her into the office to show her a replay of his brother Daniel's maiden test try, his pride in the twenty-one-year-old apparent. Then there was his coaching, and the fact he sometimes mentioned staying up late or waking predawn to catch the live feed of an international match.

"No," he said now. "Not saying it didn't hurt like a bitch when I realized I'd never play again for my country. I was twenty-five and my body refused to heal right. It didn't matter what I did, I couldn't control it."

That would've been intensely frustrating for a man like Gabriel, used to being the master of his own destiny. "How did you end up in business?"

"My parents always drummed it into my skull that playing sports was a career with a limited lifespan. Unless I wanted to go into professional coaching or sports commentary afterward, I sure as hell better have a backup plan."

"Wow, this is some backup plan." Gabriel owned the boardroom.

A grin. "No one took me seriously at first. Despite the fact I had an MBA, they figured I was playing at business." His grin widened. "Then I bought up an ailing company, turned it around, and started sweeping contracts out from under my competitors' feet."

Fascinated by this glimpse into his history, Charlotte nudged at him to tell her more about that first company, and the deep, masculine sound of his voice wrapped around her.

GABRIEL COULD FEEL CHARLOTTE getting more and more tense the closer they got to her home. When he'd offered to drive her, he'd had no ulterior motive. Once in the car though, he'd been considering if he could coax the delectable Ms. Baird into a kiss.

Now he knew that wasn't about to happen. She'd been fine all day, but something about having him near her home was ratcheting up her fear. His hands tightened on the steering wheel as his mind gave him all sorts of dark reasons why having a male in her home might terrify Charlotte.

"Which way's the best option?" he asked as he neared a fork in the road, fighting to keep his tone easy even as anger rose in a hot wave under his skin.

"Left," she said, hands locked tightly together in her lap. "It's a little quicker."

Shifting gears, he took the car left. "Are you still catching the bus in the mornings?" He would've organized a car for her except that he was sure she'd balk when she realized it was coming from him rather than the company budget.

The restraint didn't sit well with Gabriel; he liked to look after the people who belonged to him. And regardless of their personal relationship, Ms. Baird belonged to him.

"Yes." A short pause before she added, "It's pretty efficient except when it rains. Everyone seems to slow down to a crawl then." She played with the strap of her purse, the burst of conversation followed by silence until they hit her street. "There." She pointed out the long drive that serviced multiple town houses.

"Which number?" He was pleased to note the drive was well lit, security lights coming on automatically as his car passed the other town houses.

"The one right at the back."

He brought the car to a halt a couple of seconds later.

"W...would you mind waiting?" A flush of red on her cheekbones as she made the request.

"Of course I'll wait." Gabriel would've done so for any woman, but the fact Charlotte had fought her embarrassment to ask gave him another disturbing insight into the emotional scars that marked her.

Getting out, he came around to her door. She'd already opened it, but he placed his hands on her waist and put her on the ground. He was half expecting her to protest the handling; he'd done it precisely so she'd snap at him, the spark back in her eyes, but she just headed for her door, keys in hand and stride a little jerky. Deactivating the alarm using the keypad on the wall just inside the door once she'd opened it, she turned in the doorway.

Suppressed panic on her face, as if she didn't know what to do now.

It wasn't the cute panic of a woman unsure about the protocol but happy to have him there. He saw real fear in her eyes.

Shoving down his simmering anger at this further evidence of what had been done to her, he smiled and said, "Have a good night. I'll pick you up at seven thirty tomorrow."

A startled blink. "What?"

"Remember I mentioned Rotorua? I got a call about that while you were away from the office." When she'd bought him ice cream. The reminder eased his tension—Charlotte might have scars, but she liked him, even if she wouldn't admit it. Her fear wasn't directed specifically at him. "End result is that we decided to move the meeting up. You and I are heading down to Rotorua tomorrow to speak to a local Maori arts collective whose work I want to feature as part of our arts partnership deal."

That partnership, involving high-end hotels around the country as well as a select number of premier resort lodges, would not only give the featured artists a serious boost, it'd put the Saxon & Archer brand firmly back at the top of a very exclusive table. It was why Gabriel was being so hands-on when it came to choosing the artists. He'd already confirmed a gifted metal sculptor who worked at the miniature level. A painter specializing in breathtaking New Zealand landscapes was also on his list.

It was all part of his long-term plan to remind people that Saxon & Archer meant the unique and the beautiful, elegance teamed with faultless perfection. It was far from the rough and tumble of his previous position in the sustainable logging industry, when he'd worn boots and hard hats as often as he'd worn suits. However, business was business, and Gabriel understood business.

There wasn't a doubt in his mind that at the end of his one-year-contract, he'd leave behind a thriving company. The board was already making hopeful noises about having him stay on, but Gabriel had no intention of doing so—he liked playing knight for ailing corporations. The role of a captain holding the ship steady didn't suit him as well, though he'd make damn sure of his successor's skill set before he moved on.

When he did, whether it was to another business that needed his skills or to focus on his significant and growing property portfolio, he'd be taking his PA with him. Let the next CEO find his or her own Ms. Baird. Not that they would—Charlotte was one of a kind.

"A seven thirty start will get us there around ten thirty," he said to her now. "Meeting's at eleven. We'll have lunch afterward, be back in Auckland by five."

"You don't want me to hold the fort at the office?"

Staying against the car instead of closing the distance to her, he shook his head. "It's a relatively clear day tomorrow businesswise." It had taken three months and a small number of additional staff changes, but his management team was at the stage that he could trust them to do what needed to be done, even if he wasn't physically there for them to consult.

Unlike that idiot, Hill, Gabriel didn't waste his time micromanaging competent people. "You can get calls forwarded to your cell," he added. "So, seven thirty?"

CHARLOTTE COULDN'T FIND ANY reason to say no... except for her nervousness at the roughly three-hour drive with Gabriel. "Okay," she managed to get out, her nails digging into her palms as she hit her limit of cowardice.

No more, said a frustrated, angry part of her. *No more.* Her frustration was all the more intense because of how well the day had gone—she'd more than held her own with Gabriel. And now this.

"Good night, Ms. Baird."

"Good night, Mr. Bishop." Closing the door, she threw the deadbolt and double-locked everything, then ran quickly to the living room to watch Gabriel leave, the lights of his vehicle scything across windows set with bars. It was an unusual modification in her neighborhood, but she'd made sure it was tastefully done—the bars looked more like a decorative element than the rigid iron they actually were.

The sound of Gabriel's car was gone a couple of seconds later, purring into the darkness.

Taking a shuddering breath, she turned on the lights in the living room, the kitchen, the hallway, the spare room, and her bedroom one by one, including in the master bathroom. Then, as she did every night, she walked through each room to make sure nothing had been moved or disturbed in her absence and that the door from the garage remained dead-locked from the inside.

Only when she was certain everything was exactly as she'd left it, all the little booby traps she'd set unsprung, did she walk into her bedroom and change into her sleeveless white eyelet nightgown. Skimming her body to the ankle, the Victorian-inspired nightgown was embellished with a thin ribbon in the same delicate peach shade as that which separated the bodice from the rest of the gown. Overall, she thought, catching a glimpse of herself in the full-length mirror on the wall beside her wardrobe, it was sweetly romantic but not exactly sexy.

No, she was definitely not one of the red-rose women.

Brushing out her hair on that scowling thought, she walked into the kitchen to make herself a cup of tea. She'd always been a night owl, and given that it was only ten forty-five, she decided she'd read for an hour. Snuggling into bed with a Scottish historical, her teacup on the nightstand, she flipped to her bookmark but couldn't focus. Her mind kept drifting in a single direction.

Gabriel was probably home by now. If she knew him, he'd put the briefcase on a table, take off his coat, and throw it over the back of a chair. He'd no doubt kick off his shoes and socks, walk into the bedroom as he unbuttoned his shirt to reveal that glorious wall of a chest, those wide shoulders, the ink on his body only highlighting the beauty of him.

It was truly, truly embarrassing how many nights she'd fantasized about watching Gabriel dress and undress. Even with her admonitions to herself about the danger of allowing her crush to deepen into something that could hurt her, she couldn't stop herself. The book lay unread in front of her as she imagined him shrugging off that shirt to ball it up and chuck it into the laundry basket, his shoulders gleaming under the light.

Then his hands went to the belt of his pants.

Toes curling, she swallowed and watched the strip of black leather slide out, drop to the floor with a clink of metal softened by the carpet. His fingers went to the top button of his pants, undid it, lowered the zipper.

Triiiiing!

Charlotte jumped, the book slamming shut as she stared at her cell phone with red-hot cheeks and a guiltily thudding heart. No one called her this late except for Molly, and that was after her friend texted to see if she was awake. Fear sent a chill trickle down her spine, but Charlotte grabbed the phone to look at the screen. She'd long ago decided she wouldn't allow the memory of evil to terrorize her inside her home.

The caller ID showed Gabriel's name.

12

IN WHICH MS. BAIRD HAS A
GUILTY CONSCIENCE

FLUSHING EVEN HOTTER, HER breasts heavy and aching, Charlotte tapped the Answer icon. "Mr. Bishop?"

"Sorry to call so late."

"That's all right," she said, telling the giggly teenage girl inside her to shush. She didn't know why that girl had awoken after so many years, but her hopes were ridiculous. This wasn't a romantic call. It was a business one. "I'm usually awake now."

"Night owl?"

"Yes."

"Me too." It sounded like he was smiling. "What are you doing?"

Fantasizing about watching you strip. After which I would've fantasized about kissing and licking my way over every inch of your hot, hard, magnificent body.

"READING A HISTORICAL NOVEL."

Intrigued by the husky tone of Charlotte's reply, her voice breathy, Gabriel wondered if she really was reading a historical novel. "Sure it's not an erotic romance?"

"No!" A high, sharp denial that sounded so guilty he grinned.

"Why, Ms. Baird, I'm shocked."

Her breathing was rough. "Are you working?" she asked, changing the subject so abruptly that he made himself a promise that one day, he'd find out exactly what she'd been reading tonight—and then he'd make her read it aloud to him while he did naughty, debauched things to her.

"I am," he admitted, leaning back in the chair where he sat, having spread documents across the dining room table. He liked working there when at home, the vista in front of him a sparkling cityscape.

"You should take time off." A soft admonition. "You work all the time."

"I date, as you pointed out," he said, just to see what she'd say.

"I don't think what you do is considered dating."

He grinned at the coolly snippy reply, though his body wasn't impressed by his continued self-inflicted torture. The fact was, he hadn't been with a woman since the day he'd realized his PA pushed all his buttons when she wasn't terrified out of her skin.

Why go for any woman but the one he wanted?

And Gabriel always got what he wanted. "I couldn't find that memo HR sent yesterday."

"Check under this file extension." She rattled it off.

Gabriel touched the memo where it sat right in front of him. "Got it." He'd called her to make sure she was okay, that her demons weren't hounding her. "Do you watch that show with the gourmet food and the race?"

A small pause. "Oh, I know the one. I used to, but I have a very demanding boss these days, so I'm never home in time." When he laughed, she said, "Do you watch it?"

"No, but we've had an approach from them to sponsor the next season in return for advertising and in-show placement of Saxon & Archer goods. What do you think?" He knew she loved cooking. Not only had she once come back from lunch having bought a bunch of spices he hadn't even known existed, she'd refused to work last Saturday morning because she'd had a class to attend.

Something to do with fondant icing and cake sculpture.

Now she gave him her thoughts, and he leaned back and listened. Yes, smart women were his catnip—and Charlotte Baird was very, very, smart.

THE DRIVE THE NEXT morning wasn't as stressful as Charlotte had worried it might be; the fact she knew and trusted Gabriel didn't always equal control over her emotional responses, and she'd been terrified her claustrophobia would make an unwanted return. As it was, they ended up working most of the drive, thanks to the fact the company's CFO was down with food poisoning and Gabriel needed to sign off on things she'd normally handle.

The hiccup wasn't, however, that big in the grand scheme of things, and Charlotte and Gabriel stuck to their plan to head to Rotorua. Once there, the meeting with the art collective went off without a hitch. The artists were all very protective of their work, but Gabriel's personal visit and his willingness to work with them in relation to special arrangements for some pieces eased their concerns. The end result was a signed agreement and enthusiasm all around.

"Lunch?" Gabriel asked as they pulled away from the marae, the traditional meeting house set amongst velvety grass that gleamed bright green under the crisp winter sunlight.

"You'll have to return a call first," she said, having fielded everything during the meeting. "It's Brent—he just needs two minutes."

Gabriel took care of the matter using the car's hands-free phone system, then turned to Charlotte. "Trust me, Ms. Baird?"

"Not when you smile like that."

GABRIEL LAUGHED AT THE prim response that didn't quite manage to hide the twitch of her lips. It made him want to kiss her. "You know me too well." When her eyes sparkled, he said, "You have a cooking class or anything else you have to be back for tonight?"

"No, not tonight."

Since he didn't have coaching commitments either, he said, "Detour to the coast?"

A smile that made his need to kiss her almost unbearable, his heart doing things inside his chest that he was sure weren't in the least macho. He couldn't find it in himself to care, because when Charlotte smiled that way, it destroyed him.

"I'd love that."

Gabriel could feel Charlotte's pleasure in the coastal scenery the instant it opened up beside them. He, too, loved the twisted beauty of the old pōhutukawa trees, iconic against the blue-green sea that could be as cold as ice, the white sands glittering under sunlight.

Slowing down to let a mother duck and her fat little ducklings pass safely across the road, Gabriel allowed his eyes to linger on Charlotte's face as she leaned forward to watch. It was rare for him to get a chance to look at his personal assistant without her noticing. When she was aware, he made sure not to do it because it discomfited her. Any attention discomfited her.

Even in the ill-fitting clothes she insisted on wearing, men noticed her petite beauty, but every time one made any kind of an approach, she withdrew. Gabriel had quietly but harshly discouraged one particularly enthusiastic advertising executive. The man had continued to ask her out despite her earlier negative responses, to Charlotte's increasing distress.

Once Gabriel added his knowledge of that situation to her wariness when he'd dropped her home, he had a very bad feeling he knew how she'd been hurt. If he was right, he had an even harder road ahead than he'd realized. Giving up, however, was simply not an option. He had decided on Charlotte. The first time he'd decided on something, he'd been eight and it had been rugby. A seven-year international pro career later, he'd suffered the injury that took him out of play. So he'd decided on kicking ass and taking names as a man who specialized in rescuing drowning companies.

Now he'd decided on Charlotte.

"So, where are we going?" Charlotte asked after the last duckling disappeared into the reeds on the side of the isolated road.

"You'll like it, I promise." He rarely made promises, but when he did, he kept his word. It was important to him, a vow he'd made as a six-year-old who'd watched the bailiffs repossess the television his mom had worked so hard to get. Brian Bishop, Gabriel's father, had used the money intended to pay off the television, as well as two months' worth of rent money, to make an investment.

"Forget the television, Alison." A huge grin, his father's hands on his mother's upper arms. *"We'll be able to buy the fucking electronics store once I cash in these shares. I had to strike now, buy them while they were at rock bottom. We'll make a killing when they rise again, I promise."*

Only those shares had never risen. Another dud, like all his father's other schemes.

"Gabriel."

It was the first time Charlotte had used his given name. The intimacy of it sliced through the memory that marked the day he'd first understood the worthlessness of his father's promises. He'd stopped being a child that day. "Yes?"

Voice hesitant, she said, "Your expression got very dark all of a sudden. Is everything okay?"

"Just thinking over a contract situation," he said, his "father" a topic he preferred to avoid. "See that group of shops? That's our destination."

Pulling into the small parking area out front half a minute later, he got out and watched Charlotte hop out as well, stretch her legs. He wanted to put his hand on her lower back, rub to ease the muscles there. And he wanted to hold her close, alleviate his own tension by breathing her in, her soft warmth against him.

Hands fisting in his pants pockets, he led her to a tiny shop with a window to the street.

"Award-winning fish and chips," Charlotte read out with a grin. "I'm starving."

He'd taken women to Michelin-starred restaurants and never seen such open, unaffected joy. After buying the meal, which the owner wrapped in greaseproof paper, Gabriel took it to a weathered wooden picnic table by the beach while Charlotte carried over their drinks. They sat across from one another, the food on the tabletop between them, and ate in a comfortable quiet that did nothing to hide the thrumming sexual tension beneath.

Charlotte might refuse to accept it, but it was there. He saw it in her blushes when she watched him, thinking he wasn't aware, caught it in her eyes in the mornings after he returned from a run. Maybe he'd stripped off his T-shirt a few times in the office rather than waiting till the shower just to see her breath catch.

He was a guy, after all. He liked the way she looked at him.

He'd like it even better if she'd touch and kiss and handle his body like her favorite treat. Sucking would be encouraged. As would licking. Hell, anything she wanted to do to and with him would be encouraged. As long as he got to put his hands on her too. The idea of having her naked and laughing and soft and silky under his hands...

Shifting on the bench, he told himself to shut it down before his hard-on became so obvious he'd have to sit here for another hour to get rid of it. Instead, he focused on all the other things he liked about Charlotte, especially her mind. "You saw the new advertising package PR's proposing. What do you think?"

As she spoke, face mobile and animated, he watched her. The wind had tugged several of her curls free of the bun in which she'd managed to confine her hair, and he enjoyed seeing them flirt against her face as she talked and sipped her lime-flavored milkshake. They disagreed on some of her points, but it was a friendly disagreement, Charlotte sassing him more than once.

"Hey, no lip," he said lightly at one point and saw her face go stark white. "Charlotte." Getting up, he walked around to sit beside her, his back to the table.

His instinct was to touch her, comfort her, but the way she held herself—shoulders hunched in and neck strained as she stared at the tabletop—told him she couldn't handle such contact. Seeing her shiver, he went to the car and grabbed his jacket. She flinched when he put it over her shoulders and his gut clenched... but then she tugged the jacket around herself, her fingers tight on the lapels.

He sat again, and, angling his body to face her, braced one arm against the weathered wood of the table. "What did I say?" he asked when she shot him a quick look.

Her throat moved, fingers flexing and tightening. "No, it's nothing." A whisper.

"I'm not really a T-Rex, you know," he said gently and got a guilty look in response, Charlotte's cheeks flushing with color.

"How did you..." She shook her head, shoulders no longer hunched in. "You have to admit you chewed up people and spit them out that first week. Very T-Rex of you."

Relieved she sounded more like her usual self, he risked tugging on one escapee curl. "I won't use those words again."

It was obvious the term "No lip" had brought something bad to the surface.

Spark dimming once more, she bowed her head. "Sorry."

"Why?" he said, continuing to play with the curl that had escaped the bun he hated with a vengeance. It was so distant and stiff and not at all like the fiery woman who was apt to snap at him when he snarled. "I got to touch this pretty hair because of it."

Hot pink on her cheeks, her head jerking up. "That's not—"

"Appropriate?" He leaned in close enough that it was pure torture not to bridge the final inches, taste the gold-dusted cream of her skin. "Should I stop?" He had to make dead certain they were on the same page. Because he was her boss, and because he wouldn't do the same thing to her that some fucking bastard clearly already had.

The choice had to be Charlotte's.

Huge hazel eyes met his before she got to her feet in a quick movement. "We should go."

Gabriel rose with an inward smile. She hadn't said no—and she was still holding his jacket around her. It was a start.

13

T-Rex Gives Good Orgasms

CHARLOTTE CALLED MOLLY AFTER dinner, desperate to talk to her best friend.

"Charlie!" Molly's excited face filled the screen of Charlotte's laptop, her friend's black hair a wild tumble around her head and her thin, royal-blue sweater sliding off one shoulder. "I've been dying to hear everything since your text!"

Charlotte rubbed her finger over a nonexistent spot on the bedspread, the laptop on her thighs. "I overreacted."

"Wait." Molly held up her phone. "It says here that T-Rex touched you. Are you telling me that was a lie?"

Rolling her eyes at her friend's dramatic gasp, she said, "He put his coat around me... and kind of played with my hair." God, she felt like a teenager saying that. "Just the strands at the side," she clarified quickly when Molly squeaked.

"He played with your hair? Don't tell me you don't know what that means."

Charlotte's skin burned, her toes curling into the sheet. "Okay, it was maybe a signal."

"Well, I suppose he could hardly drag you into his office and do bad, bad things to you."

Charlotte's panties went damp at the idea of being behind closed doors with a Gabriel who was no longer acting as her boss. A Gabriel who surely would do deliciously bad things to a woman who gave him the green light.

If that woman wasn't a timid mouse.

Groaning, she dropped her face into her hands, giddy delight replaced by frustrated despair. "I had a flashback."

Molly's expression, when Charlotte looked up again, had changed from glee to gentle encouragement. "What happened?" asked the friend who'd walked with Charlotte through the darkness, who had seen the scars firsthand.

Drawing in a shaky breath, Charlotte forced herself to speak. "Gabriel said something in fun, but it was something Dick used to say."

She hadn't been able to say Richard's name aloud for a long time. It was Molly who'd reduced him to Dick, and in so doing, stolen his power, or that had been the plan. Charlotte hadn't quite managed to strip him of power in her mind, but she was getting there. She no longer had nightmares where she thought he was in the house, and she could get a full night's sleep ninety percent of the time.

"What did T-Rex do afterward?" Molly asked, the white lines around her mouth telling Charlotte her best friend's fury at Richard hadn't abated an iota.

Charlotte thought of the warmth of Gabriel's jacket, of the way he'd been so delightfully inappropriate with her. "He was wonderful." The fact that the ride back had felt strained and awkward was her fault, not his. She'd been so angry and tense;

the sudden flashback had come right when she'd begun to think she might have a shot at a life untainted by the ugliness of that brutal year.

"What am I going to do, Molly?" At least she had the long weekend to figure that out—with Monday being a public holiday, she wouldn't see Gabriel till Tuesday.

"Given his goal-oriented nature," Molly said solemnly, "I bet T-Rex gives good orgasms." A waggle of her eyebrows that made Charlotte splutter with laughter. "I say let him have at it. It'll be good stress relief for you."

Knowing she was bright red, Charlotte pointed at the screen. "Not funny."

"I wasn't being funny. Didn't you once tell me to go home with a rock star and have wild monkey sex?" Molly's grin was wide. "Clearly, that turned out well for me. So follow your own advice, Charlie. Have wild monkey sex with your very hot boss."

Charlotte couldn't think about being naked with Gabriel without hyperventilating, so she said, "You doing okay?" Molly and Fox had recently dealt with a horrible invasion of privacy situation, and while Molly seemed to have come through it strong and unbeaten, Charlotte liked to check up on her friend.

"I'm good." Molly touched the screen in an affectionate period to her words. "But don't think I'll let you change the subject." She put on a mock-stern face. "You're happy—I can see it. Be happy, Charlie." A deep smile. "You don't have to force yourself to be different. From everything you've told me today and over the past few months, Gabriel Bishop seems to like you fine just as you are."

Charlotte continued to think about her friend's words long after they ended the call.

Be happy.

It had been a long time since she'd been truly happy. But today, prior to the flashback that had filled her mouth with the metallic taste of fear, she'd felt like the Charlotte she'd been before Richard. That Charlotte had been shy too, but she hadn't been scared; she'd been full of hope.

In many ways, the worst thing of all was that Richard had been nice at the start. That was why it was so hard for her to trust any man, no matter how wonderful he appeared on the surface.

That first meeting with Richard, it had been so sunny, so sweet.

"HEY, YOU MIND IF I grab this seat?"

Charlotte looked up from her book, her sandwich halfway to her mouth, to see the Boy. That was the name she and Molly had given him after spotting him on campus at the start of the semester.

He was blond, the kind of streaky, summer blond that came with hours in the sun, his skin always deeply golden. From a T-shirt he occasionally wore, one bearing the label of a local surf shop, Charlotte had deduced he was a surfer. He had the lean, muscled body for it too.

Today, he slid in on the other side of the table without waiting for her reply. "I'm Richard."

His smile, it was like something out of the movies. His teeth were flawless, his lips perfect. Add in the chiseled jawline and the bright blue eyes, and he was the most physically perfect human being she'd ever seen in real life.

"Charlotte," she managed to say, not quite daring to believe he was talking to her. Boys who looked like Richard did not talk to nerds like Charlotte unless they wanted to borrow lecture notes—and as far as Charlotte knew, she and Richard weren't taking any of the same classes.

Then he said, "I've seen you in Introductory Accounting."

That was a huge first-year course with hundreds in each lecture theatre.

Charlotte still couldn't imagine how she'd missed him. "Oh." She wanted to slap herself for the monosyllabic response—you'd think she'd have gotten over her shyness by now. "Did you want to borrow the notes from today's lecture?" A whole sentence, she'd managed a whole sentence.

Shaking his head, he bit into an apple. "No, I was there. God, the prof drones on, doesn't she? I call her lectures War & Peace & Accounts."

Charlotte felt her lips tug up at the corners. "Yes."

"So you want to get into accounting?"

"I thought I might, but it's not me."

When he smiled again, it was as if the sun had come out. "Yeah, I know what you mean. I'm taking first-year law too, but I don't think I'm cut out for the life of a lawyer."

CHARLOTTE AND RICHARD HAD ended up talking for so long that she'd missed her next class. It was the first time she'd ever played hooky. The fact she'd done it with the cutest boy she'd ever met had sent her skipping across campus after they finally went their separate ways.

Now, alone in her bedroom, Charlotte wiped away a tear. Not for Richard but for herself. She'd been so *young*, so naïve. She might have been a few months past eighteen, but she'd known nothing about men, not really. If things hadn't gone so terribly wrong for Molly at fifteen, Charlotte would've learned by watching her best friend—Molly had always been the braver of the two of them. But Molly had changed after that awful year, boys far, *far* down on her list of priorities.

That was how Charlotte came to be the first of the two of them to actually have a serious boyfriend. While Molly focused on her studies, Charlotte fell dizzyingly for the beautiful boy who'd noticed the mouse in amongst all the butterflies. Unsure about her path in life and searching desperately for something to fill the hole left inside her by the deaths of both her parents two months earlier, she'd felt hope for the future. Maybe, she'd thought, maybe even shy girls with glasses got happy endings.

Molly had been so excited for her. They'd giggled in Charlotte's bedroom as they picked out outfits for her dates with Richard, trying out different makeup looks they'd found in magazines or online. Things most girls did in high school. It had been fun and innocent and hopeful.

No one could've predicted the horror to come.

Taking a shuddering breath when her heart began to thump, Charlotte got up and went to wash her face. She could refuse to allow the memories to drag her under, but one fact she couldn't avoid: she was still clueless about men. Richard had been a cruel boy under his golden looks, and she could rely on none of her experiences with him when it came to dealing with an adult male like Gabriel.

Should I stop?

The memory of his deep voice, his steely eyes holding her own, his big body so close to hers, it made her shiver. "No," she whispered into the mirror, her heart in her eyes. "Don't stop."

The phone rang.

Her heart thumped again, this time in anticipation. For so long, late-night calls had been a cause for fear, but those memories stood no chance against the reality of Gabriel's voice in her ear. "Am I disturbing you?"

Her thighs pressed together, her skin suddenly tight over her body. "No. Did you need something?"

"Yes."

Knees weak at the way he said that, though she knew she was reading far too much into a single word, Charlotte sat down on the edge of her bed. "I'll grab my laptop."

"It's not for work," he said. "Do you know how to make a pasta sauce from scratch?"

Charlotte was momentarily lost for words at the unexpected question. "Why are you cooking?" As far as she could tell, he lived on ordered meals—healthy, balanced ones created by the best chefs in the city.

"I want to impress a girl."

Charlotte's smile faded, the bubbles in her blood fizzling out. "I can talk you through it." She hoped her voice betrayed nothing of her humiliating crush. It was all her own fault for seeing too much in what had clearly been nothing but a little light flirtation on his part.

Something crashed in the background on Gabriel's end. "Shit."

She frowned, hearing pain in his tone. "Are you okay?"

"Yeah, just smashed a glass, cut my finger." He sounded like he was moving around. "I don't think I'll be practicing any cooking today."

Charlotte worried her thumb over the knuckle of her middle finger. "Are you sure you don't need a doctor?"

"Yeah, I'm a big boy."

Her toes curled again despite all her intentions and admonitions to the contrary. "Okay, good night."

"So eager to get rid of me?"

Charlotte didn't know how to deal with Gabriel when he got like this. "Aren't you sick of the sight of me?"

"Careful, I might take that as a not-so-subtle hint about your own feelings."

Her face cracked into a smile she simply couldn't fight. "Can I have a long lunch on Tuesday?"

"Meeting your friend Eggplant?"

Charlotte choked back her laughter, not about to encourage him in his determined and irrational dislike of poor Ernest. "I want to buy a few things for a care package for Molly from a couple of stores near the office." She could go into the city over the weekend, but it'd be crowded and noisy because of an outdoor festival, and she didn't do well in crowds.

"Isn't her rock star taking care of her?"

"I just thought it'd be a nice surprise to send over her favorite snacks from home." Impulsively she shared something else. "She already sent me a whole box of American chocolate bars."

"Oh yeah? Which one was your favorite? Tell me so I can buy it for you the next time you get mad."

They talked for another fifteen minutes. It was easy, comfortable, except for the stupid compulsion inside her toward him. He wasn't for her, she reminded herself—he was planning a meal for his next conquest.

That fact should've poured ice-cold water on her fantasies. Too bad her brain didn't want to listen.

That night, she dreamed of straddling his lap while they were in the office, those hard thighs under her own and his big hands on her hips as she undid his tie, unbuttoned his shirt. Dream Charlotte was confident, pushing him back in his chair while she licked and kissed her way across all that hot, satiny flesh.

She didn't mind when he fisted his hand in her hair and ordered her to her knees in front of him, told her to use her mouth on his cock. Dream Charlotte was so aroused she could barely breathe as she did exactly that, as she allowed him to direct her mouth with his grip in her hair, as she moved her mouth over the hardness of him, the veins beneath his skin plump and inviting the stroke of her tongue.

Her shirt was suddenly open, her bra gone, and when Gabriel reached down to squeeze and caress her breasts with one warm, rough hand that wasn't gentle but demanding, she moaned and—

Charlotte's eyes snapped awake on the moan, the sound cutting through her sleeping mind. Pulse a rapid thud and skin hot, she looked down to see that her nightgown was bunched at her waist, her hand under the waistband of her panties. Thighs clenching around that hand, she turned to her side and buried her face in her pillow.

Then, for the first time since she'd survived hell, she stroked herself to pleasure, all the while imagining that it was Gabriel's big hand taking care of her while his body burned hot and hard around her.

14

A Woman Named Tiffany
(Uh-Oh)

FOUR HOURS AFTER WAKING, Charlotte was still inwardly blushing over what she'd done. She was also in the office. On a Saturday. Gabriel had asked her to come in to help him finalize the documents for a major deal that had acquired legs overnight, sending a car to pick her up after her two-hour "Working with Pastry" master class. She'd been grateful—the public transport into the city was no doubt shoulder to shoulder today.

They'd been working for ninety minutes and Charlotte was in the outer office printing out a financial report on the small French company Saxon & Archer was about to purchase as part of Gabriel's plans to control production of their higher-end inventory, when security called up from the ground floor.

"Hey, Charlie," the guard said. "I gotta lady down here says she needs to speak to the big boss."

Charlotte frowned. "Who is it, Steven? I'll ask Mr. Bishop if he can see her."

A short pause before Steven came back on the line. "Says her name is Tiffany. She's pretty convinced he'll be happy to see her."

Charlotte's hand squeezed the phone. She knew of one Tiffany in Gabriel's life. The two had gone out on a date a month ago, the morning after which the requisite red roses had been dispatched; Tiffany had left the country that same afternoon, on her way to a modeling contract in Japan. Now it appeared she was back.

"Give me a second," she said and, placing the receiver down, poked her head into Gabriel's office. "A woman named Tiffany—I assume Tiffany Summer—is here to see you. Should I have Steven buzz her up?"

Gabriel looked up from his papers with a scowl. "Who?"

"Tiffany," she said again, though a tiny little evil corner of her heart was laughing in glee because he appeared to have totally forgotten the other woman. "Long, straight brown hair to her hips, blue eyes, six feet tall." What Charlotte didn't add were the woman's knockout breasts and perfect cheekbones.

In all honesty, stand Tiffany and Gabriel next to one another and they'd look like the perfect match.

"Christ." Thrusting a hand through his hair, Gabriel glanced at his watch. "Yeah, buzz her up."

Charlotte passed on the message, and two minutes later, Tiffany Summer wafted in on a wave of sultry perfume, her body clad in tight white pants and a blood-orange silk top that would've looked like a tent on Charlotte. Tiffany Summer had no such problem—she was stunning in the piece. Her black stilettos somehow went perfectly with the rest of her outfit.

"Oh," Tiffany said once through the glass doors. "I hadn't realized Gabriel had staff here."

Charlotte recognized that tone. While her family hadn't been wealthy—far from it—her mother had worked as a teacher at an exclusive all-girls private school. As a result, Charlotte had been permitted to attend the school at the discounted fee rate offered to children of senior employees. It was one of the biggest perks of the position.

Because of her mom's long service, the school hadn't kicked Charlotte out when Pippa Baird got sick and could no longer continue to work. Thanks to Charlotte's five-year stint in those hallowed halls, she'd come into contact with more than one rich girl. Some were normal kids who happened to have wealthy parents, but there was another, far more vicious group.

The Queen Bees, she and Molly had labeled them. The rich, beautiful ones who got their kicks out of humiliating or otherwise hurting girls not as genetically or financially blessed. Part of the Queen Bee motto was to never be obvious about it. Snideness, malicious gossip, and backstabbing whispers were their hallmarks.

However, give them enough ammunition and the ugliness came out into the open. The Queen Bees had attacked Molly in a rabid pack when the scandal with Molly's father had broken; Charlotte had seen the true depth of the vitriol and the poison that lived behind those perfect smiles. She saw echoes of that ugliness in this woman who referred to Charlotte as "staff" with the slightest sneer to her tone.

Not enough to be objectionable. Just enough to remind Charlotte of her place.

Too bad Charlotte had never cared what the Queen Bees of the world thought. It did make her question Gabriel's judgment, however. Then again, she thought grimly, women like Tiffany had a way of turning on the charm for male eyes. "Please go on through, Ms. Summer," she said in her usual professional tone. "Mr. Bishop is expecting you."

As Tiffany sauntered inside and shut the door, Charlotte tried to focus on work but found herself gritting her teeth, her attention very much on that closed door.

She jerked as the door opened a bare three minutes after Tiffany had gone in. Face set in hard lines, the model strode out, and Charlotte had the feeling she would've slammed the doors to Charlotte's office if they hadn't been automatic.

"Call Steven," Gabriel said, walking over to stand in that doorway, his narrowed eyes on Tiffany's retreating form. "I want to make sure she doesn't decide to cause any mischief. She's in the elevator now."

Charlotte made the call, stayed on the line until Steven confirmed Tiffany had left the building. "I think that's the fastest you've fired anyone." She didn't know where the quip came from, but it made Gabriel grin.

"I didn't fire her, Ms. Baird. I told her the position had been permanently filled." He glanced at his watch again as her stomach turned to concrete. "We're still on timetable to make the deadline."

THOSE PROVED TO BE famous last words.

Gabriel had to leave Charlotte alone in the office for half an hour not long after Tiffany's visit. "My mother just called," he told Charlotte, having taken the call on his cell. "She's in a café nearby." He shoved the phone in his pocket, gut tight at the tone he'd heard in Alison Esera's voice.

Today was the worst possible time for this, with Gabriel up against a hard deadline to get this deal finalized before the man with whom he was negotiating—the hereditary owner of

the company Saxon & Archer wanted to acquire and a bota-
nist with no interest in business—disappeared into the
Amazon jungle for six months, but he couldn't ignore his
mother. "Will you be okay alone?"

Charlotte picked up a stapler. "I'm armed and ready."

If he didn't kiss her soon, he'd go mad. "I told you," he
said as he left, "use the hole punch."

Leaving to the sound of her laughter, he made his way to
the Vulcan Lane café his mother loved. Upstairs in a two-level
building, it had windows that looked down on the wide pedestrian lane. When he glanced up, he saw her at a table by an
open window, her dark brown hair brushing her shoulders
and her gray eyes watching the people below. She spotted
him just then, and smiling, raised a hand. Waving back, he
ran up the narrow steps to the second level.

"I already ordered for you," she said when he bent down
to kiss her cheek.

"Thanks." Taking a seat, he didn't waste any time. "Did
Brian call you?"

Her smile faded. "He's your father, Gabriel."

"No, he was never that." Shoulders tense, he held his silence until after the waiter had delivered his black coffee and
his mom's cappuccino. "Why do you let him screw with you? I
know you don't love him anymore."

Sighing, his mother leaned back in the chair, hands cupped
around the white porcelain of her coffee cup. "I also have two
children with him, gave him ten years of my life. It's difficult
for me to give up on him despite the fact my feelings for him
died long ago."

Gabriel tried to understand how she could have any sympathy

in her heart for the man who'd abandoned her, abandoned them all, and came up empty. "What did he want?" Brian Bishop always wanted something.

"He's sick." Sorrow lay heavy on her face. "He asked me to go with him to his oncologist's appointment, and because he was once my friend, I did."

Gabriel's hand fisted on the tabletop. "How bad?"

"Serious enough that he might not make it." Holding his gaze with her own, she said, "He needs his sons—he has no one else."

Gabriel thought of how they'd been evicted after Brian Bishop abandoned them, of the nights in the homeless shelter, the sneer on the face of the welfare officer and the shame and humiliation on his mother's. "No," he said flatly. "He gave up all rights to his family when he stole every cent you'd both saved and disappeared." For two *years* afterward, Brian's only attempts at communication had been postcards that said he was on to "something big."

Then he'd had the nerve to be surprised when Alison handed him divorce papers after he did finally show up.

"Does Dad know about this?" he asked, referring to the man who had stepped in a year after Brian left them with no home and, because of his debts, nothing but the clothes on their backs. The only reason Gabriel and his brother, Sailor, still bore Brian's name was that Brian had refused to allow Joseph to legally adopt them, regardless of the fact he never saw his sons.

Rather than allowing themselves to be tied to Brian Bishop, Gabriel and his brother had reclaimed the Bishop name through sheer grit and determination, made it their own, until it no longer led back to the man who'd sired them. Now, it was associated with "the Bishop" and with the nationwide chain of gardening stores Sailor had set up in his twenties, after starting his working life as a landscaper.

"Of course." Alison closed her hand over his fist, her elegant manicure and soft palm a world away from the reddened and chafed skin he'd become used to seeing as a child. "Joseph and I don't have secrets." A deep and abiding love in every word. "He knows I just feel sorry for the man Brian once was—if we don't help him through this, no one will."

"Ask Sailor."

"You know your brother takes his cue from you."

Gabriel loved his mother, but she was asking the impossible. "I can't do it, Mom." He withdrew his hand, his jaw clenched so tight it felt as if his bones would crack. "I'm sorry. I can't forgive him." Everything else—the loss of their home, the fear and shock of having their belongings repossessed—he might have been able to forgive, but the beaten look on his mother's face as she asked for welfare help?

No, he'd never forgive Brian that. Alison had worked so hard, done endless double shifts as a cleaner to scrimp and save so her kids would never go without as she had, and in a single selfish act, Brian Bishop had shoved her into her own private hell.

Alison might have the heart to forgive him, but Gabriel wasn't that good; as far as he was concerned, Brian Bishop could stay out in the fucking cold.

CHARLOTTE KNEW SOMETHING WAS wrong the instant Gabriel walked back into the office. He had a temper and she'd seen him angry before, but never like this. Expression dark, he walked past her without a word, and over the next half hour didn't even growl at her once for a document or a file.

Worried, she went to the break room and poured him a glass of milk. Then, taking an apple-cinnamon danish from the airtight container of goodies she'd brought with her from her cooking class, she put it on a saucer and carried both into his office. Placing them on his desk when he didn't look up from his work, she headed back out.

It was fifteen minutes later that she heard an incredulous "Milk?" from inside.

Her lips tugged up, her teeth sinking into her lower lip. "It's good for you."

Coming to the doorway, he bit into the pastry with its flawlessly glazed top and delicate filling. It had taken Charlotte three tries to get it exactly right, and she'd given him that third, perfect attempt.

"Mmm." A deep sound of pleasure that melted things inside her it had no business melting. "This is fucking amazing." His throat moved as he swallowed before taking another bite.

Charlotte jerked her attention away from the strong, kissable column of his neck before he saw her staring. "Was everything okay with your mom?" she asked quietly, knowing she didn't have the right to poke her nose into his personal business, but worried about him.

"Yes. Some family stuff." He finished off the danish and licked up a bit of glazing that had come off on his thumb.

Charlotte's breath just stuck in her chest. It was so unfair how he could look like raw male temptation while eating a goddamn pastry. Which *she'd* given him. So she was responsible for her own torture. But it was worth it to see the shadows fade from his expression, his shoulders no longer so tense.

"Why don't you ask me?"

She felt her eyes widen. Had he realized she was imagining him naked in bed while she fed him pastries and licked up the crumbs from his chest? Good God. "What?" she managed to get out.

"Why I dated Tiffany in the first place."

Air escaped her in a quiet rush. Making a face at him, she said, "I think the letter D had something to do with it."

Throwing back his head, he laughed. "I like it when you let your snark out, Ms. Baird." Still grinning, he said, "In point of fact, I wanted to buy a property she owned and dinner was the only time she'd talk to me about it."

Charlotte's mouth fell open. "Are you telling me the Bishop was forced into a date?" She humphed. "*Right.*"

"I needed to eat, so why not?" His eyes gleamed. "I now have the property and my business association with Ms. Summer is complete."

"Not a T-Rex?" she said sweetly. "I see some very sharp teeth."

His smile deepened until the stupid melting inside her started up all over again. "Never for you, Ms. Baird." Walking back into the office and thankfully missing her blush, he said, "Let's get this done so we can both have the night free at least."

FIVE O'CLOCK AND THE deal was done. By six, Charlotte should've been at home. Instead, she found herself standing in front of Gabriel's apartment door, not quite sure how she'd ended up there.

Tired but exhilarated at their success, she'd been putting on her coat when Gabriel had unexpectedly taken her up on her offer to teach him how to make a pasta sauce that would impress his girl. Since it would've been churlish and too revealing of her own feelings to refuse, especially after she'd already admitted her exciting plans for the night amounted to a DVD and possibly some further pastry experimentation, she'd stupidly said yes.

She didn't even know why she'd made that offer in the first place. Maybe to beat it into her thick skull that he could never be hers. Gabriel accepting the offer? That she hadn't predicted—and as a result, she now stood three feet from the door to his apartment, the two of them having stopped off at the grocery store to pick up ingredients.

Her pulse raced, cheeks burning as her abdomen clenched. This time it wasn't for the reason that had given her such scandalous pleasure this morning. She wasn't comfortable being alone with a man in his home—this was the first time she'd been in this situation since Richard. However, as Gabriel keyed them in using the touchpad on the side of the door, she remembered Molly's words.

"Be happy."

Taking a deep breath, she told herself to cross the threshold when he pushed the door open. Gabriel had never done anything to make her feel unsafe.

But Richard had been like that too. At the start.

Her heart slammed into her throat at the whispered reminder from the girl she'd once been, her skin going ice-cold, and her lungs struggling for air. She fought to calm herself using every technique she knew.

She failed.

Stumbling away from the door, blindingly aware of the watchful steel of Gabriel's gaze, she fell back against the corridor wall. The words she wanted to speak wouldn't come, her throat choked up with the ugly, metallic emotion that had once again turned her into a quivering coward.

15

T-Rex Sets a Trap for Charlie-Mouse

WRENCHING HIS VIOLENTLY PROTECTIVE response under control because anger was the last thing Charlotte needed, Gabriel put the paper bag full of groceries on the floor and pulled the apartment door shut. The despair he glimpsed in the clear hazel of her eyes made him want to punch something; it took conscious effort of will to keep a handle on his temper.

It wasn't directed at Charlotte but at the person who'd hurt her. If he ever got his hands on the piece of shit, whoever it was wouldn't have any unbroken bones left in his body.

"Let me take you to dinner," he said, wanting to walk over to her, haul her close, keep her safe. The idea of anyone putting a hand on her, a bruise... His hand fisted by his side. Exhaling quietly, he worked hard to keep his tone as gentle as he could make it. "You can teach me the recipe over a glass of wine."

Eyes wet, Charlotte looked away, her shoulders slumping. He'd never seen her like this—shy or not, Charlotte had held her own against him since the day he'd forced a promotion on her. This was breaking her, he realized. And he was responsible for manipulating her into this situation, into this position.

Not only had he wanted her in his personal territory, he'd just wanted her with him. Earlier, her quiet, thoughtful care had wiped away the gut-churning anger that had gripped him after his discussion with his mother. His and Charlotte's resulting conversation had made him remember that he wasn't that lost, angry boy anymore but a man who had a beautiful, smart, deliciously sexy woman in his life. It had been selfish, but he'd wanted more of her warmth and sweetness around him.

Because of that, he'd caused her pain. Him. No one else. So he had to find a way to fix it. "Remember how I told you I have three brothers?" It had been during a late-night work session, after the two of them broke for coffee. "Sailor, Jake, and Danny."

She didn't lift her head, but he knew she was listening.

"Well," he said, "two of them are fathers, both of little girls." Tiny, fragile creatures he couldn't believe his rough-and-tumble siblings had helped create. "I babysit about once every month."

She raised her head at last, a shaky smile tugging at her lips. "Really?"

The fist squeezing blood from his heart loosened a fraction.

"Hold on." Stepping inside his apartment, he returned holding a sparkly pink purse smaller than the size of one of his palms, and an enthusiastic hand-drawn card that had the words "I love you, Uncle Gabe" spelled out painstakingly if crookedly in purple glitter pen, what looked like rugby balls raining from big, fluffy clouds.

"I didn't know rugby balls had smiley faces." Charlotte's own smile grew deeper.

"Esme thinks they should, since they're so much fun." His five-year-old niece was a ruthless machine on the rugby field, having inherited the family love for the game as well as their competitive streak.

Stepping close, Charlotte took the card, traced the glittery writing with open affection. "They adore you."

"I let them run roughshod over me, so yeah." He dared touch a finger to her cheek. "Want me to pick them up to play chaperone? Their parents would love a night off."

"No," she said softly, her smile fading to leave her eyes stark in a face that was still too pale. "I'm sorry for acting this way. You've been nothing but professional."

Gabriel realized this was it. He could either take the risk or lie to her. "No, I haven't," he said after dropping the girls' things on the small table by the door where he usually left his car keys.

Charlotte's eyebrows drew together over her eyes. "What?"

"I've been flirting with you, Ms. Baird." He saw red paint her cheeks, but when she didn't put space between them, he continued. "I told myself I shouldn't since I'm your boss, but I'm afraid I didn't follow my advice."

When she still didn't say a word, he forced himself to make an offer he didn't want to make. "I know another CEO who needs a personal assistant of your skill."

"Are you *firing* me?" Sparks in those clear eyes, her hands fisting by her sides as if in readiness for battle.

"No, damn it." It came out a snarl, his attempt at good behavior dying a quick death now that she was his Ms. Baird again, tough and with a fiery spirit. "I'm telling you that if my interest makes you uncomfortable, you can move into another comparable position."

Her eyes narrowed. "That also removes the flirting with a subordinate issue for you."

"You're the best damn personal assistant I've ever had." His voice rose. "I have every intention of stealing you away from Saxon & Archer when I complete this contract."

That made her lips part in a quiet gasp before she folded her arms. "Doesn't change what I said."

"Of course it wouldn't make anything easier," he growled, infuriated by her stubborn refusal to see what he was trying to tell her. "The hours I work, when exactly do you think I'd have time to seduce you if you weren't working with me? I like you exactly where you are."

Glaring at him—though her cheeks remained that hot pink that made him want to throw her over his shoulder and carry her off to the nearest bed to see how she tasted—she said, "I like my job."

It was the first time a personal assistant had said that about working with him. Most complained he was a bad-tempered slave driver. He wondered what Charlotte would think if he told her she was the only one who'd ever had the guts to push back, to tell him he couldn't have all her weekends and nights. Probably not believe him, she saw herself as so meek.

"Good," he said and then asked what he needed to know. "Are you going to sue me for sexual harassment if I keep flirting with you?" He had plans to go well beyond flirtation, but this was hurdle number one. And it wasn't a lawsuit he was worried about—it was whether his pursuit would scare Charlotte.

"*Why* are you flirting with me?"

The befuddled look in her eyes was adorable.

"Fishing for compliments?"

Her cheeks flushed hotter. Pushing up her spectacles and setting those soft pink lips in a prim line that just made him want to mess her up, she said, "Men like you don't go for women like me."

"How many men like me do you know?" he asked with a lingering look at her mouth. God but he wanted to kiss Charlotte, wanted to feast on her. Every part of her.

BREASTS SWELLING AGAINST HER bra and skin tight under the molten silver of Gabriel's gaze, Charlotte fought the urge to wet her lips. "You know what I mean." Her voice came out all breathy, her lungs struggling again for a far different reason than earlier.

"Do I?" He leaned in close enough that the hot kiss of his breath brushed her earlobe as he murmured. "I happen to find this particular small, smart, sexy package very, very attractive."

Small, smart, sexy.

Charlotte had been described with two of those words before. The unexpected addition made her head spin in disbelief. Except what did Gabriel have to gain from lying to her, from pretending he found her sexually enticing? He'd just had a demonstration of how screwed up she was—clearly not a fun conquest.

It wasn't as if he needed to hunt for notches on his bedpost. As displayed by Tiffany, women hunted *him* down. "Doesn't your girlfriend mind you flirting with other women?" she asked sharply before she forgot he was taken—as he clearly had.

"She's not mine yet." The last word was drawled out.

Wanting to slap herself for continuing to find the arrogant T-Rex attractive, she said, "I'll show you how to make the pasta sauce." Soon as that was done, she could go home and bake out her rage as she told Molly that T-Rex wasn't only a carnivore, he was a man who didn't value commitment when it came to a personal relationship.

Charlotte couldn't be with someone like that, even if he wasn't just messing with her for his own amusement.

Gabriel didn't get out of the doorway. "Not before you answer my question."

"No," she said through gritted teeth. "I won't sue you." She'd also not take anything he said or did seriously. A man who made a move on one woman, whom he'd asked to help him learn how to cook something to impress another woman, wasn't her idea of Prince Charming.

When his eyes glinted, lips curving in a slow and very male smile, she knew he intended to take full advantage of her acquiescence. "Come into my parlor, Ms. Baird."

How could he make her name sound like an indecent proposition? The tiny hairs on her nape prickling in an alarm that had nothing to do with fear and everything to do with another emotion as visceral, she took a deep breath and stepped past him into the apartment.

The click of the door shutting behind her made her stomach knot, Gabriel's presence at her back a heated wall that blocked escape. As if he knew, he walked past her with the groceries. Following him, she gaped. She knew this building, had seen it countless times from the road. Built on a hilltop, it had sweeping views of both the city and the waters of the Hauraki Gulf. Apartments here went for millions.

Gabriel, she belatedly realized, had the penthouse.

They'd entered on the lower floor—a sprawling space that flowed out onto a large balcony. While she couldn't see it from here, she knew the second level opened out onto another, smaller balcony. Natural light came in via the generous use of glass as well as cleverly placed skylights. The view through the balcony doors, even from here, was spectacular.

"Just how rich are you?" she blurted out.

Gabriel had already put down the groceries and now paused in the act of removing his shoes. "If I use the word filthy in my answer, what'll that get me?"

Charlotte slapped her hands over her face, mortified. "Sorry, I'm sorry." She didn't know why she'd been so rude, especially when she should've guessed at his wealth. No one played professional sports at the highest level, had major international endorsement deals—some of which were still in play—then became a sought-after business executive without accumulating wealth. In addition, she'd watched him buy property after property for his personal portfolio. Of *course* he was filthy rich.

Strong, warm hands tugging her own from her face, his smile so gorgeous that for a second, she almost gave in to the madness inside her and kissed the boss.

Then he said, "You can make it up to me by teaching me to be a maestro in the kitchen."

Right. For another woman. That infuriating reminder poured ice water on her desire. "I'll get set up if you want to…" She waved vaguely in the direction of his clothes; unlike his casual clothes most weekends when they worked together, he'd worn a suit today because he'd had to videoconference with the lawyers on the other side of the negotiation.

Charlotte was still in the jeans and mint-green cardigan she'd worn to cooking class. Below the cardigan was nothing but a white camisole with a lace edge. She hadn't thought she'd be this hot when she'd chosen the outfit that morning, hadn't thought she'd be all but pasted to Gabriel's furnace of a body.

She wanted to rub up against him like a cat.

Other woman, Charlotte! You are teaching him to cook for her!

The mental slap made her head ring as Gabriel headed to the hanging spiral staircase that led upstairs.

"Kick off your shoes," he said, "get comfortable."

"If I kick off my shoes, I'll need a megaphone to reach you," she muttered under her breath, but did in fact slip off her wedge-heeled slides, loathe to accidentally damage the warm-toned wood of the floor. Shoving up the sleeves of her cardigan, she padded over to his kitchen—separated from the living area only by a gleaming breakfast bar—and just sighed. The things she could cook in this kitchen.

Stroking the black granite of the freestanding central island, the stone streaked with gray minerals that had a faint shimmer, she took in the cooktop that blended into the counter against the wall, the inbuilt oven below sleek silver. When she gave in to temptation and opened a cupboard, the premium cookware inside made her want to whimper.

"Finding everything you need?"

Jumping, she shut the cupboard and turned to find him heading toward her. He'd changed into faded jeans and a gray T-shirt bearing the logo of the school whose rugby team he coached, the soft, well-washed fabric hugging his pecs as he moved toward her.

Gripping the counter behind her, she said, "I didn't mean to pry."

He looked up from taking the groceries out of the bag and the intricate ink on his left arm caught her eye. "Charlotte, knock yourself out. I have no idea what's in half the cupboards." She made a scandalized noise that had him laughing. "Yeah, it makes Ísa—my sister-in-law—crazy too. She, my mom, and Jake bought all the kitchen stuff after taking my credit card. I think they were hoping to shame me into cooking more."

"Really," Charlotte said, itching to explore. "I can look?"

Gabriel waved a hand. "Tell me if you find the bottle opener. I don't know where they hid it."

WATCHING CHARLOTTE MOVE AROUND in his kitchen, her face glowing and her body bubbling with excitement, Gabriel silently thanked the cooks in the family. Especially when Charlotte bent over to check out the lower cupboards and the denim of her jeans stretched over the sweet curves of her ass.

He wanted to groan.

The months of abstinence were starting to show.

Hell, who was he kidding? Charlotte Baird had done this to him since the first day she'd stopped quivering in terror and started glaring at him when he pushed too hard. He was just feeling a little extra Neanderthal today because she was finally in his space—that he'd booby-trapped for her.

His kitchen had been bare as of a month ago. His mom, Ísa, and Jake had had a field day when he told them to go wild. Of course, they'd been curious as hell about his sudden desire for supplies, but he'd managed to satisfy them with a little creative misdirection. At least for now. They'd no doubt get suspicious when his new "hobby" failed to eventuate in any actual food. Then again, maybe not.

After all, he did now have an instructor. "Did my family do a good job?"

Face glowing, Charlotte turned to him. "I could go crazy in this kitchen."

Booby trap successfully sprung.

16

IN THE LAIR OF THE T-REX

SATISFACTION UNCURLING IN HIS gut, Gabriel said, "I'll give you the door code. Feel free to break in and leave me delicious meals to eat." Having placed all the things they'd bought today within easy reach, he leaned on the central counter and watched her check out the cooktop and oven. The back of her neck caught his eye, made him want to nuzzle a kiss to the delicate skin there, draw her scent into his lungs.

Yes, he was well and truly hooked on Charlotte Baird.

"Didn't your mom teach you how to cook?" she asked absently, opening the oven to look inside.

Distracted by his fantasies of crowding her against the counter, his chest to her back as he cupped her breasts, it took him a few seconds to put his brain in gear. Thankfully, she was too in lust with his appliances to notice.

"Oh, Mom tried," he said, thinking only of the good memories and not the dark; he'd had more than enough of the latter today. "She used to say no boy of hers was going to leave home without knowing how to feed himself." Food was important to his mother, something she never took for granted. Gabriel had long ago guessed that after Brian abandoned them, she'd often gone hungry so he and Sailor could eat.

Willfully slamming the door on those memories, he thought of the years after she met Joseph, had Jake, then Danny. It made him grin. "At one point, she was riding herd on two ravenous teenagers, a ten-year-old, and an eight-year-old, as she tried to drum cooking skills into our heads instead of just eating skills." It had stuck only with Jake.

Charlotte turned with a smile. "You love your mom."

"Yep." As Charlotte came closer, he barely restrained himself from jumping over the counter to devour her. His Ms. Baird had no idea just how sweetly succulent he found her or she'd never have entered his lair. "What about you?"

It was as if someone had switched off the light inside her. "My dad was the cook in the family."

He caught the past tense. "He's gone?"

"They both are," she said quietly.

Gabriel didn't even think about it. Going around the counter, he tugged her into a loose embrace—making sure to move slowly enough so as not to startle her. That she came instead of going stiff soothed the primal craving in his soul, the one that shoved at him to protect her, take care of her, give her what she needed. "I'm sorry."

"It's okay," she said, staying against him. "My mom was sick for a long time."

He stroked his hand down her back, the delicate lines of her body holding a strength he'd always sensed but wasn't sure she consciously understood. "Cancer?" he asked, his conversation with his mother fresh on his mind.

Charlotte nodded. "I was twelve when she was first diag-

149

nosed." It hurt even now, but the pain was an old one, no longer jagged and stabbing. "She beat it at first, but it came back." Like a monster stealthily invading their lives. "I'd just turned eighteen when I kissed her good night one evening and she said 'sleep tight, baby' for the last time." Charlotte and her father had brought Pippa Baird home so she could spend her last days surrounded by the people she loved and the people who loved her.

She'd died in her own bed, held in her husband's arms.

"She wasn't in pain at the end," Charlotte said, her throat thick. That was important to her, that her sweet, strong, loving mother had left the world in peace, free of the debilitating pain that had all but crippled her. "It was as if her body knew it was leaving this earth, so it rallied itself to give her one final week where she felt like herself again."

Swallowing, her eyes gritty, she nonetheless smiled. "We laughed so hard the night before. I can't remember why, but I remember her laugh, the brightness and the life of it."

"She sounds like a strong, amazing woman."

"She was."

Charlotte didn't know why she was telling Gabriel all this. He was her boss. Who'd admitted to flirting with her and in whose kitchen she currently stood… in whose arms she stood. The instant she consciously thought about that, she became aware once again of exactly how *big* he was—all of it hard muscle and burning heat.

Gabriel was far, far stronger than Richard had ever been, and yet Charlotte wasn't scared. Nervous, a thousand butterflies in her stomach now that she was focusing on his body, but not afraid. At least not at this precise instant when she felt so safe and protected. Right now, she could almost imagine stroking her hands up his chest to his shoulders, rising on tiptoe and kissing her way along the line of that jaw dark with stubble. It'd prickle against her lips, but then she'd reach his mouth and it'd be hot and wet and so good.

Pulse a staccato beat, she pushed away from him before the fantasy led her into making a humiliating mistake. "I'll get the water ready," she said, even though they didn't need it yet.

Releasing her with a final stroke down her back that made her want to whimper and burrow into him, he said, "Even I can boil water," and moved to fill the pot.

It was oddly intimate, watching him do something so un-expectedly domestic. Though of course, he brought that raw sense of contained power and prowling strength with him—it made him appear an intruder here, a dangerous creature playing at being tame. He must, she thought with a stab of pain that shredded the anger she'd tried to foster, really like this woman he wanted to impress. He'd made no such effort with the others.

She knew without asking that there'd be no red roses this time.

Blood leaden, she took the package of dry pasta and put it on the counter beside the cooktop. When Gabriel put the pot full of water on the cooktop, she stopped him from turning it on, her fingers brushing over the solid bones of his wrist.

"We should work on the sauce first since you're new at it." She curled her fingers into her hand, hoarding the lingering warmth of him.

"You mean it doesn't come out of a jar?"

"Behave," she said, not quite able to dig up a smile.

151

He reached across her back and to the upper cupboards, his arm brushing her shoulder. She wasn't sure if he'd done it deliberately, but when he brushed his arm against her body as he brought a glass down, she knew it was all very much on purpose. For some reason, though he was seriously interested in another woman, he'd decided to continue messing with her.

Her cheeks grew hot, blood pulsing with temper. "There are glasses at the end of the counter."

"Oops, I didn't see," he said and leaned his hip against the granite. "Want something to drink?"

"No." She just wanted this done so she could leave while he no doubt hooked up with his new woman.

Going to the fridge, he grabbed a bottle of water for himself. "Hey, look what I have here. Orange-and-pineapple-juice mix."

"Do you notice *everything*?" she asked, wanting to stab the tomato she'd picked up to chop.

Pouring her favorite blend of juice into a glass for her, he put down the bottle beside his water and said, "When it concerns you, yes."

Charlotte felt her eyes narrow. *Enough.* She might be shy and tongue-tied when it came to any kind of flirtation, but this wasn't flirtation on Gabriel's part. It was a moment's amusement. Because T-Rexes didn't date mice. They stomped on them on their way to other, sexier pastures.

"Tell me about the woman you want to impress," she said, slicing into the tomato with what she thought was commendable restraint. "Is it the model who called you up for the charity dinner?"

GABRIEL CONSIDERED HIS ANSWER. He could either continue to mislead Charlotte, or he could tell her the truth. The problem with the latter was that he didn't know if she could handle the pressure of knowing he wanted her and *only* her. Hell, he'd restrain himself, hold back the full-on and relentless Bishop pursuit until she was more used to him, but she'd still be aware of his interest. It could ratchet up her nerves, make her pull away in panic.

"You don't have to tell me," she said, the blade moving faster. "I'm prying, I'm sorry." The apology was cool.

He smiled slowly at the first sign of real, deep-down temper he'd seen in Charlotte.

"She's exactly your height," he said, having come to one inescapable conclusion after weighing up all the facts: if he didn't tell Charlotte the truth, she'd roadblock him every inch of the way. Unlike many of the women who came on to him, she didn't see him as a trophy to bag and damn any other loyalty he might have. Charlotte Baird took promises seriously.

A startled look, the knife coming to a halt. "Really? I mean, you always date tall women."

"I used to." He tended to feel like a big ox around smaller women, but he'd changed his mind since meeting Charlotte. He was dead certain she could handle him—in bed and out of it. And he definitely wanted to handle her. Every small, perfectly formed part of her. "Then I met a woman with clear hazel eyes and soft blond hair I want to fist in one hand as she straddles my lap and lets me kiss her, my other hand unbuttoning her very sensible white work shirt... or her green cardigan."

Charlotte's breathing was uneven, her head slightly bent as she stared at the cutting board, her fine-boned hand tight on the knife handle.

The same part of Gabriel's brain that allowed him to make multi-million-dollar decisions in split seconds had him continuing when she stayed silent. "I now have all these extremely dirty fantasies of how easy it would be to handle her in bed." Oh, his body liked this line of talk, liked it a hell of a lot. "Though my imagination isn't confined to the bedroom."

Hoping she wouldn't glance at him and see the hard line of his cock pushing against the zipper of his jeans, he kept his distance despite his desire to do the opposite. "The lap fantasy? It doesn't end there. Sometimes," he said, "I pick her up and put her on my desk, shove up her skirt, nudge her black lace panties aside—and they're always black lace in this fantasy—and lick her until she screams my name as she comes against my tongue. Other times—"

"Stop." A breathless order.

"So," he said, wrenching so hard on the reins that his entire body protested the abuse, "you want an onion for this sauce?"

Bracing her hands on the counter after placing the knife very carefully on the cutting board, Charlotte sucked in gulps of air. His eyes, of course, went straight to her chest and to the ripe breasts he wanted to bite and suck and mold with his hands. She'd probably kick him if she learned the erotic dreams he'd had about her taking dictation while dressed only in a black lace bra on her top half, the rest of her as prim and professional as always.

He'd never had office-sex fantasies before, not even once, but now they drove him crazy; night after night, he woke sweat soaked and hard as fucking stone. Charlotte, of course, had the starring role in every single debauched dream produced by his subconscious mind. In some, she was on her knees, but his all-time favorite was the one of her in his lap or on his desk as he drove her to orgasm after orgasm.

Battling a groan and an erection that would not die—how could it with Charlotte so close, her cheeks flushed and lips just slightly parted as she attempted to temper her breathing—he grabbed the packets of seasoning he'd thrown into the cart at the grocery store while Charlotte chose the fresh ingredients. "I didn't know which ones you'd want," he said, "so I got one of most of the ones I thought you'd need."

"Chop the tomatoes." Shoving the board at him, she strode away. "Where's your bathroom?"

"Go upstairs and turn left. First door, then to the right."

It was a measure of her flustered state that she didn't question why there wasn't a bathroom on this floor. Instead, she padded quickly up the spiral staircase and into the master bedroom. He liked that she was up there, in the center of his domain. Taking the chance to grab an ice-cold glass of water in lieu of a cold shower, he managed to get his body under some kind of control.

Then he caught sight of her coming back down, her hand sliding along the polished wooden rail and her curves moving sexily in the jeans that fit snug to her butt. He loved those jeans, loved her friend Molly for talking her into them. He knew about Molly's input because he'd overheard part of Charlotte's conversation with her best friend the first weekend she'd come in wearing them. He'd been about to walk into the break room when he'd heard Charlotte inside, whispering furiously into her phone.

"They're too tight, Molly! I feel naked! I'm going to go to the department store and—"

Molly had clearly broken in then, and whatever she'd said, Charlotte hadn't disappeared off to replace her jeans—which weren't too tight. Nowhere close. They were just right, the boot cut giving her plenty of freedom to move. Thanks to what he'd overheard, Gabriel had known to say absolutely nothing about the disappearance of the two-sizes-too-large jeans she'd worn till then.

When she came in a week later wearing an elegant black jersey dress that caressed her body, he'd said only, "Nice dress, Ms. Baird," and left it at that. Even though that dress made him want to stroke her all over, then push her up against a wall and do things that would make her realize once and for all that he was completely uncivilized under the suits.

He liked it a little rough, sometimes more than a little if he was honest, and that might be a problem with Charlotte, but they'd figure it out. Gabriel had never given up on anything in his life. When obstacles appeared, he found an alternate route. Even if it meant building that route with blunt determination and immutable will.

"Find everything okay?" he asked as her feet touched the floor.

"Yes." The damp tendrils of hair curling against her ears told him she'd thrown water on her face. Her skin would feel cool under his lips, he thought as she folded her arms and said, "Did you finish cutting up the tomatoes?"

He showed her the board. "Did I do it right? I take instruction well."

"No, you don't."

"You're right, I don't." Risking it, he tugged on a wet curl. "But I'll make an exception for you. Tell me what you like."

CHARLOTTE'S BARELY STEADY HEART turned into a jackrabbit in her chest, her mind still hazy from the images he'd implanted earlier. "Wh-what?"

"In your sauce," he said, but Charlotte wasn't an idiot, even if he had left her totally off-kilter with the erotic things he'd said to her.

"Why would you do that?" she blurted out, her usual filters shredded.

"What?" said the big, gorgeous lion next to her.

"Never mind." Taking the onion, she cut off a piece. "Dice this." Then she picked up half a handful of fresh basil leaves, washed them off, and put them next to the chopped tomatoes.

Finishing dicing the onion, he left a neat pile on one side of the board. "Tell me, Ms. Baird."

Oh God, how had she gotten herself into this?

Charlotte's throat was suddenly bone-dry. Grabbing the glass of juice he'd poured, she took a long drink. And remembered what Molly had said to her back when Gabriel had first entered her life.

Be brave.

Charlotte had said the same back to Molly, and now her best friend was living a Technicolor life full of adventure, love, and passionate happiness. It was a future neither one of them could've predicted.

Being brave had its rewards.

That thought in mind, Charlotte spoke her question before she could talk herself out of it. "What you said, about the desk. Why would you do that?"

Gabriel stilled. "Because having you come against my mouth would be the biggest fucking turn-on."

17

PRIVATE GAMES WITH A T-REX

CHARLOTTE PUT DOWN THE glass, her fingers trembling. "No," she said, fighting her damn throat-choking shyness to get the words out, "I mean, there's nothing in it for you."

Charlotte knew about oral sex, knew men liked to do it sometimes, but she wasn't one of those pouting, sensual creatures who could bring the male sex to their knees. Richard had liked her at the start, and he'd had zero interest in it. Gabriel was about a thousand times more masculine than Richard, a million times sexier. Women probably went to their knees in front of him at the snap of his fingers.

She hated that image, hated it so much that she erased it from her mind with a vicious mental swipe.

"I'm not that altruistic, Ms. Baird, you know that." He played with a loose tendril of her hair again, twining it around his finger, then releasing it. "I always get something."

Swallowing, Charlotte looked up to meet his eyes, lost her breath at the dark intensity of his focus. "Wh...what"—she coughed in an effort to clear her throat—"would you get out of that?"

A slow smile that made her stomach tie itself into knots so tangled, she wasn't sure they would ever unravel. "Well," he said, shifting closer and backing her up until her spine hit the opposite counter, "quite aside from having feasted on the delicious taste of you, I'd have you all wet and limp on my desk with your skirt hiked up to your waist." He pressed closer, his erection thrusting against her abdomen. "It'd take me a second to unzip myself and—"

Charlotte was okay. She was fine. She was dealing with him, being aroused by him, and then without warning, her rational mind just shut down. Panic blinded her in a slapping wave, freezing her into place.

GABRIEL SAW THE CHANGE in Charlotte, felt it. She'd been a bundle of nerves before, but she'd also been a willing participant in their private game, her skin dewy and her lips parted. Now she was stiff and brittle enough to break. Backing off at once, he put plenty of distance between them and, because he was so fucking angry at the bastard who'd hurt her, picked up the knife and diced the damn tomatoes into mush.

He was aware of her staying as quiet and as motionless as a mouse who'd sensed a predator for at least three long minutes before she released her white-knuckled grip on the counter and turned to shakily pick up the half-full glass of juice. When she put it down after emptying it and went as if to exit the kitchen, he gave in to the snarl inside him.

"You planning to leave me to starve?"

She turned on her heel, all big, bruised eyes in a delicate face he wanted to cup in his hands as he kissed her, coaxed her, taught her he'd never ever lay a finger on her in violence.

"I-I'm s-sorry."

Gabriel could've killed at that instant—specifically the person who'd created this terrible, overwhelming fear inside his tough little assistant. "Don't be sorry," he said in a voice that wasn't as non-snarly as he'd intended. "Teach me to make this sauce, then teach me what I did that set you off so I don't do it again."

Charlotte didn't move, just stared at him through the clear lenses of those glasses that drove him nuts. He had a host of fantasies in which she was wearing nothing but the specs, her hair up in that little bun he usually hated, and maybe a string of long pearls that he—*Stop*, he told himself when his cock began to harden again. He was moving way too fast, and he needed to chill if he was going to have any chance of earning Charlotte's trust.

"Again?" she said at last, her voice small.

"Ms. Baird," he said, using her formal title because it made her pay attention, "have I or have I not made it clear that I would like you in my bed?"

Teeth sinking into her lower lip, she nodded.

"So," he said, folding his arms and leaning his hip against the freestanding counter, "why would you think one hiccup would stop me?" He raised an eyebrow. "Especially since you've been working with me long enough to know that nothing stops me when I have my eye set on a goal."

Charlotte drew in a long breath, released it slowly. "I don't know if I can."

"If you tell me you don't want me, I'm going to demand you give me your panties to prove they're not damp."

Cheeks going bright red, she stamped one dainty foot. "That is totally inappropriate!"

"No rules outside the office, Ms. Baird," he said, needling her on purpose because he liked her fiery, hated the defeat he'd seen in her. "Now come here and tell me what I did." It was important she make the decision to stay, to start trusting him.

Gabriel could push and push hard, but he'd never force.

Glaring at him instead, she shoved up the sleeves of her cardigan and said, "I'm starving. You can learn to make sauce another time." She began throwing things together in a small saucepan, the kitchen filling with a deliciously spicy scent minutes later.

A half hour after that, they were seated across from one another at the dining table located behind and to the left of the kitchen area, beside a large bank of windows that overlooked the city.

"You're missing salad," she muttered.

He wanted to haul her into his lap and tell her to stop being a hissing, bad-tempered kitten or he'd have to punish her—but he didn't think Charlotte was ready to play those kinds of games. The playful threat might actually scare her. So he got to his feet, went to the kitchen and, grabbing a bowl, opened up a pack of premade salad he'd had in the fridge. He even found the special salad-serving utensils before putting the bowl on the table.

Charlotte took some salad, ate the pasta she'd whipped together, and looked out the window. "Don't close me in."

The words were so softly spoken that it took him a second to realize she'd answered his question. "It makes you feel claustrophobic?" he asked in an effort to get the exact parameters.

"Yes."

"Any kind of crowding?"

"Sometimes… with you, it's okay"—her eyes met his—"but I can't predict when I'll have a panic attack." Her fingers clenched tight around the stem of her wineglass, Gabriel having opened a crisp white rather than a red because he knew Charlotte didn't like red much.

"I want to crowd you," he said, leaning back in his chair but maintaining the intimacy of the eye contact. "I want to pin you under me and fuck you hard, then I want to slam you up against pretty much every wall in this place. After which I want to bend you over my desk, my bed, this table. For starters."

Charlotte's skin flushed a hot pink, then paled, then went red, her eyes sparking fire. "Did you not hear what I said?"

"I heard." He took a sip of his wine. "I'm just telling you what we'll be working toward. Any problems with my goals?"

CHARLOTTE WASN'T SURE SHE wasn't hallucinating. How could she possibly be at a glossy black dining table with her big, sexy boss, talking about sexual positions? It simply did not compute. Yet he was waiting for her answer with lazy male patience.

"I don't know," she said at last, and because this was a surreal, strange half dream, she admitted to her inadequacies. "I'm not very good at sex."

Gabriel put down his wineglass and then he smiled that slow, sinful smile that made her nipples go tight and her body grow even more silkily damp—if he'd demanded her panties as he'd threatened, she'd have failed the test. Miserably.

"Ms. Baird, no one is good or bad at sex by themselves," he drawled. "It's a team effort, and you know I'm a team player."

Charlotte's breasts pushed against her bra. Those breasts weren't huge by any stretch of the imagination, but right now they felt swollen and hot, achy in a way they'd never before felt. "What if I'm not?" she asked, fighting the memory of the things Richard had said to her, things she'd never told anyone, not even Molly, she'd felt so much shame.

"I'm an excellent coach," Gabriel said, steely eyes holding a heat that mesmerized. "One who always gets the best out of my players." His foot brushed hers under the table. "I also have a close and very personal interest in making sure you perform to your full potential."

Charlotte was so out of her depth by now that she was barely treading water. Not only was she an emotional mess in general, she was so pitifully inexperienced that she'd no doubt embarrass herself if she tried anything with the man sitting across the table. The one who looked at her like he wanted to devour her in small, delicious bites.

"I have to go home," she said, putting down her fork.

She couldn't take any more, had hit her absolute limit.

Gabriel examined her with those incisive eyes. "I'll drive you," he said at last. "But finish your dinner first."

"You're not my boss here," she snapped out of her frustration with herself, with the universe.

"Not in an employment sense," he said. "But I do think you need some bossing around, especially when it comes to your health."

Charlotte had seen that look on Gabriel's face before; it was the one that denoted no mercy in a negotiation. She thought about getting up and walking out, but regardless of her inability to handle him, she wanted to do every scandalous thing he'd suggested.

While that wasn't going to happen, not with her panic attacks shutting things down more effectively than a cold shower, she could be with him a little longer. Even if he was being bossy and all around provocative. Truth was, she liked that about him, liked that he always treated her as if he believed she had the strength to stand against him.

So she ate the rest of the food on her plate and tried not to think about all the things he'd said he wanted to do to her. It was hard. Especially an hour later, when she was alone in her bed, her skin flushed and her body aching with need. She hadn't been this aroused in… ever. Not even after the erotic dream this morning.

Sticky and hot, she went to shove off the sheets so she could go have an actual cold shower when her hand brushed her breasts.

Charlotte whimpered. This was insane. He hadn't laid a finger on her and her entire body ached with need. Unable to resist, she gently cupped her breast through her nightgown. In her mind's eye, it was Gabriel's much bigger, tougher-skinned hand on her flesh. He wouldn't be this gentle, would hold boldly as he pressed her down into the sheets and thrust himself inside her, his body moving heavy and muscled above her own.

He'd be rough. The way he talked, the words he'd used, it all said he'd be rough.

Hard.

Relentless.

Breath coming in sharp, desperate pants, Charlotte pressed her thighs together and squeezed her own breast harder than she'd ever before done. Her back arched, a soft cry escaping her throat. When she came down from the shock of pleasure, it was to find her knees bent, her nightgown bunched at her upper thighs, and her hand still on her breast.

Blushing, she removed her hand, pushed down her nightgown, then wanted to kick herself. Why was she blushing? She was alone in her damn bedroom and she'd just given in to an erotic daydream. What was wrong with that? Nothing, that's what. It was great. Today was the first time in years she'd been able to truly let go. If she'd imagined Gabriel in a compromising position, it wasn't as if he hadn't done the same with her.

Dirty.

That's what he'd called his fantasies about her. *Dirty.* Breath turning shallow again as she thought about the office fantasy he'd described, the one that ended up with her screaming his name while he licked her between her splayed thighs, she got up and tugged off the nightgown, threw it to the floor, then lay back down. Her skin was too hot, her entire body aflame.

The fantasy continued to run through her head, her mind whispering that he'd called her "delicious." Turning over flat on her stomach, she tried to imagine what it might feel like to have his hands under her thighs, pulling her forward, strong and demanding. To have that sexy, dangerous mouth on her. To hear him lowering his zipper before he pulled her down on his lap and onto his cock.

Moaning, she tried to control the movements of her hips, her mind filled with images so carnal she couldn't believe they came from her. When her phone buzzed, she wanted to let it go, but its buzz kept intruding on the torturous pleasure of her imagined liaison with Gabriel. Finally grabbing it off the bedside table, she said, "Hello."

"Ms. Baird, you sound breathless again." Gabriel's deep voice went straight to her nipples and the slick folds between her thighs. "Did I make you run to get the phone?"

"No, I'm in bed," she said and barely bit back a groan at what she'd revealed.

"Ah. And breathless." His voice dropped. "You better be alone or we'll be having a very interesting talk the next time we meet."

Her skin grew tight at the rumbling warning. Inhaling jerkily, she said, "Of course I'm alone."

"Then the breathlessness becomes far more intriguing."

Charlotte pulled up the sheet to cover herself, feeling exposed even though he was on the other end of the phone line. "I was just... doing something."

"Good, keep doing it. I want to hear you do it."

Her heart kicked. "No," she said and hung up. Then she went and had that cold shower because she needed to think, needed to remember that no matter how much Gabriel thought he wanted her, he'd give up soon enough. A man that hot, that masculine, wouldn't be happy with a woman who had panic attacks before he ever laid a finger on her.

The worst thing?

It was the fact her fear had nothing to do with sex.

18

GABRIEL IS (SINFULLY) INAPPROPRIATE

MIDMORNING THE NEXT DAY and Charlotte was staring morosely at her oven, trying to convince herself that baking a tray of cupcakes would make her feel better, when the phone rang again. Figuring it was Molly, she picked it up. The name on the screen made her heart kick, her nipples go to full attention against the thin red T-shirt she wore without a bra.

Thank God Gabriel couldn't see her.

"Do I need to come in for work today too?" she asked.

While she occasionally vetoed Gabriel's weekend demands on principle, she had fun with him when they worked Saturdays or Sundays. It was often only the two of them on the floor for long periods, and Gabriel was always more relaxed—to the point that it was on a weekend that she'd first heard him laugh.

At the end of her rope with his demands, she'd picked up her muffin on a violent urge to throw it at his head. Then he'd raised an eyebrow at her and she'd actually done it. Catching it easily in the air, as he'd once caught rugby balls thrown from lineouts, he'd bitten into it.

"Banana and chocolate chip," he'd said. "Thanks, Ms. Baird, but you really don't have to bring me food."

Her infuriated scream had made him throw back his head and laugh, a big, beautiful creature limned by the sunlight. She'd wanted to touch him so badly it hurt.

Grinning as he swallowed another bite, he'd said, "I owe you a muffin. We're going for coffee in fifteen minutes."

Despite her temper, she'd gone with him. They'd ended up grabbing takeout coffee and walking to sit in Aotea Square, the central city spot that always had something going on. That sunny Sunday, it had been a skateboarding competition, temporary ramps set up for the skateboarders. Sitting on one of the benches at the edge of the square with Gabriel beside her, she'd felt almost normal.

For a few minutes.

Until she'd remembered that unlike the other women around them who laughed with their men, she wasn't brave enough to entrust herself to someone so much bigger and stronger than her, someone who could hurt her on a whim. Who could punch her and kick her and do anything he wanted. Telling herself it wasn't going to happen, that Gabriel wasn't that kind of man, didn't help—the fear was embedded too deeply in her bones.

"Do I really only call to ask you to come in to work?" he said now, his voice slicing through the darkness of her memories to make her heart skip another beat. "Today I'm calling to ask if you want to go to a game."

"A game?"

"Danny's playing tonight. The entire clan will turn up to support him."

That meant she'd be meeting his family. Her face went hot, then cold before she realized it wasn't likely that big of a deal. No doubt Gabriel's idea of a date often included a rugby game. And at the moment, he still thought he wanted her. He hadn't yet figured out how messed up she truly was.

"Okay," she said, unable to resist the invitation despite knowing it was inevitable she'd disappoint him.

"Kickoff's at six. I'll pick you up at four—we'll park at my parents' place in Mount Eden and walk the rest of the way in to avoid the game traffic."

FOUR HOURS LATER, WITH another two hours to go before Gabriel picked her up, Charlotte was having a mini panic attack—over clothing. "Molly, help me!" she cried out to her friend, whose face was currently on the laptop Charlotte had put up on the dresser so she could show Molly her choices.

While she'd made friends in the cooking class she'd joined, only Molly could she trust with her neurotic behavior.

"Charlie"—Molly grinned—"it's a rugby game. Jeans, a tee, a sweatshirt, and a windbreaker or a coat because it'll get cold by the time the game ends, and you'll be set."

Charlotte knew that. But— "I want to look nice."

Wicked amusement in Molly's brown eyes. "From what you've told me, I don't think T-Rex cares about your clothes. He wants you naked."

Glaring at her best friend, who laughed in unrepentant glee, Charlotte sat down on the bed with her chin in her hands. "What about makeup?" she asked, feeling like a teenager about to go on her first date. "Do I wear makeup to a rugby game?"

"Hmm." Molly pursed her lips. "I think a touch won't hurt if it makes you feel good. Let down your hair too—it's so pretty."

Charlotte didn't often wear her hair down, and for the first time, she realized she'd never told Molly why. Strange, when she'd shared so much with her friend, but that one thing had never come up. Even now, when she parted her lips to speak, she couldn't. How did she explain that the fear of having her hair pulled was strong enough for her to avoid risking it?

She knew logically that her short ponytail could as easily be used to savagely wrench back her head, but Richard had done it with her hair loose and so that was her secret terror. The idea of feeling the painful tug on her scalp was enough to pebble her skin, chill her blood.

Maybe because it was one of the first things Richard had done that nightmare weekend, a harbinger of the horror, humiliation, and agonizing pain to come.

The one thing of which she was deeply proud was that she hadn't shorn off her hair altogether. Richard had threatened to do that. Charlotte refused to give him the satisfaction of finishing what he'd begun. Because her soft blond hair that curled if let loose? It was the only thing about which she'd ever been vain—she'd used to think it was her one good feature.

Richard *would not* take that from her.

"Hey, Charlie?" Molly's eyes darkened, expression sobering. "I know that look. Something I said triggered a flashback."

Releasing a breath she hadn't known she'd been holding, Charlotte locked gazes with her friend. "I miss you, Moll."

They still talked or messaged every day, but she missed meeting her best friend for lunch, missed laughing with her as they threw together an impromptu dinner, missed her warm, strong presence.

"I miss you too." Molly's voice sounded thick, her eyes growing wet. "Soon as the tour wraps up, I'm flying over and kidnapping you. T-Rex can just deal."

"Don't worry," Charlotte said on a shaky laugh. "I'll sneak my vacation into his calendar and forge his signature on the approval."

"I see your boss has been a good influence." Molly grinned. "Next they'll be calling you 'the Baird.'"

Charlotte stuck out her tongue at her friend and picked up a black sweatshirt that featured the iconic silver fern emblem of the national team on one side. "I guess I'll wear this." It had been her eighteenth-birthday gift from her parents; she rarely wore it, not wanting it to fade, but they'd have loved the idea of her wearing it to a game at Eden Park, the Bishop by her side.

"Perfect." Molly's gaze lingered on her face. "It was the hair, wasn't it?" she said gently. "Did Dick do something to your hair?"

Charlotte gave a short nod. "It's a stupid thing in the overall scheme of things, but..." She just couldn't forget; so many memories of terror were tied to the wrench of hair against her scalp. "Gabriel likes my hair," she whispered, staring down at her hands. "I... maybe I'll put it down for him. Just not tonight." There were too many people at a game, too high a chance of an accidental tug.

"Hey." Molly's voice was warm, loving. "Don't stress yourself out. You're about to go to a game with a gorgeous hunk who wants to do delicious, bad things to you. Have fun."

"I don't know if I can let him do any of those things." It was a hard confession to make. "I don't know if I have the courage."

"I know you do, Charlie. I *know*." A passionate vow. "Just consider where you are now and compare it to where you were three months ago."

Put that way, Charlotte couldn't argue. "God, I have Anya's job and I'm *really* good at it. *And* I argue with Gabriel on a regular basis."

Molly laughed. "Exactly. One step at a time, babe."

"Right." Charlotte straightened her shoulders. "One step at a time." Then she gave in to a huge grin. "I did take a pretty big step last night." She fanned her face at the memory of the things Gabriel had said. He could talk dirty to her anytime.

"Are you going to tell me the details?"

"When you tell me what you did with Fox the night you went home with him after the party."

Molly fell back in her chair and sighed, her face dreamy. "Maybe when we're old and gray."

Charlotte grinned, understanding. Some things were so special you had to hug them to your heart. "Ditto."

"It's a date."

GABRIEL BROUGHT HIS SUV to a stop in front of Charlotte's town house to see her stepping out the door. Getting out of the car, he waited for her to finish locking up before walking over to cup her face gently in his hands. He was ready to break contact if she displayed any discomfort, but though she blushed, she didn't pull away.

"I want to eat you up," he said, rubbing his thumbs over her cheekbones, and when she still didn't pull away, he leaned in and took his first taste of the delicious Ms. Baird.

She shivered, her hands coming up against his chest. Fighting the urge to shove his fingers into her hair, unravel her ponytail, and thrust his tongue into her mouth like a damn marauding barbarian, he suckled at her upper lip because he couldn't resist one more taste, then broke contact. "We better get in the car before I back you right into your house and give in to my ungentlemanly side."

Though her cheeks were red, her breath shallow, Charlotte said, "You have a gentlemanly side?"

"Cute, Ms. Baird." Opening the passenger door for her, the fleeting taste of her only ratcheting up his desire, he gave in to the urge to run his hand over her denim-clad ass as she climbed in.

She inhaled sharply and turned to narrow her eyes at him over her shoulder. "Gabriel, that was—"

"—inappropriate." He smiled slowly, utterly delighted by everything about her. "You do know by now that I intend to be highly inappropriate with you?"

Charlotte fiddled with the belt tie of her black coat, but her eyes were bright when they met his. "Aren't you getting ahead of yourself?"

"Always, Ms. Baird." Closing her door, he went around to get into the driver's seat. "You want some music?"

CHARLOTTE'S TOES CURLED AT the simple intimacy of the question. Reaching out, she switched on the radio and found a station that played rock. As the throaty sound of one of Schoolboy Choir's first hits filled the car, she settled back and just wallowed in the happiness bubbling through her veins. Gabriel had kissed her, and not only had the taste of him blown her circuits, she hadn't freaked out.

In fact, she wanted to do it again. And again.

"Do you always watch your brothers play?" she asked as they turned out of the drive.

"When the game's up here, yes," he answered. "I can't make as many of the away games as I'd like, but in New Zealand one of us is always in the crowd. International matches we tend to gather together in one place to watch." He shifted gears, the car's engine a smooth hum. "Jake had a small car accident that ended his season prematurely, but when they're both playing, it's a finely tuned operation in terms of support schedules."

Charlotte heard the pride, the affection. "It must be tough for Jake to miss the entire second half of the season," she said, knowing Jacob Esera had suffered a broken arm in the accident.

Gabriel nodded. "He's healed well and the physiotherapist sees no problems ahead. The fact Danny managed to injure himself at the same time gave him some company at least."

"He has incredible footwork on the field," Charlotte said. "Daniel too. I can't believe he got the ball over the line his last game." Tackled by a huge opposition player, Daniel Esera had stretched out his arm even as he went down under a bone-bruising tackle; he'd slammed the rugby ball to the earth an inch over the try line.

"You've just proven you're my perfect woman." Gabriel's grin lit up everything inside her. "You like the game."

"I used to watch with my dad." The memories were wonderful ones. "He turned the spare bedroom into his den, and the two of us would sit on this old, comfy couch, yelling at the television until my mom poked her head inside and told us to remember we were humans, not gorillas. Then she'd bring us more chips, a beer for my dad."

Old pain had her rubbing a fisted hand over her heart. "I couldn't watch for a long time after he died." It had been too quiet without his ongoing commentary about the players' moves, too sad without her mom's affectionate head-shaking. "But then it became a way to remember him, remember them both."

Gabriel took her hand, placed it on his thigh. "Was it an accident? With your dad?"

Feeling him so strong and warm under her touch somehow made it easier to talk about it. "No, he died in his sleep." Peacefully and with a smile on his face, a smile Charlotte hadn't seen since her mom passed away. "My mom and dad were so in love, like newlyweds their whole life together." Charlotte had dreamed of the same kind of love before everything went wrong. "I knew my dad wouldn't last long after my mom, but I didn't expect to lose him four days after her."

Gabriel put his hand over hers. "Ah, baby, I'm sorry."

"It's okay." Turning her hand so she could lace her fingers with his, she found she could tell him the rest. "We came home from my mom's funeral and he said he had to lie down. I hugged him and told him I loved him, and he said the same. That was the last time I saw him alive." She blinked rapidly. "I've always been grateful for that—that I got to tell both of them how much I loved them before they were gone."

"They would've known anyway, Charlotte." He brushed his thumb over the back of her hand. "My brothers and I are firmly convinced parents know everything and have eyes in the back of their head. Sailor and Jake swear their back-of-the-head eyes started growing the instant they became dads."

She laughed wetly. "When we were about sixteen, Molly and I decided to read an erotic romance we'd found in the library. When we left the room to grab snacks, my mom sat us down and said, 'Girls, if you're going to read erotic, don't read that trash. Read this.'" Charlotte laughed at the memory of their mortification. "We were still gaping at her when she gave us three more books!"

Gabriel grinned. "I bet you were horrified."

"You have *no* idea." The two of them had scuttled back into the bedroom, red as beets. "Molly was still pretty bruised up inside with everything that had happened over the previous twelve months"—the details of which were now public knowledge—"but that day, we started giggling once we were in my room and couldn't stop."

It had been worth the mortification to see her friend laugh after the hell that had been Molly's fifteenth year of life. "What about your mom and dad?" When he moved his hand to shift gears as they hit an incline, she turned hers palm-down again. "Any good stories?"

"A suitcase full of them." His thigh flexed under her touch; Charlotte didn't remove her hand because, blush or not, she liked touching him, liked feeling all that power so close.

"Staying on the erotic theme," he said, "one time, Sailor and I decided to sneak out of bed after our parents and

177

younger brothers were asleep so we could watch porn. We'd figured out the password to get past the child lock on the TV, and we were teenagers by then anyway."

Charlotte turned in her seat to face him. "What happened?"

19

THE UNFORGETTABLE NIGHT
OF PORN

"SO THE TWO OF us are staring goggle-eyed at the screen when we hear 'Boys, real women do not look like plastic' from behind us." He shuddered. "As the oldest, I stood up, ready to take responsibility, but instead of telling us off, my mother came over and kissed me on the cheek. She told me to make sure we went to bed after the movie was over and to remember what she'd said."

Charlotte gasped. "Your mom let you watch *porn?*"

"I think she knew it was pretty tame stuff," Gabriel said. "But it was the smartest thing she could've done with two hormone-ridden teenage boys. As soon as we had permission, we didn't really want to do it that much. Watching lots of grunting and 'oh baby, oh baby' while balloon-sized tits stand out stiffly into space gets old after a while."

Charlotte clapped her free hand over her mouth, knowing her skin was going red again.

Shifting her hand higher up his thigh with a grin that told her he was about to say something scandalous, Gabriel said, "I have a feeling you've never watched a dirty movie."

Charlotte shook her head, her fingers spreading possessively over the primal heat of him.

"Hmm, I think I have a suggestion for our next date." A wicked, wicked look. "I'll do some research, find one that has a tiny, hot blonde with a big guy. Might give us some ideas."

She didn't think he needed any help in the sexual ideas department.

Thankfully, they'd arrived at their destination so she didn't have to respond to his teasing. Getting out of the SUV after Gabriel squeezed it into the already bursting-at-the-seams drive and yard that fronted a lovely wooden villa, she joined him as he walked up to the porch where everyone seemed to be gathering.

When he took her hand, she didn't protest. There were, she thought, a lot of people in the Bishop-Esera clan. Including two tiny ones who made a beeline for Gabriel, yelling, "Uncle Gabe!"

Releasing her hand, Gabriel leaned down to catch the two little girls, then rose to his feet with them in his arms as if they weighed nothing. Clearly used to this, the girls wiggled up to perch on one forearm each.

"Who's this, Uncle Gabe?" asked the little girl on his left arm, a skinny sprite with a shock of black hair and vivid blue eyes against creamy skin. She was dressed in a pink tutu over black tights. A long-sleeved black rugby jersey completed the look.

"This," Gabriel said, turning so both girls could face Charlotte, "is Charlotte."

"You can call me Charlie." She was happy to meet these small family members first, before she had to tackle the larger ones.

"Hi, Charlie!" cried the girl on his right arm, her jean-clad legs kicking to show off multicolored sneakers, her top the same as the other girl's and her skin a golden brown. "You have glasses like me!" She pushed up the bridge of her pretty blue frames, her black hair in braids on either side of her head.

"I do," Charlotte said, charmed.

"My mommy had glasses," the little girl told her. "She's in heaven now."

"Oh," Charlotte said softly. "Mine is too. Maybe she'll meet yours."

That got her a beaming smile, just as the girl wearing the tutu said, "Are you Uncle Gabe's girlfriend?"

Gabriel squeezed both girls, to their giggles. "Charlotte, meet Boo and Sweetiepie. Nosy parkers extraordinaire."

The girls giggled.

"I'm Sweetiepie," said the one without glasses. "But I'm really Emmaline. And she's Esme."

"I'm five!" Esme cried.

Smiling, Charlotte was about to reply when a gorgeous older brunette on the porch called out, "Girls! Come put on your coats. We're about to start walking."

Running off after Gabriel put them on the ground, the girls disappeared into the mass of adults. Gabriel took Charlotte's hand again and tugged her toward the noisy group. It was obvious the males she could see were all related—their skin color wasn't all the same, but their confidence, the way they interacted, it all shouted the familial link.

She saw an older Samoan man she recognized as Joseph Esera from an interview Gabriel had done where he'd been pho-

181

tographed with his stepfather and his mom. Alison Esera, the tall brunette who'd called for Emmaline and Esme, didn't look like she'd given birth to one child, much less four hulking men.

Hair in a ponytail, she came over and, standing on the top step, kissed Gabriel on the cheek. She turned to Charlotte and did the same before Charlotte could figure out how to respond. "We'll talk later—after the zoo is on its way," Alison said, gray eyes sparkling.

Gabriel's eyes, Charlotte realized.

Alison was gone in the next heartbeat, right as a booming male voice cut through the din. "Right, any stragglers will have to run. I'm not missing kickoff!"

Taking the team scarf from around his neck, Gabriel put it around Charlotte's. "There, now you're ready." He took her hand again and they fell in with the rest of the group.

Emmaline and Esme ran up ahead, skipping alongside their grandfather. The others sorted themselves into pairs so as not to block the sidewalk. The noise level didn't appreciably decrease.

"Hey, Gabe!" called one of his brothers, the one who looked most like Gabriel—though his eyes were a brilliant blue rather than steel gray. "Introduce your girl, why don't you?"

The pretty young redhead at his side, her skin even paler than Emmaline's—who had to be their child—elbowed him. "Excuse Sailor," she said to Charlotte, her smile friendly and her accent unusual. "My husband has the manners of an elephant."

Grabbing his wife's jaw in a playful grip, Sailor planted a wet kiss on her mouth. "You know you love me."

"Get moving," Gabriel yelled back. "You know Dad isn't going to wait for you two to make out."

"Jealous. I bet you want to—oomph!"

Charlotte bit the inside of her cheek at the sounds coming from behind them. Gabriel's breath brushed her cheek the next instant as he leaned down to whisper, "I want to do all sorts of things to you, Ms. Baird, just not in public."

"Sailor, Ísa," he said the next instant, turning slightly so they faced the other couple, "meet Charlotte."

"Hi," she managed to get out.

Ísa waved her over. "Come talk to me and let the boys amuse each other."

Charlotte wasn't good with new people, but Ísa was so welcoming that it would've been churlish to refuse… and she wanted Gabriel's family to like her. Letting go of his hand on a bracing breath, she fell in with Ísa, the men taking up the rear.

Gentle and warm, Ísa proved easy to talk to.

When Emmaline ran back to take her mom's hand, Alison came with her. The older woman slid her arm through Charlotte's while Emmaline and Ísa went forward to join Jake, Esme, and Joseph.

"So," Gabriel's mother said, "you're the one who's been driving my son crazy."

It was such an odd thing to hear that Charlotte responded before thinking through her words. "I don't think I'm the one who's been driving anyone crazy."

Alison's laughter said she knew her son well. "Trust me, we've all heard about his assistant who won't listen to him and refuses to work Sundays." The other woman patted her hand.

"Good on you. My sons are forces of nature—they picked that up from Joseph." An affectionately dry comment. "It's either stand your ground or end up mincemeat."

Startled at the thought that Gabriel had spoken about her to his family, she found herself saying, "Did he tell you I threw a muffin at his head?"

Alison burst out laughing again. "God, sweetheart, what had he done?"

"He kept growling and snarling at me that the documents weren't right when I'd double and triple-checked them."

"That doesn't sound like Gabriel. He's the most detail-oriented of my boys."

"Uh-huh." Charlotte nodded. "I suspected he'd 'lost' some of the pages on purpose just to mess with me."

Alison's lips twitched. "*That* sounds like Gabriel."

And suddenly Charlotte was laughing with this woman who had given birth to the most talented, infuriating, and gorgeous man Charlotte had ever known.

WHEN ESME WAS SENT back with a message that Grandpa wanted to talk to Uncle Gabe, Gabriel knew exactly what the conversation would entail even before he reached his stepfather.

"Dad," he said, "What's up?"

"You mother told me of her talk with you," Joseph said in his steady way that demanded absolute attention, his black hair grizzled with white now but his body and mind no less in shape than when he'd first come into Gabriel's life. "Have you really considered your decision, son?"

Gabriel shrugged. "You know what he did to us. Cancer doesn't change the fact that he's an unreliable piece of shit who abandoned his wife and children."

His stepfather lifted a hand to wave at another family on the other side of the road; Gabriel thought they might be neighbors. "Look, Gabriel," Joseph said. "You've always been smart and you know your own mind, so the decision's yours." Putting one hand on Gabriel's shoulder, he squeezed. "But I want you to think about what that anger inside you will do to you if he ends up dying before you've cleared the air with him."

Gabriel glanced over his shoulder to make sure Charlotte was still okay with his mom before he returned his attention to his stepfather. "I will," he said because of his respect for Joseph. "But I can't see myself changing my mind."

"Fair enough." His stepfather carried on walking. "So, tell me about your woman."

CHARLOTTE HAD GUESSED GABRIEL'S family must have really good seats, given how important rugby was to the family, but she never expected to go through the main gates and up to the exclusive top level of the stadium complex.

"You have access to a corporate box?" she whispered to Gabriel, her eyes wide. She knew Saxon & Archer didn't have one of the elite rooms, so it had to come via one of Gabriel's other investments.

Keeping her tucked close to his side, he said, "Bishop Enterprises owns the lease."

Her mouth fell open at the name under which his property empire was nested. Tipping her parted lips shut with a finger under her jaw, he leaned down to whisper, "Filthy rich, remember?" His lips brushed her ear. "Emphasis on the filthy when it comes to you, Ms. Baird."

Arousal hitting her in a hard slap, she was barely aware of walking into the box. However its spectacular view of the flawless green of the pitch had her sucking in a breath. The stadium lights bathed that green in a bright white light that made everything crisp and sharp. There were seats inside, but the tiered game seating was directly in front—on what looked to be a private balcony.

Already, the girls were outside on that balcony, standing on tiptoe to look over the rail at the bottom. Gabriel's brothers, meanwhile, were at the small bar to one side of the box itself, popping the tops off beer cans they'd taken from a well-stocked fridge. Fancy but delicious-looking canapés—crumbed prawns with sauce, for one—sat within easy reach, and there was a steward who seemed to be taking orders for other drinks.

He'd also managed to produce small bags of potato chips for the girls.

"Next thing you know, they'll be bringing up gourmet meals," Charlotte whispered to Gabriel, who'd leaned down to her.

His smile creased his cheeks. "Those have been ordered." Rubbing his hand over her lower back, he said, "You good? I'm going to grab a beer."

"Yes, I want to go look outside." Joining the girls, she just soaked in the view as the stadium began to fill, an excited buzz in the air.

"Charlotte." Joseph patted the seat next to him in the front row. "Come talk to me."

It was odd; her father had been physically slight, had worn glasses like Charlotte. Gabriel's stepfather was an ex-rugby player with twenty-twenty eyesight, a full-sleeve tattoo that she could see now he'd taken off his coat, and had a voice like a bullhorn. Yet she felt the same sense of comfort with him that she had with her father. Before she knew it, she had her coat off too and they were debating the finer points of last weekend's game.

SAILOR TOOK A SIP of his beer, his blue eyes gleaming. "She's a bit bite-sized for you, isn't she, bro?"

Gabriel imagined taking little bites of Charlotte and felt his lips curve. "Good things. Small packages," he said, enjoying watching her mobile face, her bright, intelligent eyes as she spoke to his father.

Leaning back against the bar, Sailor followed Gabriel's gaze. "You think I should tell her she's the first woman you've ever brought to a game with us?"

"Sure. If you want a black eye." Charlotte wasn't yet ready for the pressure the knowledge would put on her.

"Ísalind won't let you hurt me." Sailor blew a kiss to his wife.

Dimpling, Ísa blew one back before returning to her conversation with their mom.

"Anyway, you sure you won't break her?" Sailor asked, a dubious look on his face. "Remember that magazine called you a sexy brute."

"Keep it up and I'll break you." He knew damn well Sailor was needling him in revenge for all the teasing he'd endured after falling so hard for his English-teacher wife that he'd actually read poetry for chrissakes. As if his siblings weren't going to rag on him when that came out.

"Daddy!" Esme tugged on Jake's hand. "My shoelace is all messy."

Putting his beer on the bar, Jake bent down to fix the knotted-up lace after tapping his daughter playfully on the cheek. Jake had become a father at eighteen and it had fundamentally changed him. Gone was the boy who'd spent all his money on parts for his souped-up car, and in his place was a stable single dad whose daughter adored him.

"You talk to Danny?" Gabriel asked Sailor, at once proud of Jake and worried about him—the kid had become too serious at too young an age.

"This afternoon," Sailor said, his eyes connecting with Gabriel's in a silent understanding about Jake. "He's pumped."

Shoelace issue fixed, their second-youngest brother rose to pick up his beer. "You talking about Danny?"

Gabriel nodded. "If they win this game, they're on their way to the top of the table."

"Cakewalk as long as they watch their passes, don't allow intercepts." Jake took a drink of his beer.

Eating a piece of cheese in a single bite, Sailor returned his attention to Gabriel. "Getting back to your girl, I want to say I'm happy for you, man. I thought for sure you'd end up a sad and lonely old man I'd have to bring meals on wheels."

"I'm touched," Gabriel said as Jake grinned and high-fived Sailor. "I would've expected you to leave me to starve."

"Naw, the girls like you too much."

They talked, tried to piss each other off, let Esme and

Emmaline raid the food when the girls ran over. Kickoff though, everyone had their eyes on the pitch. Grabbing a seat in the last row after stealing Charlotte away from his dad, Gabriel put his arm along the back of her seat and gave her a plate of cheese and crackers and grapes. "I grabbed that for you before the horde could demolish it."

Esme, who'd chosen to sit next to Charlotte, giggled. "Can I have some, Uncle Gabe?"

"Only if you come give me a kiss."

Small arms wrapped around his neck seconds later as she reached up on her toes to plant an enthusiastic kiss on his cheek. Seating her on his lap afterward, he returned his other arm to behind Charlotte. That was how they watched the start of the game. Ten minutes in, Esme wiggled off and went to play with Emmaline, their parents having brought toys for them.

Gabriel turned to tease Charlotte about the effectiveness of tiny chaperones and found her eyes riveted to the pitch. He followed her gaze, saw what had her transfixed.

20

BEING PETTED BY A T-REX CAN BE
A DELICIOUS EXPERIENCE

DANNY HAD THE BALL in one hand, was barreling down the field, avoiding opponents with some seriously fancy footwork that made him seem much smaller than the six foot three, two hundred and twenty pounds of muscle that he was.

"Come on, come on."

Gabriel caught the fierce words, realized they came from Charlotte. Heart in his throat as he saw a defender heading to tackle Danny, he willed his youngest brother to pass. Danny's weakness on the field was his tunnel vision—he sometimes didn't see the teammates he had in support.

"Pass, Danny, pass!" Sailor was on his feet, yelling at their brother.

Esme and Emmaline immediately lost interest in their toys and went to their position at the front of the balcony again. "Go, Uncle Danny! Go! Go!"

"Goddammit!" Gabriel growled, up on his feet. "Pass!"

It was a sweetheart move. Danny swiveled just slightly on one foot, the oval of the ball gliding out of his hands to land safely in the hands of the teammate to his left and behind him, just as the defender tackled Danny, having committed to the attack. It left no one in front of Danny's teammate.

Two seconds later, that teammate ran across the try line with enough breathing room to slam the ball down right behind the goal posts. He did so to the roar of every single person on the balcony—including Charlotte. Pumped, Gabriel grabbed her face in his hands and smacked a kiss on her lips.

Eyes wide, she kissed him back. "That pass was incredible!"

"The little shit's learned something," Gabriel said with a grin, having spent more evenings and weekends than he could count helping Danny fix the weakness in his game. He and his other brothers had played out situations just like this, and now their baby brother had aced it.

Three minutes later, the team's fly-half converted the try, the kick sailing easily through the posts because of where the ball had been grounded during the try.

CHARLOTTE HADN'T HAD SO much fun in a long, long time. Everyone in Gabriel's family was a furious supporter of Daniel Esera and his team and had an incredible love for the game. There was passionate yelling, groaning when passes were fumbled or penalty kicks sent wide of the goalposts, and rapid-fire exchanges of opinions on the rucks and lineouts.

"Fucking offside, ref! Are you blind?" Sailor yelled at one point, only for Esme to pipe up and say, "Swear jar, Uncle Sailor."

Charlotte laughed as Sailor dug out a gold dollar coin and put it in the piggybank Emmaline had pulled out of the backpack that held the girls' toys.

"You two are going to bankrupt me." He jerked his thumb at Gabriel. "You missed him. He owes you two dollars."

By Charlotte's count, the girls made a total of twenty-seven dollars in the first half—including multiple contributions from Gabriel, Jake, and Sailor when the referee didn't award a penalty for what had been a dangerously high tackle. Then there was the scrum that collapsed twice.

Charlotte loved every second of the experience.

Everyone calmed down close to halftime, with Danny's team holding on to their lead. That was when Charlotte became aware of male fingers brushing gently over her nape.

The tiny hairs on her arms rose up, her response a mix of fear and arousal. It took conscious effort not to stiffen up under the lazy, absent caress. Gabriel wasn't threatening her, wasn't hurting her. He was… petting her. Thinking of it that way made it easier to focus on the pleasure rather than the pain.

But when he would've curved his fingers over her nape, she reached up and tugged his hand away. Giving her a measuring look, he put his arm back on the chair but didn't touch her nape again. And though the possibility of a hold there had made nausea churn in her gut, she felt as if she'd lost something precious.

CHARLOTTE SAT FIDGETING WITH Gabriel's scarf as he drove her home. "That was fun," she blurted out when she couldn't take the screaming tension anymore.

"Yeah. Danny's over the moon at the win."

Charlotte had only seen Gabriel's youngest brother for a few minutes before he had to leave with the rest of his team for the after-match briefing, but though he was sporting a cut on his eyebrow and a bruise on his jaw from what had been a hard battle of a game, he'd been in high spirits. "Did you see that fucking awesome pass?" had been his opening comment.

His family had all clapped, then hugged and kissed him. Charlotte had stayed out of the way, watching as Esme and Emmaline wriggled into the heavy mass of humanity without fear of being crushed or hurt. Danny had cuddled both girls and laughingly given them an IOU for the swear jar before heading back out, and Charlotte wasn't sure he'd even seen her.

"I heard Danny was thinking of changing teams next season," she said, wondering if the tension in the car was real or just a figment of her imagination. If Gabriel had already started to give up on her...

Ice picks stabbed at her heart.

"Charlotte, why are you determined to pick a hole in my scarf?"

She stopped her nervous motions. "Sorry." Smoothing out the wool, she looked carefully at the nubby edges, the worn weave. "Is this from when you played?"

"Dad got it for me when I was selected. It became my pregame lucky charm."

And he'd given it to her to wear. Teeth sinking into her lower lip, she stroked the weave of the scarf again, caught between hope and despair.

"You didn't answer my question."

"It was nothing."

"Ms. Baird."

She shivered. "Stop doing that."

"WHY? IT GETS YOU hot." Gabriel liked making Charlotte hot. "We'll play boss and secretary in bed one day, and you can call me Mr. Bishop and say 'yes, sir' and 'of course, sir.'" He also had a very dirty fantasy of hearing her say "fuck me, Gabriel."

"Stop putting those thoughts in my head," she ordered, chest rising and falling in jerky breaths. "How am I supposed to act naturally at work when you call me Ms. Baird in that tone of voice?"

"I won't, not unless we're alone." All bets were off in private, he thought as he pulled into her drive, parking in front of her town house a short time later.

Switching off the lights and the engine, he turned to brace his arm along the back of her seat. "Now, Ms. Baird, we need to have a conversation."

"A c-conversation." She coughed, faced him with squared shoulders. "About what?"

"About the reason you don't like certain touches and why you don't like being boxed in." Gabriel could've danced around it, but it was becoming obvious to him that that would achieve exactly nothing. They had to get this out in the open, not keep it in the dark where it haunted and imprisoned Charlotte.

She gripped at his scarf. "What makes you think you have the right to know?"

"Charlotte." He waited until she met his gaze, hazel eyes wary behind her spectacles. "You know how hardheaded I am, how determined. I can figure out a solution, but first I need to know the problem."

"What if there is no solution?" A tremor rippled over her skin. "What if I'm just too messed up?"

"No."

"No?" Her voice rose. "You can't just decide something is impossible!"

"Sure I can, when I'm the one making the decision." He gripped her chin. "Unless you've decided you don't want me anymore, then I'm making the call."

Her skin was so delicate under his touch, made him want to rub his bristled jaw against it so she'd wear his mark. He'd do it across the taut softness of her breasts too, enjoy knowing she wore him against her skin all day long. "Charlotte?"

"Not here, not now," she said, pulling away. "Are you free tomorrow?"

"Yeah." He'd intended to run some numbers on a prospective property purchase, but that could wait.

"Pick me up in the morning? Around nine?"

"I'll be here."

CHARLOTTE SHUDDERED AGAINST THE door after she shut it, watching the lights of Gabriel's SUV slice across the windows as he drove away. He hadn't kissed her good night, just cupped her face and said, "I'll see you tomorrow."

It was as if he knew she couldn't have handled a kiss. Not now. Not when she'd promised to tell him the truth.

Her heart felt ice-cold, shivers crushing her ribcage outward.

Shoving trembling hands through her hair, she walked into the bedroom after switching on all the lights in the house one by one, then stripped to change into her nightgown.

She brushed her teeth, cleaned her face using hot, hot water.

Afterward she did a second walk around and turned the lights off. For the first six months following her release from the hospital, she'd left the house ablaze all night except for Molly's room, but then it had become a matter of pride to give that up. It was still hard and she turned off the lights in a pattern that meant she was never in the dark, but it was better than surrendering to the fear.

Once behind the locked door of her bedroom, she turned on a bedside light before switching off the main overhead light and slipped into bed. Her stomach still churned; she knew she should've just told Gabriel in the car, but she hadn't been able to bear talking about it in the dark, in the night. That was the time of terror.

Given her thoughts, it wasn't a surprise she had a nightmare when she did finally fall asleep. Though most people wouldn't have labeled it that, would've seen only a memory.

CHARLOTTE LAY NAKED IN the narrow single bed in Richard's room, uncomfortable and in pain. Still, she thought, it had been worth it. It had made Richard so happy. "Hi," she said with a shaky smile when he came out of the bathroom, having pulled on his sweatpants.

"Hi." Lying down beside her, he smiled that flawless, brilliant smile. "Hey, don't worry, you'll get better."

The burgeoning happiness inside her began to fizzle. "Was I that bad?" She'd known she'd be awkward, but he'd said it didn't matter, that he was honored she was giving him the gift of her body.

He chuckled in response to her question. "Your rhythm was off, but I can teach you that." Tugging away the sheet, he looked down at her body.

It made her feel cold and exposed, but when she would've reached for the thin shield of cotton, he held it out of reach. "Richard." She fought not to cry.

"You have a good body," he said, eyes assessing. "A little skinny and your tits aren't huge, but—" He looked up, caught the distress on her face, and suddenly he was the boy she'd fallen for, sweet and caring. "I'm sorry, Charlotte. You know I love you. Here, let me show you."

She went to say no, that it hurt, but he was kissing her and she didn't want to disappoint him again, so she didn't say anything. Instead, she gritted her teeth through the pain and smiled at him when he did things to her that she knew were supposed to arouse her. They had before, but now she was too embarrassed and ashamed and feeling like a failure.

"There," he said afterward, his breath rough as he flopped down beside her. "See? I love you."

No boy had ever paid so much attention to her, told her he wanted her, told her he loved her. He probably hadn't meant to hurt her feelings; she just wasn't sophisticated enough to understand what he'd been trying to say. After all, he could have any girl on campus, and he'd chosen her.

"I love you too," she whispered.

AND SHE HAD, CHARLOTTE thought the next morning as she dressed after her shower. It had been the needy, heartbreaking love of a girl who wanted someone of her own. She and Molly had one another, but unlike her strong, determined friend, Charlotte was unsure of her path in life. She hadn't even thought of further education after high school, loathe to miss even a day with her mom.

197

The only reason she'd sent in the university application had been to make her mom and dad happy. After which, she'd promptly forgotten about it. It was only when the pre-semester letters started arriving that she'd realized her father had accepted the placement offer on her behalf and that he'd enrolled her in the classes she'd said she'd take when he'd quizzed her about them months earlier.

She'd had no intention of going... but then everything had unraveled three weeks before the start of the semester, her parents both gone in a heartbeat. She'd buried them one after the other, found herself lost. University had simply been a place she could go so she didn't drown in grief.

Two months into the semester and she'd believed she'd begun to heal, had finally started taking a real interest in her studies. Then had come Richard, and she'd learned she did still have jagged fractures in her psyche.

"Jesus, a real woman would've gotten it by now."

"I'm sorry, Charlotte. Sometimes I forget how inexperienced you are—I don't mean to be impatient with you."

"You do as I say, Charlotte. No lip."

"Don't be ridiculous. You know no one else will ever want you—if they did, I wouldn't be your first and only boyfriend."

Charlotte hadn't understood it at the time, but Richard had been a predator who'd zeroed in on her grief and her insecurities. A self-confident woman would've told him to stick it when he said those ugly things to her after her very first time. Molly probably would've punched him.

Charlotte had told herself to get over it. After all, he was so handsome, so smart, not the kind of boy anyone expected to fall for plain, shy Charlotte Baird. But the worst, the *absolute worst thing*, was how it had all begun. She might've been inexperienced and painfully lacking in confidence, but she wasn't stupid. She wouldn't have been drawn into his orbit if he'd been mean and cruel from the start. No, Richard's abuse had been slow and insidious, like a spider trapping a helpless insect in its web before the insect ever knew it was in danger.

Jumping at the hard rap of knuckles on her front door, she realized Gabriel had arrived. Shaky all over again at the reminder that she'd promised to tell him everything, she made her way to the door, opened it with hands that trembled. He was wearing jeans, heavy work boots that looked like they'd had a hard life, and a short-sleeved black shirt worn loose over his jeans. The shirt had stud detailing on the pocket flaps and the sleeves, fit perfectly over his wide shoulders.

Sliding off his mirrored sunglasses, he looked her up and down.

Her skin chilled, the memory of Richard's cold recitation of her flaws a loud hum in the back of her skull.

21

THE NIGHT THE MONSTER
WAS REAL...

"I DO LIKE YOU in a dress, Ms. Baird," said the man on her doorstep, the man who *wasn't* Richard. "Gives me all sorts of ideas about easy access."

Charlotte blushed, all thoughts of Richard forgotten. "I thought since it was so nice and sunny out..." She'd worn a sleeveless white sundress, teaming it with a pretty belt of orange patent leather. Instead of a white cardigan, she'd chosen a lime-green one. The outfit was one of the most colorful in her new wardrobe and it made her feel like spring even in winter.

"I have a new appreciation for the sun." Reaching out to cup her jaw, he said, "Shall I kiss you, Charlotte? Lick my tongue over yours, suck on the tip until you whimper?" He accompanied each word with a rub of his thumb over her lower lip. "Open."

Her lips parted almost of their own accord, her heart skittering against her ribcage. Closing her lips over his thumb when he slipped it inside, she sucked... then bit down enough to smart.

Eyes darkening, he drew his thumb out and tapped it against lips that felt kiss swollen already. "Just for that, you have to wait for your kiss." He tugged her outside. "You have everything?"

Not capable of speech just yet, she nodded and, taking her keys out of her handbag, locked up the town house after setting the alarm. Gabriel slid his hand down her back to rest on the curve of her ass as she put away the keys. It made her jump, but he didn't remove his hand, circling gently as he nudged her to the car.

"What do you keep in there?" he said, eyes on her handbag. "It's big enough for not only the kitchen sink but all the appliances."

"Ha-ha," she managed to get out past her awareness of his touch. "Don't ask me next time you need a pen or a piece of sticky tape."

He stroked her again, his cheeks creasing. The heat of him branded her, the mark pulsing even after she was in the passenger seat.

"Where to?" he asked after he was inside, sunglasses back on.

"Albert Park." It had taken her time to get comfortable in the university area again, but these days, she deliberately hopped off the bus a couple of stops early and cut through the adjacent park on her way to work. It meant something to her that Richard hadn't destroyed her pleasure in the beautiful area.

She loved the active quiet of it in the mornings, peopled by early-rising student joggers, and others dressed for work who were taking a shortcut to the central business district. Some people walked briskly, eyes on their smart phones, but most traversed the paths with a leisurely stride, smiling at one another as they passed. Every so often, she'd see a group practicing Tai Chi under the canopy of one of the larger trees and would stop to watch the graceful, slow melody of movement.

Nine thirty on a public holiday, it was busier but not crazy. Gabriel found a parking space only a couple of minutes' walk away, and they were soon entering the park, his hand on her lower back. With Auckland free of snow even in winter, the park usually had flowers of some kind or another even in the coldest season. Now, heading into the tail end of that season, the garden beds boasted a profusion of color.

"I always wonder how they keep it so beautiful no matter the season," she said, the two of them taking the pathway that would lead eventually to the covered band rotunda. Charlotte didn't want to be enclosed even that much. Instead, she turned right, taking them toward an open area populated only by a number of large trees, their limbs curving and winding and creating living sculptures.

"You should ask Sailor about the garden stuff," Gabriel said. "He's like a plant encyclopedia."

"How did he end up in landscaping and gardening rather than sports?"

"He's the nerd in the family—always was more interested in science and plants." A grin that took the sting out of the words, his pride in his brother clear. "He does play club rugby on the weekends for fun, so we haven't disowned him."

Charlotte sighed. "There's no hope for me then. I love sports, but I'm not coordinated enough to actually be any good at them."

He shifted his hand to her hip, squeezed. "What are you talking about?" he said as things went all melty and hot low in her body. "You wrangle T-Rexes, don't you?"

Scrunching up her nose at him, she fought a smile. "Only one."

"Good, because this T-Rex is possessive as hell and does not share well." He ran his hand over her hip again. "How about here?"

Charlotte looked at the natural seat formed by a spreading limb, and the bubbles of delight went flat. It was time. No more delays. She had to tell him every bit of the ugliness. "Yes," she whispered and sucked in a breath when he put both hands on her waist and lifted her up onto the tree. Instead of sitting beside her, he leaned against the branch, his arm braced behind her.

"I thought you liked crowding me," she murmured, heart bruising at the sign that he might already be pulling away.

"I love crowding you. But since you didn't want to talk in the car, I thought I'd behave and give you some space." Eyes of steel gray pierced hers. "I'm right here if you need me, and I'm more than big enough to help you fight your demons. Just say the word."

Her heart ached. She shifted closer to the reassuring bulk of him without a word. Expression softening, he cuddled her by curving his arm around her without blocking her in.

"I don't know how to start," she said, watching a girl spin around in the arms of a boy before they both raced away toward the white spire of the university's clock tower.

"Did it happen here?"

"Yes." At least it had begun here.

"Then start here. Tell me about your wild college days."

Charlotte wanted to smile, couldn't. The past was too heavy, too horrible; the malevolent shadow of it crushed any lightness inside her. "I didn't know what I wanted to do with my life, but since I enjoyed reading the business pages, I decided to do a commerce degree, majoring in accounting." She laughed softly, but the sound held no humor. "It sounds like such a stupid reason to make that big a decision, but I wasn't thinking on all cylinders."

"Was your mom sick when you had to decide?"

Charlotte nodded, the memory of loss heavy on her heart. "My mom told me to live my life, to not let her death weigh me down, and I was determined to do that—even after I lost my father too."

Her throat grew thick despite the distance of years between that moment and this. "It happened just weeks before the start of the semester. At first, I was a zombie sleepwalking through lectures, but after I survived that first burn of grief, I wanted to make Mom and Dad proud."

Gabriel stroked his hand over her hip. "Did you have anyone to lean on?"

"Molly." She cuddled even closer to him. "I wouldn't have made it without her." Her best friend had all but carried her through the weeks directly after her father's shock passing. "I'd turned eighteen a couple of weeks earlier, so I was technically an adult when my father died, but I was so lost. Molly's the one who organized my dad's funeral, who talked to the lawyers to make sure I was given access to the family accounts so I could pay for things."

Charlotte had been numb with shock, unable to forget the chill of her father's hand that day she'd gone to fetch him down for breakfast. She'd found him with a faint smile on his face, his expression peaceful.

Swallowing past the knot of old grief, she said, "I just couldn't get my mind around the fact that they were both gone." It had been one blow too many.

"What about your parents' families?" Gabriel scowled. "They should've been there for you."

"My parents were both only children, and their parents died when I was little." Charlotte had never known a rambunctious extended family like Gabriel's. "They had a circle of good friends though, and Molly later told me those friends had stepped in to help her figure things out. But she was the one who held it all together."

Gabriel touched the fingers of his free hand to her jaw, tilting her face toward him. "I'm guessing you did the same for her when the scandal tore her family apart."

"It wasn't the same." Then, as now, Molly had been tough.

"What does Molly say?"

"That she wouldn't have made it without me," Charlotte confessed.

"You were my oak tree," Molly had said once. "Enduring and protective and with a loyalty so deeply rooted, I knew no storm would wash you away. I would've drowned without you."

"I think she knows what she's talking about." Gabriel tucked a strand of her hair behind her ear. "I bet your parents wanted her to live with you after the car accident that took her folks."

Charlotte nodded jerkily. "Except the doctors had already found the new cancers in Mom's body. The social workers wouldn't approve Molly living with us." They'd said Pippa

205

Baird didn't need the stress, but Charlotte's mom had worried constantly over Molly. "She had to go live with strangers, but mostly, she just slept there." Molly's foster parents hadn't been bad people; they just hadn't had the tools to handle a teenage girl who'd lost everything.

"It was a no-brainer to share living space when we began university." Neither she nor Molly had anyone else they trusted enough to live with. "At the start, we lived in my parents' home, but I sold it a month later—they had very good insurance, so there were no bills, but I couldn't bear to live there anymore." The silence had been crushing. Her father's laughter would never again light up the room. Her mother's voice would never again rise in a silly song as she worked.

Charlotte hadn't been able to stand it.

"My father always told me I should never waste money on rent if I was in a position to invest it in a property instead," she said, her voice raw, "so I bought the town house." Going from a family home to a smaller town house had left her with enough money to put herself through university.

"Molly and I had the biggest argument because she wanted to pay me rent. I finally used guilt to win." She laughed and it was real, if a little wet. "I asked her if she wanted my mom and dad to haunt me. After all, they'd always treated her as another daughter."

"Devious." His lips brushed her temple, his hand warm and protective on her hip. "No wonder you two are close. You've been through a lot together."

Feeling safe in a way she hadn't since before Richard, she nodded. However, the warmth that came with talking about her parents and her best friend faded into a shivering chill as

206

she looked into the darkness. "I met Richard two months into my first semester." His name was like broken glass in her throat. Hard and cutting and bloodying her from the inside out. "He was smart, good-looking, and he liked me. At least that's what he made me believe."

Pressed as she was to Gabriel's body, she felt the thrumming tension in him, his muscles bunched up. "It's all right, Gabriel. He's in prison."

"Jesus, Charlotte." His arm tightened around her. "What the fuck did he do to you?"

Charlotte knew she just had to get it out—Gabriel had to know. "Four months of being in a relationship with him and I finally started to understand he was bad for me. He made me doubt everything about myself, made me think I was worthless." Looking back, Charlotte couldn't believe she hadn't seen through him sooner. "I wish I could go back and shake myself."

Gabriel scowled. "You were hurt and grieving. He took advantage of that."

Intellectually, Charlotte knew she'd been in a vulnerable place at the time Richard came into her life, but it was so hard not to look back and wish she could change the past. Still, that insecure, shy girl hadn't totally let herself down. "One day, while we were talking about a paper for a shared class, he hit me," she said past her thundering heart, conscious of Gabriel's muscles going hard as rock against her. "Said I was giving him lip."

Shocked and in pain, her lip bleeding, Charlotte had headed for the door. "I broke up with him then and there. Or I tried to." It had taken all her courage; she'd kept waiting for him to haul her back, hit her again. Richard's arrogance was what had allowed her to escape. "He refused to believe it. At first he laughed, said I'd come crawling back since he was the only one who'd have me."

A growl rumbled out of Gabriel's chest. "Tell me you reported the motherfucking piece of shit."

Patting his chest in a soothing gesture, she snuggled even closer to the furnace of his body in an effort to get warm. "Yes, but it was my word against his." And Richard was a master manipulator skilled at creating illusions that appeared real. "In the end, nothing came of it."

Gabriel's jaw was granite. "It didn't end there, did it?"

She shook her head. "When he realized I was serious about breaking up, he began to bombard me with flowers and chocolates, was suddenly the charming boy who'd first made me believe he loved me." Panic pulsed in her, causing her lungs to struggle, the air suddenly too thin. "But when I wouldn't budge, he started to get mean." Shallow breaths, her heart beating too fast. "He spread rumors about me on campus and through the online campus forums, but that didn't matter so much to me."

She'd never been a social butterfly, hadn't cared about the opinions of the popular cliques. "Molly knew the truth, and that was all that mattered." During their relationship, Richard had tried to manipulate her into dropping Molly as a friend, but that was the one thing on which Charlotte had never given an inch. "The fact that I was a nobody on campus actually helped me—no one cared enough to spread the rumors."

"Breathe, Charlotte."

"I can't. I have to get this out." Almost panting now, she slid her hand around to his back and fisted it in his shirt. "I thought that would be the end of it, but he started sitting in on my lectures, just smirking at me. And I could *feel* him following me around campus, but I could never catch him at it."

Fear licked at her, a memory of how hunted she'd felt, never knowing when he might confront her, hurt her. "Then I started getting anonymous e-mails full of pictures of women being degraded. No messages, just the vilest pictures with my head Photoshopped on the women's bodies. The phone calls started soon afterward, all from untraceable numbers." Nausea had swamped her each time she heard the ringtone. "Over and over and over and over at night and during finals, until I had to change the home line and my cell."

Gabriel's voice was hard when he spoke. "He was stalking you."

"Yes, but he was so good at covering his tracks that though the police were sympathetic, they couldn't stop him. They did give him a warning though—it enraged him. He stewed and stewed on it, and he watched me."

She shivered, continued to push the words out because she was afraid that if she paused, she'd never start again. "I didn't know that then. The incidents stopped after the warning, and when they didn't reoccur over the next two months, I felt safe again. Safe enough to insist Molly go out of town for a special seminar her lecturer had recommended. I told her I'd be fine."

Dread swallowed her in a dark cloud. "It was what he'd been waiting for. He knew I'd be alone from Friday night to Sunday afternoon when she came back." Seeing spots in front of her eyes, she tried to draw more air into her lungs, failed.

"Enough." Gabriel gripped her chin, made her meet his gaze. "I can guess the rest."

"No." She shook her head. "Please, I have to finish." He had to know exactly what he was fighting—because Charlotte didn't want him to fail, wanted a life that had Gabriel in it. "Let me finish."

Fury masked his features, but he nodded. "Go on."

22

BAD THINGS HAPPEN... BUT THEN
GOOD THINGS HAPPEN

"**H**E GOT IN USING a key he'd duplicated while we'd been together." Charlotte hadn't had an alarm then, hadn't even considered it, her neighborhood was so safe. "I never worried he might have a key because I'd never brought him to my place; we'd always gone to his."

After that horrifying weekend, she'd excoriated herself for her mistake in not thinking to change the locks, until Molly had finally shaken her and said that she hadn't either. Neither one of them had expected the depth and psychopathic patience of Richard's rage, having had no experience with his kind of a twisted mind.

"I came in after a late Friday class. It was winter, dark. And he was waiting inside." Feeling her entire body shake, she held on to Gabriel in an effort to find solid ground. "He waited for me to lock the door behind myself before he came at me." Her memories of the ensuing minutes were fuzzy at best.

"I came to, gagged and tied to a chair in the kitchen." Nausea threatened as it had then, her aching head and bruised face the least of her concerns. "He'd brought ropes, and he was wearing gloves and overalls with a hood. So they wouldn't find forensic evidence." Charlotte had known then that she was in the presence of a total psychopath.

"At first he just talked to me, told me everything he intended to do." The mental torture had been excruciating. "In the hours that followed, he'd occasionally come around to the back of the chair, pull back my head with a grip in my hair, and run a knife across my throat just enough to make me bleed."

Sometimes she still woke to the feel of phantom blood dripping down her neck, ice-cold metal across her throat. "Then he'd leave for a few minutes, walk around the town house and come back to show me things he'd found in my bedroom, things he was going to keep for souvenirs." Her panties, a ring, a picture of her parents. "Every so often, he'd hit me again."

Gabriel was rigid beside her, but he didn't interrupt. He just held her safe, and she knew he'd allow no one and nothing to get to her.

"At some point during that first night," Charlotte said, drawing her strength from his, "he wrenched back my head again and hacked off chunks of my hair." Terrified for her life, Charlotte hadn't cared about the petty act. Ironic then that it was one that haunted her.

"Eventually, he decided he wanted to sleep and went into my bedroom to do it. I thought I could tip the chair over while he was gone, make enough noise that one of my neighbors might hear. After he left the kitchen, I waited a long time, then started trying to rock the chair so it would go over. And he was there. He'd waited all that time just so he could reappear and watch the hope drain out of my face."

She'd never forget the way he'd laughed at her surprise. "Later, he hog-tied me and put me in the bedroom closet. He giggled the entire time." Her physical injuries had been agonizing by that point, but worse had been the knowledge that no one would come for her.

No one knew she was all alone in the dark with a psychopath.

"The next morning, he grabbed the back of my neck and dragged me into the kitchen." Fingers locked tight in Gabriel's shirt, she detailed exactly what had happened in the kitchen, the horrible things Richard had said, the injuries he'd caused.

"The entire time he was taunting and abusing me," she added when she could speak again. "I told myself I couldn't give in, couldn't die. I had to survive so I could testify, put Richard behind bars."

She'd still had hope then, hadn't known how much worse it would get.

GABRIEL COULDN'T THINK, COULD barely see, his vision a haze of red. He wanted to find the bastard who'd terrorized Charlotte and crush every bone in his pathetic body, pound his face to mush and stomp on his head until his brains leaked out his ears. Then he wanted to bring Richard back to life and hurt him all over again.

Jesus, Charlotte was so small. She'd have been no match for a full-grown male. Richard's blows had to have broken things in her, and the ugliness of the mental torture… He didn't know if he could stand to hear any more, but he would.

213

Because if she'd survived it, he could damn well hear it, damn well hold her safe.

He would *always* hold her safe.

"After his breakfast," she said, and she was crying now, though she didn't seem to realize it, "he hurt me again." She cradled her left arm unconsciously against her chest, and he knew the bastard had either sprained or broken it. "But he made sure it wasn't enough to push me into a blackout."

Gabriel forced himself to breathe, the red haze having morphed into pure, cold rage.

"Then he put me in the closet again." Charlotte's breath was a rasp, her body shaking. "He tied something over my nose so I could barely breathe, had to focus absolutely to get air into my lungs. I found out afterward that he left the house then, went to have coffee with friends. Setting up an alibi."

Gabriel clenched his right hand, the hand Charlotte couldn't see, around the tree branch next to him so tightly that the wood groaned. "The fucking psychopath."

"Yes, he was, but he didn't know everything. While he was out, the home phone began to ring and ring and ring. I knew it was Molly checking up on me."

Gabriel knew the other woman wouldn't have simply accepted Charlotte's sudden silence. "She called the cops."

"Yes. She directly contacted the officers who'd followed up on my complaints about the stalking and told them something was wrong. She said another student had just told her that Richard planned to come after me and that she'd been calling to warn me." A shaky smile. "She was lying through her teeth about all of it, but it got them to move."

Smile fading, her breath came shallower and faster.

Gabriel had never felt so fucking helpless in his life. "I've got you," he said, releasing the abused tree branch to brush his fingers over her tear-wet cheek. "I've got you."

A hot droplet splashed onto the back of his hand as she said, "Richard came back maybe fifteen minutes after the phone stopped ringing. I don't know the exact time—my mind was hazy. He came to the closet and told me he'd thought of a new game. How even though he didn't want me, he knew some people who might, that he'd invited them over for a party with his slut."

No, no, no.

"It was all lies," she said, sending knives of icy relief through Gabriel. "But I didn't know that. I thought it was real and it broke me. It just… broke me. I started to cry."

"Hell, Charlotte, you held out that long?" Her strength amazed him. "You're fucking incredible." He had to fight every instinct in his body not to haul her into his arms and squeeze her tight.

"I couldn't do it anymore. I started crying and it was weird. He became gentle, said how it was all my fault that I'd made him lose his temper, but now that I'd seen my mistake, maybe he'd take me back." Wet words, Charlotte's voice so hoarse it was barely understandable. "What he didn't realize was that the cops who'd responded to Molly's call had arrived right after he returned. They saw him enter the town house, but since they were certain he had me hostage, they couldn't simply bust down the door."

Gabriel understood the cops' reasoning, but those extra minutes had cost Charlotte. "Tell me they got him."

She nodded. "They made one of my neighbors turn up his music really loud, and then they broke a window under cover

215

of the noise and climbed in. The next time Richard stepped out into the hallway, they slammed him to the ground and cuffed him before he could figure out what was happening." Her entire body seemed to crumple on the last words, as if it had taken all her strength to tell him what she had.

Holding her against him without trapping her in a way that might make her panic, Gabriel tried to temper his rage. Charlotte didn't need him to be a macho stud right now. She needed him to hold her, his fierce, shy Charlotte who'd survived the horror with her soul and her spirit intact. Maybe it was a little bruised, but so many people would've just given up after such a brutal attack. She'd built a life, a career.

Hell, she'd *fought* with him.

It staggered him to realize how much courage it must've taken for her to stand up to him when she didn't know how he might react. "No one will ever hurt you again," he whispered against her hair, the promise one he'd kill to keep. "You're safe."

TEN MINUTES LATER, GABRIEL cuddling her close the entire time, Charlotte was no longer crying. She'd dried her face using tissues from her handbag, but now she didn't know what to do. She'd never felt so exposed, so naked. She couldn't look at Gabriel, terrified at what she'd see now that he knew the extent of the damage.

Not the physical, though she did bear some scars, but the psychological. Richard might not have killed her, but he'd shattered her, fracturing her psyche into countless pieces. She'd gathered up those pieces, put them back together, but the seams were jagged and rigid with scars, while other parts were hopelessly fragile.

"Hey." A big rough-skinned hand cupped her cheek, Gabriel's thumb brushing over her chin. "Look at me."

The command in his voice made her wounded soul struggle to the surface. "You're not my boss," she said, forcing up her head. "Not here."

Gabriel ran his thumb over her chin again, the tip brushing her lower lip. "You sure?" he asked, his voice a deep drawl. "It's kind of hot giving you orders, Ms. Baird."

She sucked in a breath, red-hot flames melting the lump of ice around her heart. She'd been so afraid he'd stop flirting so outrageously with her, that he'd start handling her with kid gloves, like something that wasn't strong enough to bear anything harsher—as if she wasn't woman enough to handle him. "Just don't expect me to obey," she said on the wave of her relief.

His lips curved, his thumb continuing to caress her lower lip with every stroke. "What would be the fun in that? How can I seduce you out of your panties if you take them off on command?"

"*Gabriel.*" Her skin burned, but she could feel the sunshine again, see the brilliant colors of the flowers, the shadows retreating under the raw seduction of his voice and his touch.

"*Charlotte,*" he said in an echo of her tone, and then he kissed her.

It was a brush, nothing more, but it was a kiss.

Breathless despite the short contact, she bit down on her lower lip and blurted out, "You don't mind?"

It should've been a nonsensical question, but Gabriel's

eyebrows drew together. His answer was a growl of sound. "That you're a fucking amazing woman? No."

Charlotte didn't know which aspect of his statement to respond to first. Jumping off the branch, she turned to him, her hands on her hips. "I can't believe you just growled at me after what I told you!"

Arms folded, he leaned back against the branch. "I'll do more than growl if you repeat that particular question." He ran his eyes down her body, lingering on her breasts, her hips, her thighs, before coming back up to her lips. "I might just put my hand in your panties or my mouth on your pussy and tease you until you're screaming for an orgasm and not give it to you until you say 'Sorry, Gabriel. I can't believe I'd ask such a ridiculous question.'"

Hands pressed to her cheeks, Charlotte looked around. Thankfully, no one was close enough to have overheard his sinful response. "I'm going for a walk." She needed to cool down, her breasts swollen and the place between her thighs throbbing as it never had before a certain T-Rex.

Of course he came after her, placing his hand on her lower back in a way that had already become familiar and walking with her toward the fountain. Her emotions were all akilter. She'd expected to feel broken and lost after her confession, and shards of pain lingered, but overwhelming it all was flustered delight. Charlotte didn't know if she could get over her fears to the point where she no longer had to worry about panic attacks, but it meant everything that Gabriel hadn't written her off.

"Have you had breakfast?" he asked as they reached the flower clock.

"No." She'd been too nervous. "I make really good pancakes." Cooking was her outlet, her sport, and she needed to do some right now. "I think you have almost all the ingredients—it'll only take us a couple of minutes to pick up some bananas if you'd like banana pancakes."

"Well," Gabriel said, his lips curved in a way that made her breath hitch, "I was going to take you out, but since I'd much rather have you in my lair, all to myself, I'm sold." He leaned in to press a wickedly sweet kiss to her cheekbone. "I promise I won't devour you unless you ask *very* nicely."

23

A KISS TODAY,
NAKEDNESS TOMORROW

GABRIEL SAT ON A breakfast stool he'd brought over to the freestanding counter and sliced some strawberries for Charlotte as she padded around barefoot in his kitchen. She'd taken off her shoes and her cardigan, the spaghetti straps of her pretty sundress exposing the elegant line of her throat, the gentle curves of her shoulders.

"Do you want chocolate chips in yours?" she asked with a sunny smile.

He shook his head, wanting to reach over and tumble her into his lap, have her for his breakfast. "Just plain banana for me."

Staggered by what he'd learned, by her courage, he hadn't at first known what to do. He was so angry for her, but the monster who'd brutalized her wasn't here for him to hurt, and Charlotte didn't need more violence. Then she'd refused to look at him after wiping away her tears, and he'd known exactly what he had to do: let her know she was beautiful and sexy and everything he wanted. He'd figured the woman who'd survived a cowardly psychopath could survive some blunt sexual teasing.

He'd been right.

Eating a strawberry, he lifted another perfect, glossy berry. "Come have a bite."

Leaning across the counter, she closed her teeth and lips over the bottom half of the berry, eyes closing in bliss. "Mmm, so sweet," she said, going back down on her feet.

He groaned and ate the other half. "You have no idea what it does to me to see you put things into your mouth."

Freezing in the act of turning to the black glass cooktop that was apparently something fancy that made her burst out in raptures, she shot him a look that made his cock go rock hard. Her cheeks were flushed, yes, but her eyes held sensual awareness. And then his Ms. Baird did something utterly unexpected.

She lifted a finger to her mouth and sucked on it, her cheeks hollowing.

"Fuck!" He got up, was halfway around the counter before he realized she hadn't moved, finger no longer in her mouth. Forcing himself to stop, he thrust his hands into his hair. "Pancakes," he said. "I'll have you later."

She returned to the cooktop, but her actions were jerky. He could've left it, but that wasn't who he was; walking back to his seat, he ate a few of the chocolate chips she'd bought when they picked up the fruit. "Was it how fast I moved?"

Her shoulders went stiff, but she nodded.

"So," he said, staying in position when his instinct was to go over there and stroke his hands down the smooth warmth of her arms, kiss a line up the curve of her neck, "if I walk around the counter and slide down one of the straps of your dress and press my lips to your shoulder, what happens?"

"I... I d-don't know." She poured in batter for a pancake.

He waited until she flipped it onto a plate before getting up. He expected her to turn, and she did, just enough that she could see him. Maintaining eye contact, he came close enough that her shoulder brushed his chest.

"You have such pretty skin, Charlotte," he said, running his fingers down her arm. "So soft and golden."

He drew his palm back up her arm, tugged on the strap. He could see her pulse skittering in her throat, but she hadn't gone motionless like a small animal in front of a predator. Senses on alert for any change, he bent down and did exactly as he'd said—he pressed his lips to her skin and licked out. Just a little. Just enough to make her jump.

Smiling, he broke the kiss and blew on the spot.

She shivered.

So he scraped his teeth over her before kissing her again.

A tiny whimper escaped her throat.

With any other woman, he'd have curved his hands around her front, cupped and squeezed her breasts as he got serious, his mouth ravenous on her neck, but Charlotte needed him to go slow.

Slow could be fun, he told his rigid cock, and tugged the strap back into place.

CHARLOTTE COULD FEEL GABRIEL'S kiss long after he returned to his seat. His mouth, his tongue... She shivered again, unable to imagine how she'd bear it if he ever kissed her as intimately as he'd described the first time she'd been in his kitchen.

"Don't forget the chocolate chips for yours."

His voice made her toes curl, her nipples already throbbing points. "Thanks," she managed, and turned to shake some into the rest of the batter, and a few minutes later, the two of them were feasting on pancakes.

Instead of the awkward, painful morning she'd expected, she spent it bathed in sunshine while Gabriel sat across from her. There was some outrageous flirting, but they also talked about a couple of work matters. "We should go in, do the paperwork," she said, knowing exactly how much time he'd sliced out of his schedule for her. "Otherwise you won't have time to breathe tomorrow."

"Excellent. You can tell my mother I took you to work for our date."

A date. The sound of that made her smile widen. "It'll only take a couple of hours."

Gabriel looked at her, a tenderness in his expression that made her hurt in a sweet, wonderful way. "I have something for you," he said, to her surprise. "I've had it for a while. I don't know if today's the right day to give it to you, but I want to."

Charlotte squirmed on the breakfast stool, filled with curiosity as he disappeared upstairs. When he came back down, she couldn't see anything obvious, though one of his hands was loosely fisted. Coming around the counter, he took her wrist; she bit down on her lower lip… and then she was scowling.

"I don't want a used bracelet!" Outraged, she tried to wrench back her hand.

It was the bracelet he'd made her choose in Queenstown after dragging her around all the high-end stores. Now he had the nerve to laugh and hook the platinum, emerald, and diamond piece around her wrist.

"How many women do you know who have wrists this slender?"

Still scowling at his audacity, especially given how much she'd loved this piece—the design a delicacy of flowers and exquisitely shaped leaves—she said, "Statistically, at least a number of the women you dated."

"So suspicious." Flicking his thumb against the little oval platinum tag near the clasp, he said, "Good thing I got this."

Looking down, she felt her heart slam into her ribs. It was inscribed to Ms. Baird. "Ms. Baird?" she said, a little teary.

"My Ms. Baird."

She couldn't believe it. He'd bought this months ago. Lower lip quivering, she pushed at his chest. "You are a horrible man." It had infuriated her to be asked to choose a gift for some unknown woman. "Why did you torment me?"

"I was flirting with you," he said in a growl of a tone. "I figured you'd work it out when I made it clear I wanted your opinion and your opinion alone."

"How was I supposed to figure it out?" Sunshine from the skylight sparked off the stunning piece of jewelry as she glared up at him. "I told you, men like you don't hit on women like me."

His expression altered, pure sin in his eyes. "That's one punishment," he said in a tone that was a rasp of rough silk over her skin. "We'll figure out a payment schedule you can handle."

Chest rising and falling as she inhaled and exhaled jerkily, she refused to back down. "I can't accept this." It was valued in the serious five figures. She knew because she'd taken great delight in watching him pay for it, figuring that was his just deserts for dragging her along on the excruciating exercise.

"Try to give it back." It was a dare.

Taking it, she went to undo the clasp. Tried again. "Gabriel, what did you do?"

He pressed his lips to her shoulder again in response, his hand warm and possessive on her back. "I'll show you how to take it off when you stop attempting to give it back."

"This is ridiculous. There must be a way..." But try as she might, she couldn't figure out how to undo the clasp. "I can't go around wearing a bracelet worth half my annual income!"

He shrugged and put a strawberry to her lips. "Bite down."

When she did it with force, he raised his hand to play with her dress strap. "Still doesn't put me off that luscious mouth." Stroking the remaining half of the strawberry over her lips, he leaned down and whispered, "You wouldn't bite my cock, would you, Ms. Baird?"

Chest hurting from the shallowness of her breaths and her glasses fogging up, she swallowed. "I guess you'll have to wait and see."

He groaned and fed her the rest of the fruit. "You really don't mind going in to work?"

"No—if you take this bracelet off."

FORTY-FIVE MINUTES LATER, she was at her desk printing out the documents he needed, and the bracelet was still on her wrist. Gabriel Bishop, as she'd already learned, was one stubborn male. And he'd decided the ridiculously expensive, exquisitely beautiful, one-of-a-kind bracelet was hers. Aggravated as she was, she couldn't help the melting in her bones.

He'd had it for *months*, she thought again, her eyes lingering on the pretty, delicate lines of it. She'd sighed over it in the shop, having no intention of recommending it to Gabriel so he could give it to his "girlfriend." When he'd caught her sneaking that photo of it and bought it, she'd been so frustrated. And jealous. She could admit that now. She'd been jealous he was giving the bracelet she loved to another woman.

Except the whole time, it had been for her.

Months.

Touching the tiny flowers with possessive fingers, she jerked them back when she heard Gabriel coming out of his office. "Papers ready, Charlotte?" he asked a little absently, his attention on the report in his hand.

"Yes," she said, her pulse kicking at the sight of him, so big and smart and delicious. "Here you go."

"Thanks." He took them, disappeared, saying, "Can you dig up the previous proposal for me? I want to double-check something."

"I'll have it to you in a minute." She turned to her computer, discovered that for some reason the file hadn't been input. "I'm going to have to go down to the records room," she said, poking her head into his office.

Gabriel looked up, frowned. "I'll come with you."

Stomach dropping, she gripped the edge of the doorjamb. "It's only one floor down. I'll be fine."

He was already walking toward her. "Charlotte, I know you can do it. I'm also feeling very protective today." An edge in his voice. "So just let me come with you."

Shaken by the blunt words, she spread her hands on his chest. She'd been so focused on how he was treating her that she hadn't stopped to consider how she should treat him. He was a protective, possessive kind of a man, and she'd laid a lot on him today. "Maybe I should give you a kiss," she said, finding the courage because he needed her to find it. "Come here."

He bent his head. Cupping his cheek, she pressed her lips to his, sipped gently. She was viscerally aware of the strength and the power of him, but she was also stunned to realize he'd given her control. Though his hands had come to rest on her hips, he didn't pull, didn't force, just stood there and allowed her to taste him.

His breath, however, turned uneven as the seconds passed. Charlotte thought about stopping but couldn't find any reason to do so. He smelled so good, tasted so good, his warmth surrounding her and making her feel safe and soft inside. As if her blood was molten honey.

Gabriel moved his head, fitting their lips together more firmly. Charlotte moved with him, her hand sliding from his cheek to the side of his neck. The tendons flexed under her touch, the thickness of his neck making her want to kiss every warm inch. Nipples so tight they almost hurt, she went to press up to him, rub herself against the heated strength of his body in an effort to ease the ache.

And the fear, it licked at her.

Breaking the kiss on a choking wave of frustration before the panic attack could hit, she went down flat on her feet.

Gabriel, his lips wet and his pupils dilated, said, "I like the way you make me feel better."

The cold metal hand around her chest stopped squeezing. Because Gabriel seemed not to mind that he had to go slow. If he wasn't giving up, she definitely wouldn't.

IT TOOK THEM THREE hours to get the work completed. Gabriel received a call partway through that led to a short, clipped conversation, but when she asked if everything was all right, he'd said, "Nothing to worry about."

From the tension in his jaw and shoulders, she knew that wasn't true. She intended to bring it up again when they left the office, but he was back in a good mood, so she let it slide. Still, part of her continued to worry at the question, especially given the number of calls he'd received recently from an older-sounding man with a smoker's voice. Those calls inevitably left him with shadows in his eyes.

"Gabriel?" she said as they drove out of the garage.

"Hmm?" A deep smile. "Mission Bay for a late lunch?"

Utterly undone by that smile and uncertain about their fledgling relationship, she just nodded.

Driving to the bustling group of restaurants and cafés by the sea, the water glittering under the sun and kayakers out in force in their colored craft, they decided to eat at a great Mexican café Charlotte had discovered with Molly.

Gabriel ordered what Charlotte recommended, smiling inwardly every time she touched the bracelet. She didn't seem to realize how she was petting it, and he wasn't going to point it out when her delight gave him such pleasure.

He'd been dreaming of putting that bracelet on her wrist since the day he'd bought it. She'd been so adorably bad-tempered that day, pointing him in the direction of any piece of jewelry she thought would satisfy him. But he'd been determined—and at that time, he hadn't realized the depth of the scars she bore, had expected to be able to give her the bracelet in the next few weeks.

Going slow didn't come naturally to him, but Charlotte was worth it. And that kiss. *Fuck.* He could've stood there forever, letting her taste him with a soft, sexy hunger that had enslaved him. He'd never been a man who enjoyed giving anyone control, but he could definitely get on board with allowing Ms. Baird to have her way with him.

"You have any plans for the rest of the afternoon?" he asked after lunch, the two of them walking back to the car along the pathway that edged the beach, sand gritty under their shoes.

"I was going to finish reading a novel," she said. "My boss makes me work so late that I haven't had time."

"Cute." He tapped her butt, caught the tug of her lips. "Bring the book, read it at my place. You can sit in the sun on the balcony." He liked having her to himself, where he could coax her into kisses and other delicious, naughty acts. A kiss today, nakedness tomorrow—Gabriel liked to think positive and plan ahead.

But she shook her head, her teeth sinking into her lower lip. "Do you want to come to my place instead?"

If she hadn't told him what she had this morning, he might not have understood the depth of both her courage and the trust she was offering him. "Yeah," he said, his chest aching with the force of his emotions.

Smile tremulous, beautiful, she said, "Do you like period dramas?"

He groaned. "Yes, of course. I love them."

She laughed at his obvious lie, and it was sunshine falling like rain over him. "I'm joking. I think they're replaying the South Africa-Wales game later today. We could watch that."

"Sounds good."

24

Charlie-Mouse vs T-Rex:
Round 7489

CHARLOTTE'S HEART WAS IN her throat by the time Gabriel parked his SUV in the garage she didn't really use except for storing a few things. Getting out the instant they were inside, she pressed the remote to lower the garage door, then led the way to the door into the house. This would be the first time since the attack that she'd had anyone but Molly in the house for an extended period. Even when she'd had the plumber come in last year, she'd asked her best friend to hang out at her place.

Her fingers shook on the keys, the metal jangling.

Squeezing her hip, Gabriel said, "Want me to say something dirty and inappropriate to get your mind off it?"

A giggle escaped her. "Hush." But his teasing did help, and she got the key in.

Gabriel hung back while she put in her alarm code, and she fell a little bit deeper for him that he'd done that, that he'd thought about what it meant to her. "Come in," she said and, kicking off her shoes, led him to the living room. Only then did she realize a logistical problem. "My sofa is too small." It'd make it impossible for him to sprawl with his legs up.

"I'll sit on the floor," he said easily. "Put my back against the sofa." Heading over, he grabbed the remote. "Let me check when the game's on."

Leaving him to it, she forced herself to go into her bedroom. It was hard to do that knowing someone else was in the house, but she kept reminding herself that it wasn't *someone*. It was Gabriel. Big, gorgeous Gabriel who hadn't consciously done a single thing to make her afraid. Hanging up her handbag behind the bedroom door, she put her phone into a pocket of her dress.

When she walked out, it was to find him seated on the floor, his arm on the sofa seat as he flicked through the channels. "Game's on in an hour," he said, looking over. "Aw, I'm so disappointed."

Her heart dipped. "What? Why?"

"I was hoping you went to slip into something more comfortable."

Wrinkling her nose at him, she said, "Do you find flannel pants sexy?"

His grin creased his cheeks. "Oh yeah. Especially if that's all you're thinking of wearing."

She blushed, threw a cushion at his head. Catching it, he laughed and stayed in place while she went into the kitchen to see what she had that she could put together for dinner later on. Though they'd spent most of the day together already, she couldn't wait for more.

"Ms. Baird, I'm getting lonely."

Walking back into the living area, she came down to the floor and tucked herself against him. That was how they stayed for a long time, his fingers playing desultorily over her shoulder and his body sexy and warm against her own. He teased more than one long, wet, luscious kiss out of her but didn't push for anything further, and when he said good night and left her, it was after another kiss that had her questioning her sanity in allowing him to leave.

It was the best day of her life.

CHARLOTTE FLOATED INTO THE office the next day, giddily eager to see Gabriel. He was just...

She laughed at herself, knowing she was acting like a love-struck teenager, something she'd never been at that age. It hadn't just been her shyness that had kept her from being carefree—her mom's fight with cancer had forever changed Charlotte's priorities.

Putting on the coffee in the break room since she was the first one in, she hoped her mom could see her now, see her happiness. They'd been so close, Charlotte often doing her homework sitting in her mother's treatment room during Pippa Baird's chemotherapy sessions. Her mother had also encouraged her and Molly's friendship with fierce maternal love.

"I won't let this disease steal your chance to live your life, Charlotte. To make friends and have fun."

Pippa Baird had always had so much love and generosity in her heart, even during the final stages of her disease when she'd been in such terrible pain. Charlotte knew her mother had fought to stay alive that last year only for Charlotte and her father. Pippa had been the center of their small family, the glue that held them all together.

But her father, he'd been so brave too. Three days before her mother passed away, Charlotte had accidentally witnessed a moment of heartbreaking tenderness between her parents. Her father had been holding her fragile mother in his arms, tears wet on his face. Then he'd kissed her on the forehead and said, "It's okay, Pip. You can go. We'll be all right."

Her mother had wrapped her arms around his neck, whispered, "I don't want to go."

Unable to bear any more, Charlotte had left them and walked outside to sit on the old tire swing in the garden, crying where it wouldn't hurt either one of them. Now though, she smiled through the ache of old grief—because she knew her parents would've loved Gabriel. Her dad would've been in raptures at having another rugby fan in the family, never mind the fact that it was the Bishop, and her mom would've loved him for how he treated Charlotte.

Triiiiing!

Almost spilling the coffee she'd been about to pour, Charlotte returned the carafe to the stand and dug out her cell phone. The number was unfamiliar but local. "Hello," she said, having trained herself never to answer a personal call with her name.

"Charlotte?"

Her knees trembled. Stumbling to a seat at the break room table, she tried to suck in air. "Detective Lee." She'd never forget that voice. Detective Mei Lee's was the first one she'd heard after the hours of terror, the other woman's hands gentle and kind as she released Charlotte from her bonds while telling her she was safe and that Richard was in custody.

A patrol officer then, Mei Lee was now an experienced homicide detective who'd made sure Charlotte was kept updated on Richard's parole hearings. "Is it time for another hearing?" she asked, having testified at two so far.

"No." A pause that made the hairs rise on the back of Charlotte's neck. "Charlotte, I'm sorry to tell you this, but Richard is being released next Monday. I'd have given you more of a warning, but there was a screwup and I only just got the report."

Her heart was ice. "How can they let him go? He's got time left to serve."

"According to sentencing guidelines, he's served the maximum time possible under his sentence." Detective Lee's voice was clipped as she added, "You know what I think of the judge who sentenced him."

That judge had given a lot of weight to Richard's otherwise clean record, and "bright future." *One mistake*, the judge had said, *terrible as it was, shouldn't condemn this young man for life. Other mitigating factors are his early guilty plea and his unhidden remorse.*

Both of the latter, Charlotte had thought at the time, had been carefully calculated moves to gain the court's sympathy. It had worked, Richard sentenced at the lowest end of the scale for the level and brutality of his offense.

Charlotte's hand shook, her pulse a sickening rattle. "Do you think I'm safe?" Richard had never sent Charlotte any threatening messages or letters, but she couldn't forget the way he'd looked at her the day he'd been led away by the bailiff. He'd turned, pinned her with the frozen blue of his eyes, and smiled.

That smile had haunted her nightmares for years. It said he was going to come back, and when he did, he'd finish what he'd started. But that had been five years ago. Maybe he'd forgotten her.

"No, you're not safe." Detective Lee's words punched all the air out of her. "A man with Richard Wilson's tendencies doesn't turn over a new leaf. He's still a good-looking psychopath used to manipulating people, and you beat him. He won't have forgotten that."

No, Charlotte agreed silently, he wouldn't have. As with the warning he'd received from the police, he'd have spent his time in jail stewing and obsessing and planning exactly how he'd make her pay for daring to put him, the golden boy, in prison. "Do you have any advice?" she asked, telling herself she was stronger now, could deal with this.

But terror, it had a clawed grip on her throat.

"If you're living alone, stop," the detective said. "You should also get a monitored alarm system if you haven't already. I'll have a patrol car do more regular drive-bys in your neighborhood as a deterrent, but you know he's intelligent and cunning. I'm guessing he won't target you at home, but somewhere else where you feel safe."

Charlotte nodded, forgetting the other woman couldn't see her, her mind beginning to numb over despite her admonitions to the contrary.

"I'll keep an eye on him as far as possible," Mei Lee said, "but he'll be a free man once he's out, and his lawyer's made it clear that any extra police attention will be taken as harassment. If I'm not careful, he could stop me from going within a hundred feet of him."

"Charlotte?"

Looking up at Gabriel's voice, Charlotte tried to say something, but her voice stuck in her throat as everything hit her in an avalanche. *Richard was going free and there was a very high chance he would come after her. This time he wouldn't leave her alive to testify.*

Expression dark, Gabriel grabbed the phone. "Who is this?"

He crouched down beside her as he listened, his hand on her icy one and his eyes intense. "Gabriel Bishop." Another pause after he identified himself. "Yes." This pause was longer. "I'll take care of it." An alert, focused silence, then, "You'll notify us if your patrol guys pick up anything?" Ten seconds, maybe twenty, Charlotte couldn't quite tell, her mind still not functioning right, before he said, "Yes. No, I'll make sure of it."

Charlotte stared at Gabriel as he hung up after giving Detective Lee his own contact numbers. "Can I have my phone?" It seemed very important that she have it, that it be in her hand.

PLACING THE PHONE ON Charlotte's palm, Gabriel curled her fingers over it.

"Thank you." She held it like a talisman that could ward off evil. "Did Detective Lee tell you?"

"Yes." Gabriel stood. "Come on. We're going for a walk."

"You can't. You have the Henderson conference call in"— she glanced at her watch—"fifteen minutes."

"It'll keep." His phone already in hand, he made a quick call and postponed the meeting. "Charlotte." Gabriel frowned when she didn't respond. Changing tack, he hardened his tone. "*Ms. Baird.*"

A stiffening of her shoulders, her lashes flicking up. "I'm fine. I don't need to go for a walk."

"*I* need to go for a walk." He raised an eyebrow when she still didn't budge. "There are going to be more people heading to the break room very soon."

That seemed to get through. Slipping her phone into a pocket of the tailored black trench coat that she still wore over an oat-colored linen shift, she came with him. He wanted to take her hand, but a number of other staff members had arrived on the floor and he knew the action would make Charlotte even more uncomfortable when she was already shaken. The woman who'd kissed him good-bye with a smile, who'd cuddled so sweetly next to him for hours, had been buried under shock.

Gabriel wasn't about to allow that to stand.

Taking the elevator to the ground floor, he led her out and toward the waterfront. The sidewalk was active with those who worked in the city, but not yet thronged with shoppers. Except for the coffee shops and bakeries, the stores wouldn't open till nine, so it was easy enough to stride down toward the water.

"Gabriel, did you mean sprint when you said walk?"

He looked down when he heard the acerbic question and realized he'd been taking swift, long strides in his anger. Charlotte was a little breathless but the spark, it was back in her eyes, so this was one mistake for which he wasn't sorry. "Did you get to drink your coffee?" he asked, the scent of roasting beans reaching him from a café a couple of doors down.

"No, but I don't want any."

He bought her a frothy thing with chocolate on top anyway, having seen her with something similar when she'd come back from her lunches with Molly a couple of times.

Folding her arms, she said, "Are you planning to drink one from each hand?"

"Don't be a bad-tempered cat," he said, holding out her coffee. "I even asked them to put extra chocolate on top."

Her eyebrows drew together, arms remaining mutinously folded.

"Or I'll drop it in that trash bin."

"Oh, give it to me."

Watching her sip at the frothy concoction, he didn't make the mistake of thinking she was back to her usual self. The shock had been severe, the bruises deep. But the fact she'd been able to snap at him was a good sign that his Ms. Baird was in there. Maybe a little dented, but whole.

They didn't talk as they crossed the street at the lights.

Heading past the people pouring out of the train station, they went across the street that ran along the waterfront and turned left, toward the ferry building. That section was busy with commuters. He continued to stroll onward, Charlotte a quiet presence at his side. Quiet, but potent. He was aware of her every move, her every breath.

Reaching the Viaduct, they turned right and walked through Wynyard Quarter until they came to the wide pedestrian bridge that covered the channel out of the marina to their left, the bridge's white arches sharp and stylized.

"I like watching the bridge open up to let the tall-masted yachts through," Charlotte said, leaning with her forearms braced on the railing as they faced the sea rather than the marina.

He pointed out a yacht on the water. "Someone's taking the day off work."

"I hope it stays sunny for them." Charlotte fiddled with her coffee cup. "I'm sorry for how I reacted in the break room." A shuddering exhale. "I'd managed to convince myself that Richard was out of my life forever." If she'd ever permitted herself to think about it, she'd known this day would come, but the only way she'd been able to get past the fear enough to have any kind of a life was to pretend it wouldn't.

"Hell, Charlotte, you're dealing with this better than anyone has a right to expect." His arm brushed against hers, his suit jacket a dark gray. "But you have to know I won't let anyone hurt you."

She felt her lower lip tremble. Catching it between her teeth, she shook her head. "I can't do that, Gabriel. I can't let you take over, not after I put so much effort into becoming independent."

"Charlotte—"

"Do you know why Molly moved out after she qualified and got a full-time job at the library?" She didn't wait for him to answer. "Not because she wanted to, but because we both knew I was becoming too dependent on her presence." It had gotten to the point where she couldn't relax until Molly was in the house. "The first night I spent on my own after she moved out was terrifying… and liberating."

Jaw set, Gabriel said, "I don't want to take that away from you, but we have to be smart about this—you need to take measures to protect yourself until we're certain this bastard is no longer a threat. The best protection you can have is to move in with me."

25

SHALLOW GRAVES & PSYCHOPATHS
& A PISSED-OFF T-REX

CHARLOTTE ALMOST DROPPED HER near-empty takeout cup. "What?"

"I live in a secure building. The apartment's big enough that you won't have to see me if you don't want to."

As if that was the problem. "You're not listening to me." Her fingers clenched on the takeout cup, the ensuing dent broadcast by a crackle of sound. "I can't go backward. I reclaimed my life after Richard. I didn't give up the town house I loved—I'm not going to do that now, either."

She battled the emotions that tried to rise up, overwhelm her. "Do you know how hard it was? At first, I couldn't even walk into the kitchen because all I'd see was him at the stove, at the table. Molly and I found the money to replace the table, the bed, the sofa, the carpet, anything else he might've touched, and my bedroom cupboard doesn't have any doors, but I *stayed*. I made it my home again."

Gabriel released a harsh breath. "I hope he does turn up. I'd enjoy the chance to—"

"No, don't become him. *Don't*." Voice trembling from the

force of her emotions, she put her hand on his forearm, squeezed the taut muscle. "I couldn't bear it if protecting me forced you to become like him."

"Jesus, Charlotte, it wouldn't be like that." He shoved his other hand through his hair. "I protect what's mine. Always have, always will."

The words rocked her, cut through the frustration to touch something newer, far more vulnerable. Sucking in a draft of the salt-laced air, she shook her head. "I know you, Gabriel. You're so angry, have been since I told you."

His muscles grew even more tense under her touch. "Of course I'm angry. He hurt you."

"But if you dwell on it," she whispered and laid her heart on the line, "the rage will swallow you up, and then he'll have taken you from me too."

He didn't say anything for several minutes, his jaw working and his eyes on the water that had turned choppy with the rising wind. "For you," he said at last, "I'll try not to focus on the bastard." He put one arm around her shoulders to draw her in against him, making sure not to hold too tight. "But Charlotte, I'm not a good guy when the people who matter to me are threatened. If he comes near you, all bets are off. I will crush him and bury his fucking body where no one will ever find him."

Charlotte shuddered, realizing she'd need to watch him. Because Gabriel was intensely protective, intensely determined. He was also ruthless and very, very smart. She had to make sure he didn't concentrate those instincts on eliminating Richard for good in a preemptive strike, but on her.

"If you won't move in with me," he said while she was still working through her thoughts, "I'll move in with you. Or I'll hire security for you. Whatever you want. But you have to let me protect you."

Charlotte's eyes were on the water, but her attention was firmly on the man who held her, his rage a heartbeat away from exploding and his voice raw. He'd just given her a roadmap of how she could get him to focus on her, keeping him from falling into an abyss of hate and retribution.

Petting his chest with one hand, his body heat searing through the fine cotton of his shirt, she said, "I need a few minutes, okay?"

When he didn't move, she touched her fingers to his jaw. "Gabriel."

Steely eyes locked with her own. "Fifteen minutes. Then I'm coming to find you." His hand lifted as if he would shove it into her hair, haul her in for a kiss, but he curled it into a fist before dropping it to his side. "Fifteen minutes. Not a second longer."

Heart heavy at the sign he was leashing his nature for her, she watched him walk away. Gabriel was a physical man; had she not been so screwed up, she knew full well they'd be in bed right now. She'd have eased his rage with her body, and he'd have focused all his primal instincts on her pleasure.

But she *was* screwed up. And fuck it, she'd had enough. She wanted him to be able to go caveman on her if he needed it, wanted to be able to haul him to bed herself if he was being stubborn and uncommunicative, as with those phone calls. Her instincts told her that getting physical with Gabriel would fundamentally alter things between them in a good way. The man was heavily tactile, would speak with his body if she let him.

Turning back to the water only when he was no longer in

sight, a knot of angry frustration in her gut, she took out her phone and called Molly. "Hey," she said when her best friend answered sounding a little flustered. "Was Fox doing naughty things to you?"

A guilty laugh. "Maybe, but he has to go meet Noah now anyway, so I'm shoving him out th—"

"Hey, Charlie," said the distinctive, gritty voice of Schoolboy Choir's lead singer. "Miss Molly will be a minute."

"Fox!" came Molly's faint voice. "Give me the phone."

The sound cut off, as if someone had put a hand over the speaker.

Smiling at the image of a kiss-rumpled Molly trying to deny a man against whom she had no resistance, Charlotte waited until her friend came back on the line. "Sorry about that," Molly said, breathless again. "He's in a mood today."

"I can guess exactly what kind of mood he's in, Miss Molly."

"Oh, shut up." Molly laughed. "Soooo? How was your second date with T-Rex?"

"Wonderful." The memory of the hours she'd spent with him yesterday made her want to sigh and go all gooey-eyed.

"Then why do you sound like that?"

"Do you have X-ray vision? How can you know something's wrong across a phone line?"

"Because I know you. What is it?"

Charlotte told Molly about Richard's forthcoming release, rubbing at her forehead with her fingers. "I know I need to take my security situation seriously, but I hate feeling like Richard's backed me into a corner."

"You could look at it another way," Molly said after a small pause.

Eyes on a catamaran coming in to dock on this side of the marina, Charlotte said, "What other way?"

"Last time, Dick was in control, manipulating and scheming." Her best friend's anger was a scalpel. "This time, you're the one in charge. You make the decisions."

Charlotte hadn't considered it from that point of view. "I'm still reacting to him."

"So don't," Molly replied. "Decide what *you* want. Not what will make Gabriel happy or what will roadblock that pathetic monster. What will make you feel like you're handling the situation?"

"The thing is, Molly, I *want* to make Gabriel happy." Seeing him laugh, smile, it lit up her world. "I can't bear for him to be so torn up."

"That's a choice too, you know." A smile in Molly's voice. "And it's one I understand—I like making Fox happy too. Same way I like doing things to make you happy. There's nothing wrong with caring for the people we love; the problem only comes when it's one person giving all the time. When it goes both ways, you have love."

Charlotte flushed and pushed away from the railing to start the walk back to the office. Dropping her sorely abused takeout cup in a trash can along the way, she said, "I've just started dating him."

"Charlie, you two have been doing the tango for months," her friend responded dryly. "I mean, the foreplay must be driving him nuts."

"You have a one-track mind."

"I see you're following that track, so what does that say about your own mind, huh?"

Charlotte grinned, starting to see the glimmer of a path through this. "Thanks, Moll. I'm going to think about things, act rather than react." Light sparked off her bracelet as she hung up.

Gabriel had finally shown her how to unlock the complicated clasp last night, after she agreed to keep the bracelet. She'd decided that if it didn't work out between them, if her problems made that impossible... or if he lost his desire for her, she'd simply ensure it made its way back to him.

That it hurt to even think about no longer being with him told her exactly how badly she'd already fallen.

GABRIEL WAS IN NO mood to find Brian Bishop waiting for him at the Saxon & Archer building. He'd taken the long route back to walk off his fury, but it returned the instant he walked into the lobby and saw the man who was nominally his parent. Brian looked drawn out and pale, but Gabriel also saw the yellowed teeth, the nicotine-stained fingernails, and the crooked nose from when a creditor had beat him up.

His "father" had always chosen his own poisons.

"What do you want?" he snapped after walking Brian back out to the sidewalk.

Eyes wet, the man he'd once called Dad tried to reach out to touch his face. Gabriel backed away from it. "If it's money," he said, his voice cold, "give me your account number and I'll have it transferred." Better he pay Brian off than have the man shake down Gabriel's mother by playing on her sympathies.

"No, son." The quavery voice of a man much older. "I just wanted to see my boy."

"I haven't been a boy since I was six years old." Since the day he'd had his illusions about Brian permanently shattered. Brian's abandonment a year later had only put the final seal on Gabriel's view of his father.

The other man huddled into his navy blue windbreaker. "Facing mortality makes a man look back on his life. Mine is full of mistakes—I don't expect you to forgive me, but please don't cut me out of your life."

The plea hit a stone wall. "You made that choice." Gabriel had watched his younger brother wait for their father to come home, face pressed to the window. Sailor had been adamant Brian would come back for them, his childish pain when that proved a false hope another stone in the wall. "You threw away your family—you can't just come back and pick us up again."

"Gabriel, son, I—"

Gabriel sliced out a hand. "Enough. Get out and don't come back to my workplace. I'll send you the money."

"I don't want your money." Brian's shoulders slumped. "If you ever decide you can forgive me, I'm at the Hope Hospice."

Gabriel said nothing and the man he barely knew and no longer wanted to know finally walked away.

"Gabriel."

He turned at the sound of Charlotte's voice, realized she must've taken the shortest route back. "Your talk with Molly go well?" he asked, turning his back on Brian Bishop's retreating figure.

"How did you—" A shake of her head, her eyes looking past him. "It did, but we can talk about it inside. Who was that man?"

CHARLOTTE WAS ALMOST EXPECTING Gabriel's shrug. "Someone I knew in another life." The words were cold enough to frost her glasses.

"He calls you, doesn't he?"

"It's nothing, Charlotte." His tone told her to drop it.

Her eyes narrowed. "Fine."

Glaring at her, he said, "That tone doesn't say fine. It says you're pissed."

"I've just realized this relationship apparently only goes one way," she said, her conversation with Molly fresh in her mind. "I'm to be the needy, broken one who takes, but I'm not allowed to give."

"Fuck." A growl of sound. "I don't have time for this."

"Fine," Charlotte said again, fully aware it'd prick his temper.

Gabriel's eyes flashed. "You want to know who that was? Brian Bishop. My fucking *father*. The man who left when I was seven, clearing out every cent he and my mom had in the joint account. He took the rent money, the grocery money, everything." The growl was gone, ice filming over the gray. "Now he's sick and he thinks I should give a fuck."

Charlotte hadn't been expecting this cold blast, but she'd seen Gabriel furious before. "You're still so angry at him," she said, hesitant but able to feel the pain he refused to acknowledge existed inside him. "Maybe you should talk to him, not for him but for yourself."

"I don't need or want advice on my fuckup of a father from you." He glanced at his watch after a statement that quickly, efficiently shut her down. The same way she'd seen him shut down business opponents in a negotiation. "We have to get back up to the office."

Charlotte just nodded, feeling her heart crack. It wasn't the words or the way he'd spoken them in that frigid tone. It was the fact she'd believed she was learning to deal with Gabriel on an equal basis when it came to their relationship. Clearly, that was a self-deluding lie. He'd been allowing her to handle him.

Now he'd drawn a line in the sand beyond which she was not permitted to step.

26

CUPCAKES AND KISSES

AN HOUR LATER AND Gabriel was calm enough to know he'd fucked up. Badly. He'd been so angry at Brian that he'd allowed it to spill over onto Charlotte. The fact he'd done it today of all days, when she needed him to be her rock, it made him an asshole of epic proportions.

"Goddammit." Throwing down his pen, he got up and went to find her. She wasn't at her desk or in the break room, but since her computer screen was on and showing a partial itinerary for a business trip he was taking later this month, she had to be nearby.

"Gabriel." His chief operations officer waved him into his office when Gabriel went back out into the corridor to hunt Charlotte down. "You have ten minutes to talk over something?"

"Yeah." He saw Charlotte the second he left the COO's office. She was standing farther down the corridor with another personal assistant, the two of them concentrating on a tablet. From the frowns on their faces, he thought they were trying to figure something out.

Charlotte looked okay, but when she glanced toward him, that spark he loved was missing from her eyes. Turning toward her fellow PA as the other woman made a comment, she smiled… and it wasn't his Ms. Baird's smile, rather a ghost of it.

He'd done that.

CHARLOTTE RETURNED TO HER desk after helping the CFO's personal assistant with an online meeting application, and found a fancy vanilla cupcake on her desk, complete with raspberry frosting and silver sprinkles. She stared at it. Gabriel had done this before, apologized to her with decadent treats, but it had always just been when he'd infuriated her. He'd never before hurt her.

"Charlotte."

Swiveling in her chair, she found him in the doorway to his office. He looked so ragged that her heart hurt. "Yes?" she said; she cared too much for him to push him away when he was in pain.

"I'm sorry." Shoving his hands into his pockets, he blew out a breath. "I *am* angry at Brian and it pisses me off that I can't let it go."

Charlotte rose from her desk to go to him and they both stepped into his office, shutting the door behind them. "For better or worse," she said gently, "he's your blood. It's an indelible connection."

Gabriel walked to the windows behind his desk, his gaze on the city and on the water beyond. "I don't want it to be— he has no claim on me." Shaking his head, he folded his arms. "I can't talk about this anymore, especially when I'm worried about you."

It wasn't the cold shutdown of before, simply a request for space. Charlotte had no problem with giving him that—emotional wounds this deep and complex didn't get solved in a single conversation. What continued to worry her was what would've happened if he hadn't made the first move? Would she have had the courage to push, to demand he trust her with his secrets?

"What did you decide?" Gabriel said, coming to stand in front of her, his hands on his hips.

Charlotte knew the imbalance between her and Gabriel remained a dangerous question mark over their relationship, but they had to solve this issue first. "I'm not going to let Richard turn me into a scared mouse hiding in its hole."

Gabriel didn't break the eye contact.

Wanting to touch him but not sure he'd accept it in his current dark mood, she carried on. "I'm also not going to be stupid."

"I'll organize security."

"No." When he scowled, she scowled back. "Let me finish."

Folding his arms again, he stood there, an impenetrable wall.

"You're right—your building is secure. If I move into it, it'll take a lot of the stress out of the situation." And it'd keep Gabriel's attention on her, not on thinking up ways to permanently dispose of Richard.

Gabriel unfolded his arms, his features easing. "I'm glad you've seen sense."

"I'm trying to be rational," she said, folding her own arms. "When you say things like that, it makes me want to disagree with you just to teach you a lesson."

"It's a good thing you're more evolved than I am." The faint hint of a smile.

"*Gabriel.*" She battled the urge to stamp her foot. "I did a property search on your building. There's a small apartment on a lower floor that's available as a sublet at a price I can afford. I'm going to apply for it." Not running, but being smart about her safety. "I can catch the shuttle in to work, and if anything happens, you'll be nearby."

Gabriel's scowl had become darker with every word she spoke. "I own an enormous two-level penthouse, and you want to stay in a dinky downstairs place?"

"I have to do this on my terms." She could see him gritting his teeth. Chancing a touch, she put her hand on his chest. "Try to understand."

"I'll go with you when you look at the apartment," he said at last, the words ground out. "If there's anything unsafe about it, you don't stay there. Agreed?"

Charlotte nodded. "Agreed."

"I need to kiss you."

Her heart slammed against her ribs. Pulse a roar in her ears, she rose on tiptoe. When Gabriel cupped the side of her face, it felt so tender and protective that she shivered. He ran his thumb over her cheekbone, lowered his head to hers, and pressed his lips to her own. Despite the violent tension in his body, he kept the kiss gentle, licking his tongue lightly over her lips.

She shivered again, parted her lips, and he slipped inside. A thousand butterflies in her stomach, thighs clenching, she stroked up to close her hand over the warmth of his nape. He was so big everywhere, his neck thick, but it was all perfectly in proportion. Her touch made him wrap his arm around her waist, hold her close as he deepened the kiss, his tongue licking against hers until she whimpered and licked back.

He groaned, sliding one hand up her spine to close over her own nape.

Claustrophobia swamped her in a black wave.

GABRIEL WAS SINKING INTO the sweet sexiness of Charlotte's kiss when he felt her body go stiff, the kiss no longer reciprocal. It took him a split second to release her, but it was too long. Her pupils were dilated, her skin pale, her breath so shallow it scared him.

It was almost as if she wasn't there anymore.

"Charlotte, *Charlotte.*" He wanted to shake her out of it, but wasn't sure she could handle any further contact.

Stiff, her eyes staring out at nothing, Charlotte didn't react.

"*Ms. Baird.*"

A blink… and she focused on him. Her face seemed to go even paler. Swaying on her feet, she reached out as if for a wall. Gabriel took a risk and grabbed her hand before she could unbalance. To his relief, she didn't jerk away, didn't look at him with that terrible blank stare again. "Gabriel?"

"Shh, I have you." Leading her to the black leather of his chair, he sat her down. "Breathe, sweetheart."

Charlotte obeyed the order. It was too fast, too erratic, but it was better than before.

Crouching down in front of her, Gabriel braced one palm against his desk, his other one on her knee. "That's it," he coaxed. "Deeper, slower."

It took at least five minutes before her breathing returned to anything close to normal, and his heart was in his throat the entire time, his body bunched as if to attack a predator. Except this threat was in Charlotte's mind, where he couldn't reach. He hated that he couldn't protect her from her nightmares. "There," he said, tempering his voice with sheer strength of will. "That's better."

Eyes huge and lower lip quivering, she stared at him. "I'm sorry."

"Hey." He squeezed her knee, being as gentle as he was capable of being. "Did I ask for an apology?"

NO, CHARLOTTE THOUGHT, HE hadn't. He was too good a man to make her feel bad about going to pieces, but God, he had to be sick of it. "I thought I was getting better," she whispered, the tiny seedling of hope that had grown inside her curling up and dying. "After yesterday. I thought I was getting better."

"Charlotte, I was in your house most of the damn day yesterday." Gabriel's voice was the one he used in negotiations when he wasn't about to budge from his viewpoint. "You really want to tell me that was nothing? If you do, I'll call you a bald-faced liar."

She swallowed and lifted trembling fingers to his hair, tears rolling down her face. "Why are you doing this?"

"You need to ask me that?" A growl of sound. "You haven't figured out by now that I think you're fucking amazing? You have a brain that won't quit, a smile that lights up my soul, and a body I want to do dirty things to and with three ways to Sunday."

A wet laugh broke through her tears. "You'll probably have to wait till you're eighty to do most of them at the rate I'm going." Charlotte was terrified her words weren't a joke but a prediction.

"We'll be the most energetic couple in the old people's home."

She started to cry in earnest, the sobs wracking her frame as the entire morning came down on her like a brick wall.

"Baby, come here." Gabriel's voice was raw. "Let me hold you."

Wanting nothing more, she bent forward and wrapped her arms around his neck. He stroked her back, his hand a heavy, comforting weight. Somehow, she didn't know how, she ended up on the floor too, on his lap, Gabriel's back braced against the desk as he held her and her glasses pulled off and set aside. The tears kept coming, as if she'd never cried before, years of pain and grief and anger crashing through her in a violent storm surge that made her bones ache and her skin burn.

It felt as if it would never stop, but at some stage it did. Lying exhausted and limp against him until her mind could form words again, she patted the wetness on his shirt. "This is the second time I've cried all over you."

"Since it makes you snuggle up to me, I'm fine with it."

She felt her lips curve and it was a surprise, but she held on to the quiet warmth inside her. If she'd come out of the storm unbroken, she wasn't about to turn her back on that gift. "I want to wash my face." But if she stepped out into the corridor on her way to the facilities, the other staff members would realize immediately that she'd been crying.

"Reach over to the drawer on your right. I'm pretty sure I left a bottle of water in there."

Charlotte managed to open the drawer after Gabriel leaned forward a fraction. The unopened bottle was sitting up front. Taking it out, she pushed the drawer shut and Gabriel braced his back against the desk again.

"My box of tissues is outside," she said, embarrassed about her face now. She'd put on mascara today in her continued quest to master makeup, and it had to be running.

Gabriel picked her up and put her in his executive chair. "Wait here." Exiting the office, he returned a few seconds later with the tissue box and her handbag and once more shut the door. "Weightlifting," he said as he passed the items over. "That's clearly your secret hobby."

"Very funny." Grabbing several tissues from the box, Charlotte dampened them using the water from the bottle. For now, she just wiped her cheeks clean blind. The tissues became smudged with the dark brown mascara she'd used to make her lashes stand out a little more. "My handbag isn't that heavy."

"Only half your body weight," he said dryly. "There were three notes on your desk from people who want to see me."

"Did they knock on the door?" she asked, relieved they wouldn't have heard her sobs regardless. Gabriel's office had excellent soundproofing—she never overheard any of his conversations when he had the door shut, no matter how heated.

Now he snorted. "They're scared of me, Charlotte. You're the T-Rex tamer."

She narrowed her eyes at him. "I'm sure they thought you were busy."

"Yeah." He pulled a sticky note out of his pocket. "Then why does this one say, 'Hi Charlotte—wanted to see Bishop. Can you give me a call when it's okay? I didn't want to make him mad by interrupting.'"

Dropping that one on the desk, he took out another. "'Charlotte, can you call me when the Beast is in a good mood?'" Gabriel raised an eyebrow. "That's a new one."

Charlotte scowled. "Those notes weren't for you."

"Don't worry, Ms. Baird. I won't fire the chickens. They happen to be good at their jobs." He put the final note atop the others without reading it aloud.

Feeling a little more human, Charlotte found her compact and checked her face. Her eyes weren't as badly swollen as she'd feared, and the damage wouldn't be obvious behind her glasses if she put on some makeup to replace what she'd cried off. She was no expert even after the past months of cautious experimentation, but she could swipe on a lick of mascara and powder her face, dab on a touch of lip color.

It felt incredibly intimate to do it in front of Gabriel, especially when he sat down in the guest chair on the other side of the desk and placed his feet on the scarred wood of the desk, legs crossed at the ankles and hands laced behind his head as he leaned back. "I want to watch you do that while you're naked."

Her cheeks went hot.

"On one of those pretty little benches women have in front of their vanities. Do you have one?"

"No." She'd always wanted a Victorian-style vanity, but the antiques were too expensive and the reproductions she'd found not quite right.

"Maybe I'll buy you one for your birthday. You can thank me by doing that thing with your mascara while bare to the skin."

He was flustering her, but Charlotte was used to fencing with him on this level. It made her happy that her meltdown hadn't stopped him. Not only that, she found she, too, was back on stable ground, perhaps even more so than before the tears. As if a valve that had been twisted and twisted and twisted had suddenly given way and in so doing, washed everything clean.

"You're not buying me anything for another twenty years." Raising her hand on that stern statement, she pointed to the bracelet that glittered on one wrist.

Gabriel's response was a deeply possessive smile. "Looks perfect on you, Ms. Baird."

Making a face at him for totally avoiding the point, she finished powdering her face. It was what she should've done first, but she'd felt so naked and ravaged that she'd started with mascara. She'd have to repeat the mascara now, after getting powder on her lashes.

Slicking on some lipstick, she redid the mascara and put her glasses back on. Gabriel came into crisp focus. "Will I do?" she asked the man who looked at her as if he wanted to take a greedy bite.

"Come sit on my lap."

"Gabriel."

Putting his feet on the floor, he crooked a finger.

27

GABRIEL LEADS CHARLOTTE INTO WICKEDNESS AND SIN

"WE'RE IN THE OFFICE," she said, even as she came around the desk to take a seat on those strong thighs. "We're supposed to be professional at work."

Arms loosely around her, Gabriel leaned forward to press his lips to her shoulder. "We're having a coffee break."

"We already had that this morning."

Another kiss over the linen of her shift. "I'm the boss. I say we deserve a second coffee break after all those late nights and weekends." The third kiss brushed over her skin.

Toes curling, she felt her bones start to dissolve.

Then he pressed a kiss to her throat and she turned boneless. No one had ever kissed her throat, and it was so incredibly arousing that she leaned into him in a silent request for more. He chuckled, his breath hot, and gave her what she wanted; his kiss was wet and suckling, made her whimper. "So my Ms. Baird has a hot button on this sweet neck."

Chest rising and falling in jerky breaths, Charlotte stayed shamelessly close. Gabriel continued to feed her sensual hunger, playing his fingers over her hip at the same time. Each kiss seemed to tug on her nipples, stroke her between her thighs. Charlotte found her hand was on the back of Gabriel's neck again, her throat arched for him.

Stroking his own hand over the curve of her waist and to her hip, he nuzzled the spot just below her ear. Charlotte moaned, her panties damp.

"I like that sound." It was a deep rumble against her. "Makes my cock so fucking hard."

Another moan slipped out of her throat, her nails digging into his nape. "Gabriel," she said, the single word breathy.

He kissed his way down her throat in response, each kiss accompanied by a wet little suck. By the time he worked his way back up to that spot under her ear, her panties were so wet they were sticking to her flesh, her breath coming hard and fast, her chest tight with anticipation. He paused, hot breath against her skin. "Touch yourself for me, Ms. Baird."

She bit down on her lower lip, but the moan escaped anyway. The combination of his words and the fact he'd used her professional name, it had her heart thumping even harder, her skin so hot it felt as if she'd catch on fire. "I can't."

"Yes, you can." A kiss just below that delicious spot she needed him to kiss. "I want you to come on my lap, want to watch you take your pleasure."

Lungs aching, she clenched her hand on his nape.

Another wet kiss that ratcheted up her arousal without easing it. "Put your hand under your dress."

Charlotte's heart was racing a hundred miles an hour, her mind filled with Gabriel, his scent—hot, masculine, arousing—in her every breath. And his voice, that deep voice telling her to do such a carnal thing. She didn't know where she found the courage; maybe in the protection of his arms, maybe in the fact she was so close to a pleasure that promised to be bone-searing when she'd been a wreck minutes ago.

She slid her free hand below the hem of her dress.

"Oh fuck." Gabriel's body shuddered. "Higher, sweetheart." Each word was accompanied by a kiss to her neck.

Charlotte had tried this before Gabriel came into her life, but it had never worked, as if there was a toxic block inside her made of fear and the memories of Richard's denigrating words. Then had come *those* dreams and erotic fantasies. Today, as she inched her hand up her thigh, it felt as if her entire body was alive with arousal, her nerve endings sizzling just below the surface. Breasts rising and falling in an erratic rhythm, she moaned at the feel of Gabriel sucking on her neck as he made his way back up to that spot that felt so good.

Then he was there, his tongue swirling a delicate circle against her skin just as her fingers brushed the plump bud of her clitoris through the lace of her panties. Her clit felt as if it had swollen to three times its usual size, the space between her thighs humid and hot.

"Nudge aside your panties and tug on your clit," Gabriel ordered as he continued to suck and kiss her throat. "Imagine it's my fingers doing that to you. Be rough."

Skin tight and breasts aching, she pushed aside the gusset of her panties.

"Are you wet?"

"Yes," she whispered, her fingers finding the slippery plumpness of her clit.

"Tug," he said, his voice harsh. "Harder than you usually would."

Because she could deny him nothing, she did exactly as he'd ordered. Her thighs pressed together instinctively, her lower body clenching in convulsive shivers as her eyes squeezed shut.

The pleasure was deep, sinful, sublime.

CHEST HEAVING, CHARLOTTE STARED at Gabriel after the last ripples passed through her body.

He'd stopped kissing her, was just watching with glittering eyes, a red flush brushing his cheekbones. "You are so sexy, Ms. Baird."

Blushing, she slipped her hand out from under her dress. She couldn't believe she'd done that, but even more, she couldn't believe she'd orgasmed from nothing more than his kisses and a single purposeful touch. And words. Gabriel's words. That, she thought, was the most important thing.

It had been Gabriel with her.

Closing his fingers around the wrist of the hand she'd taken from between her legs, he tugged it closer, drew in a long breath. "I can smell you, and it makes me want to lick you until you come on my tongue." Molten silver eyes met her own. "Let me."

Her thighs clamped together again, pleasure splintering her body. "I don't think I can take it today," she said when she could speak again.

He brushed the back of his hand over her breasts. "Next time."

Nipples hard and pebbled, she nodded. "Yes." Then she leaned forward and kissed him. Richard wasn't going to steal Gabriel from her. *No way in hell.*

AFTER CHARLOTTE LEFT HIS office to head to the bathroom, a hot-pink blush coloring her cheeks, Gabriel shut the door and stood with his back to it. Then he went through a step-by-step mental replay of the last professional game he'd ever played. He'd been injured two minutes before the final whistle, right after the best fucking try of his career, so he had plenty of mental footage.

Just as well.

It took the entire game to get his hard-on under control. But the agony was worth it. He'd never seen anything as hot as Charlotte coming so sweetly in his lap. And he most definitely *could not* think about that again while he was at the office.

Opening the door to see that Charlotte had returned to her desk, he smiled. "What's on the schedule, Ms. Baird?"

Her nape flushed before she turned slightly in her chair to narrow her eyes at him. He felt his smile deepen.

"Can you fit in a meeting with Geoff before your conference call?" she asked, her lips tugging up at the corners. "He says he only needs ten minutes."

"Send him in."

The ensuing workday was a merciless one. He broke for only a half hour, and that was to spend time on the phone with the principal of the school where he volunteered as the coach for the school's top rugby team—their first XV. One of his players had been caught with weed and the principal wanted to know if Gabriel would back him on a suspension from play as well as school.

"Yes," Gabriel said without hesitation. "Team's got a strict no-drugs policy." He then tore a strip off the player himself; the kid was an amazing fullback, might go all the way, but not if he fucked up.

He hung up after getting a genuinely contrite, "I'm sorry, Coach. I messed up." The boy was now aware that as a result of his error, his team might well lose its upcoming match against their greatest rivals; that knowledge would work more effectively as a deterrent than anything else.

Other than that interruption, the day involved challenge after challenge—exactly what Gabriel liked in business. Charlotte called in lunch that they both ate at their desks, then kept going. He would've pushed on if she hadn't booked a seven-o'clock appointment to view the sublet. Since there was no way he was about to let her do that alone, they headed out.

His building wasn't far from the office, and with rush hour having eased, it took them under ten minutes to make it there. Bringing the SUV to a stop in his parking space in the underground garage, he stepped out. Charlotte was already opening her door by the time he came around.

Putting his hands on her waist, he lifted her out. "Do you realize we haven't said a single word to each other since we got in the elevator at work?"

Wrinkles formed between her eyebrows. "No, that's wrong... isn't it?" She tilted her head a little to the side. "It didn't feel like it."

"No, it didn't." He cupped her face, brushed back a strand of hair. "Ready to see the apartment?"

Charlotte's hand landed on his shirt. "What happened to your tie?" A scowl. "Wait, let me grab your jacket from the back."

Laughing, he drew her to the elevators. "Trust me. The owner's not going to care if I'm not professionally dressed." Not when Gabriel owned over a quarter of the apartments in the building. Unfortunately, that didn't include the sublet.

"At least roll down your sleeves."

"You're adorable when you scowl like that."

Expression darkening as they entered the elevator, she reached up and fixed his collar, then smoothed her hands down his chest in a petting, possessive move that made him want to stretch out and ask her to do it all over his body. When she said, "Bend down," he did so without complaining.

Slender fingers brushing through his hair. "There," she said, just as the elevator doors opened on the fourth floor.

He followed her out, delighted with her. He wasn't, however, taking anything for granted; after today's panic attack, he knew Charlotte herself didn't know when she might react negatively to something he said or did. The seeds of terror were hidden within her, could burst open at any time. But then he thought about how she'd quivered big-eyed at him during their first-ever dinner.

That mouse wouldn't have sat on his lap, wouldn't have ordered him to bend down so she could fix his hair, wouldn't have slipped her hand into his and curled her fingers over his palm.

Gabriel could be patient when the rewards were so great.

"Here, this one." Stopping in front of a door in the middle of the corridor, Charlotte knocked.

It opened seconds later, the middle-aged woman inside inviting them in. Turned out the apartment belonged to her daughter. "She got a temporary transfer to Dubai," the woman told them with a beaming smile. "The rules say she can do a sublet, so she might as well. It's only for six months though."

"That's perfect," Charlotte said, because no matter what, she wasn't about to live her life looking over her shoulder. The best-case scenario was that Richard had forgotten her. If he hadn't, then she'd work with Gabriel and the police to put him back in jail, this time for so long that he'd be an old man when he came back out.

"Gabriel?" she said, glancing around to see that he'd prowled to the windows. "What do you think?"

The owner's mother patted her hand. "I'll go make some coffee while you and your handsome husband discuss it."

"Yes," Gabriel said with a glint in his eye. "Come here, wife."

Flutters in her abdomen at his teasing, she waited until their host had left before saying, "So?"

"Pros—it's not ground level, and fourth floor is high enough that no one's going to be climbing up. Fire stairs are internal. Windows don't open and the door has solid locks."

"I'd get them changed," Charlotte said, knowing she'd feel better that way. "I'm sure the owner wouldn't mind if I get the same kind or a more secure model." Since Gabriel still looked grim, she said, "Cons?"

"It's not my apartment."

"*Gabriel.*"

Brows drawing heavily together, he folded his arms. "Why are you wasting your money? I'm offering you free room and board and as much sex as you can handle."

"Hush!" She looked over her shoulder, but their host had the radio on in the kitchen nook and wasn't paying them any attention. "I'm taking the apartment."

"You'll ride to work and back with me."

"We can negotiate that." Charlotte folded her own arms. "Since I don't intend to turn into a workaholic who comes home at eleven every night."

That made him growl. "You used to be so compliant. What happened?"

"You did," she whispered, astonished by him all over again. "Come to dinner at my place?" She was finding it harder and harder to say good-bye to him.

28

In Which Gabriel Proposes
Kitchen-Chair Sex

LEAVING GABRIEL GOING OVER a contract at her kitchen table, Charlotte disappeared into her bedroom to change. Once there, she couldn't figure out what to wear, finally just grabbing a pretty dress with a blue forget-me-not print against white that she'd bought several weeks earlier. It wasn't right for work, but casual enough for home with its square neck and lack of sleeves. Slipping her feet into fluffy yellow slippers she'd bought the same day she'd bought the purple "monster claw" ones for Molly, she was about to step out into the corridor when she realized her footwear wasn't exactly sexy. "Stop obsessing, Charlotte."

With that, she made her way to the kitchen to find Gabriel had spread work all over the table, his cell phone at his ear. As he spoke, she deduced the person at the other end of the line was the head of an international cosmetics brand Gabriel had convinced to be exclusive to Saxon & Archer in Australasia. The deal was a coup for the company, but it was sucking a lot of Gabriel's energy since the head of the cosmetics firm insisted on dealing directly with him rather than with Saxon & Archer's head of merchandising.

Biting back a laugh when Gabriel smoothly negotiated a clause favorable to Saxon & Archer, she went and chopped up two apples into four slices each and placed them in front of him along with a glass of milk. He hadn't eaten since lunch, and she knew how much energy he burned.

Winking at her, he picked up a slice as he continued his conversation.

Wanting a quick but different meal, she put on some rice using the fuss-free cooker she and Molly had discovered in university, then pulled out a package of jumbo shrimp, and some fresh vegetables for a stir-fry. A hint of ginger, a dash of soy sauce, maybe a bit of spring onion, and it would be a delicious meal. She could also add in cashews for crunch.

"You really love cooking."

Looking over her shoulder to see that Gabriel had eaten most of the first apple, she smiled. "I do." Then, for the first time since Richard's attack, she brought it up while in this room. "I lost that love for two years after the attack. I managed to make myself come into the kitchen, put together basic meals, but I couldn't recapture the joy."

Gabriel's eyes iced over, but he didn't interrupt.

Having prepped everything for the stir-fry she'd make as the rice finished cooking, she began to put together a bowl of grapes and berries for dessert. "Then I had a really bad day at work. Anya," she said with a shrug. "She was being a snot. I was so *mad* I had to get it out, so I came in here and started baking." It had felt so good, so cathartic to be in here, doing what she loved, that the fear had been crushed under the sheer weight of it.

"You have Anya to thank for your breakthrough?"

Charlotte felt her shoulders shake. "God, yes." Apparently all that aggravation had been worth it. "Every time I cook now, I feel like I've reclaimed another tiny part of myself."

Biting into another segment of apple, Gabriel said, "You ever thought about doing it professionally?"

"No—it's my outlet. I don't want it to be my job." And it wasn't as if being a chef was a low-stress occupation.

Gabriel nodded slowly. "I get that."

"I've been thinking," she said, "about going back to uni part-time and completing the extra papers I need to get a full degree." Not in any state to return to university after she came out of hospital, she'd nonetheless earned a diploma through correspondence courses. It had been enough to land her the job at Saxon & Archer. However working for Gabriel required far more intellectual rigor than her previous position, and she wanted to be able to keep up. "Do you think I should?"

"There're a couple of courses at the business school you might want to check out."

His phone rang before he could continue.

"Go on," she said when he didn't answer. "I have to make the stir-fry anyway." Hearing his voice as she worked, having his presence in the house, it felt really good. Growing up, she'd always dreamed of having a family—part of her had felt guilty for harboring such an old-fashioned dream, but that hadn't changed how she felt.

Living alone had been important for her self-confidence, but it wasn't her natural inclination. On the other hand, she didn't just want roommates; she wanted people who were her own, people she loved.

Gabriel put down the phone and rubbed at his eyes. Stir-fry done, Charlotte walked over, took his phone and switched it off, then dropped it into the cookie jar.

"I'm expecting a call." It was a growl.

"Not for the next couple of hours you're not." She began to gather up the papers he'd spread on the table. "You're off the clock while we eat dinner."

Expression dark, he rose to his feet.

She flinched.

"Damn it, Charlotte." Gabriel's hands fisted at his sides, his jaw clenched. "I'm *not going to hurt you.*"

Pulse thudding against her skin and mouth dry, she swallowed repeatedly. "I know." It came out a rasp.

But Gabriel was already going to the cookie jar to pull out his phone. Shoving his papers into the briefcase after he had it, he said, "I'll see you tomorrow at the office." His voice was as hard and as unwelcoming as stone.

"Gabriel, don't go." It came out shaky, desperate. "Please don't go."

He blew out a breath, dropped everything on the table. "Shit." Thrusting both hands through his hair, he held out an arm. "Come here."

She went, curling up against his chest, a tremor rocking her frame. "I didn't mean to do it."

Gabriel wanted to kick his own ass. His only excuse for his behavior was that he'd been so fucking happy to be here, with her—her fear had scraped him raw. When he'd risen to his feet, all he'd intended to do was kiss her impertinent mouth. "I know you didn't." He rubbed his jaw against her temple, conscious this situation would come up again and he had to get a handle on it.

Because Charlotte was his. "I would've driven back," he told her. "Next time, just tell me to go calm the fuck down."

"In exactly those words?" Charlotte's response was quiet, but it held her usual spark.

Relieved he hadn't done any permanent damage, he rubbed his jaw against her temple again, fine blond hair catching on the bristles of his five-o'clock shadow. "That's my Ms. Baird."

AFTER THE MESS SHE'D almost made of what had been a wonderful evening to that point, Charlotte tried to be extra careful over dinner… until Gabriel growled.

"Charlotte, you're acting like the chickens," he said from where he sat just to her right. "You know what I think of the chickens. That they should be plucked and eaten."

Mouth falling open, she said, "You are a horrible man!"

"Yes, I am." He lifted a forkful of food to her mouth.

When she snapped her lips shut, he grinned. "Oh, this is wonderful. Now I know how to keep you quiet while I tell you all the deliciously bad things I'm going to do to you. I don't think I've told you how much I like your breasts. I'd like to squeeze them as I kiss your neck, then suck—"

"You—" The rest of her words were lost in a mumble around the forkful he'd fed her.

Chewing as fast as possible, she swallowed. "I was trying to be nice," she pointed out. "Trying to make it up to you." He'd taken the blame, but she knew it wasn't his fault. She'd hurt him. She hadn't meant to, but she had, and the knowledge stabbed at her deep inside.

"Charlotte," he said, "if you ever want to make up with me, just get naked." A glint in his eye. "If you feel like doing some sucking too, I won't say no. Otherwise, be yourself."

Her cheeks went red. Ducking her head, she squeezed her thighs against the impact of the images suddenly popping into her mind. Along with them came a whispered reminder that he was a physical man—she *could* repair things between them in a way he'd not only accept but enjoy. So, she thought, her teeth sinking into her lower lip, would she.

All she had to do was gather up the courage to try.

Gabriel tapped her foot with his under the table. "That's a very guilty look I see. What exactly are you thinking?"

"Nothing." She pretended to be very interested in her meal.

"*Charlotte.*" A coaxing murmur that reached all sorts of places it shouldn't reach. "Tell me."

"Eat your dinn—umph." Chewing on the mouthful he'd fed her, she glared at him. "Stop doing that."

"You barely ate anything you were so worried about being nice to me." He leaned back in his chair. "I know how much is normal for you, so don't tell me otherwise."

Eyes narrowed, she put some more rice and stir-fry on her plate. Not because of his words, but because she was hungry now that the knot in her stomach had been replaced by butterflies drunk on the sinful ideas circling her mind. Gabriel didn't say anything until after she was done, and the two of them were nibbling on the berries and grapes she'd put out for dessert.

"What made you blush?" He ran the back of his index finger down her cheek.

273

Charlotte immediately blushed again.

"Oh, now I have to know." His shirt stretching across his shoulders, he braced one arm over his chair back, turning to angle his body toward hers. "What makes my Ms. Baird go that sweet pink shade that makes me think about the tips of her nipples? Specifically, if they're the same color."

Those nipples throbbed as if he were tugging at them with his fingers and not his words. Rising on a hot flush, she went to clear the table, but he put his hand on the back of her chair in a gentle restraint. It didn't make her afraid, not when he had that hungry T-Rex smile on his face.

"Are you sure you want to know?" she asked, deciding to fight fire with fire.

"Of course."

"Don't blame me for your frustration then."

"I'm sure I can handle it, Ms. Baird."

Charlotte bit down on her lower lip on purpose. His eyes went straight to her mouth, and her breasts grew even tighter, her nipples stiff points. It was nerve-racking to flirt with Gabriel so provocatively, but in a good way. "Well," she whispered, leaning toward him, "I was imagining what you'd do if…"

"If?" His hand flexed on the back of her chair, the tanned skin revealed by the open collar of his shirt inviting her kiss, her caresses.

"If I served you dinner wearing an apron and nothing else." The words came out in a rush.

Gabriel's chest rose and fell in harsh breaths. "You are a bad, bad woman, Ms. Baird."

"I wasn't until I met you." Sliding out of her chair on the

side he hadn't blocked with his arm, she cleared the table. "Aren't you going to help?" she asked sweetly.

"When I can walk again, we'll talk about your new sass." He hauled her into his lap when she came back to the table, the hard ridge of his erection pushing against her buttocks. "Do I get you for my real dessert?"

Charlotte rubbed her fingers against her thighs.

Nuzzling at her throat, the roughness of his jaw scraping her collarbone and sending shivers over her body, Gabriel said, "Am I coming on too strong?"

"No." He was who he was, and she liked him that way. "I just… I want to." There, she'd managed to get it out, even if it wasn't particularly coherent.

Body going absolutely motionless, he said, "What?"

"Have sex. With you." Breath so shallow she'd hyperventilate if she wasn't careful, she stared at the wall instead of at him. "I don't want to be scared and missing out and hiding. I want to cut through the scar in a quick, clean move."

"By having sex with me?"

"Yes." Biting her lip again, this time because of nerves, she forced herself to turn to face him. "Are you mad?" Her proposal wasn't exactly romantic.

"Why would I be mad at the idea of having you hot and wet and tight around me?" It was a rough purr of a question. "But Charlotte, are you ready? I don't want to scare you off being with me because we rushed it."

"Molly says we've been engaging in foreplay for months."

"Molly is a smart woman." Another nuzzling kiss to her throat, those bristles rasping over her skin in a caress that went straight to her breasts. "How about here?"

"What?" It came out a squeak.

"Kitchen-chair sex seems appropriate after that crack about the apron."

Charlotte had been building up the guts to go into the bedroom with him, and he wanted to do it right here? Under the bright white kitchen lights? "I don't know if that would be very comfortable." It was the only thing she could think to say, her mind a mess.

29

Charlotte Confesses
Her Misdeeds

S HE WAS ADORABLE. SEXY and adorable. And his. Gabriel much preferred her flustered and blushing to scared and stiff. He figured the instant they hit the bedroom, she'd get nervous, start to worry. Right now, she was so scandalized at his suggestion that she hadn't remembered to be afraid.

"There's just one problem," he said, sliding his hand under the edge of her dress to place it on the silky skin of her thigh.

"One?" Her hand clenched on his nape. "You're asking me to have kitchen-chair sex and you say there's *one* problem?"

"Protection." He rubbed his thumb over her inner thigh. "I don't suppose you bought some?"

Her flustered expression changed, her face falling. "No."

If Gabriel had been aroused before, her obvious disappointment shoved it through the roof. Squeezing her thigh to her little jump, he said, "Good thing I'm a Boy Scout."

She shifted in his lap to angle her body toward him, but instead of pleasure, he was faced with a scowl. "Oh? You always carry around protection?" The tiny vertical lines between her eyebrows grew deeper. "For all those women you made me send flowers to?"

Gabriel didn't have to think about his answer. "I haven't fucked anyone since the day we met."

Her eyes went wide, her throat moving as she swallowed.

"At first," he continued, "you were a mouse, and I don't like mice, but I liked you. Because I could see the clawing tigress underneath." He nipped at her chin. "By the time work let up enough that I could think about women, the mouse had been replaced by the tigress, and I knew I only wanted a bite out of you, no one else."

The scowl returned. "Why did you have me make dinner dates for you?" She pushed at his shoulders. "Send the flowers?"

He nipped again, got another push. "I was trying to make you jealous, Ms. Baird. But off you went, merrily calling restaurants and choosing roses, stabbing me in the heart each time."

Scowl altering into an expression that was slightly uncertain, she smoothed her palms over his shoulders. "Did it really? Hurt your feelings?"

Gabriel had been teasing her to ease the mood, but faced with her honest question, he found himself saying, "Yeah." It had burned when she showed not even a hint of temper, at least not at the start. "I wanted you until you were all I could think about, and you didn't care."

Charlotte's face went soft and intense at the same time. "I cared." Her lashes came down to hide the look in her eyes. "That's why I always ordered the end-of-the-day leftover red roses," she admitted with a peek through her lashes. "So your dates would think you were a cheapskate."

Warmth uncurled in his gut. "Is that also why we always ended up in restaurants with abysmal chefs?" He'd thought the city's cuisine was going to shit.

A shamefaced look, but there was a glint of mischief to her. "I used to stay up nights, scanning the reviews for city restaurants and making sure to book you into places where there'd been complaints. I even kept track of which days got the worst reviews, so I'd know when the bad chef was on."

His shoulders shook, laughter in every cell of his body. "Your mind is so fucking sexy." One arm around her waist and hand still curved over her thigh, he kissed her. Hot and dark and raw. He knew she could handle it; she'd taken it in the office, showed him she liked it.

Moaning in the back of her throat, she wrapped her arms around his neck and sank into the kiss. He groaned, settled in to devour her. He hadn't been teasing—he had condoms in his briefcase. He'd been carrying the box around for a while. As with the bracelet, the goal-oriented part of his nature liked the physical symbol of his pursuit of Charlotte, despite the fact the box had driven him half-mad each time he glimpsed it.

When he removed his hand from between her thighs, she made a sound of complaint. His cock liked that. "Don't worry, Ms. Baird," he said, turned on impossibly more by how open she was about her desire once she forgot to be shy. "I just want you to straddle me."

Her cheeks went deep pink. "You really want to... here?" she whispered, her glasses fogged up.

"Yes, I really want to," he said, plucking the glasses off to put them on the table within easy reach. "Here." It was a risk, given what she'd suffered in this room, but if he could keep her mind on the sex, then maybe they could manage to make a memory that would be hotter, more vivid, than that of the horror that underlay her determined enjoyment of her kitchen. "Take off your panties too."

Her breath caught.

But he knew his Charlotte. She was stronger than she believed herself to be. Getting up, her eyes bright, she did as he'd asked. The panties were black lace, and from her shy half smile as she dropped them on the table, he knew she'd worn them for him. "Back here, now," he said, so aroused he was having trouble thinking.

Her sweet, sexy weight came down on his thighs seconds later as she straddled him.

He shuddered, stroking his hands up her thighs and taking her dress with him. "Lean back against the table." There was just enough space that her body would be slightly angled.

Charlotte did as he asked. "Why do I like this?"

Catching the seriousness of the murmured question, he looked up, met her gaze. "What?"

"Listening to you when we're like this." She undid one of his shirt buttons, another, and slid her hands inside. "I don't let you boss me around otherwise."

Drinking in the feel of her exploring him, he continued his interrupted action to bunch up her dress at her waist, baring her to his greedy gaze. She whimpered but didn't try to cover herself.

"We like what we like," he said on a harsh groan, his mouth watering at the sight of her; the fine golden curls at the apex of her thighs barely hid anything.

When he put his hands on her waist and lifted her onto the table after nudging her glasses aside, she gasped. "Gabriel?"

He pressed a kiss to one thigh. "Undo those tiny buttons down your front. Show me your breasts."

Her hands rose to the buttons, but a heartbeat later, the nervous excitement on her face turned into plain nerves.

"No?" Never would he take what she didn't want to give.

"I have scars," she whispered. "On my breasts."

Rage boiled in him at the reminder of the bastard who'd hurt her, but he wasn't about to allow Richard into this room again—or into Gabriel's loving with Charlotte.

"I have a jagged scar on my shoulder from a broken collarbone that tore the skin, more than a few others from on-field hits," he said. "A player's boot once came down on my ribs hard enough to peel off multiple layers of skin, and I've bled from more than one cut."

"That player who broke your collarbone should've been banned." A fierce statement. "I don't understand how he just got a suspension."

Smiling, he pressed his lips to her inner thigh again, felt her breath catch. "You kiss my scars and I'll kiss yours. Fair?"

"Fair," she whispered and, lifting her hands to her bodice, began to slip those tiny, tempting buttons out of their holes. He watched as each sweet inch of flesh was revealed, his hands tightening on her thighs.

"That's it, sweetheart," he murmured as the black lace of her bra came into view, the scalloped edge an erotic contrast to the paleness of her skin there. The scars were white and slightly raised, and they told him Charlotte was a fighter. He would see only her in them, he vowed, never the psychopath who'd hurt her. And what he saw was a woman who made him want to devour her.

Charlotte's fingers trembled. "When you look at me like that," she said, "I want to do everything you ask me."

"Good." He kissed her other thigh. "I have all kinds of ideas about debauching you."

She shivered. "I love the things you say." Having undone the final button, she reached up and pushed off the wide straps of her dress, baring one rounded shoulder, then the other.

The spicy, warm scent of her arousal made his hunger voracious, but he kept vicious control on himself—watching Charlotte be this confident was beautiful. In front of him, she dropped her arms and let the straps fall off her wrists. Her plump breasts were cupped in that pretty black lace she'd worn for him, the straps made of the same material.

"Should I..." She raised her fingers to the bra straps.

Pulling her closer, he said, "Bend down to me."

Charlotte's hands landed on his shoulders. He wanted to grip her nape, hold her in position, but that, he'd figured out, was what had triggered her last panic attack. In the meantime, he'd enjoy how she held him that way when they kissed, so unmistakably possessive.

Tasting her lips, he licked his tongue over hers before kissing a path down her lusciously sensitive throat. "You taste like my woman," he said as she moaned.

Leaving the bra in place, he kissed his way over the delicate lace and even more delicate skin to suck the taut pink tip of her nipple into his mouth. She cried out, her hands locking in his hair. Gripping one pebbled nipple between his teeth, he tugged, and it wasn't exactly gentle. Her whimper was no complaint. When she inched closer, her scent wafted to his nose, made his nostrils flare, his instincts buck at the reins.

Releasing her nipple, he placed his hand on her stomach and pressed. She moved back, her arms sliding from around his neck, but he felt a resistance in her abdominal muscles when he would've nudged her flat onto her back. He removed his hand, happy to have her seated with her hands braced behind her if that made her feel safer, more in control.

Pushing up her dress again, he used his body to keep her thighs spread and one hand to keep the fabric from sliding back down. "My pretty Charlotte." He ran a finger down the center of her pussy, felt his cock jerk in his pants at the slickness he found. Her hot little moan erased any doubts he might've had that she was enjoying this.

"Hold the dress, Ms. Baird."

The instant she obeyed, he slid one hand around to splay on the bare skin of her lower back, stroked one of her thighs over his shoulder, and leaned down to gorge on the delicious woman in his arms.

Fuck, she tasted good.

Her cries were shocked and soft, almost secret, but she didn't push him away. One hand came back to fist in his hair, her body rewarding each lick and suck with honey slickness. When he scraped his teeth over her, she shuddered, her fingers tightening in his hair. Yeah, Charlotte could take him.

Licking away the erotic hurt, he ran one palm along her silky-soft inner thigh. "I'm going to use my fingers on you," he said, looking up to find her giving a dazed nod. "I'm a big guy." Thumb on her clit, he circled the rough pad of his index finger at her core.

Her lips parted on another one of those quiet, secret cries that went straight to his cock.

"I," he said, nudging his finger just inside, "have to"—he rubbed her clit—"make sure"—a flick with his thumb that had her shuddering—"you can take me." He thrust his finger home.

Her back arched, her breasts gorgeously displayed. "*Gabriel.*" A husky, breathless whimper. "That's… a very thick finger."

Smiling, he pressed a kiss to her navel. "It's a clever one too." Returning to her pussy, he put both his finger and his tongue to good use until she was squirming against him, begging for release in soft gasps that made him want to growl like a damn beast and fuck her stupid, just ram into her until she forgot her own name.

Raising his head instead, he took both of her hands and put them on his shoulders, then eased her trembling thigh down from his shoulder. Lips parted and kiss-swollen, pupils dilated against the hazel of her irises, Charlotte watched him as he moved his own hands down to undo his belt, lower the zipper.

"Get the condoms," he said, wanting to make dead sure she hadn't changed her mind, was with him.

Her pulse skittered in her neck, but she turned to reach for the briefcase he'd left on another chair, one of her bra straps falling down her arm as she did so. He loved how thoroughly used she already looked, all mussed and flushed and with red marks on her inner thighs from his stubble.

While she opened the briefcase, he kept himself busy by releasing his cock.

"Where are they?" A husky question.

"Inside pocket, left side." Having given that instruction, he spread her thighs wider and suckled a kiss on the sensitive skin beside her knee while running his finger through her slickness again. Plump and wet and his, she was fucking beautiful.

Her nails dug into his shoulder. "Gabriel." It was a moan.

"Condoms." Biting at the taut flesh of her thigh, he licked, looked up to find her clutching the box in her hand.

He took it from her, then drew in her hand and tucked it between her thighs. "Keep yourself wet for me."

A choked half laugh. "I don't think I could be any more ready than I already am."

"Not ready, Ms. Baird." Tearing the box apart, he scattered flat packets all over her kitchen floor. "Deliciously wet, slick and honey sweet. Say it."

"I'm…." She licked her lips.

That was it.

Having sheathed himself during the course of her hesitation, he pulled her forward and onto his lap but held her above him. No way was he just ramming into her like he'd imagined—that would come later, when Charlotte was ready to handle the rougher side of his sexuality. Right now, it was about teaching her that his touch meant pleasure. No matter how gentle he was, or how rough, he'd always, *always* give her pleasure, never pain.

"Put your arms around my neck." Sliding his hands down to cup her ass after she obeyed his order, her fingers curling into his hair, he rubbed the blunt tip of his cock against her opening. "Control how much of my cock you take," he gritted out, his body ready to pump into her.

"Gabriel, may I please have a kiss?"

Hearing the vulnerability, he immediately lifted his face to hers, their mouths meeting in a sinful, hot, Charlotte kiss. He let her take what she needed, his hands cupping and squeezing the lush curves of her. Charlotte might be small, but she was built in sweet, curvy proportion. "Better?" he asked when she broke the kiss, one hand on the side of his neck, the other still in his hair.

"Yes." A quiet word, their breaths intermingled. Then, eyes locked with his, she sank down an inch onto him. The hitch in her breath mingled with his groan. When she said, "More," he almost lost it.

Deliberately reciting rugby statistics in his head, he said, "Ask me to fuck you, Charlotte."

Her chest rose in a ragged inhale. "I can't."

"Yes, you can," he coaxed. "I know you know bad words. All good girls do."

She sank another inch onto him, her eyes fluttering shut. "I don't know how to talk that way in bed."

The shy confession blew the statistics out of the water. "Do it with me," he said, pulling out all the way by lifting her off him, then teasing her with his eager cock. "Say 'Fuck me, Gabriel.'" The idea of those words falling from her lips shredded his remaining control. The only reason he didn't snap was because the need to protect her was stronger than his lust, stronger than anything.

Charlotte sank down on him without warning, taking a couple of inches before he could stop her. As she cried out at the pressure, he locked his spine against the searing pleasure of her scalding grip. "Naughty, Ms. Baird." Sweat stuck his shirt to his back. "Three words and you can have what you want. All of it." He lifted her off him again, to her frustrated cry.

Bringing her back down, he pushed into her slowly, lifting her off at the halfway mark. It was self-inflicted torture and it was amazing. "You are so tiny, Charlotte." It fucking turned him on how easily he could handle her, position her. "Am I hurting you?" Because the handling was only fun if she was with him.

"No," she whispered and pressed her cheek to the stub- bled roughness of his own. "Fuck me, Gabriel."

Oh Jesus!

Gritting his teeth against the impact of that breathy re- quest, he gave her control again. "As slow or as fast as you want." He had no doubts she could take him, but he had to be gentle until she was used to his size. He figured it'd be eas- ier for her to take the reins this time—but Charlotte kind of froze on him when he said the words.

He immediately put his hands back on her, realizing his sexy Ms. Baird wasn't yet confident enough to take him up on his offer. "Then again"—he sucked on the skin above her pulse, hard enough to leave a mark and make her groan—"I do like being the boss."

More kisses to coax her to melting softness against him once more. "But you'll tell me if it hurts. Understood?"

A nod against him, her body quivering.

Gripping her under her thigh with one hand to give her extra support, he pinched her clit between the thumb and forefinger of his other hand. She cried out, sank deeper on him. His cock ached, his entire body burning up from the inside, but there was no way he was messing this up. Circling his thumb around the slippery nub he'd pinched, he let her take him at her own pace.

The final inches made her shudder, her flesh so tightly stretched around his girth that when he ran his finger around the tightness, she gave a little scream and came in hard pulses that threatened to milk him dry.

He had no idea how he managed to last until the erotic ripples of her body eased enough that he could lift her off him, then bring her back down as he thrust into her. It was harder than he'd intended, but Charlotte just held on tighter, her breaths hot against his ear. "Gabriel, please. Gabriel."

"I've got you." He lifted her again, thrust in deeper and faster. "I've got you." A final stroke before his balls drew up against his body, his muscles locked in an orgasm that punched through him harder than the hardest tackle he'd ever taken on the field.

30

DIRTY TALK WITH A T-REX

CHARLOTTE WASN'T QUITE SURE how she'd ended up lying on top of Gabriel's bare chest on the sofa, the bodice of her dress mostly buttoned, but it was so very nice and warm and wonderful that she just snuggled in. Eyes heavy, she pressed a kiss to the skin under her and ran her hand down his lightly furred chest, stopping to trace the intricate lines of the tattoo that covered his pectoral muscle. "This is so beautiful."

"I think the word you're looking for is manly." A rumble of sound under her, Gabriel's hand on her bare butt.

Smiling, she kissed him again, licked up the taste of salt on his skin.

"Did it work?"

Nuzzling at him, she ran her foot down his leg—which was half-hanging off the end of the sofa—and frowned at the feel of fabric under her. "You didn't take off your pants." That seemed vaguely dirty, that he'd… fucked her without taking off his pants.

"If I take off my pants, I'll be inside you again in about ten seconds."

Skin tingling, she rubbed her cheek against him. "I won't

mind." He'd felt so good inside her, so hard and thick and hot. But he'd felt even better around her, warm and big and protective.

Gabriel petted her ass, unabashed in his enjoyment of her body. "So it worked."

This time she understood. "Yes." The scars had been well and truly cut out. "I really like being with you."

He made a deep sound in his chest and stroked her hair off her face. Only then did she realize it was out of its bun. But that was fine, wonderful… until he fisted his hand in her hair and tugged up her head. Terror screamed to life in her blood, making her lungs strain, black spots dancing in front of her eyes.

Shoving at him, she would've fallen off the sofa if Gabriel hadn't curled his arm around her waist. "Charlotte!"

She wrenched even harder, and this time she managed to get off—to fall hard onto her tailbone. The shock of pain snapped through the panic, had her staring up at Gabriel as he sat up on the sofa, his hand reaching out toward her. "Are you hurt?"

She shook her head in a quick, jerky movement. She'd ruined it. It had been beautiful and she'd ruined it. Humiliated and sad and angry, she got up onto her knees, then scrambled to her feet. "You should go." She couldn't meet his eyes, wanted only to curl up into a ball and rock herself through the pain.

He caught her hand, tugged. "Come here, Ms. Baird."

"No. I need to be alone." Her voice broke.

Gabriel curled his fingers more firmly around her hand. "Come here. Just a couple of steps."

She didn't realize she was moving until she was beside his leg. Sliding his arm around her waist, he pulled her down onto his lap. "There, you're back where you're meant to be."

Charlotte crumpled into him. "I want to be fixed," she whispered. "I want to be normal. I want you not to have to worry about every touch." He'd been so *careful* during the sex, his muscles and tendons rigid with control.

"I had a hell of a good time." He settled back into the sofa, one of his hands on her thigh, the other spread on her lower back. "Did you not feel me inside you?"

"You had to think throughout it." She sat up, twisted to face him. "Don't lie."

"I'd always have been thinking our first time together—you're damn small, Ms. Baird, and I'm a big man." He cupped the side of her face. "No matter how much I want to pin you down and ram into you, I would never have done it the first time—or the second. We'll build up to it."

Charlotte didn't know how to respond. The blunt sexual words, his determination, the tenderness with which he touched her, it all overwhelmed.

"But Charlotte," Gabriel said when she stayed silent, "you *are* hurt deep inside. Have you ever talked to anyone about what happened to you?"

Charlotte gave a jerky nod. "Right after, I did."

"And?"

"After about six months, I started to feel guilty for taking up the therapist's time when I wasn't getting better, so I stopped going to see her." The smart, well-dressed, and together woman had made her feel so small, her impatience hidden but obvious to Charlotte.

Gabriel snapped out a low, hard word. "That therapist was incompetent if she made you feel that way."

CHARLOTTE WANTED TO BELIEVE him. "I don't know if I can talk to a stranger," she whispered. "It was so hard to tell you, and I trust you."

Gabriel gently stroked her thigh. "I know someone," he said. "A doctor I talked to after my injury."

"You talked to someone?" Her eyes went huge, then turned suspicious. "Did your mom make you?"

"My dad," he admitted. "It was a good thing. I wasn't too messed up, but I might have been if I hadn't talked to Dr. Mac at that point in time." He shrugged. "He reminded me I had a whole lot more going for me than just my skill on the field."

Charlotte pressed her hands flat against his chest. "You were hurting."

"I'd been playing no-holds-barred rugby since I could run, then poof, it was all gone." Feeling Charlotte melt against him, her features soft, he realized she was a sucker for his hard-luck story. Too bad he adored her too much to use it to manipulate her. "Anyway, Dr. Mac, he's a good guy."

"A man?" Charlotte twisted her lips. "I don't do too well with men, you know that."

"He looks like Santa Claus, complete with the beard. Why don't you give it a shot? I can go with you for the first session."

Charlotte rubbed her hands up her arms and immediately found herself cuddled against the heat of Gabriel's chest. He really was very tactile—she loved it. Settling into him and hotly aware of how intimately he held her, one of his hands curved over her left thigh, she said, "Okay, I'll try it." She wasn't sure she could talk to even Santa Claus, but she was willing to attempt anything at this point.

"I'll give him a call tomorrow, see when he has a slot." Gabriel's hand moved to between her thighs.

She shifted restlessly on his lap, her pulse spiking. When she tipped up her head, his lips were there for her to kiss. Sliding her hand around to his nape, she opened her mouth to him. He thrust his tongue inside, and it was a more aggressive kiss than he usually began with; it made her wet all over again.

He cupped her between her thighs a second later, swallowed her gasp with his kiss. Rising up in an instinctive move, she pushed back down and he thrust two fingers into her. It was so hard, so fast, that it tore a rasped scream from her throat.

Biting down on her lower lip, Gabriel said, "Come back here, Ms. Baird."

She gave him her mouth again and in return, he moved his fingers in a deep, demanding rhythm, his tongue echoing the tempo. Charlotte tried to hold on, but it was hopeless. Her thighs squeezed his wrist, her internal muscles clamping down on him as the orgasm crashed over her. It didn't stop when she thought it would, because he kept doing things to her. Pressing his thumb against her clit, pulling out his fingers and thrusting them back in past her passion-swollen entrance, sucking on her tongue.

"Stop," she gasped at last, her muscles aching. "I can't take it."

A husky chuckle, but he'd stopped the instant she asked. Leaving his hand between her legs, he curved it around her inner thigh. He was sticky with her and the feel of it made her shudder again. Burying her face against his neck, chest heaving, she tried to find words, but they'd all left her brain.

"Do you mind if I use your body to get myself off?" It was a hot question against her ear.

Charlotte moaned.

"Is that a yes to my using your body?"

She nodded.

The big, sexy man who'd turned her bones molten pulled up her dress, tugging it over her head before removing her bra. She barely had the strength to move her arms, but he managed. It left her totally naked for the first time, and she should've felt vulnerable, but Gabriel's hands felt so lovely on her skin that she just let him do what he wanted.

He spread her thighs over him so she straddled him again, then cradling her against him, nibbled at her throat as he released himself from his pants. "I want your hand on my cock." Taking her right hand, he slid it over his chest and down.

Charlotte curled her fingers around the hot steel of his erection, shivered when he said, "Kiss me, Ms. Baird."

She did exactly that, part of her aware that had she been normal and not messed up as she was, he'd have hauled her aggressively into that kiss. Right now, that didn't matter. What mattered was that he was kissing her all raw and deep again while using his hand on her own to show her how to caress him. Finding strength in his desire for her, she lifted off his chest enough to look down.

Seeing her fingers on him made her lower body tighten in a convulsive shudder.

There wasn't much thinking after that.

GABRIEL REALLY DIDN'T WANT to drive home that night, but he got dressed and rose, both because he had no fresh clothes at Charlotte's and because he knew she wasn't ready.

The last thing he wanted was for her to wake up in the middle of the night and panic at having a man in bed with her.

So he kissed her on the doorstep, leaving her all sleepy-eyed and sated. It was one of the hardest things he'd had to do—especially when she reached up on tiptoe to kiss him again at the instant he would've pulled back.

"Thank you, Gabriel."

"I'm the one who should be giving thanks." He'd never been so sexually satisfied in his life. Yeah, he'd had to hold back, but that was changing. He wasn't sure she realized it, but he'd been pretty demanding on the sofa and she hadn't flinched. Sex, however, wasn't the key to Charlotte's fear. Still, it was a start.

Leaving her with a final kiss, he made his way home.

CHARLOTTE SLEPT LIKE THE dead and woke early, feeling good from the tips of her toes to the ends of her hair. She probably should've showered before going to bed, but she hadn't, not wanting to wash off Gabriel's scent. Rolling around and basking in it for another few minutes, she finally made herself go and shower, then got dressed.

Having caught an earlier bus in, she got in well before her usual time. It was as she was going up the steps to the main doors of the Saxon & Archer building that she caught sight of the man she'd seen with Gabriel yesterday. He was hiding behind one of the pillars that fronted the next building over, looking out furtively every so often.

Charlotte didn't hesitate to walk over. "Hello," she said in a gentle tone once she was close enough. "You're Gabriel's father, aren't you? Brian?"

The man, his eyes sunken and his clothes hanging off his frame, looked alarmed. "Don't tell him I'm here," he begged. "I just wanted to see him before I go to the hospital later today."

Charlotte stepped off the sidewalk and joined Brian behind the pillars so they could talk privately. "He's very angry with you," she said, understanding that anger.

"I know." Coughs wracking his frame, Brian Bishop took something out of his pocket. "Will you give him this? I don't think he'd take it from me."

Charlotte took the wrinkled envelope that she guessed contained a letter. "I will." Gabriel might yell at her for interfering, but if they were to have a relationship, she had to be strong enough to face him down when necessary.

And it was necessary here. Gabriel might not want to talk about this, but she knew the situation wasn't healthy, that he had to find a way to deal with the anger inside him. "You should go from here for now," she said, touching her hand to Brian's arm to take the sting out of the words. "I'll make sure Gabriel gets this."

Brian swallowed and nodded.

"Wait," she said when he would've turned. "When's your appointment?"

"Ten a.m. At the main hospital." He touched a hand to his chest, tremors running through him. "Cancer."

Though she'd already guessed it was something like that, Charlotte felt an ache of memory at the mention of the disease that had taken her mother. "Do you have transport home after your treatment?"

A dull smile. "Yes, a charity volunteer picks me up. It's what I deserve."

Watching him as he left, Charlotte put the envelope in her purse and headed up.

When Gabriel came in from his run, he said, "I like you in yellow, Ms. Baird," before claiming a kiss.

She waited to bring up the letter until he was in his office after his shower, the cobalt-blue strip of his tie slung around his neck in readiness for tying. Closing the door behind her, she simply sighed at the gorgeous sexiness of his smile when he glanced up.

"No office shenanigans," he said, fingers moving efficiently to get the tie in place. "Not that I can't be persuaded to negotiate that rule."

Her stomach fluttered before twisting with nerves. "I have to talk to you about something."

Brow furrowing, he watched her move toward him. "Sounds serious."

"It's about your father."

His jaw clenched. Hands on his hips and tie done, he turned to stare out at the cloud-gray sky. "That man lost the right to call himself my father a long time ago."

"I know." Charlotte touched one hand to his back, soothing the tension there with gentle strokes. "But this anger you're carrying around? It's toxic." When he didn't speak, she continued despite her worry that he'd try to shut her down again.

It wouldn't work this time, not when he'd given himself to her, but she'd have to fight to batter down his walls, and she knew exactly how hardheaded he could be. "I know what I'm talking about. I *hated* Richard for what he did. For a long time that hate drove me forward to heal myself, become stronger, and that was good, but at some point, I realized it was stealing pieces of me."

Still no response.

"The hate was making me into someone who saw only the negative in people." She shook her head. "I didn't want to be that person, so I made a conscious decision to let the hate go."

Gabriel slid his arm around her waist, drawing her against him. "How? After what he did."

"By hating him, I was giving him too much importance in my life. He didn't deserve my attention." Turning her back to the view, she touched Gabriel's freshly shaven cheek. "I don't know if you can ever forgive your father, but let the anger go, Gabriel. In the end, it'll only damage you."

Expression still grim, he nodded at the envelope in her hand. "From him?" When she confirmed that, he took it and tore it open.

It didn't hold a letter. Two checks fell out instead. One was made out to Gabriel, the other to Sailor, both for odd amounts: two hundred forty-seven dollars and fifty cents, and one hundred eighty-nine dollars and eighty-two cents.

"I DON'T UNDERSTAND," CHARLOTTE said when Gabriel just stared at the checks.

Reaching back, he dropped the checks on his desk and drew Charlotte into his arms. He needed her warmth, her tenderness. "When Brian left," he told her, "he didn't only empty out his and Mom's joint account. He took the money in Sailor's account and mine too." Miniscule amounts really, but important to two little boys.

"We put birthday money in there, and my mom used to add an extra five dollars now and then when she'd saved money on the grocery shopping or something. It was meant to pay for stuff we might need at school later on—field trips, things like that."

"And he took that?" Charlotte shook her head. "That was a low thing to do."

"He left us destitute. Then my mom lost her job because she couldn't afford a babysitter." Anger made his voice harsh. "She'd always been so proud of giving me and Sailor everything we needed, but without a cushion of savings, we had nothing. We ended up in an emergency shelter."

Charlotte didn't say anything, just held him.

"I don't think I can ever forgive him."

"Then don't." She looked up. "But don't nurture the anger. Be kind, be the better man. Be the man I know." Touching his cheek again, she said, "He's a sick old man who's lost everything and everyone. You have a huge heart, Gabriel—find room in it to be kind."

Gabriel wasn't sure he was that good, but as time passed that morning, those wrinkled checks lingered on his mind. Brian Bishop was finally trying to fix his mistakes. Too little too late as far as Gabriel was concerned.

Be kind, be the better man. Be the man I know.

Rising from his chair, he stepped out to where Charlotte worked. "What time was his appointment?"

"Ten. Are you going?"

"I don't know." He still wasn't sure when he parked the car in the hospital's parking garage, but he got out and made his way to the correct ward.

You have a huge heart, Gabriel—find room in it to be kind.

Pushing the door, he went in.

31

A Whisper of Evil

"**A**RE YOU OKAY?" CHARLOTTE asked when he returned to the office, rising to give him a tight hug.

Gabriel held her close. "He's so old and frail." A shadow of who Brian had once been. "Weak of the soul too." That, he'd realized as he spoke to Brian today, was a frailty nothing could fix. "It seems a waste of time to be angry at a man like that."

Brian had no strength, physical or emotional, was no kind of true opponent. Gabriel could destroy him in a heartbeat. Once, however, he'd have done anything Brian asked, been the son who shouldered any burden. He saw that knowledge in Brian's eyes too, the knowledge of what he'd thrown away—and it just made Gabriel feel sorry for a man who'd realized his mistakes far too late to fix them.

"I'll never see him as my father, but yeah, I can be kind to an old and sick man." The bonds of family had been permanently broken; all he could offer was decency.

"For him," Charlotte said, "I think it'll be enough. He's full of regret."

Gabriel had no intention of ever becoming the same, of waking up one day to realize he'd wasted his life in anger at Brian, so he let it go. If the anger returned, he'd make the same choice. Because Charlotte was right: holding on to it was toxic, would hurt only him and the people around him.

"How bad is it?" he asked after claiming a deep, hungry kiss.

"I'm holding the wolves at bay." She gave him two notes with phone messages. "Urgent, but I can clear you another hour if you need it."

"Do it," he said. "I need to talk to Sailor." His brother had fewer memories of the time after Brian left, fewer negative emotions, but he'd stuck loyally to Gabriel's stance.

When Gabriel tracked him to the commercial greenhouse where he was planting seedlings, Sailor gave him a disbelieving look. "You stayed with the bastard through his chemo?"

"Part of it." Yet even that had made Brian pathetically grateful. "Charlotte says he's not worth the energy of hating and she's right."

Sailor snorted. "Not worth our time either."

"No, but Mom is," he said, squeezing his brother's shoulder. "Do this for her. If we don't, she'll end up going with him because she's got a soft heart."

Sailor blew out a breath. "Fuck. I'll take him to his next appointment." He took off his gardening gloves, put them down. "I'm not inviting him into my family—I don't trust him."

"Neither do I." A tiger couldn't change its stripes. "I've made sure he has good care." For now it was as far as he could go. Perhaps Brian would one day redeem himself, but until then, Gabriel would try to be the better man Charlotte saw in him.

GABRIEL HAD BEEN BACK in the office for a couple of hours, the two of them frenetic with work, when reception called up to tell Charlotte she had a delivery. Tuck was the one who brought it up.

"Someone likes you, Charlotte," he said with a wide grin before leaving.

It was a bouquet, but each "flower" was made up of pages from old romance novels. Smiling goofily, Charlotte searched for the card. There wasn't one. A second later, she realized the writing was on the wide silver ribbon around the bouquet.

Other than her name, it had only a single line: *Our story is just beginning.—T-R.*

A little teary, she traced her finger over the signature. The gift meant all the more today, when she'd pushed her way into his emotional life, when she'd exercised her right to look after his heart as he looked after hers.

Plucking out one of the flowers, she took it into Gabriel's office. He was standing by the window, arguing with someone on the other end of the phone, but waved her in. Going up to him, she wrapped her arms around him from behind, the text flower held in one hand.

She felt his smile in the way he closed his hand over her own, though the tone of his negotiation never changed. Dropping a kiss on his back, she put the flower by the small electronic calendar to one side of his desk and was about to leave when he turned to scrawl a note to her on the back of a draft report for the board.

Expecting it to be an instruction about something he needed for the call, she was surprised to find: *Mac had an appointment cancel at three thirty.*

Her chest grew tight but she gave him a nod, and when the time came around, got in the car with him to drive to the psychologist's office. It was only when she read the name on the door of the office that she realized Dr. Mac was actually Dr. Thomas McCauley. Then his secretary showed them in, and she almost burst out laughing. Santa Claus had gone completely bald and clipped his beard.

He was roly-poly though, and short. The latter comforted her. Her father had been short. Much thinner than Dr. Mac, but of the same height and with the same gentle eyes.

"Gabriel," he said, rising to shake Gabriel's hand. "This must be your Ms. Baird."

"Charlotte."

Dr. Mac's touch was firm but not too hard when he clasped both his hands warmly around her own. "Charlotte. It's lovely to meet you—what are you doing with this guy?"

"She has excellent taste," Gabriel said.

The doctor chuckled. "And you have a healthy ego."

Smiling at the affection in the doctor's tone and relying on instincts she'd distrusted for a long time after Richard, Charlotte turned to Gabriel. "I think I'll be all right."

He didn't second-guess her, just said, "I'll wait outside."

"Take a break and read a magazine," the doctor ordered him. "Don't scare my secretary by yelling at competitors on your phone."

Since Gabriel was already sliding out his phone, that just made him grin. He pulled the door closed behind him with a look at Charlotte that said he'd be there in a heartbeat if she needed him.

Turning to the doctor after the door shut, Charlotte took a deep, shaky breath. "So, how does this work?"

GABRIEL WASN'T USED TO waiting. He was used to doing. So he did what he could—which was work. Rather than taking over Dr. Mac's waiting room, he stepped out onto the verandah of the white-painted villa the doc used as his office. He made sure he was always within hearing distance in case Charlotte had a panic attack and needed him.

But forty-five minutes after Gabriel had closed the door on the doctor and Charlotte, it opened again and Charlotte walked out. Her eyes were red, but there was a smile on her face when she said good-bye to Dr. Mac. Afterward, she came straight into Gabriel's arms.

"Okay?" he asked, pressing a kiss to the top of her hair.

"Yeah." Her voice was a little husky. "He's a nice man."

Walking her to the SUV, he gave her a boost into the passenger seat just because he liked touching her, then stood in the open doorway. "I'm nicer."

She took hold of his tie and tugged him to her for a kiss. "Yes, you are."

He tapped her cheek. "So you're comfortable with him?"

"Yes. He made me feel as if I could go at my own pace, that he was in no rush." A fierce smile. "But I'm ready to be done with this."

Gabriel wasn't sure it would be that easy, but he was in this for the long haul. Charlotte was his—it was as simple and as immutable as that.

WITH IT BEING WINTER-DARK by six thirty, Charlotte grabbed a taxi home after work. Gabriel had left at five to make his coaching session at the high school a half hour later—the interruptions to his workday meant he'd have to put in several more hours on Saxon & Archer business after the session finished, but he'd made a commitment to the team, and Gabriel took that seriously.

He'd scowled when she turned down his offer of a ride home because she wanted to finish up some work, but she stood her ground. She didn't want him to babysit her, and he didn't have to. Not yet. Because once Richard was out, Charlotte knew there'd be times when she wouldn't be able to let Gabriel out of her sight.

Not because she was afraid for herself, but because she couldn't bear it if Richard hurt him. The man she'd seen as a handsome, sunny boy so long ago knew how to hold a grudge, to stew and plan, and he was evil enough to come after the people who mattered most to her. Molly was safely out of reach, but Gabriel wasn't.

He'll be safe. He is safe.

Repeating that silently to herself, she got out of the taxi at the top of her drive. Her neighbors were outside chatting, and after she collected her mail from the mailbox, she joined them for a few minutes before heading down to her town house. She'd miss it when she had to move into the apartment, but her decision made sense.

It was time she began to pack enough things that she wouldn't constantly have to come back here. Might as well start tonight, since she had a hunch Gabriel would be dropping by after the coaching session. She'd put him to good use, hauling boxes—or maybe they'd indulge in another form of exercise, she thought with a wicked smile.

It'd give him a break before he dug into work again.

Charlotte frowned as she changed out of her office clothes into stretchy black pants and her green cardigan with the three-quarter-length sleeves. She could understand Gabriel's need to catch up on work today, as she'd understood the hours he'd pulled the first couple of months, but the man needed more balance in his life. Saxon & Archer was in a much better position, thanks to him. He could afford to take a breath now and then.

Musing about how to make that happen, she gave in to temptation and dug up one of the peach-and-passion-fruit muffins she'd frozen after making a batch two weeks ago. A quick minute in the microwave to defrost it and she put it on a saucer to nibble at while she stood at the kitchen table checking the mail.

Her electricity bill usually came now. Which reminded her, she had to switch to electronic invoices. There it was, the envelope a distinctive yellow. Opening it, she saw no surprises and set it aside. She laughed at seeing the next item in the pile. Molly had sent her a postcard from Las Vegas, the picture of a purple-jumpsuit-clad Elvis impersonator in full crotch-circling move.

Miss you bunches. Love you even more. xo Molly

p.s. Elvis says sequins are always in.

Instead of pinning it to the fridge, Charlotte kept it aside to take with her to the new apartment. The rest of the pile was made up of advertising mailers, except for a small envelope that had become stuck between the pages of a department store catalog. She frowned, not recognizing the handwriting. Then she saw the return address.

The biggest prison in the country.

Gorge rising and knees going weak, she collapsed into a chair, the half-eaten muffin falling out of her fingers to hit the table. Everything in her shook. She dropped the envelope, stared at it, jumping when a horn beeped outside. Her eyes caught the clock on the wall as her mind figured out the beep had been for her neighbor, and she realized she'd been sitting there for fifteen minutes.

No, the bastard was not stealing any more of her life.

However, when she went to pick up the envelope to throw it away, she couldn't. She had to know what it said, but she couldn't open it alone. Yesterday, that would've made her feel weak, broken. Today, she had Dr. Mac's voice in her head, telling her it was okay to need people to help her through the dark times.

"Wouldn't you do the same for Gabriel or your best friend if it ever came to it?" he'd said gently. "Strength doesn't mean never relying on anyone. And knowing him as I do, I can tell you that it would break Gabriel's heart if you didn't allow him to bear some of the weight. That's who he is."

Getting up on that thought, she left the kitchen to pack up some clothes. When Gabriel messaged to say he was swinging by and that he'd picked up dinner, she allowed herself to feel happily relieved. "Hey," she said when she opened the door for him.

He'd showered after the coaching session where he'd no doubt gotten on the field with the boys, then thrown on jeans and a white T-shirt. Not many people saw him like this, with his hair messily damp and his feet bare—he'd kicked off his shoes as soon as he stepped inside. Maybe it was silly, but it made her feel special, trusted, as if she'd been allowed to see him without his armor.

"Hey." He placed the food he'd bought on the hallway table and crooked a finger.

Bracing herself with her palms on the solid wall of his chest, she rose on tiptoe. He bent, meeting her halfway, the kiss hot and deep as it always was with Gabriel. She loved that he was so openly voracious for her, loved the taste of him. Sliding one hand to the side of his neck, the strength of him warm and solid under her touch, she gave him whatever he wanted.

Nothing felt as good as making Gabriel groan in the back of his throat, his hands clenching on her hips before he slid his fingers lower down to cup her butt. When he lifted, she wrapped her legs around his waist.

Holding her easily with one arm while sliding his other one over her thigh, he bit at her lower lip. "I like these pants." His fingers flexed under her buttocks.

She flushed, realizing the soft, stretchy fabric gave him easy access to her body. "I like these pants too," she said, because she liked his hands on her. "You shaved." His jaw was smooth under her fingertips.

"I thought I'd be civilized today and not mark up your pretty skin." A suckling kiss. "At least not with my jaw. I might just bite you instead."

Charlotte didn't know what made her do it. She leaned forward and bit down on that smooth jaw, the scent of his aftershave in her lungs. His hand flexed again. "Biting the boss, Ms. Baird?"

"I think this boss could do with some biting."

Chuckling, he said, "Want to eat? Or should I just eat you?"

"*Gabriel.*"

"Ms. Baird."

"You should put me down."

"Why?"

"I'm heavy."

He snorted, shoulders shaking. Shoving at those shoulders when he started laughing so hard he couldn't speak, she tried not to laugh with him. It was too difficult and it was the last thing she'd have thought she'd be doing when she'd received the letter. The reminder though, it stole the laughter.

Gabriel's eyes immediately zeroed in on her face. Putting her down on her feet, he said, "What's the matter?"

"Dick sent me a letter."

His expression went hard and flat. "What does the bastard want?"

"I don't know. I didn't read it. I was waiting for you."

THE WORDS SLICED THROUGH Gabriel's anger. "Want me to read it?" He didn't want that piece of scum anywhere near Charlotte, even if only through his words.

But Charlotte shook her head and led him into the kitchen. "I need to do this. If he writes to me again, I'll throw it in the trash, but I need to read this first one, find out what he thinks he has to say to me after all this time."

Gabriel could understand her need, but he still had to grit his teeth to keep from taking the envelope and tearing it to shreds. Especially when her fingers trembled as she slit the envelope open.

32

BAD, BAD, *BAD* WORDS

TUCKING CHARLOTTE CLOSE, GABRIEL said, "He can't touch you. I'll break him in half if he tries to lay so much as a finger on you."

A shaky smile from Charlotte as she pulled out the letter.

Gabriel read it along with her. The bastard had written how sorry he was, how he'd tried to write before but the prison authorities wouldn't permit it. They had okayed this letter because he was about to get out and it was considered a healthy sign of rehabilitation that he wanted to apologize to his victim to give her "closure."

That wasn't me, Charlotte. I don't know what happened that weekend, who I became, but I take full responsibility for it. It's important I do that. It's on me. It had nothing to do with you and how we broke up. It wasn't your fault you couldn't give me what I needed—I shouldn't have taken out my annoyance on you. I hope one day you can forgive me.

The fucking psychopath had the nerve to sign it "Love, Richard."

"Passive-aggressive bullshit," Gabriel snarled, unable to keep his mouth shut any longer.

"Manipulative," Charlotte said. "That's always been his MO." She lifted the letter, went to rip it up, then frowned. "I'm going to give this to Detective Lee, just in case."

"Good idea." If Richard did come after her again, Gabriel wanted him locked up for the rest of his miserable life. "You okay?"

A wondering expression on Charlotte's face. "Yes. He's been the bogeyman for so long, but now that I've read this, I see him for the pathetic, manipulative son of a bitch that he really is." She threw the letter down on the table. "He was such a big man when he ambushed me, had me alone, that pencil-dicked, scum-sucking fuckwit!"

Gabriel had never heard Charlotte swear. It was impressive.

It got even more impressive.

"Closure, my ass! That slimy excuse for a human being just wanted to get inside my head. Fuck that!" She poked Gabriel in the chest. "*Annoyance*? Annoyance? I'll show that ass-faced peckerhead annoyance! His name shouldn't be Dick. It should be Dickweasel Shit for Brains!"

Leaning with his forearm on the counter when Charlotte swept past him, Gabriel grinned as she marched around the kitchen, slamming pots and pans together and pouring flour into a bowl, taking out cocoa and chocolate chips and eggs and vanilla pods, other things he couldn't identify. He decided not to remind her he'd picked up dinner and it was going cold.

Instead, he stole chocolate chips from across the counter, said, "Yes," and "Absolutely" when she paused in her diatribe to wait for a response. The question was usually something along the lines of: *Don't you think so?* after she'd murdered Richard's character in ever more creative ways.

It wasn't until the smell of muffins baking permeated the kitchen and Charlotte had hand washed the dishes—with more banging and clattering—that she began to calm down. Exhaling, she turned to him. "I didn't know I had that in me."

He kissed her cheek, adoring her. "That's my Ms. Baird."

The blush was back, pink and pretty. "I have to remember all the bad words I used so I can tell Molly."

"Dickweasel?"

"It seemed appropriate."

Chuckling, Gabriel went and got the food he'd left on the hallway table. "Come on, let's reheat this and eat and you can tell me what some of those words mean. I grew up on a rugby field, but Jesus, baby, I have no idea where you learned all that."

"You should read more" was the prim response from the tiny blond Valkyrie he didn't *ever* want that pissed with him.

CHARLOTTE LAY IN BED that night, staring up at the ceiling. Her body was satisfied and yet not. Gabriel had touched her with the same raw tenderness he always did, but again, it had been in an armchair, with her in his lap. She knew in her gut that that wasn't anywhere close to his favorite position. A man like Gabriel enjoyed being on top, liked to have total control.

"Don't rush it. It appears you're doing very well with Gabriel."

Dr. Mac was right; she knew that. She also knew it infuriated her that even though she could see Richard for the spineless psychopathic wimp that he was, she couldn't forget what he'd done to her. It felt as if he'd branded her and she hated it, *hated* it. She wanted to wear Gabriel's brand, not Richard's, wanted to know the feel of Gabriel's hand sliding

312

around her nape to hold her close for his kiss, not the ugliness of Richard's fingers digging into her flesh as he dragged her around the town house.

And she wanted Gabriel's big, hot, protective body beside her, didn't want him walking out the door night after night because neither of them was sure she wouldn't panic in the middle of the night.

Aggravated, she shoved off the blanket and stomped into the kitchen to make some coffee. She had no idea what time it was in whatever city Molly was in now, but she picked up the phone and made the call. Her best friend came on sounding groggy. "Charlie?"

"I said Richard was a pencil-dicked, scum-sucking fuckwit."

A dramatic pause, and then Molly whooped. "That's my girl!" A rustling sound followed, with Molly whispering, "Go back to sleep. I'm going to talk to Charlie."

More rustling announced that Molly was moving about. "What precipitated this awesome assassination of pencil-dick's character?" she said after a few more seconds.

Charlotte told Molly about the letter. "All this time, I've been afraid of him, when he's a coward who could only feel good by attacking a woman half his size." Seeing his weasely words had made that truth crystal clear to her. "I think part of it is because I'm not vulnerable anymore." The grieving, insecure girl Richard had known was gone—in her place was a woman who tangled with a far stronger man on a daily basis. "He can't get at me by attacking my weaknesses."

"I'm proud of you," Molly said, fierce in her support.

Charlotte smiled. "I'm proud of me too." It had taken her years, but she'd finally stripped Richard of his power. "Whatever happens, I'll never again fear him." She wasn't naïve enough to think the panic attacks would simply cease, but surely her conscious realization of Richard's true nature would have an impact on her subconscious?

"I hope the other prisoners hurt him while he was in prison," Molly muttered. "It's what he deserves."

Coffee having finished perking, Charlotte poured herself a cup, then took out one of her "angry muffins" as Gabriel had named them, and curled up in a chair at the kitchen table. "I think I should move into Gabriel's apartment."

"Whoa." The sound of liquid being gulped on the other end of the line. "What brought this on?"

"I wanted to prove my independence," Charlotte said, her eyes on the bill she'd left on the counter. "But I've already done that. I've lived here on my own, had my own job, paid my own bills."

"You won't get any arguments from me."

"I guess I just needed to figure that out myself." Charlotte took a bite of her muffin. "The thing is, I never really wanted to live alone anyway. I want to be with Gabriel." She thought of everything she and Gabriel had already shared and of what was still missing.

"I want to feel Gabriel's hand on my nape, Molly," she said softly, her eyes hot with emotion. "I want him to tug my hair and pin me down and tie me up if that's what we want. I don't want Richard to have stolen that from me. I don't want his ugly shadow on any part of my life."

No more. *No more.*

GABRIEL GOT A CALL from Charlotte while he was shaving after his post-run shower.

"I'll be late," she said.

"Why?"

"I'm sleepy."

A ringtone buzzed in his ear a second later. He thought about calling her back, but she *had* sounded adorably sleepy, so he let it go. It wasn't as if Charlotte had ever taken a sick day. She didn't today either, coming in at eleven.

"Damn it, Charlotte!" he yelled when he saw her. "Where the hell do you keep the Paxton files?"

"Right here." Putting down her fancy coffee but not sitting, she bent to her computer and e-mailed the file to him. "I've sent it to your tablet."

He put his hands on her hips and tugged her close. She was wearing a dark pink dress with a square neckline and tailored lines, her hair in a prim bun; she looked so neat and tidy that he just wanted to mess her up. Restraining the urge, he nibbled at her throat instead.

She pushed gently at his shoulder even as her pulse thudded against her skin. "Not here," she murmured but pressed a quick kiss to his jaw before stepping back.

He released her, his entire body reluctant, but his mind reminding him of where they were. "Yeah. I have a conference call in two minutes."

It was hours later that he finally took a breath, to find Charlotte standing in his office doorway, frowning at him. "Did you come back to work after leaving me last night?"

"Yes."

Her frown deepened. "And you'd just got back from your

run when I called you this morning?"

"Your point, Ms. Baird?"

"You can't have had more than four or five hours of sleep at most. You need to break for lunch at least."

"No time." Having already folded up his sleeves, he now tugged off his tie. "Can you order me something?"

She didn't move. "This is not healthy."

"Just order the damn meal, Charlotte."

She did and, to his surprise, wasn't mad at him for snapping at her. When he pointed that out, she rolled her eyes.

"I've been working with you for months, remember?"

However, the next time she told him to stop working, there was definite temper in her eyes.

"Enough, Gabriel," she said. "You've been working nonstop since before I came in. That's not good for you."

"I'm a big boy." Scrawling his name on a contract, he held it out. "Make sure that gets in the morning mail."

"Sure."

"Thanks," he said absently, trusting Charlotte to get things done.

Looking up some time later, he said, "Charlotte?"

No response.

Figuring she must've gone to grab a cup of coffee or something, he waited, but there was still no sound from the front office. He finally stood and went out to see what was up—and found her computer shut down, her desk tidied up as she always did when she left for home.

He scowled, looked for a note. That was when his eye fell on the time displayed on her office phone: 9:47 PM.

"Shit!" No wonder she'd been so pissed.

Hauling ass, he shut down his own computer while calling Charlotte's cell. He half expected it to go to voice mail, but she picked up.

"Yes?"

"I'm sorry," he said, figuring he might as well get that out of the way. "I'll be there soon."

"Don't bother. I already had dinner, and I'm about to read my book."

He winced. "Charlotte."

"I'll see you tomorrow."

Click.

Not about to give up, he headed out. By the time he reached her town house, it was a quarter after ten, but her lights were on. He pressed the doorbell, got no response. Okay, yeah, she was pissed.

He took out his phone, decided to send her a text message rather than calling.

It's cold outside.

The response was sharp: *I'm sure your car is warm.*

What if I say sorry again?

The door opened a minute later, and at first, he thought he was in. Then he saw her face. "Hey," he said, reaching out to cup her cheek and jaw.

Turning into his touch, she pressed her lips to his palm but didn't unfold her arms. "I don't want sorry, Gabriel. I just want you to take care of yourself."

"That's what I have you for." He kissed her, taking the chance that she wouldn't push him away.

She didn't, the kiss red-hot.

Pressing her hand to his chest even as she softened against

317

him, she said, "You need to get some rest."

"I'm starving." He deepened the kiss, made sure she understood his hunger had nothing to do with food, his tongue stroking aggressively against hers.

Her nails dug into him through his shirt, and it was so damn good. He wanted Charlotte's nails scratching him up, wanted to get wild and dirty and sweaty with her. Locking his muscles when his body urged him to haul her close, get rougher, he just kissed her until she was melting and soft; she didn't resist when he nudged his way inside and kicked the door shut.

Stroking his hands down to her gorgeous ass, he lifted her up and pinned her against the wall, alert for any sign of fear. "Finally I see the sexy flannel pants," he said as her legs came around him.

She bit him. It was a tiny bite on his lower lip, but it was a bite. He grinned, bit back. It made her shiver, the shiver rippling over her body when he slipped his hand under her tank top to fondle her bare breast.

She moaned. "We can't just keep having sex."

"Why not? We've got months of frustration built up." Since he had no scruples when it came to being naked with Charlotte, he went for her throat.

"Oh, God, *Gabriel.*" Fingers tight in his hair, she seemed to lose her train of thought for several long, pleasurable minutes. He busied himself getting her tank top off, then leaned down to suck and taste the pretty breasts that made him want to do bad, bad, *bad* things.

"Touch my nape."

He froze. Giving a final suck of one pouting nipple, he lifted his head to look into her eyes. "That makes you have a panic attack."

Chest rising and falling in a jagged rhythm as her fingers flexed on his shoulders, she said, "I know. But I don't want it to."

"I'm not going to do anything that hurts you."

A stubborn glint in her eye, teeth gritted. "I want to do this, Gabriel. I want to do everything."

Gabriel pressed his hands palms-down on either side of her head, holding her up by the simple pressure of his body, her thighs locked around his hips. "What did Dr. Mac say?"

Her expression mutinous, she folded her arms over her naked upper body. "I know better than Dr. Mac what I need. I'm ready!"

Gabriel gripped her jaw, tilted up her face. "Do you know what it does to me when you flinch or go all stiff and scared?" Seeing the shadows, he shook his head. "I'm not saying I'm giving up, Charlotte. I'm saying I *will not* do something that I know will hurt you."

She closed her hand over his wrist, her slender fingers holding him in place more effectively than any manacle. "It hurts me to be like this, to know that you're always thinking." Raw emotion in her voice, in her eyes. "I don't want you to think when we're intimate. I want you to let go."

He couldn't dispute her statement. He *was* always thinking, always making sure he didn't handle her too roughly or touch her in any of the areas that traumatized her. But he also knew something else. "You couldn't have handled any of this when I first started trying to get you naked."

No smile at his words.

"We could do more damage than good by pushing it," he said.

"I'm sick of being stuck in the past!"

The fury of her was a beautiful thing. "I'll do what you want," he said, holding up his hand when she began to smile. "*If* Dr. Mac tells me it won't hurt you."

A little scream. "Let me down."

He did as she asked. There might be times he'd playfully hold her prisoner, but this wasn't the right time for games. "Why are you mad? I'm trying to look after you!"

Pulling her tank top back on, she stomped off to the kitchen. "I want you to listen to me! Dr. Mac has only met me once. I *know* me! I know I'm ready!"

He watched her pull open her freezer, take something out. "What are you doing?"

"Defrosting a stew I made." A glare. "Don't expect to get fed next time you come home at a ridiculous hour."

Warmth and anger combined inside him. *Home.* He liked her talking of them as being at home. He was also still pissed at her for trying to force him to hurt her. "What if we do this and it destroys all the healing you've done so far?"

"I'm not that weak." She stabbed the buttons on the microwave, set it to humming. "If I fall, I'll pick myself back up."

"I don't want you to fall!" he roared.

"You're an overprotective Neanderthal," Charlotte muttered but came over to cup his face in her hands. "I'll talk to Dr. Mac tomorrow, and then you can go and talk to him. But we *are* doing this."

"When did you get so bossy, Ms. Baird?"

"Self-defense against a certain T-Rex."

33

SNARLING AND GROWLING AND A
BAD-TEMPERED T-REX

GABRIEL WAS NOT IN a good mood the next day. He'd had to leave Charlotte again last night when all he'd wanted to do was hold her in his arms the whole night through. He'd barely slept, his mind raging at the fact that it was only a few more days till that piece of shit who'd hurt her would be out in the world once again.

He wasn't sure he could stop himself from hunting down and killing Richard.

Then as soon as he arrived at work, he had to handle a holdover fuckup from the previous CEO's reign that had suddenly taken on new life.

"When are you moving into the apartment?" he asked Charlotte in the car on the way to Dr. Mac's, the doctor having squeezed them in during what should've been his lunch break. It was the first time they'd had a chance to speak about anything other than fixing the fuckup.

"We'll talk about it after the visit."

Once at Dr. Mac's, Charlotte went in and he paced the waiting room until the receptionist gave him the evil eye.

Scowling, he went outside and forced himself to deal with his e-mail as he paced. When Charlotte came out, her cheeks were hot with color and her eyes sparking. Gabriel didn't ask what had happened, just went straight in to see the doctor. "Did she yell at you too?"

Dr. Mac chuckled. "A little, but it's good for her. Sit, Gabriel."

"I can't." He was too wound up. "She tell you what she wants me to do?"

"Yes." The doctor rose to come stand with Gabriel. "She's right in one way—she does know herself far better than I do, and I think the incident with the letter was a significant breakthrough."

Gabriel blew out a breath. "It fucking *kills* me when she gets that scared look in her eyes, Doc." Like being stabbed over and over.

The doctor patted his arm. "You're a strong man." Solemn eyes. "Now you have to be strong enough to help her through this next stage of her healing. She's made the choice, and we have to honor it."

Muscles tense, Gabriel nodded.

Charlotte glared at him as he stepped out of the doc's office. "Well?"

He kissed her smart mouth, needing the contact. Arms unfolding, she spread her hands on his chest and rose on tiptoe to sink into the kiss.

"*Ahem.*"

Gabriel barely stopped himself from snarling at the receptionist. Wrapping his arm around Charlotte, he led her out to the car, which he'd parked in front of the villa.

"Fine," he said, "we'll do this at your pace. But I reserve

the right to call things to a halt if it's breaking you." He put his fingers over her lips when she would've spoken. "I can't hurt you and live with myself, so just deal with it."

Eyebrows drawing together, she bit at his fingers. "Do you think I want to hurt you?" she said, and tugged on his tie until he bent to her. "Next time you tell me to just deal with something in that tone of voice, I will throw more than a muffin at your head."

He kissed her again, thrusting his tongue deep and pressing her against the warm metal of the car, his emotions raw. It was only the screech of tires on the road past the shrubbery hedge that had him pulling back. "Go for it," he said, taking in her swollen lips with intense satisfaction. "I like fighting with you."

"I'm moving in with you." She smoothed out his tie, that fire still in her eyes. "We'll be fighting more often in the future."

His bad mood was gone in a heartbeat. Pressing into her with his palms braced on either side of the car behind her, he smiled. "Game on, Ms. Baird."

SIX HOURS LATER AND a trip to Charlotte's place to move some of her stuff over, and Gabriel leaned against the doorjamb of the spare bedroom as Charlotte finished her phone call. "What did she say?" he asked, knowing Charlotte had finally managed to touch base with the woman who would've been her landlady if Charlotte hadn't decided to move in with him.

"She was lovely," Charlotte said with a smile. "I offered to pay a penalty for changing my mind, but she wouldn't accept it, said she already had someone on a waiting list who'd be delighted to take it."

"Good." He watched in possessive satisfaction as she put away some of her things. This room was right next to his, and while he had every intention of seducing her into his bed, this was good for now. "You like it here?"

A delighted laugh. "Gabriel, I have a penthouse room with a view!" Walking to the sliding doors that faced the balcony, she pushed them open. "Wow."

He walked through and out onto the balcony with her. It had a solid concrete wall around it that hit him at waist height, higher on her. Above that was a gap of about five inches, topped with a smooth railing that was comfortable to lean against. Charlotte did just that, the night wind tugging at her curls as the city sparkled not far in the distance.

Gabriel thought of what the doctor had said, what Charlotte had demanded, and tensed his abdomen. "I'm going to come up behind you."

Her spine went stiff; he could almost see her forcing herself to relax. "Okay." A husky response.

Not drawing out the suspense, he shifted to stand at her back and put his hands on either side of hers on the railing. Her small body went rigid again.

"Hey." He nuzzled a kiss to the side of her face. "Gabriel, that's who's holding you right now. Say it."

"G—" She swallowed. "Gabriel." A deep inhale, a slow exhale. "Gabriel."

CHARLOTTE HAD NEVER FELT so scared and so good at the same time. Gabriel was an impenetrable wall of protection around her. He was also trapping her.

When he leaned forward, his chest pressing along her back, her muscles threatened to tense regardless of her attempt otherwise, but then she caught his scent and it was raw and hot and Gabriel. "Come closer," she murmured. "I want to smell you."

A chuckle rippled through him, but he shifted his arms closer and bent so that his breath brushed her temple. "What do I smell like?"

His voice made her sense of safety deepen. "Good."

"Look," Gabriel said, "there's the office."

She followed the line of his arm, got distracted by the muscular strength of it. Turning to brace her back against the railing, she ran her hands up his chest. Big and gorgeous and hers, he'd made her an addict. When she undid a couple of buttons on the work shirt he hadn't yet changed out of, he stayed in position, head lowered to watch her.

Breasts swelling against her bra, she rose on her toes to press a kiss to the triangle of skin she'd bared. He shifted his arms closer but didn't otherwise move. Charlotte undid a couple more buttons, nuzzled at him, his scent making her drunk. "We should go inside."

"Not into public displays of affection?" His voice was rough with arousal.

Charlotte licked at him, nuzzled again. "My best friend ended up splashed across the tabloids making out with her guy. I don't think anyone has a zoom lens on us, but you are a rugby god, so you never know." It was pure luck the gossip magazines hadn't caught on to their relationship—her position as his PA added to his notoriously intense work habits had helped explain away the times they were seen together.

That wouldn't work if she was caught kissing the boss.

Gabriel shifted back, ran a finger down her throat. It made her shiver.

"Come on then, Ms. Baird. Let me suck on you in private."

She tripped as she stepped forward, but he caught her wrist, tumbled her against his chest before tugging her into the bedroom. "Stay." It was an order.

Charlotte stayed. She really had no reason to disobey—not when she wanted Gabriel so very badly. Her heart kicked at hearing him shut the balcony doors and flick the switch to close the blinds. This time when he stepped behind her it was a little easier.

Her pulse still went into overdrive, her spine still locked, but she knew it was Gabriel behind her, was no longer so blinded by terror that she didn't see or hear or smell anything but the horror of the past. A rustle of sound and when he slipped his arms around her, he wasn't wearing his shirt. She turned her face deliberately into his arm, breathed him in as her skin brushed his.

Running his hands up her body, Gabriel shaped her hips, her ribs, her breasts. He squeezed, and it made her moan, try to get closer to him. His breath kissed her throat, his mouth wet as he sucked. Shivering, she reached back for him, touched the hard bulk of his thighs.

"I like your hands on me."

The rumble of his voice was another caress.

"I like your hands on me too," she said. "And your mouth."

That got her more suckling kisses on her neck before he lifted one of his hands from her breasts to gently collar her throat. "Yes?"

Her lungs strained, though he wasn't restricting her airway. *Gabriel, this is Gabriel with his hand around my throat.* Oh, God, she was starting to hyperventilate. If she did, he'd back off, and she didn't want him to back off. She wanted him exactly where he was. "Gabriel," she managed to get out, the sound thin but audible.

Kisses along her shoulder, her throat. "That's it, sweetheart. Stay with me."

Chest heaving, she dug her nails into his thighs. "Don't stop." Her heart beat so hard it felt as if it would punch out of her ribcage. When she tried to say more, it was to find her throat had closed up.

No, no, no.

Her body wouldn't obey her mind, panic a trapped bird inside her skull.

"I think," Gabriel said, his voice rough, "this'll work better."

Charlotte was still trying to process the words when he shifted them both. He was still behind her, but she now faced the other side of the room and the full-length, freestanding mirror that stood beside the vanity. In that mirror was an image of a blond woman who had a big male hand at her throat, another on her breast; those hands with their blunt tips and square nails were hands she knew, the eyes that held hers a familiar steel gray.

"Gabriel," she said on a rush of air.

"I like my name on your lips." He moved his hand in a petting motion but didn't take it off her throat. With his other one, he continued to mold and shape her breast, tugging at the nipple that pushed at her dress through the lace of her bra. "My pretty Charlotte," he said, each word spaced out with

327

a kiss on her jaw, her cheek, her throat. "You have no idea the ways in which I want to fuck you."

She jerked at the harsh word, but her thighs clenched at the same time.

"I used to dream about bending you over my desk, shoving up those ugly skirts you used to wear, pulling down your panties, and using my hand to push you to orgasm before I drove my cock into you."

All she could hear was his voice, all she could feel was him, the images he painted flashing on her retinas. "Th...that's—"

"Inappropriate, I know." More kisses. "But a man can be inappropriate in his mind, especially when his balls are turning blue." Another kiss, this one on her nape.

It wasn't, she realized, the first one. He'd distracted her with his words, seduced her with his mouth, was teaching her body that a touch from him in that place wouldn't mean pain and humiliation. "*Gabriel.*" She moved restlessly. "Let me take off my dress."

He tightened his grip on her throat the slightest fraction. "No."

Her breath sped up, her heart rate rocketing as her chest squeezed in panic.

"Shh." Easing his grip, he kept kissing her. "We're just playing, Charlotte."

Playing.

It was such an unthreatening word that it cut through the grip of fear. "Playing," she whispered.

"Yes." He reached across to torment her neglected breast. "Pull up your dress."

Mouth dry, she did as he asked, to reveal panties of black

lace. She'd bought three different lingerie sets, all in his favorite shade on her flesh.

He traced the waistband of her panties with a single finger, brushing over the tiny pink rosette in the center. "Is this
for me?" A pleased sound against her ear. At her nod, he said,
"Such good behavior deserves a reward, don't you think?"

"Yes."

Chuckling, he used his hand on her throat to urge her to
bend her head back toward him. The instant she did, he
kissed her. The position left her intensely vulnerable and yet
feeling intensely protected. Breaking the kiss after a long,
deep taste, Gabriel allowed her to straighten. "Keep holding
up your dress."

Charlotte's fingers tightened on the fabric as he slid his
free hand into her panties. A whimper escaped her; that got
her kissed once more in that painfully vulnerable position as
he touched her with possessive confidence, tugging at her
clit, stroking through her folds, thrusting a finger, then two,
into her body.

"Come for me, Ms. Baird."

The low, deep, rough order sent an electric surge through
her body. Gasping, she tried to fight the rising edge of need,
but it was coming too fast, too hard, Gabriel's sinful fingers
playing her body like a favored instrument. Pleasure arched
her spine hard enough to snap, and through it all, Gabriel
kept his hand on her throat, his grip gentle but firm.

She shuddered into boneless limpness afterward, held up-
right by his body and by the hand he'd kept between her
thighs. Cupping her damp heat, he kissed her nape again,
licking over the spot before saying, "On the bed." When he

removed his hands from her, she would've stumbled to the bed, but he took her hips and nudged her out the door.

"My bed. That's where you belong."

She thought maybe she should protest his high-handedness, but since she wanted to be in Gabriel's bed anyway, that particular idea stood no chance of success. Her knees were so weak she didn't know how she made it to the master bedroom. Climbing onto the sprawling bed, she would've turned over onto her back but he said, "Stay there."

Her stomach knotted, the pleasure of a few moments ago buried under increasing strain. "I don't know if I can take your weight," she said, his earlier statement stark in her mind: she would not hurt Gabriel by freaking out. Better to warn him in advance.

"Why are you always trying to rush?" The bed dipped. "That's graduate level, and we're at the freshmen stage." A tug on her dress told her he was pulling down the zipper. "Now you can turn."

When she did, he slid her dress off her shoulders and down her body to strip it off. Coming down beside her, he braced himself on one arm and stroked his hand from her chest down to the tops of her thighs. His skin was a little rough, his palm big enough to easily span her breastbone. It felt good, but...

Gripping his wrist, she brought his hand to her throat. "There too."

His eyes darkened as he curved his hand around her throat once more.

It made her rub her feet against the sheets, her blood hot with nervous arousal. Those nerves sizzled under his kiss. He thrust his tongue deep, moving his hand back down her body only to return to collar her throat in a more aggressive hold.

"Okay?" His lips brushed her own.

She arched into him in a silent yes, her hands buried in his hair. Kiss even deeper, he came over her, using one fore-arm to brace himself so his weight wouldn't crush her. For a second, Charlotte thought she'd be all right, that they'd fig-ured it out, then black spots danced in her vision, claustrophobia choking her until she couldn't even tell him to get off.

34

GABRIEL AND HIS MS. BAIRD

GABRIEL FELT CHARLOTTE'S BODY go motionless underneath him. Her breathing told him that this time it wasn't the incipient panic he'd sensed in her earlier. This was the real deal, a full-blown panic attack.

Shifting immediately to his back, he pulled her on top of him. "Charlotte." Chancing a light grip on her chin while leaving her otherwise free, he held her gaze.

Her eyes were dangerously blank.

"Charlotte, it's Gabriel." His heart twisted inside his chest, his anger at what had been done to her as violent as his need to protect her. "The man who wants to love you every possible way there is on this earth, but who will *never* hurt you."

No response.

He repeated his name, reminded her that they were just playing, trying to figure out what worked for them. "Come on back, Ms. Baird. It's no fun playing solo when I can do it with you."

"Gabriel." A whisper so husky he could barely hear it, but it was there: his name on the kiss-swollen plumpness of her lips. "Gabriel." Shuddering, she collapsed against him like a frightened kitten.

The wet he felt against his neck the next second threatened to break him. "Why are you crying?" he growled, almost curving his hand over her nape before he remembered that was a danger zone.

Instead, he shifted her onto her back again and, staying on his side, collared her throat. "Quiet."

Jerky sniffs, one hand lifting to wipe away her tears. "Sorry."

"You can cry whenever you want," he said. "But you damn well don't do it because you're beating yourself up. Understood?"

Her eyes glittered. "I told myself I was done with the memories, done with fear." As much anger and frustration as self-directed disappointment rippled through her words. "But my brain won't listen!"

"Charlotte." She drove him crazy. "You have my fucking hand at your throat." Tightening his grip to make his point, he kissed her, used his teeth, his tongue, until she moaned and kissed him back as hotly. "How exactly," he said when they came up for air, "do you think you messed up?"

Tiny vertical lines formed between her eyebrows. "Stop snarling at me," she said, lifting one hand to fist it in his hair.

"I'll stop when you begin to listen to reason." He moved the hand on her throat down to her stomach, caressing her as he kissed her again. Her ribcage was so delicate under his touch, her breasts exquisite through the fine lace of her bra. "We're not going to do everything in one night, and what the hell fun would there be in that anyway?"

Making an aggravated sound in her throat, she pulled at his hair. "I *said* stop snarling at me."

"You have a temper, Ms. Baird."

A scowl. "I have to, with you around." Shoving at his chest, she pushed him to his back. "I want to do things to you now."

His cock, already rock hard, jerked to attention. "Oh yeah?"

"Yeah."

She straddled him low on his thighs, the view a gorgeous one, especially since her hair had started to come out of that bun. When her hands went to his buckle, he sucked in a breath. Her teeth sinking into her lower lip in sexy concentration, she undid the belt and stripped it off to throw it on the floor, clever fingers on the fastenings of his pants.

He cooperated when she moved down his body, taking his pants and underwear with her. Dumping his clothing on the floor, she straddled his thighs again, her eyes on the hard length of his cock.

"I don't know how this gets inside me," she murmured, capturing him in her small, competent hands.

He groaned.

A small, wicked, slightly shy smile on her face, Charlotte began to jerk him off. His eyes closed, his hips rising toward her. He wasn't the least prepared to feel the hot wet of her mouth close over the head of his cock.

"Fuck!" He had his hand on her nape before he could stop himself, his actions instinctive.

Tearing it away when she went stiff, he groaned and fell back on the bed with his arms thrown wide. "Well, fuck. Now you're not going to suck me off, are you?"

Muscles easing to softness again, Charlotte sat up, stared at him. Her pulse was erratic in her throat but her lips, they held that tiny, wicked smile. "That's all you're worried about?"

"Charlotte, when you have your mouth anywhere near my cock, my brain cells turn into gibbering idiots."

She laughed, ran her nails down his chest. "You have to behave." A playful statement, but there were shadows in her eyes.

"I will," he promised. There would come a day when he could fist his hand in her hair, direct her to do exactly what he wanted, but she'd already gone far beyond what either one of them could've expected.

So he lay there and took it, and fuck, it was good.

CHARLOTTE KEPT BLUSHING AS she stood on the sidelines with Gabriel early the next day. A cold Saturday morning, and the high school team he coached was playing its heart out. Then she blushed through her eleven-o'clock pastry class, causing her new friends Juliet and Aroha to teasingly question her about her Friday night.

That just made her blush deepen. She couldn't believe what she'd done with and to Gabriel. Not only had she taken him in her mouth, he'd then hauled her to the end of the bed and returned the favor with interest, one of his hands tight on her breast, her thigh thrown over a heavily muscled shoulder.

God, the man could be deliciously merciless when he had a goal in mind.

"*One more time, Ms. Baird.*"

The memory of his roughly coaxing words vivid in her thoughts, she certainly couldn't look his parents in the eye when she and Gabriel joined the entire Bishop-Esera clan for an afternoon barbeque at a local park.

Full of tall trees, including cheerful cherry blossom trees that had anticipated the coming spring, the park, located at the foot of a dormant volcano like so many of Auckland's parks, also had plenty of open space.

The barbeque was in honor of Joseph's birthday, and Charlotte had bought him a DVD of great rugby moments that she hoped he liked. Before any presents were opened or food eaten, however, there was to be a "friendly" rugby game. It was why she'd worn a pair of jeans and a light sweater over a T-shirt, rather than a dress. Though she had her doubts about her skills on the field, no "shirking" was allowed.

"Game's a tradition," Gabriel had said, placing a hard kiss on her mouth. "Everyone plays except the one who's refereeing. We occasionally excuse pregnant women and those with broken limbs, but that's on a case-by-case basis."

Now he stood with the oval-shaped ball under one arm, his other one slung loosely over Charlotte's shoulders. "Where the hell is Sailor?"

Looking around, Charlotte saw that Sailor's wife and daughter, Ísa and Emmaline, were already here.

It was Alison who answered Gabriel's question. "I asked him to bring Brian. They should be here soon."

Charlotte expected Gabriel to lose his good mood at the mention of his father, but he just shook his head. "Don't let him scam you, Mom, okay?"

Alison smiled, expression poignant. "I've learned that lesson well—but for better or worse, he did help give two of my boys life." She came over to hug Gabriel. "Two wonderful boys who have hearts big enough to let him in even after what he did."

Squeezing his mom, Gabriel said, "Those hearts come from you."

Charlotte spoke only once Alison was out of earshot. "You're a good man, Gabriel Bishop."

A shrug, but he smiled. "I'm a better man because of you." Kissing her to the accompaniment of giggles from Esme and Emmaline, he said, "You were right about the anger eating me up. It was poisonous."

Sailor arrived then with Brian. Gabriel helped get the frail-appearing older man settled into a chair, a blanket over his lap, then put two fingers just inside his mouth and whistled. "On the field. Brian's refereeing."

Everyone tumbled out onto the open playing area. When Charlotte hesitated, Daniel, whom she'd met properly earlier, grabbed her hand and tugged her forward. "We're playing touch, no tackling. Esme, show everyone an example touch."

The little girl ran to Emmaline and tapped her cousin on the hips with both palms before breaking contact. "No holding, Uncle Danny," she said seriously. "Just touching."

"Jeez, Boo, I only did that once."

Biting back a laugh at Daniel's aggrieved tone, Charlotte listened as Gabriel said, "Normal rules. Pass before you're touched, six touches to score or ball has to be turned over, no forward passes. Did I forget anything?"

Emmaline jumped up and down. "You gotta tap to start again."

"Right." Tugging one of her pigtails, Gabriel demonstrated the tap.

Alison was the one who split them into two teams, dividing the couples. "A little healthy competition," she said with a wink.

Charlotte ended up on the team that got to wear pink armbands. Also on her team were Sailor, Esme, Daniel, and Alison.

"I'm the slowest," Alison said, "and Danny's got wings on his feet, so we even out."

"You've also got me," Charlotte pointed out. "I love rugby, but I'm not a player."

"Give us a few years and you will be," Sailor predicted. "Always pass to Esme if you can—the munchkin's slippery when she gets going."

"Here we go," Gabriel called out and the game began.

The first time Danny passed the ball back to Charlotte, she dropped it forward, leading to it being turned over to the opposing side.

Esme patted her hand. "It's okay, Charlie. I do that sometimes too."

"Hey, less talking, more playing, Butterfingers!" Gabriel called out.

Charlotte narrowed her eyes at the grinning taunt. "You're going down, T-Rex!"

He winked at her and, tapping the ball with his foot to restart the game, spun it back into Jake's steady hands. From there it went to Joseph, then to Emmaline, who pumped halfway down the field before yelling, "Mommy!" and passing to Ísa right before Alison tapped her.

Ísa would've made it over the try line if her husband hadn't gotten his hands on her.

"Sorry, honey," Sailor said, stealing a kiss, "this is war."

"Watch it, mister." Expression fierce, Ísa restarted the game, but a series of touches by the pink team meant they regained possession of the ball.

Charlotte caught the pass this time, got it to Esme, who was a tiny rocket. She passed to Sailor, who threw to Danny, who sent it back to Charlotte again, their team moving across and up the field. Able to see the try line, Charlotte ran her hardest. She was almost there when strong arms lifted her off her feet.

"Uncle Gabe is cheating!" Esme cried out while Charlotte tried not to laugh.

"Here!" She threw the ball down into the little girl's hands.

Face gleeful, Esme grounded the ball on the other side of the try line just as Gabriel finally let Charlotte down. "I thought this game had rules," she said to him.

He kissed her. "Most of the time."

They played for another twenty minutes, Emmaline scoring for the other side when Gabriel fed her the ball right on the try line.

All other try attempts were foiled by quick, legal touches, or very illegal body blocking—or in one case, by Sailor throwing Ísa over his shoulder and running off toward the trees.

"I don't think I've ever laughed so hard," Charlotte said afterward, having collapsed on the grass to soak up the sun, Gabriel on one side and Danny on the other. She really liked Gabriel's youngest brother. Despite the fact he was starting to build up a serious profile, with all the attendant media and female attention, he was a genuine sweetheart. She hoped he never lost that gentleness of nature.

"I love playing for my team," he said right then, "but these are my favorite games. I reckon Esme's got what it takes to make a rep team."

"She's good," agreed Gabriel. "Em's doing well at soccer—I caught one of her school games a month back."

Feeling content, Charlotte lay there under the sun as the two spoke. A dragonfly buzzed somewhere, and she could hear the girls playing with Jake and Sailor, the atmosphere warm and alive and happy. This, she thought, was what she wanted. A big, rambunctious family that welcomed everyone, even prodigals who'd made awful mistakes.

Gabriel's phone buzzed into the hazy quiet. He'd left it on the sideline during the game but now slipped it out of his pocket. "Bishop," he said, then paused. "What's the situation?"

He left ten minutes later, heading to deal with an unexpected supply issue that could derail a nationwide campaign set to launch tonight. "No, stay here," he said to Charlotte when she readied herself to accompany him. "I'll sort out this headache and be back in time to eat."

"Can't Arnett handle this?" He was Gabriel's Chief Operations Officer, and highly competent.

"He's meeting me there. I want to make dead sure we put out this fire." A kiss and he was gone.

Charlotte frowned after him, thinking once again of family. What kind of family would they create—if her hang-ups didn't sink them after all—if Gabriel was never around or always obsessed with work when he was around?

35

A Slight Glitch (Okay, Fine, A Big Freaking Glitch)

GABRIEL DIDN'T, IN FACT, return in time to eat. Charlotte caught a ride home with Jake and Esme, and didn't confront Gabriel about his work habits when he came in late. He looked so stressed that she didn't want to add to it.

There was kissing and petting, but she went to sleep in the spare room that night and on Sunday, the latter being a quiet day where Gabriel only spent a few hours on work. It worried her, but again, she let it go because he finally relaxed in the afternoon—bringing it up at that point would've likely led to an argument, wiping out any mental rest he'd managed to get.

The next day at the office, she was still musing over how to handle things when a dozen red roses were delivered to her desk. Her heart threatened to crack, but unable to believe he'd break up with her so callously, she reached for the card, opened it.

"Gabriel!"

He was beside her in a heartbeat. "What's the matter?" Seeing the flowers, he picked up the card she'd dropped.

"That pathetic piece of shit!" Though the words were hot, his tone was ice-cold. "You okay, sweetheart?"

She patted his chest. Her heart still raced, but now that she'd calmed down from the first stab of shock, she was angry more than anything. "I'm good," she said, taking the card and putting it in an envelope so she could pass it on to Detective Lee. "I'm going to give these to Tuck for his girlfriend. No point in good roses going to waste."

Wanting the bouquet out of her sight, she carried it to the mail room herself. Tuck was over the moon.

"You sure you don't want them?" he asked, touching his fingers to the petals of one. "They look real expensive."

"I'm sure." Charlotte smiled, pleased that Richard's sliminess hadn't had the intended effect. "Hope you get lucky."

Tuck grinned. "No question. She's going to love me today."

Gabriel was looking out the window in his office when she got back, his hands on his hips and his shoulders so tense he was like a stone statue. Ignoring her ringing phone, she shut the door to his office, then went over to him.

"I'm fine," she said, her hands on his chest. "Come here." She petted his nape, kissed his jaw, claimed his mouth.

It took time, but his muscles finally began to ease. "You're really okay?"

"I am. A whole lot of that has to do with you." She'd come a long way on her own, but she'd become stuck in stasis at a certain point. It had taken Gabriel challenging her, expecting her to handle him, that had pushed her to go further. "So thank you."

His arms came around her, and they stood there for a long time. Charlotte had never felt safer, and the fact that

Richard had sent her flowers right after his release, along with a card that said "I miss you," was not about to change that. "Don't let him inside your head," she said to Gabriel when they drew apart. "That's how he gets you. He's a bug, and we ignore bugs or we squash them. We don't think about them."

Gabriel's lips curved

"That's my Ms. Baird."

"Yes, I am."

RICHARD MADE FURTHER ATTEMPTS at mental manipulation over the next two weeks, but Charlotte shrugged them off while continuing to pass everything on to Detective Lee. Richard was being very careful not to cross the line that would shove him back in jail, but eventually, he wouldn't be able to help himself, and then they'd have him.

In the interim, she settled into Gabriel's apartment and into his arms. He kissed her on the back of her neck every morning, rippling a shiver through her body. And he kissed her there when he walked her to her room every night. They made love in his bed but she slept in her own.

The one time they'd tried sleeping together, she'd woken so panicked that she'd given him a black eye. Of course, that was only because he'd been trying to calm her without holding her down. Her resulting emotional mess of a mind threatened to unravel all her progress.

"Does it hurt still?" she asked at breakfast two days later.

The bruise under his eye blue and green, Gabriel sighed. "I'm crushed, fragile flower that I am."

"It's not funny." She hated that she'd hurt him.

"Sweetheart, I took worse hits than this in training." He cuddled her close, big and strong enough to not care that she'd gotten in a lucky shot. "We will sleep in the same bed one of these days." A deep, demanding kiss that left her breathless. "In the meantime, we'll amuse each other in other ways."

She couldn't be as sanguine, but as the bruise faded and they continued to become more entwined as a couple, she listened to Dr. Mac's advice and forgave herself for the incident. Festering over it would only hold her back. It still hurt though. Deep in the night, when she lay alone in her bed, she couldn't help the tears sometimes.

She hated, *hated* knowing that something inside her remained fractured. But for that one huge obstacle to the life she wanted with Gabriel, things were good. The man she adored felt the same about her, and they were an incredible team at work. That Friday, he was at a meeting with all the regional managers while Charlotte held the fort at the office.

When she did need to contact him, she sent through a quick message, received a response. A couple of times, he called her back during breaks in the meeting in order to give her more complicated instructions, which included her having to deal directly with CEOs of supply companies, VPs, and other high-level people.

A few months ago, she'd have quivered and stuttered and curled into a ball at the very idea of it. Today she was greeted by name, she chatted easily with the people on the other end of the line, and got matters sorted out one after the other. The T-Rex at whose head she'd once thrown a stapler, then a muffin, had been good for her.

No one could travel a hard road all alone.

Not even Gabriel.

She called him at two. "Have you eaten lunch?"

"Yes, since it was delivered right to my hand."

"Good." She'd organized the catering for the meeting and given very specific instructions about making sure Gabriel's was handed personally to him. "How's it going?"

"No one's been an idiot so far" was the short answer. "I'm giving it another hour, then heading to the North Shore store to speak to the staff."

That was the thing about Gabriel—he was consistently noted as one of the most approachable CEOs of a major corporation in the country. Everyone on the staff, from the most junior new hire to the old guard, had his e-mail address. She'd seen his inbox. She also knew he answered every one of those messages. That's often what he did at night and on the weekends.

Aware that it was important to him, she'd started to figure out ways to clear time during the day so he could deal with the e-mails at the office rather than constantly taking work home. Part of that meant handling more things herself. "I need an assistant," she said to him now. "What I was to Anya."

Gabriel snorted. "You were doing her job."

"Yes, fine. I need someone who will actually be my assistant."

"Hire someone."

That was that. Instead of making up a job ad, she promoted from within, reaching out to a staff member who'd shown potential. The other woman didn't have the qualifications that would've made her an automatic shoo-in for the position, but she did better work than others who were technically more qualified.

It felt good to make someone's day and to make a silent statement that hard work would be noticed and rewarded. "You'll officially start next week," she told the younger woman. "That'll give HR time to get someone to fill your current position."

Beaming, the other woman left to share her good news with her friends, and Charlotte got back to work. Gabriel still wasn't back at five thirty. When she called him, he said he was taking the store's managerial team out to dinner and asked her to meet him at a restaurant over the bridge.

Heading downstairs to the lobby around six, she smiled at the security guard on duty. "Bye, Steven."

"Hey, Charlie. I have to walk you out—boss's orders."

"The car's two feet outside the door." She could see the idling cab, her favorite cabbie's bearded form in the driver's seat.

"I'm not about to argue with Mr. Bishop."

"You should. It's good for him."

That made Steven laugh as he pushed the button that opened the doors after hours. "You have a good night."

"You too." Right before she was about to slide into the cab, something made her look around. It felt as if someone was watching her, the feeling so visceral she knew it wasn't paranoia.

For a second, she thought she saw Richard at the end of the block, but when she looked again, there was no one there. Though the incident disturbed her, she put it out of her mind by the time she arrived at the restaurant; she would not let Richard win by allowing him to dominate her thoughts. As long as she was smart and careful, he couldn't get to her. Gabriel, too, knew not to let down his guard.

"Ms. Baird," Gabriel said when she reached the table, a glint in his eye. "I'm glad you could join us."

He was a wicked, wicked man. The two of them weren't hiding their relationship any longer, but no one at work had twigged to it. Charlotte was glad she didn't have to deal with media scrutiny, and it made sense to remain professional during work situations—which Gabriel didn't make any easier, tapping her foot with his under the table and making the odd double-edged comment designed to tease her but that went right over everyone else's head.

She shot him a glare now and then for form, but she felt like laughing. The dinner was fun overall, the people around the table a mix of both those she dealt with regularly and several new faces.

When the store manager—seated beside her—leaned over and said, "I don't suppose you'd have a private dinner with me another day?" she smiled and shook her head.

"I have a guy."

"Ah well, my loss. Should've scooped you up earlier."

It was only when Charlotte glanced across the table that she realized Gabriel had tensed up, his good humor for show. Discreetly taking off her high heel under the table, she ran her foot over his leg. The gleam returned to his eye, but she could tell he was annoyed by the fact another man had hit on her.

Gabriel, she realized suddenly, wasn't as onboard with the whole "under the radar" thing as she'd believed. He'd agreed only because of her discomfort with being in the spotlight. Her heart expanded—yeah, she was pretty stupid in love with her guy. And she wanted people to know he was hers, enough to handle any resulting pressure; she'd make that clear to him later tonight.

He was definitely possessive when he ushered her into his SUV, the two of them the last to leave the restaurant after Gabriel took care of the bill. Tipping up her chin after backing her up against the car in the dark parking lot behind the restaurant, he kissed her, his hand at her throat. It made her shiver, wrap her own arms around him, her mouth opening under his and her fingers tight in his hair.

Biting her lower lip, tugging, Gabriel smiled. "I'm thinking diamonds and skin."

Feeling scandalous, she whispered, "I'm pretty sure you could convince me to get naked in the backseat."

Another wet kiss, his hand tugging up her dress to slide up her thigh before he stepped back and opened the passenger door so she could get in. "Hold that thought," he said after getting into the driver's seat and throwing his wallet on the console. "But not in the backseat. I'm too damn big."

She put the wallet in her handbag so he wouldn't forget it in the car. "I like you big."

"Naughty, Ms. Baird."

"I didn't mean—"

"So you're saying I'm not big?"

"You should've been a lawyer," she said with a laugh.

He put his hand on her thigh, the warmth and weight of it intimate and familiar. Closing her hand over his, she leaned back in the seat and just enjoyed the drive, enjoyed being with her guy. Even the thought alone made her grin like a giddy schoolgirl.

When he brought the car to a stop at the apartment building, she got out and they headed to the elevator. She slapped her forehead just as the doors opened. "Damn, I forgot to ask you to stop for milk. We're all out."

"Want me to go grab it? It'll only take a few minutes." Gabriel held the elevator open. "Go on up and get into something slinky." He leaned in close to whisper, "I vote for the tiny black thing that's all straps and skin."

Blushing, she crooked a finger. "We don't really need milk."

He chuckled. "You're not human until your first latte. I'll be back in five minutes."

"I'll be waiting." Blowing him a kiss, she pressed the button for the penthouse after swiping the keycard.

She had a smile on her face when she exited onto the penthouse floor, but she'd only taken five steps when her blood ran cold. "How did you get up here?" she said to the handsome blond man standing by the apartment door. His face was older, meaner, and he had a new scar across his cheek, but there was no mistaking Richard.

36

TAKING OUT THE TRASH

"I WAS WAITING FOR you," Richard said with a flawless smile, leaning his body against the wall. "We have something to talk about."

"We have nothing to talk about." Charlotte's heart thudded in her throat, her rage a roar beneath the skin. "Get out."

"You bitch." Richard's mask fell off far faster than it had the first time. "I spent years in prison because of you, and you can't give me five minutes?"

"You spent that time in prison because of what you did."

"Only because you made me," he retorted. "If you'd been a real woman—"

"I'm not the one with inadequacy issues." Charlotte would not back down, would not run. She was no longer prey—and she was no longer vulnerable. "I'm with a real man now, and guess what? He doesn't need to hurt a woman to feel good about himself."

"Some stupid rugby player." He sneered. "I guess a dumb whore like you would want a dumb boyfriend."

"You're a pathetic loser who doesn't deserve to breathe the same air as Gabriel." She curled her fingers around the strap of her handbag. "I have nothing more to say to you. You aren't worth the time."

"Oh, we'll talk," he hissed, launching himself at her. "You'll crawl before I'm done with you."

His hand went for her throat, but hell no, he was *not* holding her there. That was Gabriel's right and his right only. Swinging her handbag, she slammed it against the side of Richard's head. He staggered; she kicked him between the legs. Then she gave him a second hard whack just as the elevator doors opened behind her.

The next thing she heard was a roar of sound, and then Richard was flying back to slam into the wall, his nose crooked and gushing blood. Gabriel's second punch took him to the floor, the knife in Richard's hand dropping soundlessly to the carpet.

The third punch cracked bones in Richard's face.

The fourth punch smashed out several of Richard's teeth and turned off his lights.

It all happened so fast that she barely had time to blink before Gabriel was turning to her.

"Did he touch you?" It was a ferociously quiet question.

"No." Deeply conscious that he was on a razor-thin edge, but not the least afraid he'd turn his anger on her, she went into his arms. "I whacked him with my handbag—it came in useful, see?"

He didn't laugh, just crushed her against his chest. Breath harsh and pulse thumping, he held her for long minutes, his muscles vibrating against hers. She held him back, knowing her presence was all that was keeping him from beating Richard to a pulp. Not about to let Gabriel go to jail for a psychopath like Richard, she stroked his back until he got himself under enough control to say, "Call Detective Lee. I'll keep an eye on the trash."

THE DETECTIVE LAUGHED AT a newly conscious Richard's snuffling, barely understandable accusations of assault against Gabriel. "He was protecting a woman against a psychopath armed with a knife. The psychopath would be you." A grin that bared very sharp teeth as she put the knife in an evidence bag and held it in front of Richard's face. "Mr. Bishop only used his fists. No prosecutor will *ever* touch him."

Charging Richard then and there, she snapped the cuffs on him even as the paramedics lifted him onto a gurney for transport to the hospital. Gabriel had broken Richard's face worse than Charlotte had initially realized—Richard would never again be as pretty, would wear his ugliness for the world to see. That seemed fitting. People should have a warning of his kind of evil.

"The fact he came after you so soon after his release is a significant aggravating factor," Detective Lee said. "Hopefully we'll get a judge who'll throw the book at him this time."

Charlotte hoped that too. She could handle Richard now, of that she was certain, but she hated the effect the attack had on Gabriel.

"Hey," she said in bed that night, rising up on her elbow to look down at him. "You're still furious. I can feel it."

"Of course I'm furious. If I hadn't forgotten you had my wallet and come back up, he would've had you alone."

"I was doing a good job of beating him up," she pointed out. "Richard expected me to be who I was, not who I am."

"You're fucking amazing." Hauling her down, he kissed her, and it was all tongue and heat. "But he should've never been able to get to our floor. I'm getting the woman he charmed into bringing him up so he could 'surprise' his girl-friend kicked out of the building."

Scowling, Charlotte shook her head. "He played her. He's good at that. The poor woman already feels terrible." That woman lived directly below the penthouse and had the keycard to use the same elevator. "Leave her be."

One arm behind his head, Gabriel ground his teeth to-gether. "I wanted to pulverize him until he didn't have a single unbroken bone in his body."

"I understand the urge." She had the same one. "Now, forget about Richard. He isn't worth the time or the energy."

Gabriel wrapped his arm around her, his fingers on her bare hip. "It'll take me a while to get to that point."

"Want to spend that time being naked together?"

He took her up on her offer, but when it came time for him to leave her at her bedroom door, she held on to his hand. "Stay with me."

"No." A flat answer. "I'm sorry, sweetheart, but if I see you afraid of me today—" He shook his head, then kissed her hard. "Go to sleep."

She tried, but she tossed and turned for the next two hours, a jagged hole inside her formed of the knowledge that she couldn't give Gabriel what he needed. When she heard movement, she got up and stepped out to find him seated with his back to the wall of her bedroom, his head in his hands.

"What are you doing here?"

"Making sure you're safe. That fucking monster almost had you."

He was breaking her heart. "No," she said, "he didn't." Taking his hand, she tugged. "Come on. Since neither one of us is going to sleep, let's go lie on the couch and watch movies."

It was a rough night. Charlotte fell asleep in patches against him, and he dropped off now and then, but neither one of them could fully wind down. She was frustrated with herself, and he was still riding a wave of fury.

IT WAS A GOOD thing the next day was a Saturday when Gabriel's high school team didn't have a game. Grumpy and sleep-deprived, neither one of them was in the best of moods, and it didn't help when she came downstairs after her shower to find Gabriel already on his laptop working.

Seated at the dining table, he'd grabbed a cup of coffee from the pot she'd put on to perk before her shower, but hadn't bothered to get any food.

"Gabriel, it's Saturday!" She threw up her hands. "Can you not forget about work for a single weekend?" He'd already brought work home every night this week.

A scowl over his bare shoulder. He was dressed only in sweatpants, his hair rumpled, and his jaw shadowed. "I'm just checking my e-mail."

"Work e-mail." Tightening the belt on her thin red robe, she began to crack eggs to make omelets. "None of it urgent if I'm guessing right—and even if it is, you *pay* people to take some of the load off. *Delegate.*"

He slammed the laptop shut and got up, shoving his chair

back. "Jesus, Charlotte. You've always known how much I work."

"And I've always thought you were heading for an early grave." She began to whisk the eggs. "You didn't belong to me before, so I couldn't say anything, but now you do, so I am."

"I'm as healthy as an ox."

"You don't rest, you don't relax—"

"I feel very relaxed after we fuck."

"Stop trying to make me back off by using words like *fuck*." She poured the omelet into the pan, so angry that she didn't even blush at getting the word past her lips. "I want to have a life with you. I don't intend to have a life with your job as a silent partner."

He growled at her, actually *growled*. "I am who I am, Charlotte."

"So am I—doesn't mean you haven't helped me heal." She put the omelet on a plate, shoved it onto the counter. "Eat."

"I don't need healing." He ignored the omelet.

It just made her angrier. She found a fork, put it on the plate. "So you're telling me I'm the only flawed one in this relationship?" After all, she was the one who couldn't even sleep with the man she loved beyond life.

"Fuck." He thrust a hand through his hair. "That's not what I said."

"It sure sounded like it." When he continued to ignore the omelet, she picked it up and began to eat herself. "Go then, work," she said after swallowing the first couple of bites. "I'm going to go out."

"Where?" He came around to loom over her.

"Wherever the hell I want." Charlotte slammed the plate with the half-eaten omelet on the counter.

Gabriel followed her upstairs to her bedroom when she stalked off. "Damn it, Charlotte, this discussion is not finished."

"If you want to finish it, you can come with me. Otherwise, go stare at your laptop!" She slammed the bedroom door—or tried to. He'd blocked it with his hand. "Go away. I'm about to change."

"I've seen you naked, Ms. Baird, and I intend to keep on doing it." Folding his arms, he filled the doorway, a big, brooding male who didn't think she'd take the dare.

Infuriated with him, she shrugged her robe to the floor.

FUCK.

Gabriel's cock went as hard as rock between one heartbeat and the next. Charlotte hadn't been wearing anything under that robe, and now she was standing all sweet and curvy and flushed with temper in front of him, her hair tumbled around her face. He didn't even think about it, just strode to her and picked her up, then threw her on the bed.

She gasped, her eyes flashing at him. "What do you think you're doing?"

Coming over her after tearing off his sweatpants, he braced himself on his forearms. "Finishing our argument." He tore off her glasses and threw them in the vague direction of the nightstand.

"Hah! I'm—"

He swallowed her words with his mouth, one of his hands gripping her breast. She shoved at his shoulders. Lifting his head, he said, "What? You want me." She always wanted him, and that was the hottest thing on the planet.

"I am really, really, *really* mad at you!"

"Good, we'll have angry sex." He kissed her again, thrusting his tongue deep into her mouth and squeezing her breast harder than he'd ever done before.

Shoving her hands into his hair, she pulled.

He jerked up his head. "What?" It was a snarl.

"We are not having sex," she said, chest heaving. "I'm going out."

He nudged his hips into hers, his cock shoving against her passion-damp entrance. She whimpered, her throat arching. He kissed it, suckling hard enough to leave a mark before tugging on her nipple and rolling the plump nubbin between his thumb and forefinger. Then he gave in to the beast inside him and moved down to bite at her breast while he firmly collared her throat with one hand.

She wrapped her legs around him, opening herself up to his possession. "Gabriel."

"Yeah?" Stroking his free hand along the back of her thigh, he shifted his voracious mouth to her other breast, sucking hard on her nipple before using his teeth again. He scraped up her soft flesh to her moan, fingers digging into her thigh.

Sucking in gulps of air, Charlotte finally said, "Please."

"Please what?" he demanded, rocking himself against her so that the very tip of his cock pushed into her before he pulled back out. It was torture, her grip scalding and possessive and so, so good.

Her nails dug into his shoulders, her hips lifting toward him. "You know."

"Say it." Kissing his way up her chest and to her throat, he squeezed the hand around that slender column just enough to get her attention. "*Say* it."

She moaned. "Fuck me, Gabriel."

It was all he needed to hear. Gripping her under her knee, he shoved her leg up and wide before he thrust into her in a single aggressive push. She gave an erotic little scream, then hauled his head down to hers for a kiss as wet and as raw as the sex. He rode her hard, made her come with rough caresses of her clit while he pumped in and out of her, and then, while her body was limp and sweaty, he pushed up both her thighs, spread her even wider, and drove himself to the hottest fucking orgasm of his life.

37

CHARLIE-MOUSE VS T-REX: CHAMPIONSHIP ROUND

COMING TO ON TOP of Charlotte, his body pinning hers down and his happy cock snug inside her, Gabriel finally started to think. *Shit.* "Charlotte?"

"What?" She bit him on the shoulder. Hard.

It made him grin. "You're okay."

Glaring at him, she tightened her legs around his hips. "I'm still mad at you."

Rocking into her, his cock in fine form today, he squeezed one swollen little breast again. "You'll wear some bruises." Faint, but very clearly from his hand gripping her breast. Then there were all the reddened patches on her skin where he'd marked her up with his stubble, the dark pink stripes his teeth had left on her other breast, not to mention the kiss-swollen plumpness of her lips.

She looked thoroughly used, thoroughly his.

"Can you feel your back?" was the sassy response, hazel eyes sparking.

"Some hellcat clawed the life out of me." He kissed that same hellcat, got his tongue bitten for his trouble. "And she bites too."

Charlotte scraped her nails up his back again, over the ridges she'd already created.

He hissed out a breath and thrust hard into her a couple of times. When she shuddered, he kissed her throat before reaching down to fondle one of her ass cheeks. "That was fucking incredible sex." Hard and rough and primal.

"You didn't touch my nape."

"So? We'll work on that." He kissed her sulky mouth. "As long as I can throw you on the bed like a caveman and pummel you to orgasm with my love-club, I'm good."

Her shoulders shook, a little snort escaping her as she said, "I am *not* laughing."

"And I'm not about to give you a love bite on your pretty breast." Which he then promptly did.

She demanded a kiss after, tussling with him as she threatened him with a love bite where he couldn't hide it, then arched her back in shivering pleasure as he began to move in and out of her once more.

He wasn't as rough this time, the caveman satisfied enough to have mellowed out. Instead, he petted her all over, kissed the marks on her skin, bit her playfully, and generally had a great deal of fun driving his Ms. Baird crazy. She got her revenge by digging her heels into his butt, sinking her teeth into his shoulder, and coming so fucking hard around him that he had not a prayer in hell of holding out.

AN HOUR LATER, HE finished washing the soap off his body while watching Charlotte dry her petite one. He'd made her deliciously sweaty and sticky. Sated, he wanted nothing more

360

than to just sprawl on the couch with her, but she'd given him an ultimatum. Either they went out together, or she was going to go out on her own.

Gabriel didn't react well to ultimatums, but Charlotte seemed to think she was doing this for his own good. He had to set her straight.

Dressing in jeans and a striped rugby jersey while she put on a pretty yellow sundress teamed with a sky-blue cardigan, he ate the rest of the cold omelet as well as three pieces of toast. Then they went out.

He stopped at a coffee place to buy her a frothy thing, getting himself a plain black one.

"You should try this," she said to him. "It's yummy."

"Black coffee puts hair on the chest."

"In that case, I'll keep on avoiding it. But you go right on ahead, Mr. Love-club."

God, he loved her wit, loved even more that she trusted him enough to let down all her walls. "Where do you want to go?" he asked once they were back in the SUV.

"How about the Wintergardens?"

He pointed the car toward the Auckland Domain, the sprawling green space in the center of the city. Coming in through the entrance nearest the two huge old greenhouses known collectively as the Wintergardens, he drove past a small pond with a fountain and found a parking spot down the hill from the museum.

The majestic building at the top of the hill dominated the skyline, the lawns sloping down from it sheets of manicured green. Beyond the landscaped areas, complete with playing fields that included a cricket pitch, the Domain was full of old trees, the limbs thick and twisted and interesting.

"I love it here," Charlotte said, slipping her free hand into his with a cheerful smile.

Suddenly, it didn't seem so bad that he wasn't working on the files he'd intended to go through. Breaking the hand-clasp, he wrapped his arm around her shoulders instead. "Are you over the mad?"

"Nope." She drank more of her coffee. "We're going to talk about this."

"About what?" Finishing off his own coffee, he dropped the cup in the trash can right before they walked into the first greenhouse.

"Funny, Gabriel." Her face lit up at the profusion of blooms inside the glass structure built in the early 1900s, the vaulted ceiling high enough to be home to a number of large trees alongside the flowers.

"Oh," Charlotte said, "look at the daffodils."

Gabriel wasn't really a plant guy, but he was a Charlotte guy. He enjoyed her enjoying the plants, got rid of her disposable coffee cup when she was done, and made her stand under a hanging fern so he could take a photo with his phone. Laughing, she pretended the ferns were her hair, the resulting image making him grin.

"Let me see," she said, tucking herself under his arm.

"I demand payment." Leaning down, he took a sweet, hot kiss before the two of them walked out of the first greenhouse and outside. The long, rectangular decorative pool that separated the temperate greenhouse from the humid tropical one was full of lilies, the sunshine bright on the green of the lily pads.

The area around it was relatively empty except for a small girl who leaned on her hands and knees at the edge of the pool, looking intently within while her parents watched over her from a nearby wooden seat. Vines wound through the large pergola behind them. Running parallel to the pool, it offered fleeting glimpses of the marble statues within.

"You want to go into the other greenhouse or the fernery?" he asked Charlotte.

"Fernery."

Turning left, they walked into the cool enclosed garden covered only by crosshatching beams and filled with native ferns and trees, the pathway spiraling down in a gentle slope. An enthusiastic tui, the bird's song distinctive, was their sole companion. Charlotte didn't say anything as they walked around, then down the steps to the wooden bench on the second level.

"Sit with me."

Going down beside her, his arm along the back of the seat, Gabriel stretched out his legs. "I have to admit, this was a good idea." He felt no urge to go for his phone, the peace of the cool quiet seeping into his bones.

Charlotte put her hand on his thigh as she turned to face him. "Of course it was a good idea," she said, face solemn. "You needed to take a breath."

He frowned. "I like working, Charlotte."

"I KNOW." CHARLOTTE FOLDED a leg up on the bench. "But you don't give yourself any time to just enjoy life. You're always going ten thousand miles an hour."

She could see the annoyance on Gabriel's face, feel the tension gathering in his thigh. He always got like this when she pushed him about how furiously he worked, but this time, she wasn't about to back down. "I love you," she said quietly, "and—"

Steely gray eyes locked with her own. "What did you say?"

It was so easy to say because it was him. "I love you."

Hauling her into his lap, he smiled, his cheeks creasing in that wonderful way she adored. "I love you too."

Bubbles of sunshine in her blood, she cupped his face. "I love you," she repeated. "That's why I can't bear knowing there's something inside you that hurts you." She had a good idea what it was, but he had to confront it himself if they were to make any headway.

The smile faded into masculine exasperation. "I'm fine, Charlotte."

"Hey." She wrapped her arms around his neck. "Don't do that. Don't shut me out." When he stayed stubbornly silent, she decided that since gentleness wasn't working, she'd take a page from his own book. "You're acting like the chickens."

That got her a narrow-eyed look. "Say that again."

She smiled. "Say what?"

"You're a riot, Ms. Baird."

"You know why you work so hard," Charlotte said. "Don't tell me you don't."

He blew out a breath. "I need to walk."

Getting up, they headed out of the fernery and the gardens altogether. Charlotte gave him the lead and he took them toward the beautiful old trees in the Domain, leaves rustling in the wind as they walked.

He spoke without warning. "It broke something inside my mother when we ended up in the shelter."

In him too, Charlotte thought—he'd been made utterly helpless, his foundations stripped away. It made her so angry at Brian. Never had she been more aware of Gabriel's strength and heart in finding a way to allow his father back into his life. "How rich are you?"

"Thinking of the divorce already?"

Elbowing him, she said, "I know you have lots of zeroes after your name. The apartment was a giant flashing sign, even if I didn't realize what you must've been paid as a sportsman, and what you're paid as a CEO, forget about your property portfolio and the stock options."

"Your point?"

"I'm getting there. A lot of your money, is, I'm guessing, either in banks, or in stable investments no one can touch without your consent."

That got her a curt nod.

Stopping, she came around to face him. "You can afford to take a breath," she whispered, her hands on his chest. "You don't need to constantly keep making money. Even if I decide to demand a diamond bracelet every month, I'm pretty sure it wouldn't make a dent in your zillions."

Lips tugging up slightly at the corners, he gripped her hips. "You can have a diamond bracelet every month, but you have to wear them all at once, naked in bed—no wait, I have a better idea. You have to take dictation while wearing only diamonds."

"*Gabriel.*"

He ran his thumbs across her hip bones. "I'm not sure I know how to stop."

"So," she said, "we'll work on it."

The echo of his own words had him smiling. "Meanwhile, you'll drag me out to look at flowers and canoodle in a public park?"

"We aren't canoodling."

"We will be." However, instead of a kiss, he reached into his pocket to pull out a piece of paper. "It's a prenuptial agreement."

Mouth dry, she said, "You're asking me to marry you?"

"No. You *are* marrying me." Taking her hand, he thrust a ring onto her finger. The diamond was huge enough that she could've used it to bash Richard over the head, the design around it so delicate and the size so perfect that she knew it had been made to suit her bone structure.

"These," Gabriel said, holding up the paper again, "are the terms."

She scowled at him and took the folded piece of paper. "I have nothing against signing a prenup, but that was the least romantic non-proposal in the universe." Opening up the single sheet of paper, she found a handwritten list.

PRENUPTIAL AGREEMENT BETWEEN
GABRIEL BISHOP AND CHARLOTTE BAIRD

1. You (Charlotte) will wear your engagement ring and/or your wedding ring at all times so other men do not hit on you.

2. If a man hits on you regardless, you are to tell your husband so your husband can kick his ass.

3. You will change your last name to Bishop.

4. You will agree with everything your husband says and never argue with him.

5. You must never wear anything but black lace underwear.

6. You agree to take dictation half-naked at least once so as to fulfill one of your husband's office fantasies.

7. In return, your husband will fulfill one or more of your own dirty fantasies—all of which you promise to share with him in intricate detail.

Charlotte looked up without reading the rest of the list. "This is a ridiculous list."

"We can negotiate."

Putting her fisted hands on her hips, the paper crumpled in one, she said, "Don't you try that with me, Gabriel Bishop." He had a sneaky tendency of inserting clauses into contracts that he didn't really care about—his opponents were usually so infuriated about negotiating them out that they gave him what he actually wanted.

What he actually wanted right now was for her to marry him, and likely, terms one and two. And okay, probably six and seven. "I am not marrying you." She tugged off the ring and put it back in his jeans pocket when he wouldn't take it.

He bared his teeth. "Yes, you are."

"No, not until I can sleep the night through with you." Folding her own arms, she stood toe to toe with him. "Husbands and wives do not sleep in different rooms in my world." It was hard enough now, but if she took vows, if she became his partner in every way, it would cut at her each night she slept alone.

"Fine," he said. "You agree to marry me the minute you sleep the entire night through in my bed."

Having the vague feeling she'd been outmaneuvered after all, she nodded. "After you ask me properly."

A shark smile that made her skin prickle, her blood hot. "Done."

38

DON'T EVER NEGOTIATE WITH A
DETERMINED CHARLIE-MOUSE

"I'M STAYING," CHARLOTTE TOLD Gabriel that night. His smell, the feel of him, everything was familiar, made her feel utterly safe. It was time her subconscious got with the program.

And damn it, she wanted to marry him.

"Okay," he said suspiciously agreeably.

Eyes slitted, she watched him, but when he yawned and closed his eyes, she snuggled close and let her own lashes grow heavy. She was almost asleep when it clicked. Her eyes flicked open. Sitting up, her butt on her heels, she poked at his pretend-sleeping body. "You sneak!" He'd made her agree to marry him if she slept the entire night through in his bed, conveniently forgetting the words *with him*.

An unrepentant grin as he opened his eyes. "You knew who you were negotiating with. Now"—a pat on her butt as he rose up onto his elbow—"I'm going to your room."

"You do that and I'll follow."

"I'm bigger than you," he said smugly. "I can pick you up and put you right back here."

"I have legs. I'll come back."

"No."

"Yes." Snuggling down against his shoulder, one leg thrown over the deliciously hair-roughened skin of his, she closed her eyes. "Try to make me leave."

A distinct snarl of a sound as he curved his arm around her, his hand on her bare butt. "You need a goddamn spanking."

It was her grin that was smug this time. "I love you too."

Yawning, she closed her eyes. They snapped open what felt like a heartbeat later, her pulse in her mouth. She was frozen, her muscles so stiff they felt as if they'd snap. She drew in a breath when her lungs protested, and the scent of Gabriel filled her lungs.

Gabriel.

Shuddering, she felt her muscles ease, her body aching. It took her a minute to realize what had wakened her. She was still on top of Gabriel, but he had his hand around her nape. Warm and strong and heavy and Gabriel. That's all she had to remember. This was Gabriel. Breathing in and out, in and out, she closed her eyes.

It took conscious focus, but she eventually fell back asleep.

There were two more panic attacks, and Gabriel woke both times. "Shit, sorry," he mumbled the first time and went to take his hand from her nape.

"Leave it," she ordered, bad-tempered from lack of sleep. "I'm dealing."

He massaged the back of her thigh. "You're all tense."

"I'll get untense. *Leave* it."

More massaging, and then he began to do that to her nape too. Gentle and firm, the rhythm eventually lulled her

370

exhausted mind into slumber.

The next time she woke it was because she'd ended up under Gabriel and he had her pinned down with his leg and thigh.

"I know," he mumbled. "Leave it."

She just made an incoherent sound, her eyes gritty.

THE NEXT NIGHT, SHE woke them four times.

The night after that, it was twice.

The one after that, it was five times.

Exhausted to the bone by the time Friday night rolled around, she flopped into bed and said, "I'm not giving up."

Lying on his stomach beside her, Gabriel reached out to twine his fingers with her own. "Neither am I. I already booked the fucking wedding venue."

She started to giggle, but it was slightly hysterical. Fighting back the tears, she kissed his knuckles. "I love you."

Steel-gray eyes held her own. "You're my heart."

Holding the words to her own battered heart, she allowed her eyes to close.

She woke to find that they'd been so exhausted that neither one of them had moved, their hands entwined under the sunlight.

The sunlight!

Blinking, she stared at the clock on the nightstand. It was nine a.m. on a Saturday morning, and she was in bed with the man she loved. She turned very quietly and saw he was still asleep, his skin dark gold under the sunshine pouring through the skylight and his hair gleaming blue-black. When his lashes lifted lazily a half hour later, she said, "Never argue with my husband?"

A sleepy smile. "I was hoping you'd negotiate that out. You know I like fighting with you." Tugging her into him, he reached into the bedside drawer on his side and, after taking out the ring, slid it onto her finger. "The black lace underwear clause is nonnegotiable, though I will permit red lace underwear on special occasions."

Curling her fingers into her hand, the ring warm against her skin—as if it had absorbed his heat, she lay on her back with him leaning over her. "That's a pity," she said. "I'll have to throw out that pretty blush-pink G-string set I bought."

His eyes gleamed. "Like I said, Ms. Baird, there's room for negotiation." A slow, luscious kiss, his hand cupping the side of her face. "Marry me?"

"Yes," she said, her heart wide-open. "Yes, I'll marry you."

WHEN THE PHONE RANG in the middle of the night a month later, Charlotte groggily searched for it. The past four weeks had been good and not so good—she still woke some nights in a cold sweat, but those times were getting less and less with each week that passed. Tonight, she'd been in a full, deep sleep, in spite of the fact Gabriel had his hand around her nape as she lay sprawled on his chest.

"I've got it."

Letting Gabriel pick up, she closed her eyes and snuggled back against his neck.

"When?" he said after answering. "It's confirmed? Can't say we'll mourn the fucker."

"Who was that?" she mumbled once he'd hung up.

"Lee. Turns out Richard couldn't handle being locked up again. He's dead."

The bastard had hanged himself the night after his transfer from the hospital to the jail, a judge having ordered he be held on remand until his trial. The scum had left a note to be passed on to Charlotte, a note she would never see. Detective Lee had made that call, told Gabriel about it, and he fully agreed.

He didn't think Charlotte would believe a word of it, of how Richard was killing himself because she'd rejected his love, but he didn't want that creep's words in her head. "It's over."

"Good." A jaw-cracking yawn. "Now go back to sleep."

He was dumbfounded for a second at her response until he realized that for Charlotte, it had been over the day she'd decided not to be scared of Richard. Whether he lived or died had made little difference to her stability, but Gabriel was sure as hell glad the bastard wouldn't be around to threaten her ever again.

Curling his body around hers, he closed his eyes.

39

PRENUPTIAL AGREEMENT: CHARLOTTE BAIRD'S TERMS

1. You (Gabriel) are to always wear your wedding ring so no women ever hit on you.
2. If any woman hits on you regardless, you are to tell your wife so she can kick that woman's ass.
3. You have to walk around shirtless at home so your wife can ogle you to her heart's content.
4. Under no circumstances are you to ever send your wife red roses. Do it and she will throw far worse than a muffin at your head.
5. You will not work after seven at night unless it is an emergency situation requiring immediate remediation. Late-night international calls can be negotiated on a per-call basis.

GABRIEL BISHOP'S COUNTEROFFER

Done and done. You're mine now, Ms. Baird. And I'm yours. Always.

I hope you enjoyed Charlotte and Gabriel's story! You met Charlotte's best friend Molly in this book. Molly's story, which takes place partly at the same time as Charlotte's, is told in ROCK ADDICTION. And if you like the sound of a shy drummer and some sexy memos, then check out ROCK COURTSHIP.

*I'm currently at work on the next book in the Rock Kiss series. For exclusive sneak peeks and bonus content, including free short stories, and deleted scenes from my books, swing by my website (*www.nalinisingh.com*) and join my newsletter. Also on the website is a special section dedicated to the Rock Kiss series, complete with photos of many of the locations used in this book.*

Any questions or comments? You can contact me at any time through the e-mail address on my website. You can also find me on Twitter (@NaliniSingh) & Facebook (facebook.com/Author NaliniSingh). – xo Nalini

Turn the page for an excerpt from

ROCK ADDICTION

EXCERPT FROM
Rock Addiction

S HE WANTED TO BITE HIS lower lip.

Wanted to tug on the silver ring that pierced one corner of that delicious, toe-curling mouth.

But mostly she wanted to bite down with her teeth, taste the badness of him.

"Um, Molly?" A hand waved in front of her face. "Molly?"

Blinking, she forced her gaze away from the man who made her want to do bad, bad things and toward the petite form of her best friend. "What?" Her skin flushed until she wondered if her fantasies were visible to everyone in the room.

"You mind if I bug out?" Charlotte took a last tiny sip of her pomegranate martini before placing it on one of the small, high tables scattered around the room. "I want to spend tomorrow making sure all the files are in order for the new boss."

Molly scowled, all embarrassment fading. "I thought you were trying to take it easy on weekends?" The fringe of the black flapper-style dress she'd pulled out of her closet in a moment of whimsy swirled just above her knees when she shifted to give Charlotte her complete attention. "Isn't making sure everything's up to standard Anya's job anyway?" It was Anya who was personal assistant to the CEO; Charlie officially worked in the records department, but Anya had a way of treating Molly's best friend as her own assistant.

"New boss has a rep," Charlotte said. "I don't want to be fired because Anya didn't bother to do what she should." Narrowed hazel eyes behind fine wire-rimmed spectacles made it clear Charlotte had no illusions about the other woman.

Nodding, Molly considered the cherry that decorated her nonalcoholic but very pretty cocktail. "Let me get my coat." Disappointment whispered through her veins, but really, what would've happened if she'd stayed longer? Zilch. Zero. Nothing.

Okay, maybe another blush or two inspired by the rock god across the room, but that was it. Even if he, for some wildly inexplicable reason of his own, decided he wanted her, the one thing Molly would never *ever* do was become involved with someone who lived in the media spotlight. She'd barely survived her first brutal brush with fame as a shocked and scared fifteen-year-old; the ugliness of it had left scars that hurt to this day.

"Oh, no, don't." Charlotte put a hand on her arm, squeezed. "I'll order a cab. You're having too much fun staring at Mr. Kissable."

Molly almost choked on the cherry, lush and sweet, that she hadn't been able to resist. "I'd say I can't believe that came out of your mouth"—cheeks burning, she fought not to dissolve into mortified laughter—"but you have been my friend for twenty-one years and counting."

Charlotte grinned as she took out her phone and texted a cab company. "You know who he is, don't you?"

"Of course. He's only one of Thea's most important clients." And on the cover of every second magazine that came across Molly's desk at the library, all sleek muscle and tattoos and a sexy smile curving those dangerous, bitable lips. If she couldn't resist reading the articles and sighing over the photos, that was her guilty little secret.

"You two talking about me again?" Her sister's sultry voice sounded from behind Molly, followed by her slender body—currently clad in a tight red designer sheath.

"About your raking-it-in client," Charlotte clarified.

"That's *über*-client to you." Raising her champagne flute, Thea clinked it against the glass that held Molly's frothy concoction. "Here's to rock stars with voices like sex and bodies like heaven."

Molly felt her stomach clutch, and even though she knew it was none of her business, said, "You sound like you're speaking from personal experience," grateful her voice came out steady.

"Molly, m'dear, you know I never mess around with money." Her older sister's uptilted eyes, a burnished brown, were suddenly dead serious. "And Zachary Fox, known to his gazillion and one fans as Fox, and to any woman with a functioning sex drive as hot with a capital *H*, is serious money. As are the other members of Schoolboy Choir." Putting down her empty champagne flute beside Charlotte's cocktail glass, she said, "Come on, I'll introduce you both to him."

Charlotte shook her head. "No thanks. You know me and gorgeous men—I turn into a Charlie-shaped statue." Having kept her phone in hand, she now looked down as the screen flashed. "That's a message from my cab driver. He's downstairs."

"You're sure about going home alone?" Molly couldn't help but worry about her best friend. Charlotte was fierce and strong and the only person who'd stood by her when the scandal broke, but she knew Charlie's own past had left invisible wounds that had never quite scarred over.

"Yes—I use this driver a lot for work stuff. He always waits while I unlock the door to my place and disarm the security." She hugged Thea good-bye before doing the same to Molly, leaning up to whisper, "Live a little, Moll. Take the hot rock star home, then tell me all about your night of wild monkey sex."

Molly's breath caught at the idea of it, foolish and impossible though it was. "If only." Over an hour into the party and Fox hadn't even looked in Molly's direction, that's how high she registered on his radar.

"Fox knows who you are," Thea said after Charlotte had left. "He saw a photo of us in my L.A. office—the one from after we went through the caves."

Molly groaned. "You mean the one where we both look like drowned rats, have giant black inflatable rings around our waists, and dented helmets on our heads?" The trip through the waters of the underground cave system had been fun, but it did not make for alluring photos. "Let's not forget the ancient gray wetsuits that made it look like we were molting."

Choking on her laughter, Thea nodded. "He was interested in doing the black-water rafting thing when I told him where we took the photo. I'm sure he'd love to talk to you about it."

Molly fought the temptation to get close to him any way she could, and it was one of the hardest things she'd ever done. "No thanks," she said, her mind awash in visions of what it would be like to meet him in a much more private setting, run her fingers over the firm lines of his body... bite down on his lip. "I'd like to keep standing over here with my fantasies." Distance or not, the needy, achy feeling in the pit of her stomach continued to intensify, her response to the rock star across the room scarily potent.

Thea raised an elegant eyebrow.

"If I meet him," she added through the shimmer of heat that licked over her skin when he laughed at something one of his bandmates had said, the sound a rough, dark caress, "and he's an arrogant snob or worse, a stoned-out idiot, there go my fantasies."

"Fox is neither a snob nor a stoner." Thea's lips kicked up. "The man is the whole package: intelligent, talented, and a nice human being unless you piss him off by pushing too hard about his private life—and I don't think there's any chance you'll go paparazzi on me."

"That just makes it worse," Molly pointed out, trying not to watch as Fox bent his head to speak to a bombshell brunette in a dress the size of a handkerchief. "How can I fantasize about him ripping off my clothes in a moment of reckless passion if he politely shakes my hand and says it's nice to meet me?"

Molly had learned her lesson about reality versus dreams as a teenager—once destroyed, some dreams could never be resurrected. And for some reason, she couldn't bear for this silly, unattainable dream to be splintered by reality.

"If you change your mind," Thea said with a shake of her head, "speak up soon. Fox never stays long at these things."

She picked up a gorgeous cobalt blue cocktail from the tray of a passing waiter. "I'd better go make nice with the other guests."

Watching her publicist sister expertly work the room, Molly smiled in quiet pride. Though they'd joyfully connected after a lifetime of not knowing the other existed, the bond was yet new, fragile, and no one who wasn't aware of their family history would ever guess they were related. Twenty-nine to Molly's twenty-four, not only was Thea naturally slender in contrast to Molly's curves, she had the smooth golden skin of her Balinese mother as well as Lily's eyes, but she'd gained her height from Patrick Buchanan, topping Molly by a good five inches.

Their shared father had put his stamp on Molly in a far stronger fashion, giving her the black hair she constantly fought to tame, creamy skin that burned easily, and eyes of deepest brown. Every time Molly looked in the mirror, she remembered what Patrick had done, and each time she wrenched her hair into a tight twist—as she'd done tonight— it was in silent rebellion of the shadow he threw over her life even from the grave.

Patrick Buchanan, "family values" politician and vicious hypocrite, was the kind of man who'd have taken a stranger home for a night of uninhibited passion.

Fingers tightening on the stem of her glass, Molly made the deliberate decision to turn away from the rock star whose presence made her body sing. It was just as well that Fox was oblivious to her existence, because should he turn those smoky-green eyes in her direction, Molly had the heart-thudding sense that she might break every one of her rules and give in to the other Molly who lived inside her. That dangerous woman was Patrick Buchanan's irresponsible seed, someone who might well wreck everything Molly had built brick by brick after her world fell apart.

Releasing a shuddering breath, she wandered over to the plate-glass window that functioned as one wall of the exclusive penthouse suite Thea had hired for the party. The bright lights of New Zealand's biggest city sparkled in front of her, a cascade of jewels thrown by a careless hand and bordered by the black velvet of the water that kissed its edges.

"Stunning, isn't it?"

She glanced at the man who'd spoken. "Yes." Rangy, with eyes caught between gold and brown, he was only a few inches taller than Molly, but there was a contained energy to him that made him seem bigger.

"I'm David."

"I know." She smiled. "David Rivera—you're the drummer for Schoolboy Choir."

"Wow." David rocked back on his heels, hands in the pockets of the tailored black pants he wore with a stone-gray shirt. "You actually recognize the drummer. Big fan?"

Her smile deepened. "My sister's your publicist." Based in L.A., the only reason Thea even had an "office" in New Zealand was because of Molly. That fictional office had alleviated some of the pressure during their first nervous meetings, making Thea's flights to the country about something other than the relationship they were trying desperately to build.

"I didn't know Thea had another sister." David's eyes skated to where Thea stood with Fox, the lead singer's arm around her waist, and all at once, he wasn't the charming, well-dressed man who'd been talking to her, but one with a stiff jaw and rigid shoulders.

"Thea," she said softly, as the rich darkness of Fox's hair caught the light, "has three very specific rules."

Sharp interest, David's attention snapping back to her. "Oh?"

"One: never sleep with clients." The words weren't only for David's benefit—the idea of her sister in bed with Fox caused her abdomen to clench so tight it hurt.

"What's the second rule?"

"Never sleep with clients."

"Why do I get the feeling I know the third one?" Thrusting a hand through the deep mahogany of his hair, he blew out a breath. "She ever made an exception?"

"Not as far as I know." Having forced her gaze back to the multimillion-dollar view in a vain effort to control the visceral pulse of her physical response to a man who could never be hers, she followed the path of several blinking lights in the distance, a plane en route to the airport.

"You want another drink? I definitely need a beer."

Molly shook her head. "No, I'm heading off." She didn't trust herself to stay any longer, didn't know what she might do; every cell in her body continued to burn in awareness of the rock star on the other side of the room.

Putting her glass on a nearby table, she dipped into her little black purse to find the keycard Thea had handed her that morning. The card gave her temporary access to the building's parking garage.

"Thanks for the advice on Thea's rules," David said with a rueful smile.

"Don't mention it." Molly wondered if her sister had any idea of the drummer's feelings. "Will you be flying home soon?" Schoolboy Choir had played a sold-out concert three days ago as part of a new outdoor music festival that had attracted bands from around the world.

"No, we're staying in town for a month."

Molly froze.

"It's been a tough year," David continued, "and we need downtime before the tour we have coming up. We liked it here, figured what the hell, we'd just stay on instead of flying somewhere else for a vacation."

It made perfect sense... and Molly knew she'd spend the next month obsessing over whether she might run into Fox again. Her cheeks heated at the sheer ridiculousness of her response. God, she had to go home.

"I hope you enjoy your time here," she said as she turned away from the view. Of course, her gaze went straight to Fox. A leggy blonde was currently whispering in his ear while several other women looked on grim-eyed. It was a stark visual reminder of the gulf that existed between them, regardless of her body's potent response.

David's voice broke into her thoughts. "I'll walk you to your car."

"No, that's okay." When he frowned, she added, "There's a guard on duty in the garage. It's safe." Smiling her good-bye, she began to tunnel her way out of the packed room.

Skirting around the tall form of the guitarist for Schoolboy Choir, an almost too-handsome blond male in the midst of charming an actress Molly recognized from a local soap opera, she managed to snag Thea for a quick hug. "I'll call you later in the week," her sister said in her ear. "I'm staying in the country with the band for the first part of their vacation."

"Oh, that's wonderful." Molly loved spending time with her older sister now that the initial awkwardness had passed. "If you're in the city anytime, come into the library and we'll sneak out for a coffee."

"Deal."

With that, Thea returned to her guests while Molly continued on to the exit—where she gave in to the inexplicable ache inside her and craned her neck for one last glimpse of the man who'd turned her blood to molten honey. Fox, however, was nowhere to be seen. "Not exactly a surprise," she muttered under her breath, recalling the gorgeous women who'd been buzzing around him.

More than likely, he was in a shadowy corner of the building, pinning one of those women to the wall while he pounded into her. The image poured ice-cold water on her fantasies.

Stabbing the button to summon the elevator at the end of the corridor, she tried to think of anything but Zachary Fox's muscled body flexing and clenching as he drove himself into that nameless, faceless woman.

Her pulse fluttered, her breathing choppy.

"Thank God," she said when the elevator arrived and, stepping inside, scanned her keycard over the reader before pressing the button for the garage.

"Hold up!"

Automatically pressing the Open button until the other passenger had ducked inside, she turned to give him a polite smile. It froze on her face.

Because there in the flesh stood the sex god whose lip she wanted to bite. All six feet four inches of him. Masculine heat, golden skin... and smoky, sexy dark green eyes focused on her mouth.

About the Author

NEW YORK TIMES AND **USA Today** bestselling author of the Psy-Changeling and Guild Hunter series **Nalini Singh** usually writes about hot shapeshifters and dangerous angels. This time around, she decided to write about a gorgeous rugby player turned brilliant CEO. If you're seeing a theme here, you're not wrong.

Nalini lives and works in beautiful New Zealand, and is passionate about writing. If you'd like to explore the Rock Kiss series further, or if you'd like to try out her other books, you can find lots of excerpts on her website: www.nalinisingh.com. *Slave to Sensation* is the first book in the Psy-Changeling series, while *Angels' Blood* is the first book in the Guild Hunter series. The website also features special behind-the-scenes material from all her series.

CPSIA information can be obtained
at www.ICGtesting.com
Printed in the USA
FSHW010507061020
74512FS